Shining City on a Hill

Book One

Priests & Plowboys

Karen Edmonds

Cover design by Benjamin Devey

Shining City Publications
ISBN-13: 978-0692912010

To pilgrims, pioneers and patriots past, present and future

Aux Etats-Unis, pays de ma naissance
To the United States, land of my birth

A la France, pays de mon éveil
To France, land of my awakening

Preface

On June 22, 1630, a fleet of eleven English ships, led by the flagship Arbella, landed on the coast of Massachusetts with some two-thousand souls fleeing religious and political persecution. Approximately 20,000 men, women and children followed over the next ten years to settle Boston and the surrounding areas, in a movement that would come to be known as the Great Migration. From this body emerged statesmen and writers, patriots and military leaders— pioneers of a new civilization based on hard work, independence, morality, and Biblical law.

What unfortunate circumstances moved these souls—many of whom lived in relative luxury in England—to embark for a wilderness across the sea? *Shining City on a Hill* tells a portion of that story—an epic tale, filled with courage and cowardice, triumph and tragedy.

During the first half of the sixteenth century, in England and the rest of Europe, cruel burnings, beheadings, torture, imprisonment, and deprivation of property were the order of the day for people who simply wished to read the Bible in their own language or worship according to the dictates of conscience. Reading the Bible often led to disagreement with the doctrines and practices of the Roman Church and subsequent charges of heresy. Concepts of freedom of religion, speech, and assembly did not exist. Church and state worked together to persecute unrepentant heretics. The concept of basic human rights had not yet dawned in the darkness of a world that demanded conformity of thought.

Toward the middle of the sixteenth century, a contingent of well-placed Puritans in England fled intense religious persecution under the reign of Queen Mary for exile in Geneva, Switzerland. There in Geneva, exiles from England, France and other nations studied at the feet of French reformer John Calvin, while working to establish a godly society.

When Queen Elizabeth inherited the English throne in 1558, exiles returned to England to pursue reform within the English parliament and society at large. Meanwhile, violent and bloody wars of religion raged in France. Thousands of mercilessly persecuted French reformers—Huguenots—found refuge in England. The word *refugee* entered the English language as a result of the French Protestants who fled their homeland.

By the early seventeenth century, King James I and his successor, Charles I, considered the Puritan influence in England a growing nuisance. Puritans criticized corruption in the English culture and political system. Once again, clouds of persecution gathered as tensions between Puritans and the rest of English society grew. With the horrors endured by Protestant martyrs fresh in the collective memory—throughout England, John Foxe's book of martyrs, *Acts and Monuments,* was chained to church podiums along with the Great Bible—Puritans sought refuge in the Massachusetts Bay area, recognizing the hand of God in opening the way for them to establish a Christian colony across the sea.

With the Bible and Calvinism as their guide, Puritan colonists set about to establish a society that would serve as an example to England and the rest of the world. Aboard the ship Arbella their leader, John Winthrop, delivered a sermon entitled, "A Model of Christian Charity." In his sermon, Winthrop exhorted his flock to remember that the eyes of all nations would be upon them and that if they succeeded, their godly society would serve as a "city upon a hill" (Matthew 5:14) to the rest of the world. Puritans believed God led them out of cruel bondage to the shores of America, as He led the children of Israel out of Egypt. The concept of America as a city on a hill has become immortalized since the Puritan founding.

Through a series of serendipitous events, I discovered in the 1980s that my tenth great-grandfather, Thomas Dudley, was an influential English Puritan involved in organizing the initial migration to Massachusetts. He sailed with his family to America aboard the Arbella, serving as deputy governor (second in command to John Winthrop), and also as governor several times of the Massachusetts Bay Colony. As I immersed myself in the life stories and writings of the Puritans, I felt moved upon to tell their story from the context of the times in which they lived. Adding to my drive was the many people I met while living in France in the 1980s who looked to America as something special—a place of freedom and opportunity—even a city on a hill.

Priests & Plowboys is the first episode in the *Shining City on a Hill* series. Using a mixture of historical and fictitious people and events, the story illustrates the Bible's profound influence on common people in the sixteenth century. Translation of the Bible from Latin to the common languages of the people laid the groundwork for the cultural, political and religious revolution that followed.

Along with the exhortation to shine as a city on a hill, John Winthrop included a warning in his sermon aboard the Arbella that I believe speaks to us from the dust: *But if our hearts shall turn away so that we will not obey, but shall be seduced and worship other gods, our pleasures and profits, and serve them, it shall be propounded unto us this day, we shall surely perish out of the good land whither we pass over this vast sea to possess it.*

As storm clouds of antagonism to Christianity and threats to freedom of conscience once again cast an ominous shadow over the human family, the tragic and triumphal stories of those who stood firm against shackles of tyranny for adherence to conscience is a poignant message, for central to the American founding is the concept that freedom comes from God.

John Foxe's *Acts and Monuments*

Popularly known as *Foxe's Book of Martyrs*, the influence of this book on the minds of the English people cannot be overstated. For more than four centuries, it was widely read and preached from the pulpit. I relied on Foxe's book in putting together accounts of persecution and trials of Protestants.

Sixteenth-Century France

Until the end of the nineteenth century, a mishmash of Latin and regional dialects were spoken in France, and regional dukedoms led by prominent families still wielded power. However, to preserve the flow of the narrative, I approached the tale from the perspective of one country under a common French language.

What's Historical and What's Fiction?

Priests & Plowboys makes every attempt at historical accuracy, and draws heavily upon real-life figures and events. I made two trips to Europe, visited Dartford and London, England, as well as La Rochelle, Bordeaux, Périgueux, and Paris, France (I also lived in France from 1984-1986). I visited the London National Archives, stood at Smithfield and the Tower of London, where countless martyrs suffered, corresponded with researchers in both countries, and read more books, academic journals, and websites than the average reader would care to see documented. In a few rare instances, I placed historical events a bit before or after they occurred, such as the Rood of Grace early in the book. It was actually paraded around market towns and destroyed several months before it appears in the novel.

Christopher Wade and Nicholas Hall were actual historical figures, but nothing is known of their daily lives except that Wade was a married linen weaver and Hall was a bricklayer. A search of genealogical records and a trip to England's National Archives revealed no lists or names of family members for Wade;

therefore, I used creative license to build a story based on the times in which he lived. The end of their lives is a matter of historical record.

Priests & Plowboys

"If God spare my life, ere many years
I will cause a boy who drives a plough
to know more of the scriptures than you do."

~

William Tyndale
1494-1536

August, 1538

—

Market Day in Dartford came one day each week. It was a day when the village's population of a thousand souls swelled like lungs filling with oxygen; a day when folks from all over the countryside and neighboring towns within six miles brought goods to sell and scouted for others to take home; a day when performers juggled and acted and played their instruments for work-weary residents; a day for petty criminals to be humiliated in the Market Square pillory; and a day when fourteen-year-old Christopher Wade popped awake looking forward to a break from weaving linen to take in all the things his favorite day of the week offered.

On this particular Market Day in late August, with his mouth watering at the prospect of devouring one of Abby Wellington's lemon-infused taffaty tarts for breakfast, Christopher rose at the break of dawn without any prodding from his father, William, or his mother, Elizabeth. He slopped Miss Piggle, tidied up the pallet where he slept, stocked the kindling bucket, and sat outside next to the front door on a stool, scratching the head of his black and white spaniel Dart, waiting impatiently for William to get dressed.

The Wades lived in a one-room daub and wattle cottage on East Hill built by Christopher's grandfather near the turn of the century, nine years before Henry VIII was crowned king. A loom passed down by Grandfather Wade stood before a stone fireplace that took up most of one wall, where Grandfather Wade passed the linen weaving craft down to his son William, and where William was passing it on to Christopher.

In the same room, next to a lead-paned window that afforded a view of the fertile Darent Valley and wooded West Hill, Elizabeth spun thread and, when she had time, embroidered towels and handkerchiefs to sell at the market. Near the

1

spinning wheel stood a heavy oak bed where William and Elizabeth slept, and under the bed rested the straw pallet pulled out each night for Christopher.

It was in the cottage on East Hill where Christopher entered the world. He wasn't the only child born to William and Elizabeth but no others survived, except a precious red-headed girl who lived to almost four. Elizabeth refused to speak of her.

Each Friday night, father and son packed up their cloth in a two-wheeled wooden cart to prepare for Saturday morning when they took turns wheeling it down the knobby road to High Street, and parked on the cobblestone between Holy Trinity Church and Market Square. Sometimes Elizabeth would place a basket on top with a few things to sell such as eggs, embroidered linen towels and handkerchiefs, apples from the tree, surplus vegetables and herbs from her garden, or her locally famous lavender salve for pox scars.

From the cart, Christopher could watch folks coming and going in and out of town on Watling Street, an ancient Roman road that ran from the West Midlands of England all the way to Dover. He had a clear view of Market Square, where townsfolk relieved pent-up tensions pelting thieves in the pillory with raw eggs or shouting and clapping at traveling minstrels. Christopher especially relished jugglers, despite his mother's warning that they were a coarse lot barely a step above sorcerers.

The sweet aroma of Abby's taffaty tarts wafted from her stand a half-minute's walk away, on the corner of Lowfield and High Street. Just to the west of the cart, Simon Nix's Pilgrim Hat shop offered pilgrims on their way to Canterbury a place to purchase souvenirs such as pewter badges or carved statues of Saint Thomas Becket. Between the Pilgrim Hat and Holy Trinity Church, Amy Coppinger's two-story, timber-framed Crown & Anchor Inn beckoned folks inside to sip a homebrewed ale, enjoy a hot meal and catch up on the latest happenings.

As soon as they parked the cart on High Street, William took to arranging the linens while Christopher watched a swarm of flies fighting over a sliver of shade cast by the cart's shadow. He wiped the perspiration from his brow and surveyed Market Square, where a crowd was already gathering around the stone market cross. Twenty-year-old Thomas Nix emerged from The Pilgrim Hat to assess the commotion, with a carving knife in one hand and a partially completed statue of Thomas Becket in the other. Amy Coppinger peeked out the Crown & Anchor door, clutching a wooden stirring spoon, to peruse the goings-on. Father Garrett, Dartford's parish priest, stood in front of Holy Trinity Church in his black cassock, squinting toward the square, his right hand held up to protect his puffy, sleep-deprived eyes from the morning sun.

Nudging his father's side Christopher asked, "May I go see what is drawing the townsfolks' attention?"

Not bothering to look up, William muttered, "Yes, but don't tarry. I need your help here."

"I'll be gone but a moment. I promise."

Squeezing his lanky body through the crowd, Christopher arrived a few feet away from a creaky wooden platform upon which a speaker with curly blonde hair, dressed in a brown robe cinched at the waist with a cord, addressed his curious onlookers. Thomas Nix found a place around the side where he wouldn't block the view for shorter folks. Father Garrett worked his way to a spot next to Thomas as folks pressed in to discover the visitor's purpose in coming.

The spindly, bearded speaker held up a life-sized wood crucifix. Above the scuffle of folks going about their business and over the bleats, moos, and snorts of animals held against their wills on ropes and in cages, he shouted, "This is what popish idolatry has brought us. This work of a man's hands, pretending to be something holy. The monks of Boxley Abbey are nothing more than money changers in the temple. 'Rood of Grace' they call it. I call it the Rood of Disgrace!" Murmurs rippled across the crowd. A group of folks in the back booed, while others clapped in approval.

The speaker manipulated wires in the back of the figure to demonstrate the puppet-like movements of the image on the cross. "Look at the springs and wires here on the back. They allow our Lord to move his eyes, bow, wiggle his hands and feet, nod his head, smile and frown."

"Can the puppet pardon sins?" The question came from Edward Bartholomew, the village baker, who towered a head above the throng. William Wade nicknamed him "The Burning Bush" in reference to his bright red hair and fiery temperament. Edward's clownlike appearance gave Christopher the urge to laugh, but anyone acquainted with Edward knew better than to trifle with him. He'd served an apprenticeship with a baker in Paris, married the baker's daughter and brought her back to England, taught both of his young children to read, and could entertain folks performing large passages of *Piers Plowman* from memory. As if all that weren't enough, his breads, cakes and pies were good enough to make a grown man weep.

"For enough money, he can pardon sins!" the speaker proclaimed. "Give him gold and he smiles, silver and he frowns. All the work of idolatry to part fools from their money."

"'Tis criminal!" Edward shouted back, his green eyes flashing with anger.

Thomas Nix watched the proceedings with pursed lips and arms folded tight across his chest, the chip on his shoulder oozing from his penetrating, dark brown eyes. After King Henry's break with the church in Rome four years earlier, Thomas conducted himself as if the world owed him restitution. Nix's older sister, a nun, resided at Barking Abbey in London. His mother passed away from scarlet fever several years prior, leaving only Thomas and his father to run the souvenir business. Thomas offered a faint smile when Amy Coppinger waddled up next to Father Garrett, wearing a soiled apron and with her stirring spoon still in hand. The three whispered amongst themselves and turned their attention back to the speaker.

"Aye!" replied the speaker. "And to think, ignorant pilgrims from all over the kingdom worshipped this graven image, taking time away from planting and harvesting—passing through your very village—letting their crops rot in the fields to pay it homage. Popish idolatry it is, and the monks pretend to know nothing about its workings. Money changers in the temple, they are! The second commandment says, 'Thou shalt not make unto thee any graven images. I am the Lord thy God.'"

"Down with popish idols!" Edward Bartholomew shouted, his right fist raised.

Christopher turned to see if his father noticed the commotion in the square, when the sight of an unfamiliar freckled face stopped him. She stood a couple inches taller than he, with her eyes fixed upon the speaker, nutmeg hair cascading like a waterfall to just above her waist. Returning his attention to the speaker he no longer heard the man's words, obsessed with finding out whether her eyes were brown or hazel. When he spun around, pretending to flag his father's attention, an unwelcome sight met him: John Whitfield and Edwin Taylor standing side by side, directly behind her. Edwin glared at Christopher. They had noticed her, too.

"Why, look, John," Edwin sneered, smoothing his black velvet jerkin. "A rodent at the marketplace."

"Ho, Lollard's knave," John taunted, his face scrunched.

Christopher winced. John and Edwin, sons of wealthy merchants, lived on Overy Street, just across the Darent River that cut past the church on the east side of the village. Christopher turned back to the speaker, wondering how to extricate himself from the humiliating situation.

With a puzzled look, the maiden searched for the unfortunate "rodent" to whom Edwin referred. She glanced back at John and Edwin. John lifted his feathered cap and introduced himself.

Christopher's chest tightened. Fighting the urge to pummel John to the ground, he turned toward the linen cart to watch her response to John's flirtation.

"Anne. Anne Cooper," she responded, her face flushed. The light sprinkling of freckles across the bridge of her nose accented her sage-colored eyes. Christopher's heart did a cartwheel.

"Are you visiting from another parish?" John continued.

"No, my family and I lately moved here from Tonbridge. My father is a fishmonger." She pointed over her shoulder. "He works over there in the Shambles."

John flashed a wide grin. Anne Cooper giggled and twisted a chunk of her hair around her forefinger. Christopher took in the scene with a knot in his stomach. Right under his nose, John Whitfield moved in on the prettiest girl he'd ever seen.

Turning back to the speaker, Christopher no longer heard the message. Nothing mattered except finding a way to talk to Anne Cooper without the two bullies around.

September, 1538

—

Dartford

Breathing out a soul-weary sigh through his thin, taut lips, Father Garrett shuffled some papers on his pulpit and lifted his gaze above his parishioners' heads, to a crucifix on the stone wall near the church's arched entry door. *How impossibly sad Jesus looks*, he thought. With renewed determination to bear his own cross, he squared his narrow shoulders and declared, "The following injunctions have gone forth to all the clergy of the realm. Per Thomas Cromwell, the king's chief minister, parishes are to secure a large volume of the Bible in English." A predictable wave of murmurs stirred the congregation. Tapping his dainty fingers on the podium, he waited for voices to still before continuing. "The Bible will be set up in a place where all of you can easily read it."

"An English Bible? 'Tis blasphemy," Thomas Nix whispered, elbowing his father, Simon. Simon looked to his right for the reaction of Matthew Cooper, father of the new girl in town. Cooper rocked back and forth on his heels, twitching the corner of his mouth. Simon detected a faint aroma of whiskey wafting about the fishmonger.

As the murmuring rose to a fevered pitch, Father Garrett shifted his weight back and forth from one leg to the other, swatted at a fly circling his head, studied the crucifix near the front door, shuffled his papers on the podium, and finally cleared his throat loudly to get his parishioners' attention. With a heavy sigh, he continued, "I am to recite with you each Sunday a portion of the Lord's Prayer in English, until you have it memorized, as well as the Ten Commandments."

Garrett focused for a moment on Teresa Willoughby. With a firm arm around her six-year-old boy and a handhold on the collar of her two-year-old son, she struggled to keep the unruly imps from stealing the congregation's attention away from the priest. *Poor maid!* Garrett thought, sympathetic to the dark circles and sallow skin that cast a shadow across her otherwise lovely countenance. He couldn't help but notice a wisp of long, black, lustrous hair that had untucked itself from her coif and teased her lips. Her husband had lain ill for the past several months, leaving her with the burden of caring for his homely duties as well as her own. The Father stepped in to help with tasks such as chopping wood and slopping the pig. He looked up from the widow to see his parishioners gawking at him. His face and chest flushed.

Edward Bartholomew reacted before the priest could catch his breath. "When will we have the English Bible, Father?"

Forcing a cough to clear his throat, the priest replied, "Ah, yes. We were to have it by All Saints' Day. 'Twas being printed in Paris until French authorities seized portions of the book under charges of heresy. With production back in England, methinks it won't be long."

Thomas Nix's hand shot up. "Not two years past they burned William Tyndale for translating the word of God into English. If putting God's holy word into the common tongue was heresy then, why is it not so now? Why, now even a common baker will be able to read scripture." He cast a contemptuous glance at Edward. Edward's pupils narrowed.

"It says here," the priest traced along a paper, his forefinger shaking. "It says here I am to encourage you to read from its pages, but you are to avoid contention and altercation." He rubbed his eyes and continued. "There is more. I shall quote from the injunctions. 'Such feigned images as you know to be abused with pilgrimages or offerings of anything made thereunto, you shall, for avoiding the most detestable offense of idolatry, forthwith take down, and without delay.' It reads that I am to exhort you to works of charity rather than wandering to pilgrimages, offering money and candles to images or relics, kissing or licking them, speaking over beads, and so on."

Simon and Thomas cast each other an alarmed glance. Elizabeth Wade fingered her rosary, head bowed, while her husband gazed up at the light streaming through the stained glass windows with a broad smile. Christopher stared wistfully at the back of Anne Cooper's head, oblivious to the banter surrounding him.

"Has His Majesty gone mad?" Thomas Nix barked.

"I suppose that is for you to decide," Father Garrett sighed. Christopher looked away from Anne to the priest. If it were not for Garrett's thin moustache and beard, and the three furrowed lines in his forehead, one might mistake him for an adolescent boy.

As parishioners filed out after the service, Thomas grabbed the back of Edward's tunic. Edward spun around, knocking Thomas' grip loose. "Hands off!" he barked.

"When shall we have a Bible?" Thomas mocked in a nasally tone, wrinkling his nose. "Fancy yourself a priest, do you?"

Edward's eyes narrowed. "If the king wills that we have the Bible in our mother tongue, only a fool would not wish to drink from its pages."

"The same king burned Tyndale for putting out an English Bible," Thomas scowled. "Perchance he will return to his senses before the book comes out."

"Tyndale's last prayer when he embraced the stake was for God to open the king of England's eyes. It seems to me God honored his servant's prayer."

"A heretic quoting heretics, you are. By God's teeth, what is to become of us when a lowly bread baker considers himself holy enough to read the word of God for himself? You and your ilk—you fancy every man a priest. 'Tis for God's servants to teach the word of God, and not in the vulgar English tongue." Thomas grabbed the front of Edward's tunic with both hands and shook forcefully enough to poke a hole in the wool fabric. A thrust of Edward's knee met Thomas' groin. Thomas' knees buckled.

"The Son of God offered his people living bread and free salvation," Edward declared, towering above his nemesis. "The papists offer dead traditions and pardon sins for money. Tyndale said he would cause a plowboy to know more of the scriptures than the pope. 'Tis God opening the eyes of the people, stubborn mule! Will you keep yours closed?"

Matthew Cooper rushed over to extend a hand to Thomas. Once on his feet, Thomas barked, "You can quote scripture, can you? Here's what I think of Tyndale!"

At the loud *smack* of Thomas' fist against Edward's cheek, men and boys formed a circle around the brawlers and chanted, "Cock fight! Cock fight!"

Father Garrett galloped out of the church like a palfrey in a jousting contest, to discover a scowling fishmonger and a flaming redhead staring each other down like two felines in a tussle. The crowd parted as he approached the scuffle and demanded, "What in God's name is going on here?"

Wiping blood from his nose with his tunic sleeve, Edward responded, "An English Bible will soon be made available to all. My desire to read from it offends him." He pointed his chin at Thomas. "He wishes to seal off the well of living water to those who thirst." Thomas listened with both fists clenched, the veins in his neck bulging.

"I pray you—both of you. 'Tis incumbent upon all of us to do the king's bidding." The beleaguered priest turned to Thomas. "Cromwell ordered that an English Bible be placed in all parishes. No one will force you to read it." Thomas kicked at the ground, frowning.

Garrett looked up into Edward's eyes. "Mister Bartholomew, 'twas not long ago, the tide was against those of your opinion. I suspect you can understand Mister Nix's sentiments. Now, if you will excuse me, I pray you, let the fighting cease." He slinked into the church massaging his temples, his cassock swishing around his ankles.

Edward gathered his wife and two children. Matthew Cooper called on Anne to collect her three siblings, while he lingered to speak with Thomas.

Leaning against an oak on the riverbank, Christopher took note of the entire encounter, studying Anne's reaction. She didn't notice him, her attention absorbed with corralling her two brothers and sister.

"Nathan! Come here! John! Maria!" Shrieking, they chased a panicked hen toward the river. "Come here this instant!" Anne demanded. She stomped toward nine-year-old Nathan and reached for his cloak. He darted away, leaving her empty handed. As Anne approached the riverbank, Christopher's chest tightened. He struggled to think of something to say, words jumbling in his head like churning butter.

Matthew looked away from his conversation with Thomas to check Anne's progress, and discovered the three children ignoring their older sister. "Anne!" he shouted. "I told you to get the children!"

"They refuse to listen," she moaned.

"Nathan! John! Maria! Here, now!" At the sound of their father's voice, they abandoned the chicken and ran to Matthew's side. Anne trudged toward her family.

A mixture of relief and disappointment washed over Christopher. He felt sorry for her. He had to speak with her, but how?

ငဒ

Leaning forward against the wall of an arched stone bridge spanning the Darent River, Thomas Nix watched a yellow oak leaf meander along the water toward him and disappear under the bridge. His thoughts turned to The Pilgrim Hat's scant sales last Market Day. Melancholy engulfed him.

9

A hound barking in the distance on East Hill drew his attention to movement on the horizon, where Watling Street crested the hill and descended into the village. The ancient road had transported pilgrims back and forth between London and Canterbury—through Dartford for lodging and souvenirs—for hundreds of years. *Until now*, Thomas lamented, tucking a few strands of curly black hair behind his ears and brushing curled birch wood fragments from his jerkin.

The dimming light of dusk signaled suppertime. He slipped an unfinished Thomas Becket statue and knife into a leather purse strapped around his waist. Squinting toward the horizon, he made out the first of a large company of carts emerging over the hill. The first was followed by another, and then another, in a long caravan. *There must be more than twenty*, he thought. *One, two, three…seventeen, eighteen… twenty-six, twenty-seven, twenty-eight!* Twenty-eight carts! An entourage of men escorted the procession, some in front, some behind, and others on either side, while several men armed with pikes, spears and halberds carried large coffers.

What in Jove's name? he muttered.

"The king's men."

Thomas turned, startled to see Father Garrett standing a few paces away. "Father—I had no idea you were there," he stammered, returning his attention to the approaching company. "Who are they?"

"The king's men sacked Canterbury Cathedral. They're on their way back to London with everything—the precious relics, the jewels—everything." The priest punctuated his concern with a heavy sigh.

"God help us. The devil reigns over us now," Thomas whispered.

Father Garrett started to respond, but caught himself. He scratched his head, displacing a section of shortly cropped brown hair.

"It appears they looted the entire cathedral." Thomas straightened and stood rigid. "What right does the king have to rob God's holy church?"

"You know as well as I that His Majesty, and not the pope, is now the supreme head of the church in England. We've no choice but to bend with the times—or to be broken by them, as the case may be." The priest surveyed the surrounding bushes and lowered his voice. "Lollards and Lutherans prowl in our midst, wolves among the sheep." He pursed his lips.

Thomas hissed, "His Majesty is dancing with devils." Studying the priest's careworn face in the dimming light, he added, "Father, there is no one here but

10

you and I. This conversation need not travel any further. You agree with me, don't you? I detect it in your sermons."

Garrett's countenance darkened. "To speak ill of the king is an act of treason. If you value your life, you must mind your tongue. We can no more hold back the changes that howl around us than tame the wind."

"But Father, must we accept this sacrilege in God's church? Destroying holy altars? Burning sacred relics, breaking centuries-old stained windows and looting holy treasures to fill His Majesty's coffers? Can we stand helplessly by as heretics pollute the church—and destroy livelihoods? How will father and I survive without pilgrims?" He fished the Saint Thomas statue from his purse and turned it back and forth in his hands. "Who will be left to buy my souvenirs, with Canterbury laid to waste, and Saint Thomas' shrine destroyed?"

"I share your concern, but consider the fate of those who speak up—even in the king's closest circle. They're burned. Drawn and quartered. Beheaded. The head of Sir Thomas More, King Henry's finest, ended up on a pole on London Bridge. Is that the fate you seek?"

"My poor head on a spike on London Bridge? I think not."

"Your lot would be different. They hang, draw and quarter commoners. They don't even spare the maids. Think of Sister Elizabeth Barton, our dear Maid of Kent. Need I remind you what happened when she prophesied that evil would befall the king if he divorced Catherine?"

"Word was she went out of her mind with strange visions and prophecies."

"Fables. The king's men spread rumors that she engaged in wanton behavior with priests, and branded her lunatic. First defame, then arraign—that's what they do to those who dare to speak out. Cromwell's agents arrested her, and five others with her, and hung her at Tyburn gallows. Her head came to rest on a spike on London Bridge. Poor Elizabeth, she was the first woman to earn that honor. His Majesty intends to make an example of those he deems traitors. Do you think he would spare a lowly commoner like yourself?"

Thomas' heart raced. As always, he had been too quick to speak. "I spoke out of line, Father. I pray you, let it be as if this conversation never happened."

"Put your mind at ease." Father Garrett nodded. "But, by my truth, you must learn to mind your tongue. One must profess the proper opinion or suffer the consequences. You won't find me falling on my sword. I intend to keep my head down and my lips tight, I do."

"Long live King Henry," Thomas muttered.

"God save the king." Father Garrett took a deep breath and watched the company approach.

October, 1538

—

"What did you think of the rood displayed at the market last month?" William asked, peering over Christopher's shoulder while his son practiced a tabby weave.

"I didn't pay it much heed," Christopher muttered, his mind occupied with Anne Cooper from Tonbridge with the long chestnut locks.

"What is this rood you speak of, William?" Elizabeth stopped spinning and looked up.

"The Rood of Grace. 'Twas a wooden puppet of our Lord that the monks at Boxley Abbey used to swindle folks out of their money. It was paraded around market towns so folks could learn the truth about the papists. Last I heard, the Bishop of Rochester broke it to pieces in London."

"Hmm." She fingered the ridge of rosary beads beneath her green wool robe. "Well, maybe 'twas an honest mistake, and the monks truly believed in it." Watching Christopher flick the shuttle back and forth, she noted that he was becoming more like his father. Both had a rugged and sober demeanor, not quite brooding, but thoughtful. Christopher's translucent blue eyes reflected light like the surface of a brook—captivating eyes that made folks do a double take. He got them from her, along with his sandy blonde hair. *He's a good-looking young man*, she thought, even if she was a bit biased.

As the oldest in a family of eight children, Elizabeth grew up in nearby Maidstone, charged with the care of her younger siblings while her mother worked as a housemaid and her father as a blacksmith. William could forgive her if, taking care of all those children, she developed a bit of a bossy streak.

One couldn't sit at a spinning wheel day in and day out with nothing to think about, so she often entertained herself contemplating the whys and wherefores of things. For instance, who first looked at a field of flax, with its long stems and dainty blue flowers, and thought, *those plants would make a nice tunic*? Did Eve learn

13

to make cloth in the garden and teach it to her daughters, who passed it down from generation to generation until Elizabeth, herself, was taking part in something as ancient as creation? Thank goodness *someone* invented cloth, she thought, picturing William and Christopher traipsing around Dartford clad only fig leaves. At the image of herself wearing a fig leaf, she gasped. "Oh my! Methinks it would take a dozen fig leaves to cover this ample body."

"What did you say, Mother?" Christopher wound the horizontal weft thread over, under, and over the vertical warp thread, concentrating on making his tabby weave tight and even. The simplest of weaves, clothiers used it for basic items such as sheets.

"'Twas nothing." Elizabeth rested her spindle atop a small table and stretched her fingers, stiff after a day's work. Smoothing her apron, she gazed wistfully at her expansive lap, longing for the days when she took up less space on her stool.

William arranged his tools in a row on a table near the loom, grateful for Christopher's eagerness to learn. William, too, had been eager to learn as a boy, and would be working with his father if not for a sweating sickness outbreak that claimed the life of his father and three sisters. The tragedy left William's mother with two boys to raise alone. She sent William to work with his uncle Nathan, a linen weaver in Maidstone.

It was in Maidstone where William met an intriguing young woman on a hot July day at the St. Swithun Day's feast. He and Elizabeth chuckled about it ever since—how he had his head submerged in a pail of water, bobbing for apples. When he came up gasping for air, his eyes met a pair of bewitching blue eyes belonging to a blonde-haired maiden who stole his heart from first glance. He wasted no time in discovering that she was Elizabeth Page, and thus the courtship began. She liked to tease that he was in over his head when he met her.

Their courtship wasn't without wrinkles. The constable's wife warned Elizabeth of rumors that the Wade lad took part in secret meetings at his uncle's house to study the forbidden writings of men who wanted to reform the church. Whispers of Lollardy cast suspicion on the young man from Dartford. Elizabeth paid no heed; after all, William attended the parish church with her faithfully. Her mother thought Elizabeth must have feared becoming a spinster; why else would her daughter embrace the attention of a man flirting with heresy? But her mother was wrong; in fact, Elizabeth admired much about William. He worked hard, possessed ambition, and valued her opinion. After a church wedding, they moved to Dartford. William quickly established himself as a weaver, taking over what was left of his father's business.

14

Corralling her thoughts to the present, Elizabeth watched William run his hand across Christopher's practice piece, grateful for her husband's diligence in teaching Christopher the art of weaving.

With a pat on Christopher's shoulder William remarked, "Good work, son. Your tabby weave is near perfect. Tomorrow we'll start a twill. How about we celebrate with a cup of ale at the Crown & Anchor?"

Christopher set the shuttle on his lap with a wry smile. "The tavern?"

William winked.

Elizabeth stood abruptly and crossed the room to the cooking area, her footsteps heavy on the straw-covered dirt floor. The faint perfume of lavender and sage rose from the straw as she walked. She retrieved her cutting board from a small oak cabinet next to the fireplace and plopped it on the table, biting her tongue for several seconds until she could no longer hold back.

"You need not be cartin' him off to the tavern to keep company with ruffians and vagabonds. Why, just the other day the sheriff had to break apart a brawl there. Amy Coppinger said two lads were intent on killin' one another over the injunction abolishin' pilgrimages, and if the sheriff hadn't got there just when he did, Father Garrett would be preparin' for a funeral. If Amy doesn't know what's goin' on in this village, no one does. Tendin' to the inn as she does, she hears all."

Yes, things that happen as well as things that do not, William thought. "You know well enough what happens to tale bearers, Lizzie. Amy should be wearing a gossip's bridle, with that loose tongue of hers. I'm surprised her husband hasn't bridled her himself."

Elizabeth scolded her husband for speaking of a good Christian woman that way, while she retrieved her kitchen knife from a wooden box next to the butter churn.

"Soon Christopher will make his own way in the world," William persisted. "We might as well introduce him in small doses."

Elizabeth frowned her disapproval, but she rarely won an argument when it came to William's opinion on raising a son. A heavy sigh signaled her surrender.

"Before you go, Chris, there's supper to be preparin'. Run out to the garden and fetch me three turnips and an onion. I'll get the fire goin' and porridge in the pot. Then you and your father can run along."

Christopher glanced at his father. William winked. "I'll fetch some water from the well. Do what Mother asked."

Approaching the garden, Christopher was reminded that his mother took as much pride in growing things as his father did in weaving. The family's winter vegetables—onions, carrots, turnips and parsnips—stood in carefully cultivated rows, while a couple sections of herbs provided seasonings and ingredients for salves and potions. A beehive William placed a stone's throw from the cottage produced the sweet honey Christopher loved to drizzle on barley bread and porridge. Miss Piggle, the hog, inhabited a sty William built adjacent to the hive.

At the edge of the yard, a sturdy apple tree planted by Grandfather Wade provided the perfect place to survey the village. Forgetting his mother's request for turnips, Christopher scrambled up to the highest branch capable of supporting him and spied a cluster of boys racing along the Darent River behind a hound. He strained to see what the dog was chasing when a sharp sting in the back of his head jarred him from his mission. A rough stone, just larger than a robin's egg, bounced to the ground and landed next to the gnarled tree trunk.

"Ho, Lollard! Did your father give you heretic lessons today?"

Christopher turned to see John Whitfield and Edwin Taylor speeding downhill toward the village like two rabbits at the chase. He weaved his way down the branches and jumped to the ground, rubbing the developing welt on the back of his head.

"Come back, you lousy milksops!" he yelled at the top of his lungs, his voice cracking in mid-sentence. He had just started back up the tree when the pounding of footsteps stopped him. He leaped to the ground and picked up a couple stones, determined to not be caught off guard a second time.

Struggling to catch his breath, Nicholas Hall—Christopher's lifelong best friend—skidded to a stop at the base of the tree. "A fight is brewing at the Crown & Anchor!" he panted. "Thomas Nix thinks he can take on a whole company of king's men from London!" Nicholas' bushy brown eyebrows danced up and down like two caterpillars when he spoke.

Christopher let the rocks slip from his fingers, wiped his hands on his trousers and stepped forward. "Is there a fight?"

Nicholas shook his head. "Not yet, anyway. Father and I were laying brick on Bullace Lane when we saw a company of men enter the tavern—six or seven, at least—dressed to the hilt. Thomas watched them from his storefront and stormed straight to the tavern, with his poor father shouting after him to stop."

William rounded the corner of the cottage with a pail of water. Christopher waved his arms to get his father's attention.

"Mister Wade," Nicholas shouted, "Thomas Nix is fixing to take on a whole company of king's men at the Crown & Anchor."

William set the bucket down and leaned against the cottage to catch his breath. "Slow down, lads. What about the tavern?"

Nicholas sped across the yard with Christopher at his heels.

"Thomas Nix—I saw him shouting at his father about some royal visitors going into the tavern. I could see his spittle in the air. Mister Nix tried to pull him back."

William plopped the bucket against the cottage door and struggled to keep pace with Nicholas and Christopher in a dash down the hill toward High Street.

Hearing a thud, Elizabeth cracked the door open. She was greeted by a half-empty pail of water and a rear view of William, Christopher, and Nicholas. With hands on her hips, she sighed. "Good Lord. Not even a couple turnips. Methinks I have two children and no husband."

C&#x08;

"Twenty-eight wagons of loot! His Majesty will be pleased!"

The man boasting at the table nearest the tavern's front bay window reminded Christopher of a rooster crowing. Christopher leaned sideways and whispered, "Father, who is that?"

"He's one of Cromwell's commissioners."

"Cromwell?"

"Thomas Cromwell, the king's chief minister. He helped the king secure a divorce from Queen Catherine and pushed for the break with Rome. Remember Father Garrett reading injunctions directing pilgrimages to be abolished?"

"Yes. The townsfolk have been at odds since."

"The injunctions came from Cromwell. He charged that churches and monasteries 'round the realm be visited to expose corrupt behavior. Commissioners have been traveling England the past three years to uncover abuses and report back to the king."

Christopher raised his eyebrows. One of the king's men, just inches away from him! He elbowed Nicholas. The two watched, transfixed.

Pacing back and forth, the commissioner crowed, "We've got hundreds of years' worth of idol worship in our carts and coffers. Kings and princes, lords and ladies, pilgrims and dolts, all leaving their treasure for popish robbers. Ignorant beasts! It took eight men just to carry the coffers." He held a mug of ale to his lips and threw back his head. Christopher watched his Adam's apple bob up and down. The man slammed the mug on the table and wiped his wet lips on the shirt ruffle at his wrist.

Thomas Nix narrowed his eyes at the intruder. "Strutting like a peacock," he whispered to himself. Tapping his fingers on the table, Thomas cleared his throat and snipped, "Had a little too much ale, have ye?"

A livery worker at the table next to Thomas stared into his cider, vibrating the table as he shook his right foot. "He's one of the king's men," he whispered without looking away from his drink. "Mind your tongue!"

Thomas sized up the deficit in height and girth between the commissioner and himself. "I could take him," he boasted.

"Canterbury tops everything, I tell you," the commissioner went on. "We found enough treasure at the cathedral, I could buy myself a pope if I had a mind to. Ignorant dolts worshiping a traitor, Thomas Becket."

After a deep breath and a slow exhale, Thomas piped up, "With all due respect, sir, you're mistaken. Thomas Becket was a saint, he was. Still is, in fact."

The commissioner turned toward Thomas with a smirk. "A saint! By Jove, here we have a lad as ignorant as they come!"

"I beg to differ," Thomas countered. "My mother made a pilgrimage to Canterbury after two years of marriage as barren as Sarah. She kissed Becket's skull and prayed for a miracle, she did. Ten months later she delivered me and named me Thomas, in his honor. I'm living proof that Saint Thomas works miracles, blessed be his name." His right hand skimmed his chin and his chest, then his left shoulder and his right, while the commissioner watched the young man's display of hubris with a look of incredulity. Thomas figured his words had struck a chord.

Nicholas cast Christopher a sideways glance that said, *what is Thomas thinking?* Christopher shrugged his shoulders.

As the evening sun dipped below the horizon, darkness flooded the room. An awkward silence ensued until Amy Coppinger emerged from behind the counter, retrieved a long wood taper, held it to live coals in the fireplace, and waddled about illuminating lamps and candles. She retreated back behind the counter, her eyes filled with apprehension.

Eerie shadows filled the commissioner's eye sockets and the hollows of his cheeks. He locked eyes with Thomas and sneered, "Saint Thomas brought you into this world, you say?"

Thomas nodded. "He, himself, didn't bring me into this world, but he healed my mother's womb."

Letting out a howl that ricocheted off the tavern walls, the commissioner strode to Thomas' table, planted his hands palms down, and leaned in close enough that Thomas could smell the ale on his breath. "Idol worship is coming to an end in the realm. Your days of worshiping a false saint are over. You might as well kiss the skull of that yapping hound outside as to kiss Becket's. Yea, that dog is more of a saint than Thomas Becket." He pointed his thumb over his shoulder in the direction of the barking.

Thomas slowly rose to his full 6'2" stature, a head taller than the visitor. With his facial muscles tensed like a bow string pulled back, his head slightly lowered, and his eyebrows raised, he aimed a verbal arrow straight at the commissioner.

"I've a riddle for you. Tell me, sir, what is the difference between you and a donkey's arse?"

An icy silence filled the tavern as palpable as cold fog in the Darent Valley after a frigid November rain. One of the commissioner's traveling companions, a rotund man with an oily, egg-shaped face that reflected the candlelight, jumped up and stood next to his companion with his chin in the air, defiant.

William arose from his table and approached the scuffle. In a low voice he pleaded, "If it please you, gentlemen, the lads and I came for a pleasant cup of ale."

Without warning, Thomas shoved William backwards. Amy ducked behind the counter. William tripped over a stool, hit the wall and slumped to the floor. "Be quiet, you stinkin' Lollard," Thomas hissed. "'Tis you and your ilk bringing about this rubbish in England!"

Christopher stumbled around the table and extended a hand to pull his father up. Rising stiffly, William dusted off his buttocks and cast a solemn glance at the impetuous young man who assaulted him. "Look at us. Neighbors, countrymen, fighting in a tavern. We sit at mass together on Sunday reciting the Ten Commandments, but raise our fists every other day of the week. The good Lord said a house divided against itself cannot stand."

"Heresy divides us," Thomas growled, "and heresy will not stand! Lollards and Lutherans brought this curse upon us, and every last Lollard mongrel in England should be burnt, along with their Wycliff Bibles!" Snatching his cloak,

19

he spun around and stormed toward the tavern door while Amy peeked her head above the counter to watch.

"Traitors to his Majesty will not stand," the commissioner shouted.

Thomas turned. Pointing a finger directly at the king's representative, he shouted, "Traitors to God's holy church will burn in hell!" He slammed the door behind him, rattling mugs, dishes and wall hangings throughout the tavern.

☙

In the faint light of a half moon, Thomas scanned High Street from his vantage point at the cemetery next to Holy Trinity Church. A tilted stone cross, speckled with moss, partially obstructed his view. He shifted from his squatting position behind a tombstone and sat on his buttocks, stretching his legs straight in front of him. Tender calf muscles rebelled with spasms of pain.

He studied the inscription on the grave marker next to him. Many of the characters were too weather-worn to read, but he made out a name and date. "Margaret Poole, 1330." *I may soon be joining you, Maggie*, he thought. He eased up to a standing position, the loud pop of his knees sending a bolt of fear through his body. After a tentative glance in all directions, he tiptoed to Holy Trinity's vine-covered stone wall, flattened himself and wished he could melt into it. A dog barked near Market Square. His heart flip-flopped.

The Pilgrim Hat stood a leisurely two-minute walk from the church directly past the Crown & Anchor Inn, but it was a tortured fifteen-minute maze for a fugitive who had spoken against the king's reforms in the very presence of one of His Majesty's key enforcers.

Muffled voices came from the direction of the inn. He darted for cover in a patch of tall grass next to the river, a stone's throw from the church. A loud splash sent his heart pounding. He spun around to face his pursuer. A coot flapped it wings and ran across the water upriver. He almost laughed with relief.

Working his way along the riverbank through the grass, he cut around the back of the church, stopping every few seconds to listen. He snaked his way down an alley behind the Crown & Anchor, slinked next to the wall of the building, and finally made it to his back door. Surveying the area one last time, he slipped inside and eased the door closed behind him. With his back against the door, he slid down like a snail descending a blade of grass and cradled his forehead against his open palms.

20

He felt his father's presence beside him. "Where have you been?" Simon demanded. Thomas didn't bother to look up. "Talk to me. What is happening?"

"I'm done for!" Thomas lifted his head and rubbed his temples. Dark circles under his eyes betrayed his lack of sleep.

"What in Jove's name is the matter? I've never seen you like this. Catch your breath and tell me what is going on."

"A party of king's men was drinking at the tavern. Their leader spouted off blasphemies about Saint Thomas. He boasted on and on about his company stripping the entire shrine at Canterbury. They're spending the night in Dartford before they head back to London this morning with the holy relics—twenty-eight carts full." Thomas wiped his brow with his sleeve. "All doubt is gone. Our livelihood is done for."

Simon's face reddened. "His Majesty will stop at nothing to poke a finger in the pope's eye. But what does this commissioner have to do with you showing up like a chased stag in the wee hours of the morning?"

"Has anyone come by looking for me?"

"Yes, two men—the justice of the peace and another I didn't recognize. I thought perhaps you'd been involved in a brawl."

"A brawl it was, at the tavern. I stopped just short of calling Cromwell's commissioner a donkey's arse."

Simon's shoulders slumped. "A man must learn to bridle his tongue," he lamented. "I was trying to tell you that earlier, before you stormed off. God have mercy. What have you done?"

"Treason!" Thomas moaned. "Speaking against the king's reforms is treason!" He sprang to his feet, scrambled up the stairs to his chamber and knelt beside the wooden chest where he kept his most precious things. Throwing the lid open, he tore through the contents, leaving a litter of items about him on the floor like leaves scattered in a tempestuous wind.

"Here it is!" Cradling the Thomas Becket badge his mother purchased as a souvenir from her pilgrimage to Canterbury, he whispered, "Mother, you gave this to me when I turned twelve. You told me Saint Thomas helped bring me into this world, and would help me make my pilgrimage through life safely, so long as I'm faithful to him." He kissed the badge and tucked it into his leather purse.

Simon's silhouette darkened the doorway. "The king's men will be scouring Dartford. They've probably set a snare for you," his voice cracked.

"I intend to flee. I don't yet know where. If anyone comes looking for me and you say you have no knowledge of where I am, your answer will be truthful. Forgive me, Father. I hope I haven't brought ill upon you."

Simon crossed the room and plopped on Thomas' bed with a heavy sigh. "I can't believe this is happening. My only son, fleeing because of edicts that change so fast we can't stay on top of them." He thought for a moment and brightened. "What am I saying? We'll talk to Father Garrett in the morning. You had too much to drink. You can confess your error, pay your penance—perhaps a day in the stocks—and 'twill be forgotten. Everyone knows too much barley loosens the tongue. It can be forgiven."

Thomas shook his head. "At the tavern last night—'twas the king's men. They saw me. They heard me. They know who I am. I must flee while I've yet a chance. Besides, I have no future here. You intended for me to inherit the shop, but with the king's reforms, we're done for."

Simon scratched a large bald circle on top of his head while he frowned at the wood floor's uneven planks, stumped for a response.

After they descended the creaky staircase in silence, Thomas embraced his father and slipped out. Simon checked to see that the latch was securely fastened and dropped to his knees. A crushing pain tightened his chest, expanded into his soul, and worked its way out in the form of a wail.

"First my livelihood. Now my son. It is too much!" Looking up, he complained bitterly, "God, you ask too much!"

&

"A ha'penny for a poor man?"

The raspy voice gave Thomas a start. Cramped beneath the stone footbridge across the Darent, he had thought himself alone.

In the faint light of dawn, Thomas discerned the outline of a man's face. Warts and coarse grey stubble covered the wrinkled visage. The beggar's faded blue eyes, veiled with a thin white film, peered out from behind bushy salt-and-pepper eyebrows that resembled tufts above the eyes of a Scottish terrier. Part of his right ear was gone, the first penalty for begging without a license.

"Harry?"

"By Jove!" Harry's whole body shook. "Thomas?"

"Shh," Thomas warned. "The justice of the peace will be looking for you. Where is your license to beg? You can ill afford a second offense, unless you want to be hung."

"After they cropped me ear, I made sure to get a license, I did. Dropped it outside the tavern last night. The wind kicked up and carried it away like a swallow in flight. Look at me. Ye think I could run after it?"

Thomas gazed at the arthritic old beggar. He didn't care whether Harry was telling the truth about his license, but worried about Harry's witness to his flight.

Leaning next to Harry's ear he whispered, "I shall give you a ha'-penny, but you must be quiet. You never saw me here."

"Eh?" Harry screeched. Thomas recoiled at the stench of Harry's breath and pulled a worn ha'-penny from his pouch. With a wide grin, the old man revealed a collection of twisted teeth and toothless gums. "Thanks be to you, lad. The good Lord bless you." When Harry looked down to put the coin in his pouch, Thomas slipped his hand around a large stone and thumped the back of the vagabond's head. The coin rolled from Harry's limp fingers and came to rest in the mud a few inches away.

"Sorry, Harry, but I couldn't take any chances." Working quickly, Thomas dragged Harry out from under the archway and removed the beggar's tattered hemp cloak. It would make a good disguise—knee length, with a full hood to pull over his head. He rummaged through Harry's pouch. A water-stained piece of parchment at the bottom rewarded his efforts. He stuffed the begging license in his purse.

The approach of horses' hooves stopped him cold. He crouched under the bridge, barely breathing. As the ground vibrated above him, he waited in dread anticipation for the rider to stop. The clip-clop of hooves continued over the bridge into town. After a few seconds, the sound faded away.

Breathing a sigh of relief, Thomas pushed, pulled and tugged Harry's limp body partway under the bridge and laid his cloak over the man's legs. Next, he swung Harry's cloak around his shoulders and pulled the hood over his head. He took two pence from his pouch and laid them on the ground next to the vagabond. "I hope when you wake up—if you wake up—these will compensate you for your trouble," he whispered. He stood and jogged southward along Watling Street, staying close to gorse bushes and heather along the roadside to duck for cover if necessary.

A tug on the ankle startled Harry from his slumber.

"Wake up, sirrah. Up!" Andrew Barnes, a member of the king's company, dropped Harry's ankle and pushed the toe of his boot into Harry's side. "Is he alive, Luke?"

"Probably had too much to drink last night, like the rest of us. 'Tis his normal state in the morning." Luke Tisdale, Dartford's justice of the peace, knew Harry all too well. "We should have taken a few extra winks of sleep this morn, rather than getting up early to give that mouthy lad from the tavern a scare. He had some nerve calling the commissioner an arse, but I wager Master Throckmorton has been called worse—behind his back, at least."

Andrew grinned in agreement. He wrapped his hands around Harry's ankles and pulled the beggar out from under the bridge. "The young man is a disgruntled papist. Let him rant. 'Tis the clergy we need to worry about—the ones with power to stir up dissension among the flocks." Andrew dropped Harry's ankles and heard a moan.

Nudging Harry's side with his toe, Luke opined, "I daresay, the best way to push fear down the gullets of the commoners is to make an example of one of their own. Hits closer to home. 'Tis the impetuous young laborers with an appetite for uprisings. Think Wat Tyler and the peasants' revolt; those unruly ruffians wrought havoc in this very town."

"Another group of disgruntled peasants who didn't want to pay their taxes to the Crown." Andrew feigned a yawn. "We behead them, burn them, jail them to quiet them down for a few decades, until the horror of what befell their grandfathers fades away in the memories of the grandchildren. At any rate, I have more pressing matters than to pursue an impulsive, overgrown urchin. The company is headed to London as we speak. I wish to be along to see the tormented expressions on the papists' faces when they see cartloads of treasures making the pilgrimage back from Babylonian captivity."

Luke Tisdale glanced sideways at his companion. "You're pure evil, Master Barnes, finding joy in others' suffering. Pure evil, I say." He chuckled. "A good trait to have when in the king's employ. At any rate, we must at least make a token effort to find the lad, or it might appear we're shirking our duty."

"You make a good point; appearances are everything, after all."

Struggling to shake the fog from his brain, Harry pushed himself up to a sitting position and slumped back against the bridge. When his eyes fluttered open, he saw two men standing over him.

"Ho! What is all the hurly-burly?" Harry groaned.

Andrew responded first. "Have you seen a lad pass by between last night and this morning? Quite tall, about my height. He was sporting a yellow doublet with sleeves slashed in the German fashion. I don't recall the color of his trousers. Luke?"

"Methinks they were tawny."

Harry squinted against the blinding morning sun. "By Jove's footstool, if such a lad passed through, I slept clean through it."

Andrew looked Harry up and down. "Do you trust the word of a vagabond, Master Tisdale?"

"I have no reason not to. He got caught begging outside the parish and had his ear snipped years back. Been an honest man ever since."

"No one passed across the bridge, about this tall?" Andrew held his right hand in the air almost level with his horse's head. "Black wavy hair, muscular build, olive skin—resembles a Spaniard more than an Englishman. Methinks he would have appeared panicked—like a hare at the chase—unless he's a very good actor."

Harry scratched his head, wincing when he touched the welt from the rock with which Thomas hit him. "No, in truth, I haven't seen anyone fittin' that description."

"Do I see dried blood on your head?" Luke inquired.

"Blood?" Harry ran his fingers over the right side of his head.

"Other side," Luke pointed.

Harry felt the left side of his head, stopping at the rough, crumbly texture of dried blood. "By Jove, I must've stumbled and knocked meself out. 'Tis curious, it is. I don't remember falling."

Growing impatient, Andrew mounted his white palfrey and gathered the reins in his hands. "'Tis a waste of time talking to this lunatic while a heretic runs free. Shall we go southward on Watling? Most likely a rebel to the crown would head toward Spain. The Spaniards enjoy nothing more than harboring English heretics, except perhaps discovering new lands to expand their empire."

While Luke contemplated Andrew's question, Harry spoke up. "Ah, come to think of it, a lad did pass by here. Me head was fuzzy when ye first roused me. Whether he was wearing yellow, I don't recall, but his breeches was tawny in color, and I do believe he had curly black locks. Said he was going to London, I believe it was. I saw him go that way." Harry pointed north.

"Are you sure?" Luke inquired.

"'Pon my honor, I recall such a lad, and he said he was bound for London. 'Twas before the cock crowed." Harry ran his knobby fingers through his wiry grey hair to feel the dried blood, and then over his cloak to smooth it out, when he stopped short. "What in…" He swallowed his words, looking up at the two gawkers.

"The cloak appears a bit above your station," Luke noted. "I seem to recall seeing you in a tattered hemp covering."

"By God's teeth, I don't know where this came from. I laid me down with my hemp cloak, and awoke with this." Harry ran his cracked fingertips across the fine wool garment, stopping at soft rabbit fur along the edges.

"Dare we trust a man whose clothing magically changes overnight?" Andrew smirked.

"What else have we to go on?"

"Perhaps you're right. Looks like our mouthy rogue paid Harry an unfriendly visit. For what Harry's memory is worth, the fugitive said he was going to London. Risky as it might be, at least it is a lead." Andrew scanned the wooded horizon to the north.

"Toward London we go." Luke mounted his chestnut mare and gave her a gentle kick.

Andrew pulled a couple of coins from his pouch, not bothering to check their value, and tossed them in Harry's direction. "For your trouble," he said. Harry's face lit up.

Luke watched with a scowl. "You realize he will waste that on ale?"

Andrew chuckled. "The town beggar sees everything. 'Tis beneficial to be in his good favor."

ℭ

"How long will mother be gone?" Christopher washed down his last bite of breakfast porridge with a sip of watered-down ale.

"I reckon most of the morning," William replied. "Shall we work on a twill this morning?"

Christopher watched intently while William demonstrated a twill weave, taking the weft thread under two warp threads, then over one, offsetting the pattern by one warp thread on each row to create a diagonal design called a wale.

"Perhaps you would like to try your hand at a herringbone after you finish this one?" William asked. "'Tis a twill weave variation, and really quite easy. You simply alternate the pattern back and forth to create a zigzag."

"I would." Christopher began to practice a twill, and settled into a comfortable rhythm. "What will we use this piece for, Father?"

William thought for a moment. "Your mother might want to make some towels. She could stitch them with blackwork and give them as gifts, or sell them at the market and give you a share of the money."

Christopher nodded and continued, biting his lower lip. A question had been troubling him, but he was waiting for the right moment to bring it up. Elizabeth had to be away, as the topic would raise her ire. Any time she injected her opinion into a question he asked his father, a squabble ensued between his parents that sidetracked the entire matter. This morning, she was at the church with other women from the parish planning a church-ale to raise money for the leper hospital. Now seemed as good a time as any.

"Father, what exactly is a Lollard?" Without breaking stride, he prepared himself to be disappointed in the event William skirted around the topic.

William stared at the fire Elizabeth built earlier that morning to chase the damp chill from the cottage. He strode to the wood bin and selected a log, stirred the fire with the tip, and carefully placed the log where the coals were hottest. Turning toward his son, he contemplated the reflection of flames dancing in Christopher's inquisitive eyes. *A Lollard is someone with a fire in the soul*, he thought.

"Why do you bring up the topic?"

"John and Edwin call me a Lollard. And the other night at the tavern, Thomas Nix called you a Lollard."

"I regret taking you there. 'Twas an ugly scene."

"Did you know the king's men would be there?"

"No, I hadn't the slightest inkling. Since His Majesty has been closing shrines and monasteries, I've heard rumors that he might take Canterbury. But I wasn't aware, until they showed up in Dartford, that he carried it out. I imagine he'll be reveling in his new treasures—a dragon hovering over his lair."

Christopher visualized the scene he'd witnessed at the tavern. "Thomas Nix spoke with so much hate, Father. What is a Lollard, and why does Thomas blame them for what is happening to the church in England?"

27

William poked at the fire one last time and picked up an empty shuttle on the mantle to fiddle with. "You've already tasted a bit of the hatred some folks have toward those they call Lollards, and for that I am sorry. 'Tis not right that you should have to suffer because of their ignorance."

"People call us Lollards." Christopher's voice cracked. "I don't understand why. We go to mass, the same as everyone else. We do everything the others do, so why do they hate us?"

"'Tis not us they hate. Some folks are afraid of new ideas that challenge what they've always believed, though Wycliff's ideas aren't exactly new…"

Christopher interrupted. "Who is Wycliff? And what does he have to do with folks calling us Lollards?"

Rolling the shuttle between his hands, William paced back and forth in front of the fire. "Some two hundred years ago, John Wycliff taught at Oxford. His study of the Bible convinced him that the church had clean strayed from Christ's teachings. He went to work translating the Bible from Latin to English because he wanted folks to have Christ's word, to see for themselves what he saw. Without the Bible in their own tongue, folks have to rely on their priests to interpret scripture, and not a few priests are more ignorant than their parishioners."

"But Father Garrett preached in Latin until a couple of months ago."

"Cromwell's recent injunctions instructed parishes to conduct services in English. But for most of my life and yours, and for hundreds of years before that, services have been in Latin."

"But what good are they if folks can't understand them?"

William looked at the smoke-stained ceiling with a smile. "Wycliff thought exactly that. He grew critical of the Roman church and its officers, and believed some in the clergy held power over the people and robbed them by keeping them in ignorance. Some folks loyal to the church thought—and still think—if common folks had the Bible in English, they would misunderstand it and corrupt it. I give them one point—now that the English Bible is spreading throughout England, it is the source of much dispute. Even the king and his officers can't seem to settle on what we're to believe and practice."

"But where does 'Lollard' come from?" Christopher was growing frustrated. He wanted a simple answer.

"'Tis a nickname given to people who agree with Wycliff's teachings—some say it comes from the Dutch, meaning a babbler of prayers."

A shuffle outside the door signaled Elizabeth's return.

28

Christopher stopped weaving and whispered, "Father, I wanted to have this talk without her around."

William nodded. "We'll pick up where we left off." When Elizabeth entered, father and son looked at her blankly.

"Did I interrupt somethin'? You both look as if you've seen a sprite." She plopped a bundle of parsnips on the table. William and Christopher cast sideways glances at one another.

"We were just discussing supper," William teased. "Roast pork and peacock?"

"William Wade, I know you, and I suspect you were discussin' a good deal more than supper." She eyed them both with suspicion. "Amy gave me some fresh parsnips, and I was thinkin' of parsnip and leek pottage."

Christopher brightened. "With raveled bread?"

Elizabeth strode to his side and laid her hand on his shoulder. "No raveled bread today—we can't afford the wheat—but I stopped by the bakery for yesterday's cakes. No matter what I think of Edward Bartholomew, he did give me a discount."

Christopher shrugged his shoulders. "Day old cakes suit me."

William set the shuttle on the mantle and poked the fire. "Christopher and I need to fetch some wood. Do you need anything from outside, Lizzie?"

"If you happen upon an onion, my arms were too full to pull one up." With a look of reproach, she scolded, "Now, don't you be fillin' the poor lad's mind full of heretical ideas! He'll have enough strife in this world without you fillin' his mind with such notions!"

William tickled Elizabeth's ample waist. "Not filling up on Mother's pottage—now *that* would be heresy!"

"Oh, stop that!" Elizabeth slapped William's hand away.

"We won't be long."

Elizabeth cast William a warning glance, picked up a crate next to the fireplace, and thrust it toward him. "Get dry wood from the bottom of the pile. The wood from the top will smoke us out. You'll want your cloak. It's cold and damp outside."

As soon as they were outside crossing the wet grass to the wood pile, William continued. "As I was saying, Wycliff criticized the Roman church, as well as its clergy. He made it his life's work to put an English Bible in folks' hands so they could see the errors of the church."

"Is that why King Henry ordered the Great Bible to be in all the parishes?"

"Well, I think the king's motives are more complicated than that. That's a topic for another day."

They arrived at the wood pile. William stopped and lingered, waiting for Christopher to make eye contact. "Son, what I tell you here might not matter to you now, but some day you will likely have more questions. 'Tis important to question, and I will never fault you for it. Lots of folks who heard Wycliff's teachings agreed with them. Many in high positions were threatened at hearing the church criticized. They came up with the nickname 'Lollard' to make light of Wycliff's followers. When people call someone a Lollard, 'tis no compliment. They mean a heretic—someone they consider ignorant for following Wycliff, and guilty of leading others astray."

Christopher filled the crate with split wood, then picked up a few pieces to cradle in his arms. William lifted the crate with a grunt. They were halfway to the cottage when Christopher stopped. Searching William's eyes he asked, "Are we Lollards?"

Taking a deep breath, William adjusted his grip on the crate. "We must be careful what we call ourselves. Would that we could speak as we think, and worship as we believe, but this old world will never welcome that idea. The Son of God was crucified between two thieves, and his greatest crime was teaching the truth."

He set the crate down and shook out his hands. "As more and more people accepted Wycliff's teachings and spoke out against the church, Parliament passed a law called *de heretico comburendo*, Latin for 'regarding the burning of heretics.' The law made Wycliff's ideas a crime, and called for the destruction of all books and writings in support of his ideas. It also ordered those who refused to recant to be burned as heretics. You understand what heresy is?"

"Speaking ill of the pope or the king?"

"Partly. A few years after Wycliff died, King Henry IV passed a law that made translating or owning a Bible a crime. The law deemed those who disobeyed heretics, and they faced burning at the stake unless they recanted."

"For having a Bible?" Christopher's eyes widened.

"For the crime of having a Bible," William nodded.

"Is someone who owns a Bible a heretic?"

"Not presently, but just a few years ago 'twas so, and it could be again."

"Father, *you* have a Bible."

William swallowed and looked down at the crate. "Is there something else?" he asked. He picked up the crate and took a couple of steps toward the cottage, when Christopher's voice stopped him.

"Father, are *you* a heretic?"

Setting the crate down again, William sighed, "We forgot to get Mother an onion. Run along and tell her I'm on my way with one."

Maidstone, England

Thomas swiped his hand across his cheek to chase away a pesky gnat. "Be gone," he demanded, swatting again. A missed night's sleep and a fretful day's travel southeast toward Maidstone left him weary and ill-tempered. Illuminated in the setting sun, the bluish-grey ragstone tower of Maidstone's All Saints' Church towered in the distance.

Spotting a grove of oak trees far enough off the road to hope that he might rest undetected, he made his way there and settled in for the night, using the tattered cloak as a covering. Sleep eluded him. He fancied every noise an enemy. The faraway bark of a dog was the king's hounds tracking him; the whir of a bird passing overhead was an arrow flying past. When he finally drifted off around midnight, he awoke every hour or so and laid awake for several minutes, listening.

He had just drifted back to sleep when he felt a tickle on his side. Brushing it away, his hand encountered cold metal. His eyes blinked open to see two men staring down at him, one with his dagger drawn.

"By Jove, methinks he's a runaway."

"Sir George, you be too easy on the rogue. I know gutter scum when I see it."

"Gutter scum is too gentle, Sir Robert. Perhaps he's a heretic!"

"Slay the heretic! Slay the heretic!" George—a portly, middle-aged man—accompanied his singsong chant with jabs from the butt of his dagger to Thomas' side.

Thomas pulled the cloak around him, bolted upright and exclaimed, "By God's teeth, let a poor beggar alone."

"Beware how you speak to the constable!" George puffed out his chest. "A young and able-bodied lad, a beggar?" Placing his dagger blade next to Thomas' right ear, George leaned close and growled, "Bet you committed a crime. Who are you running from?" He studied the tattered cloak and sneered, "Did the hounds drag you through the countryside and tear up your clothes?"

31

Robert chimed in, "Just where did you get that rag, sirrah? Steal it off a vagabond, did you? You'd best tell the truth. 'Tis no light crime to deceive Maidstone's justice of the peace."

Beads of perspiration formed around Thomas' hairline. Justice of the peace? Constable? Had the news of his crime preceded his arrival in Maidstone? As the two men cackled, George's dagger blade vibrated against Thomas' ear.

"Swipe his ear, George," Robert chirped. "He's pretendin' to be a beggar."

Thomas stiffened. "I pray you, sirs, lower the dagger and hear the truth."

"'Lower the dagger,' he says. What do you think, Robert?"

"''Tis a ruse," Robert snipped. "He wants us to put our guard down."

"I come from London," Thomas lied. "I know nothing of heresy or vagabonds." George tickled his ear with the dagger blade.

"Let him speak, George. Perhaps he's got good cause to be hidin' outside Maidstone. Whether it be truth or not, the dagger will decide."

George lowered the dagger to his side. "Say on. What's your name, lad?"

With a polite nod, Thomas began. "Name's Harold…Harold…" He spotted a broken arrow in the grass behind the men. "Harold Archer, good sirs. My father died of a fever, he did, and left behind my mother with a suckling infant and five more including me, six in all. Mother got the pox and died shortly after. Saint Helen's in London assisted us, until the king ordered her doors closed year past. I searched for work in London to take care of my poor brood, but alas, methinks half of England is looking for labor there. Presently, I'm making my way to…"

"Enough!" George raised the tip of his dagger to Thomas' ear. "Methinks you're a liar. A young man finding no labor in London? Lies, I say!" A second too late, Thomas raised his arms in self-defense.

"I beg your mercy!" he demanded, wiping a warm trickle of blood from his earlobe.

"Get your tale straight, or we'll flog you and cart you through Maidstone!" George demanded, wiping the bloody tip of his dagger on his breeches while Robert circled Thomas, his head cocked sideways. Thomas nearly choked on the pungent odor of perspiration wafting about Robert like a cloud.

Robert stopped directly in front of Thomas, and rested his hands on his hips. "As Maidstone officials, it behooves us to let the lad explain. With King Henry throwin' nuns and monks out on their arses to roam the countryside in search of a livin', labor is hard to come by. Let me question 'im." Like a cow chewing its cud, he twisted his mouth and spewed a wad of spittle past Thomas' head. Thomas' heart skipped a beat.

32

"Ye claim to be a beggar?" Robert blinked.

"I do not 'claim' to be, but I am in truth."

"Have ye permission to beg? Your beggar frippery looks real, I'll give ye that. Whether the rags be your own, or stolen, is the question." Robert eyed Thomas' purse on the ground nearby.

Willing his knees to stop shaking, Thomas explained. "Sister Mary, one of the nuns at Saint Helen's who knew of my plight, sent me to seek work in the wool trade with her brother in Calais. She pleaded with the London justice of the peace to grant me a begging license to sustain me until I arrive there."

"The king's law prohibits begging without a license. Show your license, if you be a legal beggar." George stuck his hand out, waiting for Thomas to produce the piece of paper.

Thomas crouched down to retrieve his purse from the dew-covered grass where he laid it the night before, keeping a hawkish eye on his two inquisitors. Standing up slowly, he slipped his right hand inside the bag and felt the pilgrim badge, praying silently to Saint Thomas for protection. Taking pains to avoid jingling the groats and pence in his purse, he fumbled for the stolen begging license.

George grunted, "If you be an imposter, you will soon regret it."

"'Tis here, I swear it."

"You have three seconds to produce the license before we hobble you and flog you on High Street in Maidstone." Tugging up on his sagging tights, George flashed Robert a twisted grin.

Perplexed, Thomas rummaged through his purse one more time. He'd checked to make sure the license was there the night before.

"Three. Two…"

A tattered paper fluttering in a hawthorn bush several feet away caught Thomas' eye. He lunged toward the bush. "This is it." Shaking the license in front of Robert and George, he pointed at the lettering. "You see my name, Harry, right there. Harry, Harold, 'tis all the same." Before they could reach for it, he stuffed the paper into his pouch.

"Not so fast." George took a step forward. "What are you hiding? Show us the license."

"I showed you. Now, if it please you, I must be on my way to Calais. Good day." Thomas stepped sideways. Robert shuffled directly in front of him. "I shall be on my way," Thomas nodded, forcing a smile. "Kindly step aside, sir. I'm sure others are more deserving of your attention." Robert pawed at Thomas' pouch. Thomas hopped backwards.

"What is it ye be hiding, lad?" Robert growled. "Give me the paper."

George stabbed his dagger into the grass to free his hands while he strode with outstretched arms toward Thomas, as if ensnaring a wayward chicken.

"Let me alone!" Thomas backed away. "I have nothing of value to you."

"He doesn't trust us, George. See the fear in his eyes?" Something about Robert's demeanor raised the hair on Thomas' arms. "Now why would two of Maidstone's officers be out on the highway molestin' unsuspecting travelers? That wouldn't be proper behavior now, would it?"

George crept toward Thomas while Robert chattered, "Who are ye, lad? Ye show up in Maidstone parish claimin' to be a beggar, yet we never saw the likes of you before. The law forbids beggin' outside of your own parish, even if you do have a license. Are you a highway robber, lad? A cutpurse? Tell the truth."

"I told you the truth. Name's Harry. I've nothing to hide."

"At the very least, we'll have to send ye back to your own parish. If ye can't show your license, we'll cut off your ear. I say, Harry, show the license. George, back off and give him a chance to show the license."

Seeing no other option, Thomas pulled the license from his purse. Robert approached slowly and deliberately, like a cat stalking a bird. Extending the license to Robert, Thomas kept a close eye on George. Robert snatched the paper and backed up, sounding out the words while George looked over his shoulder.

"D..Dar...Dart...f..ford P...Par...ish. Look here, George, it says, 'Dartford Parish.'" He handed the license to George.

George stared at the paper blankly. "What do you want me to do with this? I can't read."

"The word 'Dartford'? Right here, Dart..."

"I said I can't read!"

Seizing the opportunity while the two men were distracted, Thomas lunged for George's dagger. Gripping the handle with both hands he diced the air, waving it back and forth in front of him. George dropped the license and froze. Robert made his way forward, one deliberate step at a time.

"Halt," Thomas growled.

George's eyes widened. "Robert, listen to him. He looks like a tethered bear—got a wild look to his eyes."

"Now, calm down, lad," Robert cooed. "We mean you no harm." Robert moved a step closer.

Seized with adrenaline, Thomas aimed the dagger directly at Robert's chest and lunged forward. Robert stumbled backwards, blood spurting from his wound.

"He got me!" Robert gasped, his eyes wide with panic. Covering the wound with his hands, he fell to his knees.

Enraged, George tackled Thomas. The dagger went flying.

"Please God, help me!" Robert screamed. "George," he wheezed.

Thomas dove for the dagger and sprang to his feet, daring George to come closer. After several seconds of tense stare down, George stumbled toward his partner.

"I warned you," Thomas' voice quivered, "leave me to go my way and you'll have no further trouble. Threaten me again, and you'll be wearing this dagger in your chest."

George swung off his cape and knelt beside his companion, pressing the garment tightly against Robert's chest. Turning his face toward Thomas he growled, "You'll pay for this. You may get ahead of us for now, but you will pay."

Փ

Thomas stumbled to a stop in a grove beside the Medway River, figuring he'd been running for at least an hour. Pain seared his lungs. His thigh and calf muscles burned. Taking solace in the likelihood that he successfully escaped—a rider would have caught up with him by now—he crawled under an alder tree and leaned back against the trunk, listening to the cadence of his own hard breathing. The spongy soil provided a welcome cushion for his aching body.

Justice of the peace. Constable. He shook his head. Imposters, both of them. Ah, the devices highwaymen concocted to separate travelers from their belongings. They had him fooled at first. He pulled an apple from his purse, took a greedy bite, and contemplated his conundrum. How could it be that in the space of two days, he'd gone from a respectable merchant's son, to a disobedient subject, to a potential murderer? If not for his aching muscles and foreign surroundings, he might believe it all to be a bad dream.

How bitter the irony that he, who had always considered obedience to the laws of church and king to be of utmost importance, found himself fleeing because of those very laws. How did allegiance to the centuries-old Christian faith suddenly become a crime? Taking another bite of apple, he wondered how he was supposed to respond when his conscience told him the king stood in open

35

rebellion to God's church. Did God expect him to submit for the sake of being a peaceful subject? Should he obey his king, or God's pope?

An image came to mind, that of a large black bear tethered to a post with a chain around its leg. His father took him to a bear baiting in Southwark when he was a young lad. He recalled the agony of watching adults cheer on bloody and wounded bullmastiffs tearing at a bear's flesh while it swiped frantically in self-defense. Now he was that bear, chased by the king's dogs. Perhaps it was a blood sport the king enjoyed, chaining his subjects to impossible edicts and sending out human bullmastiffs to enforce them. *Like the bear, I will fight to the death*, he told himself.

After flinging the apple core aside, he wiped his sticky fingers on the cloak, licked the sweet residue from his lips and pondered his next move. Calais was out of the question; the region fell under King Henry's rule. Germany harbored too many Lutherans; he could never pretend to sympathize with their cause. France was a possibility. His uncle hunted truffles there and returned to tell of beautiful ladies, rolling hills and green river valleys. And Spain would no doubt always remain loyal to the Holy Mother Church.

Fishing the Saint Thomas badge from his pouch, he squeezed it in his hand with a silent prayer and worked his way through oak trees and thick undergrowth. When he reached the riverbank he knelt and laid the badge on the grass next to him. With the hood of his cloak drawn back, he cupped his hands into the water and splashed his face, neck and forearms. A few seconds after the water settled, he gazed at his reflection and gasped. Dark blood stains covered the front of the cloak.

He picked up the badge, kissed it, and whispered, "We fly to thy protection, O holy Mother of God. Despise not our petitions in our necessities, but deliver us always from all dangers, O glorious and blessed Virgin." After making the sign of the cross, he pulled back his arm and hurled the badge into the water for good luck.

Dover popped into his mind. If all went well, three days' journey would take him there, to cross the English Sea into France.

Dartford

"Elizabeth? Elizabeth! Have you heard?" Amy Coppinger sang her words as she shuffled up the pathway to Elizabeth's cottage, lifting her moss-colored skirt with both hands to avoid tripping. Elizabeth paused in her task of hanging freshly washed towels to give Amy her full attention.

"What is it, Amy?" Elizabeth inquired. "What do you know?"

Amy stopped a few steps away, leaning forward with her hands on her thighs. "Whew! Let me catch my breath," she panted. "My heavens," she heaved, "I used to run up this hill when I was a girl. Anyway, I saw Simon Nix in Market Square just now, cursing your husband for chasing away his son. He had a crowd about him, stirred up into a frenzy. 'Lollard this' and 'Lollard that,' he shouted, his arms waving. That new fishmonger in town—what is his name?—'tis on the tip of my tongue…"

"Cooper!" Elizabeth chimed in, leaning forward. "Matthew Cooper."

"Yes, Matthew Cooper—he stepped forward from the back of the crowd, shouting in support of Simon and shaking his fist in the air. That girl of his—I feel sorry for her—she stood off and watched the entire scene, looking as if she wished she could hide under a rock."

Elizabeth lowered her voice. "Now don't say this to anyone, Amy," she flashed her eyes left and right, "but I do believe Christopher has taken a likin' to that girl. And I'm just not sure how I feel about my son takin' a fancy to the daughter of a man like that. Why, the man is always red in the face. Wouldn't be surprised to see the top of his head blow off like the lid from a boiling kettle next time Father Garrett reads from the injunctions."

Christopher watched from the pigsty, just finishing up his daily chore of dumping slop into the feeding trough. The mention of Matthew Cooper pricked his ears.

"That girl needs a womanly influence in her life, by my troth," Amy declared, licking her fingers to stuff a renegade strand of prematurely grey hair under her coif. The gesture called Elizabeth's attention to deep pock marks across Amy's forehead. "Imagine, a young maiden like that being brought up by a fishmonger. She does all the tasks of running a household, from tending the children to washing the clothing. Poor thing. A wife to her father, she is."

"Yes, 'tis indeed pitiful. Now, you were sayin', Simon was publicly blamin' my William for his son's disappearance? I've a mind to have a word with that man." Elizabeth pinned the last towel to the line with a disgusted *humph*.

"Stay clear of him, Elizabeth. He's an unsteady man." Amy cracked her knuckles with a smug look on her face, a habit she had when she finished sharing especially juicy gossip.

With the slopping finished, Christopher set the bucket in its proper place, snuck behind a patch of gorse bushes, and ran down the hill toward the village center. Amy could talk for hours, and so could his mother. They wouldn't miss him. He ran until he reached High Street, hid around the corner of the candle maker's store kitty-corner from the church, and peered toward the market cross. Simon was still there, along with Matthew Cooper and a crowd of a dozen or so townsmen.

He watched a boy about eight years old chase Anne's siblings in the churchyard, while Anne stood with her back against the Crown & Anchor Inn, her eyes cast down at the street.

"Psst!" Christopher tried to get the boy's attention, but the children's laughter drowned out his voice. Picking up a small pebble, Christopher tossed it at the boy's torso. The lad looked in all directions with eyebrows raised, until his eyes rested on Christopher. Holding a ha'-penny high, Christopher raised and lowered his eyebrows to tantalize the lad. The boy trotted toward him, the other children following like baby ducklings. Shaking his head no, Christopher motioned for them to stay. They returned to their play.

"What is your name?" Christopher asked when the boy reached him.

"Howard."

"Howard, how would you like to earn this halfpenny?" Christopher flipped it in the air and caught it.

The boy's dark brown eyes opened wide. "How?"

Pointing to Anne, Christopher said, "Go tap that maiden on the shoulder and tell her to look my way."

"Miss Anne? Her father will be angry with her if she leaves," the boy objected. "He told her to watch the children."

"Do you want this coin or not?" Christopher pretended to return it to his pouch.

"Just tap her on the shoulder?" With an approving nod from Christopher, Howard bolted forward.

"Wait!" Christopher grabbed the back of the boy's cloak. "Try not to attract attention. Pretend you're the king's spy, and you must not be noticed."

"I will." Bubbling with enthusiasm, Howard demanded, "Now, give me the ha'penny."

"You must first follow my instructions. Be careful to not draw any attention."

"I will." Howard glanced across the street at Anne.

38

"Good. Now, go do what I asked. I'll be watching. Then come back for your money." Christopher picked up three stones and juggled them, thinking *getting her attention is the bravest thing I've ever done.* All activity around him blurred except for Howard walking toward Anne, and Anne leaning against the wall of the Crown & Anchor, wrapping and unwrapping a section of her hair around her forefinger.

As Howard spoke with her, she looked toward the candle shop. Christopher stopped juggling to watch from the corner of his eye, feigning disinterest. Howard ran to Christopher for his coin before rejoining the Cooper children.

A shout went up in Market Square. Matthew Cooper motioned with his right arm for the crowd of men to follow him. The entire group moved like a pack of feral dogs toward the Crown & Anchor. Anne started toward Christopher. Christopher shook his head no. She studied him quizzically. A deep voice behind her stopped her in her tracks.

"Where do you think you're going?"

Anne spun around, her heart racing. "Father! You startled me!" She cast a quick glance across the street. Christopher was gone. "I wanted to be closer to tend to the children at the church." Matthew surveyed the churchyard, satisfied to see his children playing tag on the grass.

"I'm going into the tavern to discuss urgent matters with the townsmen. Watch the children until I come out. Understood?"

"May I go over to the churchyard with them?"

"Yes, but don't go anywhere else. Understood?"

"Yes, I understand."

"Very well. I won't be inside long." The rest of the men were already in the tavern when Matthew disappeared inside.

Anne ran to the churchyard, turned back to look across the street where Christopher stood minutes earlier, and then surveyed Market Square. The town center was calm.

"Miss Cooper?" Christopher's head appeared above the tall grass on the riverbank behind the church. She cast an astonished look in his direction, then checked her siblings in the churchyard. Howard was playing Robin Hood while the other children dodged his imaginary arrows. She ventured to the riverbank.

"Ho there." Christopher suddenly wished he could duck down and hide.

"Hello." Mildly vexed, she blurted, "Why are you hiding?"

"What about your father?"

"He'll be in the tavern until he's wearing a barley cap. It's always that way."

Christopher emerged from the grass. "Christopher Wade," he said, brushing weed debris from his tunic before removing his wool flat cap. "Pleased to make your acquaintance." He sneezed.

She covered her mouth and giggled. "I know. I've seen you before."

Feeling foolish, he argued, "But we didn't speak. John butted in."

"Yes, you were the rodent, come to behold the Rood of Grace." Her eyes twinkled when she smiled.

He thought she looked lovely in her sage-colored dress, but didn't dare say so. Instead, he rolled his eyes. "John and Edwin live to torment me."

"Don't worry. I know their kind. You bear no resemblance to a rodent."

They looked each other squarely in the eyes. His heart danced.

"Your father is a…" both spoke at the same time. Christopher shrugged his shoulders. "I pray you, speak first."

"Fishmonger." Anne smiled.

"Linen weaver." His chest tightened. He had no idea what to say next.

"I see you and your father every Saturday. Your linen is beautiful."

"Thank you." He picked up an egg-sized stone and tossed it back and forth between his hands.

"Are any of the linens yours?"

"Some of the towels are mine." He picked up a second stone and juggled it with the first. "I'll soon be moving on to larger things, like sheets and sailcloth."

"The blackwork towels are lovely." She watched the stones circle round and round between his hands, wishing he would keep his eyes on her instead.

"My mother stitches them."

Anne's younger sister, Maria, ran up and tugged on Anne's frock. "Nathan keeps pinching me!" she complained.

With a threatening look in Nathan's direction, Anne warned, "Tell him he must leave you alone, or Father will give him a lashing when we get home."

Before she ran off, Maria stopped to watch Christopher. "Are you a juggler?" she inquired, wide-eyed.

He dropped one of the stones and blushed. "No, but I enjoy practicing." No longer impressed, Maria rejoined her siblings.

"I must be going as well." Anne bit her bottom lip and looked toward the Crown & Anchor.

"But you just arrived."

"Father will whip me if he finds out I spoke with you."

"Your father knows me?"

"No, but he knows who your father is—a Lollard."

Undaunted, Christopher blurted, "Meet me here on Market Day."

"Father would never allow it."

"Find an excuse. Please?"

"It just won't work. My father is…" she stopped.

"A fire-breathing dragon?" Christopher finished her sentence.

A glance toward the tavern dimmed her countenance. "I really must go now." She turned and ran, reaching her siblings just as Matthew peeked his head out the tavern door. "You mustn't do that again, Nathan," she shouted, approaching the children.

"What?" Nathan looked at his sister quizzically.

She raised a hand toward the tavern. "All is well, Father."

Matthew nodded and disappeared behind the door. Anne breathed a sigh of relief and looked at Christopher as if to say, *do you see what I mean?*

Christopher looked, but he didn't see. Planning their next encounter occupied his thoughts.

November, 1538

Dartford

The adoration English subjects showered upon Thomas Becket might have chafed at the pride of any monarch, but for King Henry VIII, locked in a power struggle with the church in Rome, his subjects' devotion to the saint was especially irksome. Because of Becket's stand with the church and against an English monarch three centuries earlier, the saint represented precisely that which King Henry loathed: the church's affront to his royal power.

Reverence for Becket saturated the hearts of Englishmen as rain saturated the kingdom's soil. All of Christendom celebrated Becket's feast on December 29, the fifth day of Christmas, but the English held an additional feast day in his honor on July 7. Churches bearing Becket's name outnumbered those named after any other holy figure, except God himself. Statues and altars erected in Becket's honor everywhere seemed to thumb their noses at the king. Primers and psalters included prayers to him and images of him. Calendars lauded him. Dartford's Holy Trinity Church had a special chapel and altar dedicated to the saint where pilgrims worshipped on their way to Canterbury.

All of which made the task in front of Father Garrett this blustery morning especially daunting.

The deceased archbishop was nowhere near Christopher's thoughts as he stood in the nave, feeling giddy. He was supposed to be focused on memorizing the sixth commandment, *Thou shalt not kill*. Concentrating on four short words should have been easy, but his problem had nothing to do with the phrase itself, or the frigid November wind howling outside the church door, or the torrential rain pelting the windows. The problem stood directly in front of him, with cascading chestnut locks and a blue frock.

Father Garrett raised his voice and commenced the recitation of commandments from the beginning. "Thou shalt have no other gods before me." He surveyed his flock to ensure that all who were able participated, and moved

42

to the second, "Thou shalt not make unto thee any graven image." By the time parishioners reached the sixth commandment, restless nine-year-old Nathan Cooper shouted each word with an exclamation point: Thou! Shalt! Not! Kill! The boy's antics drew a crooked grin to the weary priest's face, but a frown to Matthew Cooper's. Upon reaching the tenth commandment, "Thou shalt not covet," the priest cast a quick glance at Theresa Willoughby. She looked up at him with a half-smile. Garrett blushed.

"Ahem. Yes, very well. If you find yourself unable to recite all of the commandments, please do what is necessary to learn them. We're to have the Lord's Prayer and Creed memorized by Easter. You should accomplish this before you come to confession or partake of the host, per Cromwell's injunctions." He glanced at Jesus on the back wall to buoy himself up, and cleared his throat. "In addition, I have a new proclamation to announce."

"More?" William whispered to Elizabeth. He saw her jaw muscles tighten.

Father Garrett bit the inside of his cheek, a pained look on his face. "The September injunctions instructed the king's subjects to discontinue divers feast days and cease the worship of such saints as were then named. We have additional word in regard to Saint Thomas Becket." He glanced up at the lofty stone ceiling, begging heaven for help, before resting his eyes on a paper on his podium. The congregation hushed.

"It says here, Saint Thomas' death was wrongly called martyrdom. His own stubbornness created the riot that led to his death. There appears to be nothing in his life that justifies his being called a saint, but rather he was a rebel and a traitor to his prince." Matthew Cooper gasped. Like frogs croaking in a pond at dusk, murmurs erupted across the congregation.

Father Garrett continued, "Henceforth Thomas Becket shall not be esteemed, named, reputed and called a saint. His images and pictures throughout the realm shall be plucked down and removed out of churches, chapels and all other places. From henceforth, festivals in his name shall not be observed. The prayers in his name shall not be read, but erased out of all books."

Matthew Cooper could no longer restrain himself. "All books, Father? Even the primers?"

"All books," Father Garrett said, his voice sharp with aggravation. "Yes, yes, even the primers."

"But my primer came down to me from my mother, God rest her soul." Cooper lifted the primer in his right hand and exchanged glances with Simon Nix before he continued. "The king is asking me to deface my mother's book. 'Tis

43

not proper, Father. No one should ask this of us." Not knowing what else to say, the priest shrugged his shoulders.

Elizabeth whispered a silent *amen* to Cooper's objection. She, too, revered her primer. Erase Saint Thomas? 'Twas blasphemy!

Simon Nix cried out, "But what about our Saint Thomas feast? We've always kept our Saint Thomas feast, and Saint Thomas has kept us!"

"'Twill be held as an ordinary day." Father Garrett stood before his parishioners feeling like a shriveled snakeskin from which the life had slithered away.

"'Tis scandalous!" Matthew Cooper shouted, his face red. "What of my Saint Thomas badge from Canterbury? Shall we do away with our badges—what they now call idolatry?" Father Garrett looked at the church door. For a split second, he imagined slithering out.

"How will the king enforce these edicts?" Cooper demanded. "Will he send officers to check on us in our cottages and shops? Will the constable come calling to inspect our primers? Or is it you, Father? Will you check our coffers to make sure we've done away with our badges?" Matthew wiped beads of perspiration from his forehead with the back of his hand.

Simon Nix chimed in, "The holy altar in our church—why, 'tis named after Becket himself. I suppose the king will sack our church, as he did Canterbury?" For the first time Christopher could remember, Father Garrett looked like a boy about to cry.

A group of men standing in the back of the nave murmured loudly among themselves, while directly in front of the Wades, Simon Nix raised his right hand. Father Garrett glared at him, his eyes hollow. "The Fifth Day of Christmas, Saint Thomas' feast, is barely a fortnight away. Am I to understand we can't celebrate it? Shall we now be required to labor on that day?"

Father Garrett shrugged his shoulders.

Simon turned to address the congregation. "We might as well build a moat around the village," he shouted. With a contemptuous look at William, Nix continued, "The king has chased away our pilgrims and abolished our feasts. What next? Will he close the priory and run the nuns out of Dartford? He's already closed the smaller religious houses. Mark my words, he'll drive my daughter clean out of Barking Abbey, as he drove my son from Dartford."

"England is bein' sacked from within!" The booming voice of Amy Coppinger's husband, Tom, bounced off the walls from the rear of the nave. "The inn and tavern are already suffering from lack of pilgrims to spend the night.

44

I have only one thing to say. The king is mad!" He grabbed Amy's hand and stormed out the door. Several others followed, including Matthew Cooper and Simon Nix. Anne made eye contact with Christopher and smiled as she passed by—at least he thought she did. Mark Whitfield followed with his family. John Whitfield cast a disparaging glare at Christopher on his way out.

Father Garrett waited for the murmurs to subside, leaning forward upon the pulpit for support. "Do I rule in the king's stead?" he asked in shrunken voice. "These are difficult times for all of us. I am a man, like you, and I must submit as well."

Those who he figured most needed to hear the message were gone.

☙

With the wooden trenchers washed and dried, and the fire covered for the night, Elizabeth retrieved her nightshirt from its peg.

"Did you hear the curfew bell?" William cocked his ear toward the door.

"No." Elizabeth slipped the nightshirt over her head. "But judgin' from the dark, methinks it to be after nine o'clock." She writhed and contorted her body to remove her frock from under the chemise, then unpinned her coarse blonde hair and proceeded to comb it.

"I heard it a few minutes ago." Christopher pulled his straw pallet from under the bed and dragged it next to the fireplace. He preceded his parents to bed by a few minutes, after stocking the kindling bucket for the morning fire.

"How did I miss it?" William enjoyed the curfew bell's ring each evening. To him, it was a symbol of closure for the day's labors and an invitation to rest. To his progenitors, the bell represented an ever-present reminder of bondage. After William the Conqueror crossed the channel with his Norman armies and subjugated the Anglo-Saxons, he required his subjects to cover their fires— "curfew" from French *couvre feu*—every evening at the ringing of the curfew bell. The law's intent was to keep townsfolk from conducting secret nighttime meetings and planning a revolt against their oppressors. The curfew bell still rang, but as a tradition and marker of hours rather than a reminder of oppression to a conquered people.

Christopher, William and Elizabeth lay in silence for several minutes listening to the crackling coals, each lost in thought. Elizabeth finally voiced the question that had troubled her all day. "What do all these injunctions mean?" She rolled onto her back and stared at faint flickers of fire light on the beamed ceiling.

45

"Where will we end up? How can I cross Saint Thomas from my primer? I fear God will strike me down for such blasphemy."

William turned on his side to face her. "'Tis for the better. The tide is turning, as I always hoped it would. I never could believe Hitton gave his life in vain." William referred to Thomas Hitton, burned at the stake in Maidstone just a few years earlier for smuggling forbidden English devotional books and writings into the realm. The loss left William with a lingering melancholy that the passing years had not diminished.

Irked at his disregard for her angst over the injunctions, Elizabeth nevertheless swallowed her pride and snuggled next to him for warmth against the cold sheets. "How can you be sure these changes are for good? I fear what is coming."

Running his fingers through her hair, he opined, "One can never be entirely certain. But I have to believe in the end, things always work for good."

"Would Thomas Hitton say that? Or Thomas More? On opposite sides of reform, they were, and the king executed them equally."

William turned onto his back with a sigh. Only an occasional pop from the coals broke the silence that settled over the room.

Stretched out on his pallet, Christopher intertwined his fingers and rested the back of his head on his hands. He stared at his parents' silhouette against the wall in the faint glow of the fireplace, his thoughts entertaining the smile he was quite sure Anne cast in his direction earlier that day. At least a dozen times since he retired to his bed he ran the scene through his mind, and perhaps a hundred more throughout the day. A small log flared up, the flame dancing softly in a stubborn refusal to be extinguished. The flicker paled in comparison to the flame in his heart as he mused upon Anne's glance in his direction. Dared he entertain the thought that she took a fancy to him? She did, after all, come talk to him when he sent Howard after her. Perchance...

A loud thud against the wood shutters opposite the front door shocked William upright. Christopher's heart skipped a beat. Footsteps pounded across the grass and faded in the direction of the village.

"William!" Elizabeth gripped his hand, quivering so violently the bed shook.

He put a finger to his lips. The family was silent for a full minute or two before William dared to whisper, "Probably rogue lads playing a prank. Rest here while I check." He gently peeled his wife's hand off of his.

"No," Elizabeth whispered. "Please, wait until morning."

Christopher scooted to the pallet's edge and slipped his breeches on under his nightshirt. William motioned with his hand for Elizabeth and Christopher to move by the fireplace, and tiptoed across the room to pick up an axe resting against the wall next to the door. He lifted the tool across his right shoulder and reached for the door latch. Christopher held his breath.

☙

After several minutes, William came inside and set the axe next to the door, distraught. A waft of cold air followed him inside.

Elizabeth rushed to his side. "Did you find anything?"

He held a black bird upside down by the legs. "A dead rook beneath the shutters."

Elizabeth gasped. "A rook in flight would never hit the house at this hour. It portends evil, William. Evil! Who would do such a thing?"

"Someone who wishes us ill."

Christopher approached to get a look at the bird. "I would wager 'tis Simon Nix. He can't leave you alone."

"Perhaps. But let's withhold judgment until we know for certain." William opened the door and laid the rook on the ground. After closing the door and hooking the latch, he crossed the room to Christopher's straw mattress, excusing himself while he fumbled through the straw for his Bible. Feeling it there, he breathed out a sigh of relief and returned to his bed, book in hand.

"Why?" He spoke just above a whisper. "I've done nothing. Why will they not let me alone?"

January, 1539

Wobbling precipitously, Thomas stretched his right leg from a weathered fishing boat onto the Seine's snow-dusted right bank before carefully extricating his left. He slipped the fisherman ten sols and blew out a puff of relief, watching his breath dissipate into the frigid Parisian fog. Anxious to stretch his legs after a cramped float along the Oise River, to the Seine, and finally to the Parisian port of La Grève, he took a step in the direction of Les Halles markets.

The shout of *Monsieur Englich!* stopped him in his tracks. With a stiff turn, Thomas removed his cap and scratched his head.

The fisherman gestured to several buckets in his boat that were brimming with herring. "You aid me, Monsieur Englich. *Oui?*"

"Uh, *pardon*," Thomas nodded. In his haste to put the wearisome leg of the journey behind him, he forgot his agreement to help unload the catch. The physical labor came as a welcome relief to his stiff muscles. With the cargo safely onshore, the fisherman tipped his cap. Thomas returned the gesture. The fisherman evaporated into the crowd to search for the merchant who was to buy his herrings.

Thomas turned his back to the river. A pillory and gibbet standing in the middle of the Place de Grève taunted him like twin malevolent spirits with arms outstretched. The dark malaise that lingers in a place where infernal deeds have occurred saturated the space between the quay and the mismatched buildings surrounding the square. He shivered, whether from the cold or the haunting ambiance, he wasn't sure. A sickly odor tainted the air—the hint of burnt flesh mingled with decomposing cadavers from the nearby cemetery, Saints-Innocents.

A fine greeting, Thomas muttered under his breath.

He pulled his cloak tighter and massaged his hands together, cursing the holes he'd worn in his gloves after four months of travel. From Maidstone to Dover, across the channel to Calais, he stopped in a village here and there to earn money and rest, until his final job assisting the fisherman landed him in Paris.

Not sure where to go next, he followed a motley throng to Les Halles, intent on finding victuals to satisfy his rumbling stomach. A short walk atop a thin layer of crunchy snow took him from the port to the complex of seven covered halls that housed the city's fresh food market, where one could also shop for cloth, leather goods, wine, grain, and other of life's necessities.

A ray of light skipped past him in the form a blonde-haired, blue-eyed girl who looked to be about seven years old. A meat pie in her hand diffused its tantalizing aroma as she flitted by. The joy in her demeanor lifted his heart after the grisly scene at Place de Grève. She stopped and showed the meat pie to a tired looking man cradling an infant in his arms. Thomas assumed the man to be her father.

Winding his way through the market halls, past cloth and leather, wine and pots, the exhausted traveler finally happened upon meat pies. He purchased and wolfed down two mussel pies and washed them down with red wine before turning back to peruse the Italian leather gloves he passed on his way in. He pointed to a pair made of brown calf-leather.

"You estranger?" The olive-skinned vendor spoke in broken English while judging his customer through bloodshot, Basset hound eyes.

Thomas nodded. "English."

The Basset hound collected Thomas' money and, with an icy frown, handed him the gloves.

Hoping to surround himself with brighter company, Thomas backtracked for a small cylinder of brie cheese and a round of rye bread, stuffed them in his purse, and proceeded towards the Île de la Cité, an island in the middle of the Seine River.

Making his way across the river's congested Pont Notre Dame, he was soon impeded by a flock of pilgrims who stopped and started, pointed and gawked, to the chagrin of all anxious to cross the bridge to the other side of the river. Each pilgrim wore a wide leather hat and a cape, and carried a leather bag decorated with a scallop shell. A thin, red-headed young man directly in front of Thomas measured his steps with a tall walking stick, on the top of which rested a hollow pumpkin for holding water or wine.

Thomas made a quick decision to follow them as they meandered their way to the square in front of Notre Dame Cathedral. Huddled together in the yellow pastel evening light, the sightseers marveled at the imposing gothic structure.

After taking a moment to admire the cathedral's two soaring towers, Thomas tapped the back of the young man he had followed across the bridge.

The pilgrim turned to reveal a freckled, acne-covered face. Thomas offered a faint smile.

"Yes?" The young man looked up into Thomas' eyes, startled.

"You speak English?"

"Yes, I hail from Canterbury."

Relieved to find an English speaker, Thomas let his guard down. "On the Way of Saint James, are you?"

"Yes." The young man leaned on his walking stick and extended his right hand. "Charles Blythe's the name. And you?"

"Thom—er, Harold Archer, it is. From London."

Charles tipped his hat. "Pleased to make your acquaintance, Mister Archer. What brings you to Paris?"

"I'm making my way to Périgord to hunt truffles." Thomas decided to take a chance. "Say, do you know where I might find a night's lodging in the city?"

Stroking the indention in his cleft chin, Charles gave the question some thought. "At a hostel offered by the church of Saint Julien-le-Pauvre, on the left bank, perchance. 'Tis where we're lodging for the night." He pointed across the river with his walking stick. "It's for pilgrims, of course, but perhaps they'll take pity on you because you're a foreigner." He eyed Thomas with suspicion. "In France to sell truffles, are you?"

Thomas leaned close and confessed, "By my troth, my name's Thomas Nix, from Dartford, but you mustn't let on that you know. My father sold souvenirs to pilgrims in England before the dissolution. I fled for speaking against the reforms."

Charles wagged his head. "'Tis a pity, having our faith stripped from us. Methinks if the priests who run the hostel know you're fleeing heresy, they should be kindly disposed. Where are you going, in truth?"

"To Périgord, as I said. I do hope to make a living selling truffles, as my uncle did."

"You may travel along with us, if you wish. 'Twill be safer for you. I certainly wouldn't want to travel alone, what with highwaymen prowling the roads. We're following the Vézelay route to join a group of pilgrims from Germany. It passes directly through Périgord." Feeling the weight of worry lift from his shoulders, Thomas uttered a silent prayer of thanks to Saint Thomas.

As dusk's yellow glow succumbed to the silver shadows of nightfall, the pilgrims—with Thomas following—traversed the left flank of the river and hastened to a hostel nestled between the College of Sorbonne and Cluny Hotel. Thomas stood back while Charles spoke with Father Marcel, a beast of a man who bore an air of resentment. The priest's eyes darted back and forth between Thomas and Charles. Finally, he nodded his approval.

They settled for the night on a cold, straw-strewn floor, recounting their adventures in low tones. Charles told of how his father—a cloth merchant in Canterbury—sent him on the pilgrimage, wishing for him to experience the strength and beauty of the Roman church away from the turmoil of King Henry's reforms. Thomas, in turn, expressed his devastation when the king's reforms stripped away all hope of inheriting his father's business. He told of the night in the tavern when he stood up to the commissioner, playing up the surprise on the man's face at being asked the difference between himself and a donkey's arse. Charles laughed out loud.

While they chatted in the candlelight, enjoying their newfound friendship, the silhouette of Father Marcel darkened the doorway. The cleric headed straight in their direction and knelt on the floor beside them.

"You, Englishmen—heretics are taking over your country, no? You are in France to flee?" His black eyes bore into Thomas.

"Yes. The whole realm is teeming with them," Thomas replied. Charles nodded in agreement.

"Here in France, we have them as well." The priest watched Thomas' eyes widen, and repeated, "Yes, we have Lutheran heretics, and they are bold as serpents. Just four years ago, they posted placards—posters—all over this city and in others—Blois, Orléans, Rouen and Tours—blaspheming the holy mass in the most vile language imaginable. A poster appeared even on the door of King Francis' bedchamber—yes, I said his *bedchamber*—at his Ambois residence. Alas, the heretics cut their own throats with that move. Until the placard affair, the king tolerated Lutherans."

His curiosity piqued, Thomas sat upright. "What did the posters say?"

Father Marcel thought for a moment, gathering the words in his memory. "It was titled, 'Genuine articles on the horrific, great and unbearable abuses of the papal mass, invented directly contrary to the Holy Supper of our Lord, sole mediator and sole savior Jesus Christ.' They claimed Christ's true body is not in the Eucharist. The whole thing was vile. Too vile for me to repeat."

Thomas and Charles exchanged looks of disbelief.

Enjoying his captive audience, the priest seemed to relax a bit, the cloud of resentment lifting. "You know well, the Lutherans speak poison and infect God's body. The king offered a reward to catch those involved with the placards, and many good souls came forward to turn in the guilty. I'll never forget the procession three months later; this city had never seen such a spectacle! The king, his court, and all the clergy attended. Six barefoot heretics, dressed in white chemises and holding lit tapers, led a grand procession to Notre Dame. One of them, an architect—Anthony Poille, I recall—they cut his tongue out so he could no longer spout blasphemies or sing their damnable hymns. He stumbled along, his white frock stained red. I almost had to look away.

"At Notre Dame, the procession ended. His Majesty delivered a most stirring address, exhorting his subjects to protect themselves and their little ones against heresy. Afterward, a marvelous new invention awaited them. They were chained to chairs attached to levers, and suspended over the flames. Over and over again, they were dipped in the fire—I counted twenty-five dips, myself—until they expired. It was good for them to get a taste of the flames here above, to prepare for the fires of hell awaiting them in the underworld."

Thomas gulped.

Father Marcel eyed Charles and Thomas, respectively, a brooding darkness once again shadowing his countenance. "Do you think that silenced the heretics? No, they still walk among us."

Thomas rubbed the bumps on his forearms with his palms while he watched eerie shadows dance on the hostel's stone wall. "I thought to get away from heretics," he said in a low voice.

Father Marcel shook his head, rose to his feet and dusted off his cassock. "You won't get away from them. But here in my country you will find that His Majesty, King Francis, knows how to deal with them."

February, 1539

Elizabeth cracked six cinnamon-hued eggs into a bowl before whisking in milk and butter. With the liquid ingredients combined, she sprinkled in flour and a pinch of salt and stirred vigorously, her belly jiggling as she moved. The fat from Monday's bacon collops rested in a crock nearby, to be used along with the remaining butter for cooking the pancakes.

Like other housewives across the realm, Elizabeth made pancakes every year on Shrove Tuesday to use up rich and fatty foods forbidden during Lent. The forty days of abstinence from eggs, butter, milk and meat commemorated Jesus' forty days of fasting in the wilderness. French nuns at Dartford priory called Shrove Tuesday *Mardi Gras*, or Fat Tuesday—the last day to indulge in rich, fatty foods until the Easter feast. For an adolescent lad, Easter loomed a painful distance away from Ash Wednesday.

"Have you decided what to sacrifice for Lent?" Elizabeth handed Christopher a trencher graced with three large rolled pancakes, drizzled with honey and lemon juice.

"Taffaty tarts," Christopher answered, dangling a bit of bait he knew she would latch onto. Elizabeth remained silent for a few moments, digesting his answer.

"Taffaty tarts, is it? Methinks it hardly a sacrifice to give up somethin' you eat only once a week. It would please God if you offered Him a bit more. And have you thought of your misdeeds the past year to confess before you take the Holy Communion in a few weeks? What about your Pater and Creed? Do you have them memorized?" Christopher shrugged his shoulders.

"Let me help you. Remember the time you stole eggs from my basket, and the constable caught you with Nicholas throwin' 'em at folks on Watling? Or puttin' my stockings on Miss Piggle?" The sound of stomping outside the front door diverted her attention. William entered, soaked from head to toe. He

53

stomped to shake the remaining mud from his shoes and extended his right hand toward Elizabeth with two eggs. Water ran down his arm and onto the floor. Elizabeth took one look at the muddy mess and opened her mouth to scold him.

William held up his hand to stop her. "I'll clean it up." She held her tongue, visibly relieved. William continued, "I hope 'tis not too late to use them. No one seems to have told the hens that Lenten season is upon us."

"The batter is already made, so I'll be settin' 'em aside for Easter. Perhaps Christopher would like to paint them then." Elizabeth placed the eggs in a basket on the floor near her kitchen cupboard. She returned to the fireplace and removed the pancake skillet. Working quickly, she slipped a spatula under two cakes and placed them on a trencher, drizzled them with honey and lemon juice, and rolled them. She handed the steaming treats to William. Smiling appreciatively, he sat at the table next to Christopher. She poured two more scoops of batter into the pan and returned it to the coals.

"Delicious, Lizzie. No one makes pancakes like yours." William smacked his lips.

"Not even Abby Wellington?" Elizabeth winked, but William and Christopher both knew she was a bit jealous of their love of Abby's tarts.

William stuffed his mouth full of pancake and chewed slowly, exaggerating his enjoyment. "I haven't tasted Abby's pancakes, but I daresay hers would not hold a candle to yours. Perfection. Absolute perfection."

"Now William, speakin' with your mouth full is poor manners, and you must set the example for Christopher." She smiled as she watched bubbles form on the tops of the cakes in the skillet before sliding the spatula underneath to flip them. After a couple of minutes she removed them and placed them on a trencher for herself, drizzled them with lemon juice and honey, rolled them, and joined her husband and son at the table. "Speakin' of Abby," she spoke while pouring herself a cup of ale, "Christopher was just sayin' he thinks to give up taffaty tarts for Lent."

William feigned shock. "No one should have to make a sacrifice that terrible! How could you even consider such a thing?"

Christopher grinned. "By my troth, 'tis no small sacrifice. Mother, are we out of ale? The pitcher is empty." He shook the pitcher upside down over his mug.

"Check the barrel. I think it has a bit more. Let me know; I started another batch a few days ago."

Not wanting to keep his friends waiting, Christopher decided he wasn't so thirsty after all. "Never mind. Thank you for breakfast."

54

"Of course," Elizabeth replied. "Would you like more pancakes? I've two hot ones in the pan."

"I'm full, thank you. May I be excused?" She nodded.

"My stomach has room for another." William spoke with a bite of pancake in his mouth and half a pancake still on his trencher. Elizabeth started to get up before he laid his hand on hers to stop her. "Stay there and eat. I'll get it." He pulled the skillet from the coals and pushed a spatula at one of the cakes. "It seems to be a bit stuck." He scraped vigorously until it came loose, and showed Elizabeth and Christopher the charred underside.

"Throw 'em in the slop bucket. Miss Piggle will eat 'em, and 'twill fatten her up." Elizabeth stuffed her last piece of pancake in her mouth and asked, "Will you men be cheerin' for me at the pancake race?"

Christopher had just swung his cloak around his shoulders to leave. Watching apron-donned women race through town flipping pancakes in frying pans was not his idea of an enjoyable Shrove Tuesday activity. He tried to slip out while her head was turned. Her voice stopped him.

"And where would you be sneakin' off to?" He stiffened.

"Uh, nowhere. Well, to meet Nicholas. Perhaps we'll come back to watch the pancake race."

"You have no plans to play football, do you?" Christopher stared at her blankly. "'Tis a ruffian's game. Do you hear me? Not one good thing will come of it. Bruises and broken bones are the fruits of that evil game, and I'll not be robbin' money from my crock to take you to the apothecary. Our kings have banned it time and time again, for good reason. Do you understand?"

"I hear you, Mother."

"You know lyin' is the devil's art, and football is his game. Understood?"

Christopher cast William a sheepish glance and slipped out the door into the drizzling rain. Nicholas waved at him from the bottom of the hill.

"Ho, Christopher! The lads are waiting! Make haste!" Christopher broke into a sprint.

ॐ

An odd assortment of boys and young men swarmed Watling Street, halfway between Dartford and the neighboring village of Crayford. Christopher sized up his opponents and made a mental checklist—those he could dominate, and those to avoid.

"On with it!" Adam, a well-built Dartford adolescent, shouted, anxious to start the game. He threw his head back to force the hair out of his eyes, exuding the overblown confidence of a seventeen-year-old who had not yet met his match. The majority of boys failed to hear Adam's rally cry, swallowed up as they were in the chaos of hurling insults, burping, shoving, and slashing the air with imaginary weapons. A trio of rascals hovered at the roadside, throwing rocks at a yellow cat in the gorse bushes. The feline bounded away in a full-speed panic and disappeared.

"Play ball!" Adam shouted louder. A few heads turned in his direction. He clapped his hands. "Shall we get on with it?" Those who heard rallied others in their immediate vicinity to gather in. Gradually, the young men formed a loose-knit pack in the center of the road.

"Here are the rules," Adam bellowed. "No hitting above the shoulders. No weapons. Did anyone bring a weapon?" He waited several seconds. A sallow-complexioned Crayford lad with sunken eyes fidgeted nervously, then pulled a knife from under his coat and tossed it to the roadside. He kept one eye on it, then trotted over to cover it with grass and twigs. "Nobody touch that," he warned, casting a menacing glance to all in attendance.

"No more weapons?" Adam scanned the crowd again. "Anyone caught with a weapon will be out of the game. Ready?"

"Wait." Willie Malden from Dartford pulled a knife from his pouch. He ran several yards off the road and hid it beneath a heather shrub while the bloodthirsty pack watched.

"Same goals as usual?" Nicholas shouted, drawing an X in the mud with his toe.

James Romney, on Dartford's side, stepped up to assert the unchallenged authority his six-foot-one-inch stature and twenty-three years afforded him. Years of labor at Dartford's lime kiln had hardened his muscles and stamina, and he happened to be the only player with a beard. "Same as always," James confirmed. "Crayford must touch the ball on the door of Holy Trinity, and Dartford on the door of Saint Paulinus. Aye?"

Adam took a step back, scowling at the affront to his leadership. A few boys nodded and a few shouted 'aye,' while others simply waited for someone to give the signal to start the game.

"No fair!" The soprano complaint came from Johnny, a delicate, pre-pubescent Dartford lad, whose hand-me-downs hung loosely on his frame like a collapsed tent. "No fair!" he whined again. "Our team has to climb the hill to get to Saint Paulinus. Holy Trinity lies at the bottom of the hill."

"Boo hoo," Michael, a thirteen-year-old merchant's son from Crayford, chided. "If you can't play by the rules, go home and hide behind your mother's apron. You'll never keep the ball anyway, because you'll trip on your breeches and fall and skin your knees. What ever will you do without your mother here to bandage them for you?"

Johnny puffed out his chest, scowling.

"Where did you get those breeches anyway, off a giant?" John Whitfield poked Johnny's side. Laughter erupted in all directions.

Like storm clouds that gather in the sky before releasing their fury, the boys pulled into teams, each tensing his muscles and projecting his most threatening look. James scanned the crowd to make sure he had their full attention. Satisfied, he pulled a groat from his pouch, examined it carefully, and laid the coin flat across his outstretched fingers.

"Ready?" he shouted. With all eyes fixed on him, he threw the groat in the air and caught it with his right hand. "Cross or pile?"

"Cross," Adam hollered.

"You should have said pile!" Johnny whined.

"Quiet, Johnny!" a boy on the Crayford side moaned, throwing a stick in Johnny's direction. Johnny stuck out his tongue.

James slapped the coin on the top of his left hand, while players on both sides held their breath. "Pile!" he shouted, raising both arms. Adam spit in disgust.

A Dartford teammate threw James a well-worn football crafted from an inflated pig bladder encased in leather. Grass and blood stains told the grisly tale of past games. He threw it in the air and caught it again repeatedly, until a teammate named Guildford swiped it in midair.

"Let's get on with it!" Guildford complained.

"I'm waiting for them to look at me."

"Atten-tion!" Guildford shouted. The command worked.

"On the count of three," James bellowed. "One!" Christopher's heartbeat quickened. "Two!" His legs felt wobbly. "Three!" Christopher watched the ball fly upward. The annual Shrovetide game began.

Nicholas bounced skyward and snatched the ball. Cradling it loosely under one arm, he sprinted forward. A Crayford player dove for the backs of his knees. Elbows and legs gyrated in all directions, while the ball escaped into a mud puddle. Crayford boys piled on top. Christopher threw himself atop the human mound and clawed for the leather. His fingertips made contact. A Crayford chandler's son wrestled it away.

"I got it!" the Crayford lad shrieked, clutching the ball against his stomach. "Off! I have the ball!" One by one, the players peeled off and hovered over him. The chandler's son jumped to his feet and raced toward Dartford, nursing a slight limp.

Johnny dove forward, wrapped his arms around the ball carrier's torso, and used his head as a battering ram into the lad's back. The ball popped loose and wobbled toward Adam. Adam scooped it up and lobbed it over the heads of two Crayford players into Christopher's arms. Cradling the prized possession against his side, Christopher sprinted toward Crayford until a deep pock in the road swallowed his right foot. He hit the ground with a thud and immediately felt as if someone threw an anvil on his back, and then another. Gasping for breath, he felt his chest press into the road. He tried to spit out the dirt on his tongue but couldn't breathe in enough air to muster an exhale. The weight piled on. A sickly *crack* echoed in his head. His eyes fluttered closed.

"Christopher." The muffled call of his name was followed by a *whack* on his cheek. "Christopher, wake up." *Whack.* "Christopher. Your mother is going to kill you."

Christopher's eyes fluttered open. Nicholas hovered over him, poised to slap his cheek again. "Stop it," Christopher shouted, swatting the hand away. He strained to sit up, but fell back to the ground with a moan. "Who has the ball?" he grunted.

"Adam. He latched onto it after you dropped it. Last I could see, he outran the others."

"Hurrah!" He started to sit up again, but wilted back to the ground. "Oh," he moaned, "something is horribly wrong. My chest." He drew his knees up.

Nicholas pressed softly on his rib cage. Christopher reacted with a groan. "I wager you broke a rib. We'll have to carry you home."

"No, I want to finish the game."

"No more playing for you, not this time." A stone's throw away, a teammate sat by the roadside, rocking back and forth with his arms wrapped around his knees. With a raised hand Nicholas shouted, "Ho, Miles!" The lad struggled to his feet and limped over. "I think Christopher broke a rib," Nicholas explained. "Help me get him home, will you?"

"My foot is lame," Miles protested, scratching at a patch of mud clinging to his brow.

"I need your help. One way or another, we must get home."

"Well, I suppose I can try." With a grimace, Miles knelt next to Christopher.

"Easy does it." Nicholas slid an elbow under Christopher's right armpit, while Miles slid an elbow under his left. Grunting, they helped him to his feet and hobbled toward Dartford, stopping every few steps to rest.

Picturing his mother's face, Christopher sighed. "I survived the game, but will I survive my mother's wrath?"

"Mine warned me not to come," Miles frowned. "I'm afraid to go home."

A mud-saturated pack of Crawford players approached. They puffed up their chests and stopped to gawk at the lame trio making their way toward Dartford. "You're a pathetic lot," one of them scoffed.

Christopher squared his shoulders and looked the lad up and down derisively. "Better luck next year," he snorted. As soon as the Crayford lads passed, he slumped forward and fought back his tears.

C&#x8;

"My goodness, I've a mind to send you to the stocks. 'Twould serve you right," Elizabeth complained, "disobeyin' your mother this way. Add another thing you can do penance for." She pushed lightly on her son's rib cage. He winced and curled into a ball.

"'Honor thy father and thy mother, that thy days may be long upon the land which the Lord thy God giveth thee.' Have you memorized that?" She rolled him to his side more roughly than she should have.

"Ouch!" He bit his lower lip.

"I barely touched it. Now lift up your nightshirt, and give me a look at it."

"Mother!"

"You can cover up where it matters." She handed him a linen towel.

"Turn your head first." Elizabeth looked away until Christopher gave her the go-ahead. When she turned around and saw his bare torso, she gasped.

"What in heaven's name were you lads doing to each other?" she complained. "Playin' the part of Roman gladiators, were you? Looks like you got the worst of it. Your whole left side is green and purple. You look like the cock that was beat to death in Market Square this morning. Football and cock throwing—what's the difference, except one involves roosters and one involves boys? Barbarians! You lads are barbarians!"

An intelligent response escaped him, so Christopher suffered in silence.

"How did this happen?" she demanded.

"I tripped and fell to the ground, and the lads piled on me. I heard a crack and fainted."

"Who did this? You don't have any enemies, do you?"

"I haven't done anything to them, but John and Edwin have been calling me names, throwing rocks at me, and such."

"Your own teammates?" Elizabeth's heart sank. She would never be happy with William's leanings toward the new learning, but she knew she wouldn't change him so she held her tongue as best she could. This was different. Her son was paying a price.

"I wager you have cracked a rib. Let me fetch a cool compress."

She grabbed a cloth from the cupboard and disappeared outside. A couple minutes later she returned and gently placed the damp cloth, neatly folded into a rectangle, on his left side.

"Lie there and rest while I make a poultice. Goodness knows, you'll be laid up for a few days."

March, 1539

—

Father Garrett lay on his back, arms outstretched, wishing the mattress could swallow him up. Weary of shepherding a flock of goats, he cursed his father's decision to steer him into the clergy after his mother died. Given a choice, he would have picked adventure. The enviable lot of some men! To stretch their wings, discover new lands, and return to tell the tales. His lot? Angry parishioners and an out-of-control monarch. It was a miserable quandary.

He arose each morning dreading what the day would bring, and retired at night with a gnawing anxiety about the morrow. Who could have predicted the rise of the irrepressible Martin Luther and the others who followed? Lollards and Lutherans, Wycliffites and Anabaptists—he feared the reformers were molten magma oozing from the cracks of an underlying volcano.

Lately, a painful pinch in his stomach radiated waves of pain into his back. Each night he tossed and turned with mounting anxiety as he witnessed colleagues disciplined for refusing to acknowledge King Henry as head of the church in England. Charges of corruption forced the closure of religious houses. Displaced nuns and monks scrambled for a place to go.

He envied those with the means to flee to friendly places on the Continent. If the axe were laid to his neck, what would he do? Never, he vowed, would he so much as flirt with behavior that might imperil him. He would make the king's wishes his wishes. His life and livelihood depended upon it.

The turmoil of the times reflected on the countenances of many in his parish—in the nervous tic Goodman Miller developed on the left side, and in the shadow hanging over Mistress Adams' previously sunny disposition. Widow Willoughby—ah, the widow—came to him for help with increasing frequency since her husband passed, and he would not be a good shepherd if he withheld it. *The whole of England is under duress*, he thought, massaging his abdomen. *Surely*

61

God understands that his humble servant stands as much in need of comfort as do his parishioners.

As he lay wallowing in his distress, his eyelids grew heavy and had just flickered closed when the door latch rattled. Two loud knocks jarred him from his longed-for repose to a sitting position.

"Father! Father!" The voice on the other side of the door sounded plaintive, even desperate.

"What now?" the weary priest muttered under his breath. He forced his legs over the edge of the bed and dragged his feet across the cold floor to a hook where he hung his robe. The insistent knock grew louder. "Fie and fie again. Break the door down, will you?" the priest cursed. Swinging the robe around his shoulders he shuffled to the door, lifted the latch and found himself eye-to-eye with Aaron Potter.

"By God's teeth, what ails you, Mister Potter?" Father Garrett massaged his eyes.

"Emma! She delivered a healthy boy, but she lies gravely ill—struggling for her very breath. Please Father, make haste. I fear she's almost gone."

The priest's gaze traveled from Potter's stubbly face, to his sweat-stained wool cap and threadbare tunic, down to the man's soiled hose and tattered shoes. Potter constantly pestered him for one thing or another. Garrett kept the man's family fed with goods set aside for the worthy poor, but he was starting to question whether Potter might be more deserving of a day at the whipping post.

The prospect of venturing out into the cold night air filled the priest with dread. Some parishioners rewarded him handsomely for his services, but Potter had nothing to give. Take, take, take—a bucket with a hole in it, he was. A quick call would have to suffice, so Garrett could hasten back to the warmth of his bed and hopefully get a few winks before facing tomorrow's misery.

"Go on ahead. I'm just a moment behind you." Garrett eased the door closed, leaving an opening the width of his right eye. "I must get dressed. Run along; I will be right behind."

"Please, Father. She is suffering terribly."

"Is the midwife there?"

"Yes. Mistress Willoughby said she can do nothing more."

What makes you think there is something I can do? Father Garrett thought it, but he didn't utter the words out loud. He closed the door and splashed his face with cold water, praying silently, *God, grant me strength, strength to carry on in these insufferable circumstances.* If nothing else, at least he could be of assistance to the widow.

Aaron Potter glared over his ale mug, clenching the vessel so tightly his knuckles were pale. The priest found the widower's cold, steely eyes entirely unnerving. *Was it my fault Emma Potter passed into Purgatory last week?* he thought. The wretched man Potter should be grateful to have a healthy child, and he had Teresa Willoughby to thank for it. What thanks did Potter show? Nothing. Not one penny of reimbursement to the priest or to Teresa for getting up in the middle of the night to minister to him. Nothing but a cold glare. A man of his station should be grateful to have help at all.

Father Garrett lifted his mug to his lips. *Some priests are marrying*, he thought. *The king himself is married, and declares himself head of the church. He wants marriage for himself—the supposed shepherd of God's church—but not for the undershepherds.*

April, 1539

—

Perched beneath a street sign in St. Louis Square, six trail-weary pilgrims—two English, two German, and two French—congratulated themselves upon reaching the village of Périgueux in the hilly, southwestern Dordogne region.

One of the group, a short and stocky peasant from Dijon with the face of a bulldog, jubilantly raised his staff toward heaven and exclaimed, "O God, be merciful to me, a sinner." It was his most dramatic display of energy since he joined the group in Vézelay. When a group of nuns in the square curiously looked his way, he cast his eyes to the ground as if nothing had happened. Thomas thought it peculiar that the peasant remained tight-lipped all along the way, while the rest of the group shared tales about their lives before the pilgrimage. The man admitted that he came seeking penance, but nothing more. As folks are wont to do under such circumstances, Thomas assumed the worst, slept with one eye open, and never let his purse out of sight.

Claude Marot, the other French pilgrim, also joined the group in Vézelay, volunteering as a guide. Unlike his countryman, Claude chattered non-stop in a manner Thomas found taxing. Neither tall nor short, Claude stood at Thomas' shoulders, while his thin-as-a-broomstick body stayed that way because he spent all of his time either coming or going along the pilgrim route between Compostela and Vézelay. Early in the journey, Thomas began to suspect that Claude was secretly in the employ of souvenir sellers along the route. Upon approaching each village, Claude touted the virtues of certain merchants while slandering others in a vile manner unbecoming a man on a holy journey. All the while, the costly Italian leather purse he wore across his body grew heavier with coins as the trip progressed.

"Rue Egui—Eguiller—Eguillerie—I give up. It's Threadneedle Street." Charles read the name of the street out loud from a sign above Thomas' head, shielding his eyes from the midday sun.

"Five months in France, and you speak no better than that?" Thomas teased. His French had come along nicely, well enough that he found it pleasant to converse with the locals.

Brushing the comment off, Charles continued, "We need to find Rue Limogeanne—it's the main pilgrim route through town. A priest at the Saint Front Cathedral will direct us to the hostel, and bless us in the morning as we leave."

"Look at the shells above the doorway there." Hans Bauer, a stone mason from Württemberg, Germany, pointed to a striking limestone building embellished with a narrow, overhanging turret that hugged the upper corner of the building's square tower. Thomas gazed up at the structure, thinking of how much he liked Hans. His fellow pilgrim had lived a comfortable life loyal to the Mother Church until Ulrich, the expelled duke of the region, returned to power in Württemberg and chased out Catholics. Along the Way of Vézelay, Hans explained how a series of maneuvers by Francis, king of France, restored Ulrich to his dukedom. The two rulers formed a strange alliance, Thomas thought. King Francis befriended German Lutheran dukes while persecuting reformers in France.

Bit by bit, as Hans told it, Württemberg succumbed to Lutheran heresy. First, Ulrich invited theologians to the region's churches to teach Luther's religion. The duke then dissolved the monasteries, confiscated lands belonging to the Holy Mother Church, and turned universities and schools into Lutheran indoctrination centers, all while King Henry was making similar changes in England. Until he came on the pilgrimage, Thomas had no idea so many others were suffering at the hands of Lutherans. Curse the reformers! He resolved to find a way to fight them.

Claude Marot stopped to ask a peasant woman with friendly eyes and dimpled, rosy cheeks for directions to Rue Limogeanne. She pointed across the square to a street teeming with folks churning back and forth, like a fast-moving river current.

The pilgrims proceeded at a leisurely pace along Limogeanne Street, admiring its tympanum-embellished doorways, stately courtyards and cupola-topped roofs, a display of the village merchants' wealth. As they wound their way to the church, Thomas fought a growing sense of melancholy.

Charles caught up and met his stride. "Is all well, Thomas—I mean, Mister Archer?" he winked. "Do you know how guilty I feel for misleading others about your name? At any rate, you look forsaken."

Grateful to unburden himself, Thomas replied, "I have no idea what lies ahead. How will I get to Sarlat, or find work as a truffle hunter? I find myself wishing I could continue on with the group."

"What is to stop you? You've been banished. You're free to go where you will."

Banished. It was such a lonely word. Up ahead, Thomas spied the lofty Romanesque bell tower of Saint Front Cathedral. "I reckon I have a night to think about it," he said heavily.

"'Twould be a pleasure to have your company all the way to Compostela." Charles offered a reassuring pat on the shoulder.

They found Father Gaston, the parish priest, behind the church pruning a vine. After exchanging pleasantries, Gaston led them to a hostel in an upstairs apartment across the street from the cathedral. From the window they had a grand view of the cathedral and the Isle River meandering its way below, along with the red tiled rooftops, winding streets and stone buildings of the walled village.

After a hearty dinner of cassoulet and rye bread they followed Claude's lead in singing ballads—all except for the peasant from Dijon, who ate his day-old bread and slurped his soup in the corner of the chamber with his eyes down. The pilgrims retired on straw-stuffed mattresses and covered up with wool blankets provided by the priest, commenting on how the accommodations were the best they had encountered thus far.

The next morning, standing with the group of pilgrims on the riverbank in the cathedral's shadow, Thomas watched a mother duck preen in the river before gliding downriver with a trail of ducklings behind. Wafting past his nose, a sweet aroma more poignant and lovely than lilac infused the brisk morning air. He spied a cascade of lavender-hued flowers on a stone wall across the street. Ah, wisteria. His chest expanded to its full capacity as he filled his lungs with the intoxicating fragrance.

A light breeze scattered some papers in front of the church and sent one fluttering downhill toward him. Seized by curiosity, he trotted up the hill and picked it up. After wiping a dusty footprint from the back of the paper, he flipped it over and almost choked.

"Monsieur Archer!"

Blinded by rage, Thomas failed to hear his assumed name. He glanced about to see who might be responsible for the abomination he held in his hand.

"Monsieur Archer!" Father Gaston shouted. Thomas glanced downhill and saw the priest with his hand on the shoulder of a tall, stately man dressed in the manner of a wealthy merchant. Swallowing his anger, Thomas crumpled the piece of paper and hastened down the hill, careful to avoid tripping on the rough stone pavement. When Thomas reached the group, the priest introduced him.

"This is the truffle merchant I told you about last night. Monsieur Bonner, meet Monsieur Archer."

Following Bonner's lead, Thomas extended his hand. The salt-and-pepper haired merchant offered a firm handshake, exuding an air of self-assurance. A warmth emanated from his close-set, brown eyes that Thomas thought a contrast to the stern lines on his weathered face.

"I understand you're seeking work as a truffle hunter?" Thomas nodded, clutching the wad of paper tightly in his fist. "We won't hunt truffles until fall, but I have other work on my estate outside of Sarlat. I understand you're English?"

"Yes, Monsieur."

After a quick sizing-up, the merchant determined the muscular young man who stood head-to-head with him appeared capable of a good day's labor. "I'm leaving for Sarlat tomorrow at the break of dawn. Would you be available to accompany me on horseback?"

Thomas nodded, blubbered a thank you, and stuffed the paper in his purse.

Offering a warm smile of encouragement, Charles stepped forward. "It appears providence has given you an answer. This is where we part ways. I won't forget you."

"Nor I you," Thomas replied. As an afterthought, he pulled a sol from his purse. "Buy a candle for me after you arrive at Compostela, and touch the pillar inside the church doorway for me. And please, remember me in your prayers."

Monsieur Bonner tapped Thomas on the shoulder. "Pardon me for interrupting. You'll find me on Rue Aubergerie, number eight. I'll wait for you."

"Yes, Monsieur, I'll find you." After watching Bonner ascend the street past the church and disappear into the heart of the village, Thomas lingered to bid Charles farewell, then took a stroll along the river to contemplate the twists and turns he'd experienced the past few months.

The deafening toll of St. Front's noon church bells made it necessary for him to tap the doorknocker four separate times at 8 Rue Aubergerie. Finally, a freckled, red-headed maiden he guessed to be in her mid-teens opened, and ushered him into a spacious room dominated by a central spiral staircase. After

67

inviting him to be seated in a green velvet chair, she disappeared down a narrow corridor behind the stairs. Running his hands across the velvet, Thomas fixed his eyes on a painting of a ship moored in a harbor guarded by two crenelated white towers.

Upon entering the room, Monsieur Bonner walked directly to the painting. "That's the port of La Rochelle." Stroking his thick, greying beard, he suddenly looked faraway. "Lovely, isn't it?"

"Yes, Monsieur. La Rochelle—is it far from here?"

"A week or two, depending on the horse and the weather. I have business there on occasion. But for the task at hand—I'll need help through the summer, tending my geese and ducks, weeding the gardens, mending fences and such. If we mutually agree for you stay on, truffle season begins in late fall. I offer room and board in my guesthouse, and a stipend generous enough to make it worth your while."

Silently thanking Saint Thomas for continued watch care, Thomas spied the top half of a piece of paper peeking from Bonner's travel bag. Emblazoned across the top in Latin were the words, "*Ego Sum Papa*. I am the Pope." Below the words rested a woodcut image of a frightful beast, grasping a pitchfork in its clawed fingers. The beast had serpents in its ears, sharp teeth, talons for a nose, and a crown embellished with flames. He gulped. It was the same handbill he found fluttering in the breeze earlier that morning.

"Is all well, lad? You look as though you've seen a ghost."

Taking a deep breath, Thomas forced a smile. "No, Monsieur. I gladly accept your offer of work."

May, 1539

—

With the linen cart ready for market and five taffaty tarts in his stomach, Christopher summoned his courage. Feeling a tad guilty about both his gluttony and the breaking of his Lenten vow to abstain from taffaty tarts, he wiped the crumbs from the corner of his mouth and straightened his cap.

"Something bothering you?" Suppressing a smirk, William watched Christopher pace next to the cart.

Christopher stopped to crack his knuckles and blurted, "May I take a few minutes to wander about the market?"

"Looking for anything in particular—perhaps a certain brown-haired girl?" William peered past Market Square in an effort to see the Shambles, but Cooper's fish stand stood around the corner, outside his range of vision.

Christopher blushed. "I just thought I'd stretch my legs."

"Yes, but be wary around Cooper. He won't take kindly to you."

Raising an eyebrow Christopher asked, "What have I ever done to him?"

"You? Nothing. But remember our discussion about Lollards?"

"Mm-hmm."

"He despises anyone who supports the king's reforms, and lumps them all into the Lollard category, whether they're followers of Wycliff, Luther, or Robin Hood."

"Robin Hood?"

William shrugged his shoulders.

A look of concern flashed in Christopher's eyes. "Since he fancies you a Lollard, he holds it against me as well?"

"Sadly, yes."

Christopher sighed. Lowly weaver. Rodent. Lollard's son. It was his father's choice to be associated with Lollards, not his.

"Very well, Father. I'll be back soon."

William tipped his hat. "Godspeed."

Christopher plucked a few daisies next to the churchyard fence and arranged them into a small bouquet. After tucking them into the sleeve of his tunic, he cradled the stems with his cupped hand. Now, to work his way to the fish stand undetected. The boisterous crowd would work in his favor.

Past stands and carts, squealing pigs and clucking chickens, shouting vendors and gossiping country folk, he staked out a place near the center of Market Square where he could watch Cooper's stand from a safe distance. A portly woman stopped in front of him to shout at her young son, who was caterwauling for a snack of oysters. She dragged him by the hand toward the Shambles. Snaking through the crowd, Christopher crouched behind Twisden's meat stand. A couple of skinned rabbits suspended upside-down gave him cover while he watched Anne help a lad about her age select an eel.

Why can't it be me speaking with her, he sighed. *The prettiest girl in all of England.* She looked beautiful in her lovely sage dress.

Mister Cooper turned his back to stack barrels and crates. Seizing the opportunity, Christopher flexed the fingers on his left hand to confirm the presence of the daisies and darted forward. He ducked behind a barrel, where he could hear the conversation between Anne and her customer.

"My father intends to send me to Cambridge," the lad boasted. "'Tis my choice, of course."

John Whitfield! Christopher's heart plummeted from his chest to his feet.

"When would you go?" Anne pulled three eels from a small barrel and laid them in front of her admirer while he studied her graceful movement.

"Next year, when I turn sixteen."

"Wouldn't you be anxious to go so far away from home?"

John rolled each eel from front to back to inspect the length and thickness. "Father says Cambridge is where the best and brightest go, so I think staying in Dartford and missing out would be worse." He selected an eel and slipped it into a bucket dangling from his elbow.

Christopher pulled the flowers from his sleeve and made his way toward Anne at precisely the same moment the Cooper's tabby cat sprinted across the street with fish entrails dangling from her mouth. He stumbled forward, breaking his fall with his hands, while daisies scattered across the street in front of him.

70

Anne looked past John just in time to see Christopher's hands and knees hit the street. Undeterred, the feline ran under a bush across the street to gobble down her feast.

John turned to see Christopher sprawled on the ground with marketgoers stepping around him. "Why, look at that," he quipped. "He fell for you, Anne." Anne felt her cheeks; they were warm and moist. Christopher sprang to his feet, dusted off his breeches, and searched for the quickest exit from the humiliating scene.

"Ho Lollard, did you bring the flowers for me or Mister Cooper?" John shouted through the bustling crowd. "Or were the pathetic, wilted things for Anne?"

Matthew Cooper stopped stacking crates and turned to investigate the commotion. At the sight of William Wade's son, he frowned and stepped forward. It was no secret Christopher had an eye on his daughter; the lad turned into a bumbling fool in her presence. Cooper accepted the inevitability of suitors, but God forbid William Wade's son to be one of them. He had better plans for his daughter, and John Whitfield fit in with them perfectly.

He picked up a filet knife and ran his thumb along the blade. "Methinks you're on the wrong street, lad," he growled.

Christopher's eyes widened. "I was taking a shortcut to bring my mother some flowers," he stammered. He bent down to collect a cluster of daisies that survived the stampede of marketgoers.

"You're on the wrong street entirely." Matthew laid the knife on a barrel that stood between him and his daughter's would-be suitor. Christopher tensed. "Whatever your intentions, Tizzie did a fine job interrupting them."

Christopher stepped sideways to pick up his cap, keeping an eye on Mister Cooper. After dusting off a footprint and punching the trampled crown open, he stole a wistful glance at Anne, plopped the cap on his head, and hurried down the street. With arms folded, Matthew watched Christopher disappear around the corner before addressing his daughter.

"Keep a good distance from that lad. Comes from a long stock of Lollards. Blasphemers, they are. Satan's minions, destroying the Holy Mother Church. I forbid you to talk to him." Anne bit her lower lip.

Straightening his leather jerkin, John opined, "Sir, I agree with you about the Lollard problem. After mass last Sunday, I overheard Christopher tell Nicholas Hall that Mister Wade keeps a Tyndale Bible in his cottage. Wade hides it because, he says, you never know when the king will sour against it. Apparently, the elder

Wade carries on suspicious and fearful-like any time he thinks his Bible is threatened."

Matthew returned to his task of stacking crates. "Nothing but trouble will come from that family. Stay as far away as you can, Anne. Made a pact with the devil, they have."

"I will, Father."

"I must get back to the manor," John interjected. "Thank you for the eel, Anne. It will make a fine supper tonight."

After bidding farewell, she watched John turn west on Spyttal Street. His attention flattered her. Unlike Christopher, he exuded confidence. Christopher conducted himself like a puppy that hadn't grown into its paws. Still, the linen weaver's son intrigued her.

"John's a good catch," Matthew said. "A well-bred lad like that can lift you out of a life of fishmongering and into the life of a lady. Don't let him get away."

"Oh, Father." She picked up a rag and wiped the counter. "Is hooking things all you think about?"

"I only want the best for you."

"How about what I want?"

He ignored her comment. "Did I hear him say he is going to Cambridge?"

"He said his father wants to send him there."

"Imagine yourself, married to a Cambridge graduate! Perchance some light will shine in the midst of all this darkness after all."

"I like John well enough. But talk about marriage? I barely know him."

"I know a good catch when I see one. Remember, I make my living catching things." She rolled her eyes and wiped up eel juice with her rag.

☞

Christopher threw the wilted daisies into the river and plopped down on the bank with a huff. *I'm a fool!* he whispered, tearing up a handful of grass by the roots and hurling it haphazardly into the air.

"Ha'penny for a poor man?" The raspy voice startled him. Harry sat a few feet away, his back against an oak tree.

"I have no ha'penny," Christopher retorted, sullen.

"Ye got problems, lad? The whole world's got problems. What problems ye got?" Harry pried a rye seed from his teeth with his little finger.

72

"I'm the world's biggest fool." Christopher buried his head in his knees with a groan.

"If ye be a fool, ye be in good company. The world is full of 'em." Tearing off a piece of rye bread donated by a housewife who sold her bread at market, he chuckled at the wisdom of his own observation.

"You wouldn't understand." Christopher didn't bother to look up.

"Packed a lot of life in my years 'ere on this orb, lad, I have. What is it? Did ye commit a crime? Steal a chicken? Got the sheriff after ye? Problems with a maiden?"

Christopher raised his head and studied Harry's leathered face. "What would you know about maiden problems?"

"Maiden problems is my specialty. Founded the Great Guild of Suffering Menfolk, I did. Ye ever hear of it?"

"No."

"Had a lovely maid, I did, years past. Took her to wife and we set up housekeeping. Did my best to make her happy, and methought she was. But not six months after we united in holy matrimony, she hankered to make a pilgrimage to Canterbury. Said she felt God's pull to be a nun. So I said to her, I said, 'Ye got Dartford Priory right 'ere, just join up and you can have the best of both worlds—ye can do your duty by the church and by me.' She wouldn't have it. If she could just get to Canterbury, she said, Saint Thomas would help her. Haven't seen her since. I'd a mind to put the law on her, I did. A married maid has no right to run off like that. Found out she become a mistress to a vicar down in Dover. No denyin' she was the religious sort—went for the godly types of men. Been doin' my best to stay away from women and ratsbane ever since. Bachelor life suits me fine. Ye should try it."

Christopher smirked. "I'm only fourteen." He buried his face in his knees.

"Fourteen! By Jove, ye still got time. Stay away from women and ratsbane, and ye'll do just fine, lad." Christopher lifted his head and gazed into Harry's eyes, amused by the old man's tufted eyebrows. Harry tugged at his coat sleeve. "Fancy my coat, lad? Got it from a strange fellow in the witching hour, during a cold night November last. Seemed gentil, he did, until he thumped me head with a rock, took me cloak, and left me two pence and this." He ran his fingers across the fur trim. "Fair trade, I would say. A bump on the head for two pence and a coat. Life is fair enough, lad. Ye just got to see the bright side."

Christopher picked up a pebble and lobbed it into the water. "There is no bright side."

73

"Aye, there's always a bright side. What problems ye got? Am I right? Is it a maiden?" Harry fluttered his bony fingers over his eyes, imitating eyelashes. "Got you to grin. So 'tis a maiden, indeed?"

"Of sorts."

"Speak up! Remember, ye speak with the founder of the only guild solely dedicated to troubles with the womenfolk."

Moved by a desire to relieve his burden, Christopher scooted closer to Harry. "Anne Cooper is the loveliest maiden in Dartford. She moved here last fall. John Whitfield—the son of a gentleman—won't leave her alone. Me? I'm but a lowly linen weaver's son. My father is a Lollard, and Anne's father hates Lollards. A few minutes ago I went to the Shambles to give her some flowers, tripped over a stinkin' cat and fell, right in front of her. John Whitfield and her father saw it. I want to crawl into a hole."

For a few seconds Harry stared into the water, then shook his head. "By Jove, son, ye do got problems. Let me see if I got this straight. First off, ye fancy a maiden and her father hates you. First blow against you. This John lad fancies her, and her father fancies him. Two blows. Ye tripped on a cat and fell in front of her, and now they all think ye a fool. Three. Fourth off, ye think yourself a fool. I say, ye do got problems—at least four, anyway."

"'Tis no use." Christopher stood and kicked a dirt clod.

"What do ye mean, 'tis no use? Has she run away on a pilgrimage? Does she want to be a nun? Has she married the Oxford lad? Has she taken up housekeeping with a vicar?"

Christopher shook his head.

"Then ye have hope, lad. Ye got to fight for what ye want. Fight for the maiden! 'Tis all about chivalry—the maids fancy the chivalrous sort."

"Do I look like a knight to you?"

"Sir Galahad, no. But knights is made, not born. Is that John What…Whatnot a knight?"

"No, but he's a gentleman's son."

"Then ye must act like a gentleman, and think like a knight. Let's take stock of your knightly virtues. Have ye got courage?"

"Well, it took courage to bring her daisies, and I spoke with her a few weeks past."

"Courage, check. Do you believe in justice?"

"I'm not sure what that means."

74

"A knight has to believe in justice. In other words, do ye believe wrong should be punished and right rewarded?"

"I suppose so."

"I'll give ye a check. Justice. Are ye merciful in dealing with others?"

"Well, my father says Jesus taught us to be merciful so we would obtain mercy."

"Good. Ye passed the first three questions. Also, a knight must be generous. Ye aren't the stingy sort, are ye?"

"I once gave away my taffaty tart to a beggar."

"Excellent! Now let me recall, what other knightly virtues have I missed? We got courage, justice, mercy, and generosity. Can ye think of any?"

"Sir Galahad had faith in God. I have faith in God, although I'm not sure who is right, the pope or the king."

"Join the crowd, lad. Only God knows what is right. Perhaps all paths lead to him, or we are all gone astray. What do I know? Regardless, ye do believe in God. What are we missing?"

"Knights know how to woo the maidens. I can't woo a snail."

"Come lad, your days with the maidens are just beginning. You've plenty of time to hone your skills. And ye be not sore on the eyes."

"The maidens swoon over John Whitfield. No one looks at me."

"Ye got to think in terms of what ye have, not what this Johnny Whit— Whitnit has, son. 'Tis called 'assets.' Ye got to think of your assets."

"He's older, richer, taller, more handsome…"

"No, no, no! Assets, lad."

"I have no assets," Christopher frowned.

By fits and starts, Harry worked his way to a standing position. Once upright, he tapped the brim of his cap and said, "Alas, lad. I'm trying to assist ye, but ye are not making it easy. I wish ye luck. Now I must drum up a drink of ale. G'day, and keep your chin up."

"Godspeed." Christopher watched Harry limp toward the tavern, then moped for a good quarter-hour before summoning the wherewithal to return to the linen stand.

At the sight of his son, William frowned. "You've been gone a long time," he complained.

Christopher grunted something unintelligible. William sensed it best to not pry.

"I would like to speak with Christopher, if you please."

Elizabeth raised an eyebrow. If someone had given her a hundred guesses as to who might show up on her doorstep on a Sunday afternoon, Mister Cooper's freckle-faced daughter would not have crossed her mind.

"You're Matthew Cooper's daughter, if I'm not mistaken?"

"Yes." Anne peered sideways past Elizabeth into the cottage, hoping to catch a glimpse of the blonde-haired, blue-eyed lad who had caught her fancy.

"Remind me," Elizabeth searched the young maiden's hazel eyes, "your first name is?"

"Anne."

"Anne. Yes, that does ring a bell. Christopher stayed after church today, but he's never late for supper. Would you care to wait for him?"

"No, thank you. Father will be anxious for me to get home." Anne looked down at her toes, stumped for what to say next.

"May I give 'im a message?"

"I'd hoped to speak to him myself."

"You might find him at the church, or somewhere between here and there."

With a slight curtsy, Anne thanked Elizabeth and made her way down East Hill. Once the damsel disappeared from view, Elizabeth closed the door with a *humph.* "Maidens callin' on lads. I tell you, the world is upside down. Next thing you know, dogs will be mewin' and cats barkin'. Isn't that so, Dart?" Christopher's spaniel cocked his head and wagged his tail. Elizabeth patted his head before arranging bread trenchers on the table for Sunday supper.

As she descended East Hill, Anne debated whether to stop at the church or hurry home. Convincing her father to allow her to go to town by herself took her last drop of persuasion, and she didn't dare incur his wrath by staying away too long. She'd already stretched the truth when she told him she forgot her grandmother's primer at church. Truth was, she left the book on purpose.

She stopped to pull a small bouquet of daisies from her purse, dismayed to discover the petals starting to curl. *If I don't do it now, I may never have the nerve—or the chance—again*, she thought. Gazing ahead at Holy Trinity's lofty ragstone tower and crenelated walls, standing fortress-like in contrast to the timber-framed buildings around it, she whispered, *it's now or never.* She bit her bottom lip and forced one foot in front of the other.

The rattling song of a warbler perched on a nearby gorse bush caught her ear. She glimpsed its rust-colored belly and grey head plumage seconds before the bird took flight toward the heath. Bleating and the occasional ring of a sheep's bell drew her gaze to the fields and hills surrounding the village, while the delicate aroma of apple blossoms saturated the air. Over the wooded horizon lay the Thames River, with the famed city of London sprawled on its banks a few miles upriver.

When the stone bridge came into view, her heart fluttered. She hastened to the middle of the bridge and stopped to collect her wits, when a tap on her shoulder startled her. She turned and gasped.

"John. How did you know I was here?"

Panting, John rested his hands on his hips. "I stopped by your cottage first, but your father told me you came to the church to fetch a primer. I ran as fast as I could."

"Your timing is unfortunate—I'm in a terrible hurry." She turned and continued toward the church.

Grabbing a fistful of her kirtle, he pulled her to a stop and circled in front of her. "This is very important." He noticed the flowers in her hand. "Daisies?"

She held the flowers to her nose and inhaled. "They're so lovely, I couldn't resist. I pray you, tell me your news. If I'm late, father will—well, you know his temper."

"I'm fortunate to be on your father's good side. Surely you've noticed?"

"Yes, he thinks well of you. Tell me, what is your news?"

"Father made all the necessary arrangements. I'm Cambridge-bound." He studied her reaction, hoping for a sign of disappointment that he would be leaving Dartford. She offered only a cordial nod.

"Cambridge! 'Tis what you wanted."

"Yes. It's a great opportunity for my advancement, but I fear the place is teeming with heretics."

"What do you mean?"

"William Tyndale attended Cambridge. You do know what happened to him?"

"He was burned for translating the Greek testament into English." Her eyes darted between John and the church.

"Yes. Father told me Cambridge is filled with those of Tyndale's ilk, sowing seeds of heresy. He bid me to beware of the company I keep."

"I'm sure they're but a small group that will soon fade away. You'll find like-minded folks at Cambridge."

"I hope so."

From the corner of her eye, Anne saw two young men leave the church. Lifting her skirt hem, she pressed, "I must go. Congratulations on your news." She managed only a couple steps before John took a long stride and grabbed her right elbow. With a firm grip, he forced her to face him.

"I must speak with you now," he insisted. She shook her arm. He squeezed tighter.

"Let go!" she implored.

Christopher saw the commotion and poked Nicholas in the side. "Let's go."

At the approach of his two inferiors, John sneered, "The Lollards have come to your rescue."

Planting himself in front of John, Christopher demanded, "Let her go."

As he let Anne's sleeve slip between his fingers, John inched his nose next to Christopher's and growled, "This is none of your affair, Lollard."

Feigning a choke, Christopher waved his hand in front of his nose. "Phew! Out grazing with Jack Miller's asses again? Your breath smells like a dung heap." Christopher stepped sideways to extend the primer to Anne.

Her eyes lit up. "Thank you. Father let me come fetch it, but I must hurry home." Blushing, she extended the daisies toward Christopher. "These are for your mother. I felt awful when Tizzie tripped you. 'Twas all my fault. I gave her the fish just as you were coming."

"The daisies were actually for you," he confessed. "I thought I would die of shame after tripping over your cat, so I made up the story about my mother. Keep them." She smiled at the daisies, then at Christopher.

"Daisies from a Lollard!" John howled, stepping between Christopher and Anne. "If only your father could see you now, Anne. I've a mind to tell him his daughter is chasing a heretic."

"Leave her out of this, dung breath." Christopher planted his palms against John's chest and heaved. John took one step sideways, wiped the dusty handprints from his velvet jerkin, and snickered.

"Are all Lollards that weak, or just you?" He looked down at Christopher, a flash of anger in his eyes.

"I'm not a Lollard. Stop calling me that."

"How dare you lay hands on me, Lollard. How would you like to take a dip in the river?"

78

"Go ahead. Try it."

"Go ahead, Whitfield." Nicholas stepped forward. "Send us both into the river. Come on, I dare you."

At 5'9" Nicholas stood a scant taller than Christopher, and was of equally slight build. The victim of perpetual hand-me-downs from his older brother, he sported a russet-colored wool doublet that would have fit perfectly were he to gain ten pounds and sprout a few inches. Whereas fashion dictated that a man's breeches should reach to the knee, Nicholas' breeches reached to just above his calves. He owned one article of properly fitting clothing: the linen shirt his mother made for him.

Sizing up his opponents, John lifted his chin in the air with a snort. "'Tis unbecoming for a man to take advantage of maids."

"Maids?" Nicholas glowered.

John looked about. "Do you see anyone else here?"

Nicholas lunged forward, thrusting his palms against John's chest with a force that propelled John backwards against the bridge's rough rock wall. Christopher rushed forward to pick up one leg, Nicholas another. They lifted him backwards over the wall into the river. A loud splash rewarded their efforts.

Nicholas slapped Christopher's back with a hoot. "Now what?" he beamed.

"We celebrate!" Christopher shouted.

John trudged to the bank, his shoulders coated with green slime. "On second thought," Nicholas gulped, "we better get away while we still have breath, and celebrate if we live to tell about it."

They raced across the bridge, Christopher in the lead, and stumbled their way up East Hill. Christopher cast a quick glance behind him just in time to see John pulling himself onto the bank. John shook a slime-covered fist in their direction, accompanied by a slew of expletives.

"Faster!" Christopher accelerated, watching his step on the knobby grass, when a sudden realization struck him. Anne had disappeared.

⚃

"But he did nothing wrong." Anne eased her right hand open and closed. It ached, bearing red lines from the blows sustained trying to protect her buttocks from the birch switch. Her father left the switch perched against the wall, a sober reminder of the consequences of crossing him.

Matthew paced back and forth in front of the fireplace, wringing his hands. "Tush! I have it on good word that he followed you to the church."

"Whose word? 'Twas only John who came to find me yesterday at the bridge."

He stopped. "As I said, I have it on good word. Now mind my words, or you'll feel the sting of the switch again."

She knew she should bite her tongue—obedient children did—but the injustice of his accusation compelled her. "Someone is lying. Christopher was inside the church when I arrived. Father Garrett had him and Nicholas tidy up, when Christopher found my primer. They saw me standing on the bridge with John when they came outside. John had hold of my arm and wouldn't let go, even though I told him I needed to get home. Please believe me. Christopher only wanted to give me Grandmother's primer and tell John to leave me alone. He was defending me."

"'Tis scandalous!" Matthew barked. "Sneaking behind your father's back to meet up with a lout. The Wades are nothing but trouble, the whole cankered lot. The lad has brought public disgrace upon you, upon us, and you're too headstrong to see it. I've a mind to send you away! If your mother were alive, I doubt she could endure the shame of it."

Before she could stop herself, the words spilled out, "Father! You refuse to listen!"

She failed to duck in time. Warm liquid trickled from her nose. Choking back a sob, she rushed her palm to her cheek to cool the sting, and turned her back to dab the blood with her apron hem.

"I'll not have my daughter shaming this family, parading around the village like a strumpet with lads of questionable reputation. Don't you dare be seen with him again." Matthew slapped his hand against the kitchen table for emphasis.

She fled outside, to her favorite hideaway in a cherry orchard overlooking the valley. Finding safe haven under a tree, she held the apron to her nose with her left hand while cradling her cheek with her right. Her seething rage toward her father was matched only by fear of what he was capable of doing next.

With bowed head, she whispered her mother's favorite scripture passage from the hundred and first psalm. "'*O Lord, hear my prayer, and let my cry come to thee. Turn not away thy face from me. In what day soever I am in tribulation, incline thine ear to me.*' My Father, who art in heaven," she prayed, "father has grown so harsh since Mother passed away. I'm afraid. I have nowhere safe to flee."

80

She gazed through swollen, stinging eyes across the valley, skimming scores of thatched rooftops, wondering how many fathers like hers resided under those roofs. Children expected correction, but to be whipped for telling the truth?

Rays of sunlight diffused through the branches of the cherry tree, drawing her eyes toward heaven. *Father expects me to take the place of my mother, and I simply can't do all that she did. God, why did you take her? Oh Mother, why did you leave us?* Tears flowed down her cheeks to her neck and chest, making a wet circle on the front of her frock. *How will I ever face Father again?*

He finally did it—he threatened to send her away. She'd anticipated this day. A redbreast on a branch above cocked its head at her, when an idea struck. If her father intended to threaten her, she would help him make good on his threat.

June, 1539

—

"By God's teeth, stop the yapping!" Thomas smothered his head with a pillow, gritting his teeth with every nerve-wracking *woof-woof* thundering inside the manor house.

Zeus, Monsieur Bonner's Great Pyrenees, couldn't have picked a worse night for a barking marathon. Already bone-tired from a long day harvesting foie gras—fattened goose livers—Thomas dreaded pushing through the day ahead with no sleep. He would have to rise before dawn to deliver the foie gras downriver to Baron François at Beynac Castle in time for a feast in the afternoon.

Throwing off his indigo coverlet, Thomas stormed to the window of the guest house chamber and gazed up at the full moon, calculating the hour to be near midnight. A scan of the area revealed nothing out of order. Huddled together in the walnut grove, the geese reposed with their heads tucked beneath their wings, bright moonlight illuminating their white feathers. In a nearby coop, the chickens were roosting peacefully. He saw no commotion in the pig sty. Across the lawn, not even a flicker of light appeared in the shuttered windows of the manor house.

Zeus barked again. *Strange*, Thomas thought. *How are Bonner and his household sleeping through the noise?* Perhaps wild boars were rooting in the walnut grove again, or a wolf was on the prowl. No, if that were the case, the geese would raise a ruckus.

Thomas slid his breeches on under his nightshirt, grabbed his dagger from its resting place on the nightstand, and slipped outside. The bright moonlight made a candle unnecessary. He stood on the porch for a few seconds, listening. A horse stamped and nickered in the stable behind the manor house. Tiptoeing, Thomas made his way around the main dwelling and stopped. The faint hum of voices tickled his ears. Voices in the stable at midnight? How odd! He'd seen no visitors come or go during the day, and surely no one would brave the dangerous

82

trip through the forest after dark. With his heart pounding loudly in his ears, he crouched behind a stone wall within earshot of the stable, straining to hear.

"Master Calvin taught that if the early apostles had lived to avoid danger, Christ's church would have never been planted. Our own Nero, King Francis, intends to exterminate us. Shall we recoil like worms?"

Bonner! Thomas' heart caught in his throat.

"Since the placard affair, the king has doubled down against us. It was a miracle that you escaped from Amboise with your life." Thomas recognized the raspy voice of Luc Lemoine, a Sarlat bookseller.

So Bonner took part in posting placards against the mass at the king's Amboise residence—a crime that could get him swiftly executed! The handbill depicting the pope as antichrist peeking out of Bonner's bag in Périgueux made perfect sense now. Thomas inched his way up to peer over the wall and began counting silhouettes of folks gathered in the stable, when his knees popped. He crouched, praying that his knees would cooperate.

"Did you hear that?" Lemoine whispered.

"I didn't hear anything. What was it?" Bonner stiffened.

A minute of deafening silence passed before anyone dared to speak.

"Perhaps there's a bird or squirrel in the trees." Lemoine gazed up at the branches of a large oak next to the stable.

"Did you bring any French Bibles, Monsieur Lemoine?" The woman spoke just above a whisper.

Louise! She worked as Bonner's housemaid. Women, attending secret midnight meetings. Thomas had the urge to spit in disgust.

Lemoine hesitated for several seconds before whispering, "I have three French Bibles, smuggled from a bookseller in Paris." He pulled a Bible from his leather knapsack.

"Praise God!" The woman realized her exclamation had been too loud, and glanced fearfully in all directions before producing a handful of coins. Lemoine slipped a Bible into her eager hands. She held it to her chest.

"You know what can happen to both of us for having forbidden books," Lemoine warned.

"I'll be careful. I've been wanting to ask you, Monsieur Bonner," Louise inquired, "did you distribute the handbills in Périgueux?"

"I intended to, but a breeze whipped them from my bag and scattered them in front of the cathedral."

"Perhaps God distributed them for you." The bass voice belonged to Christophe Villon, a Sarlat tanner. Thomas would have never suspected him of heresy.

"Where's the Englishman?" Lemoine inquired. "He doesn't join our meetings."

"He's a Babylonian," Bonner stated matter-of-factly. Thomas raised his eyebrows. "The lad is secretive about what brought him to France. I suppose he fancies he's fooling me. When I first met him, he was with a group of pilgrims on their way to Compostela. My gut instinct warns me to be wary. I see evil in his eyes."

"He came into my bookstore last month to purchase papist writings," Lemoine remarked, "and asked if I have any writings of Luther or Calvin. I couldn't tell whether he was laying a trap, or genuinely curious."

"Perhaps we should try to enlighten him," Villon offered. "Can we rest when the fires of hell threaten his soul?"

Bonner snickered. "When I traveled with him from Périgueux in April, he knelt down to pay homage to a shrine of the Virgin along the way, beating his chest as if she could forgive him of some terrible deed for which he felt guilty. Fool!"

Thomas felt his chest pulse into a raging cauldron of anger. A Babylonian? The fires of hell? Evil in his eyes? How dare they!

"I don't care for him. He's full of himself and acts as if he's above me." *Louise just had to join in the feeding frenzy*, Thomas thought, bristling.

Bonner nodded. "Nix is a good worker, but I don't trust him." He paused for a moment to wait for Zeus to stop barking. "Shall we end our meeting? I fear Zeus will wake him and he'll discover us here."

Thomas tiptoed as fast as he could back to the guest house, his mind reeling with questions. How long had they been gathering, undetected? What should he do with the revelation that Bonner played a prominent role in the placard affair? Should he keep his head down, look for other working arrangements, or inform and let the chips fall where they may? He slipped between the sheets, but didn't sleep a wink.

Dartford

Christopher set his father's goose quill pen on the hearth and checked his note to Anne one last time.

84

Meet me at the Brent, next Market Day
Noontide
Nod your answer - Yea or Nay

On second thought, she probably wouldn't want to get this note from him; in fact, she might find it insulting that he even thought he had a chance with her, considering she could choose John Whitfield. Holding the scrap of paper between his fingers he started to tear it in half, then stopped himself. He was fairly sure she smiled at him in church. She positively did go out of her way to leave the primer at the church and look for an excuse to retrieve it. And, she brought him daisies.

If he didn't at least try, he would never forgive himself. What was the worst that could happen? Could any indignity top sprawling out, face down, in front of the fish stand? No, and he survived that misfortune.

"Take stock of your knightly virtues. Look at your assets," Harry said. But what assets? A Lollard father and measly hands that were learning to weave. Brushing fear aside, he whispered encouragement to himself, folded the paper and tucked it in his pouch.

"Mother, are you almost ready? Father will be waiting."

Tying the laces on her bodice, Elizabeth responded in the affirmative. "Oh, wait. I need to get somethin' for Amy." She retrieved a small clay pot from the cupboard. "She wanted to try my salve for Rose's pox scars. I hope 'twill help the poor imp. Wouldn't hurt Amy to try some herself." She set the salve in her purse. "Let's go."

Mother and son started downhill toward the church, Elizabeth chattering along the way. "I wonder what bad news Father Garrett will have for us today? I miss the olden days, when we knew what to expect." She tightened the string on her coif and continued to babble.

His mind occupied with the myriad of things that could go wrong with his plan, Christopher tuned out Elizabeth's chatter. What if Anne were only pretending to like him? What if her father caught him giving her the note? They arrived at Holy Trinity's front door. His true test of courage lay just on the other side. He took a deep breath.

Heads turned to see who was coming in late, including Anne's. Christopher's heart fluttered. Mother and son took their place next to William, while Christopher uttered a silent prayer for success. After an annoyed glance in their direction, Father Garrett proceeded with the mass. Christopher rocked from heel to toe, sure the interminable service would never end, when the words "thanks be to God" snapped him to attention. He willed his legs to stop trembling.

He lingered outside near the door behind a small group of parishioners who stopped to gossip about a recent string of burglaries on West Hill. Two feather beds, a brass pot, two pewter pots and a chopping knife went missing from John Fenton's house around the same time Gilbert Brock discovered twelve pewter plates missing after he'd been away helping John Fenton birth a calf.

Matthew Cooper exited the church without noticing Christopher. The Cooper children followed like baby ducks. Anne emerged last. Christopher tapped her shoulder. She jumped. Without a word, he slipped the note into her hand and waited to make sure she held it securely before he ducked into the crowd to watch from a safe distance. She opened the note and smiled. When their eyes met, she rewarded him with a nod.

CB

After enduring the longest week of his life waiting for Market Day to arrive, Christopher made his way to the Brent, sat on a grassy mound with his legs straight in front of him, and waited. The church bell signaled noontide. A steady parade of folks passed by, leaving and approaching the village.

Christopher twiddled his thumbs, stood up, sat down, removed and straightened his cap, chewed at a callus on his middle finger, and checked in the direction of the village every few seconds. Finally, he saw her top the crest of East Hill. His excitement gave way to disappointment at the sight of her three siblings trailing behind. She gathered them around her and said something that appeared to excite them. They scattered to scour the ground on hands and knees.

She hurried to Christopher, out of breath. "I haven't much time. Father won't let me go anywhere without them after what happened with the primer. I told them I would give a ha'-penny to the first to find a four-leaf clover." He detected a mix of pain and determination in her eyes. "Nathan will tattle if he catches on that I came to meet you. He fancies himself Father's sheriff." She kept her eyes on her siblings.

"Is there no way you can meet me without them?"

"If we were to meet closer to the Shambles, perhaps. I don't know."

Nathan looked up from his hands and knees in Anne's direction.

"Did you find one?" she shouted. He shook his head. "Keep looking," she encouraged. "We must get back soon."

Nathan stood and pointed at Christopher. "Who are you speaking with?"

She looked directly into Christopher's eyes and let out a frustrated sigh. "You see what I'm up against. 'Tis no use. I need to go."

Before she could take a step, Christopher grabbed her hand. Her cheeks flushed. "I want to speak with you again." He glanced at Nathan. "Without them around." Nathan's eyes narrowed as he watched the exchange.

"I don't know how. Really, I must go."

He let go of her hand and watched her return to her siblings. Nathan took a final look at Christopher before getting down on his hands and knees.

"I found one!" Maria jumped up, shaking a clover in the air. Christopher watched Anne inspect it and slip her sister a coin. After rounding up the children and starting back to the village, Anne cast a wistful glimpse at Christopher before disappearing over the hill.

"She fancies me," he smiled, a thrill coursing through his body. "Methinks she truly fancies me."

October, 1539

——

"*Monsieur?*"

Thomas barely heard her words, as he was gazing into the hypnotic chestnut eyes of a fawn. She wore her voluptuous russet hair in a braid, wrapped like a crown on the top of her head, with ringlets spiraling tantalizingly above her shoulders.

"*Monsieur. Que puis-je faire pour vous?*"

Her voice rang like the song of a lark. His heart leaped and his stomach growled at the same time. He rushed his hands over his abdomen.

"What can you do for me? Eh, *je suis femme, mademoiselle.*"

She covered a smirk with her hand, noting that his expression resembled that of a scolded puppy.

"*Monsieur,*" she explained, "you say, what is in Englich, 'I am woman.'"

His face felt hot. "You speak English?"

"*Un petit peu*—a little." She made a pinching sign with her fingers. "You want to say, '*J'ai faim,*' I have hunger."

"Merci, *mademoiselle…mademoiselle…?*"

"Isabelle LeBlanc, monsieur."

Thomas licked his lips and extended his right hand. "Mademoiselle LeBlanc, I am Mister Archer. Harry Archer. Pleased to meet you."

"*Enchanté.*" She averted her eyes with a modesty he found alluring. "Monsieur Harry Archer, what may I get for you?"

"Bread, please." He pointed to a dark, round loaf stacked alongside breads of all shapes and sizes, thinking it fortuitous that of all the stands at the Sarlat market, he picked this one.

"*Du pain.*" She lifted the loaf with both hands in front of her. "Bread."

"*Du pain,*" he repeated. He knew one thing for certain. She was the prettiest teacher he'd ever had.

"You are Englich, then?"

"Yes, from Calais."

"*Oui, oui*, Calais. What brings you to our ville, to Sarlat?"

"Perhaps you did, mademoiselle."

"*Moi?* But Monsieur Archer, I have never made your acquaintance before today."

His overture was lost on her, but he let it go. He aimed to become better acquainted with this woman, not scare her away.

"I came to this country last November, a year ago, after my mother succumbed to a long illness. We tried everything to balance her humors. A wise woman gave her wormwood and mint. Parishioners donated to help pay for a doctor. He tried everything, including leeches. 'Twas no avail—she passed away last September."

"Your mother? She died?"

"Yes, it is a pity. I felt compelled to leave Calais and put down new roots. I'm her only living child. My mother's dying wish for me was to find a good woman and raise a family."

"So you come to Sarlat, and not stay in Calais or go to England?"

Relieved to finally have a true story to recount, Thomas explained, "A few years ago, my uncle came to this region to hunt truffles. He grew rich working with a partner from Sarlat. One night the partner snuck into my uncle's chamber, stole the money they made together, and disappeared. With no money to start over, my uncle returned to London. He spoke often of this beautiful area and thought he might return, but he found success in London. I came here because of the stories he told me."

"And you have found truffles?"

"*Oui*, I live near the river on a truffle merchant's estate. He provides hogs to sniff out the truffles, and I dig them up and transport them to markets up and down the Dordogne River, as far as Bordeaux."

"*C'est bon.* Is good." Isabelle extended the loaf. "That will be three sols, *s'il vous plaît.*"

Thomas handed her three coins.

"*Merci bien.*"

She wore a rust-colored kirtle with half sleeves. A wide, square décolletage bodice accentuated her feminine form. He wished to inhale her beauty, but instead he held the rye loaf to his nose and breathed deeply. "I will see you again." It was a declaration rather than a question.

"I'm here next Saturday, Monsieur Archer. *A bientôt.*" Her trusting nature left him feeling guilty for lying to her.

Thomas bowed and backed away with a doltish smile, oblivious to a smattering of truffle-filled baskets behind him. He tripped and fell backwards, scattering an entire bushel basket of the prized delicacy across the cobblestone square.

A short, heavy-set man who was talking to a wine merchant ran toward Thomas, waving his arms in the air like an angry mother goose flapping its wings. He removed his cap and shook it in the air, revealing a balding crown on his head.

"*Allez! Allez, imbécile!*"

"*Pardon, Monsieur.*" Thomas apologized profusely, squatting to set the baskets upright and scrambling across the bumpy cobblestone on his hands and knees to gather scattered truffles. The man spit out a string of expletives Thomas was grateful he could not understand. After retrieving the truffles, Thomas took several sols from his purse and offered them to the man. The vendor's countenance softened as he wrapped his hand around the coins.

Isabelle watched intently while the incident played out, eager to learn more about the polite English gentleman. Thomas looked her direction. She blushed and averted her eyes.

03

Harry Archer. Thomas berated himself for thinking up such a ridiculous name. *Imbecile!* He sliced his canoe paddles through the placid surface of the Dordogne River, leaving ripples in the wake.

Toned by manual labor, his biceps bulged with each thrust of the oars. His hardening physique pleased him. He wondered if his appearance appealed to Isabelle, until he looked down at his legs. They were muscular, but skinny—bird legs, to be precise. A sense of insecurity gripped him as he began counting his follies, starting with tripping over a basket and introducing himself as Harry Archer. Harry Archer! *I'm neither hairy, nor an archer*, he thought.

As he paddled past the imposing limestone cliffs towering above, a brisk breeze swirled around him like a graceful dancer, waltzing with dried leaves and debris swept from the bushes and cliffs above. This kingdom of rolling hills and fruitful fields stirred affection in his bosom, not only because of the beautiful young woman tantalizing his thoughts, but also because of the land's fidelity to the Mother Church, in contrast to her rebellious neighbor to the north.

The two lands, England and France, had a long history of conflict. The very river on which he glided had, eight decades earlier, formed a border between the two kingdoms when the English occupied the region north of the Dordogne. A century earlier and two-hundred miles north, Joan of Arc sacrificed her life to liberate her people from English rule. Some of the French folks he encountered resented any English presence in France, but the occasional animosity he encountered as an Englishman paled in comparison to the hostility back home between reformers and traditionalists. Then again, the French kingdom had dangerous folks like Monsieur Bonner lurking in the shadows. *Wolves*, he thought.

Château de Beynac loomed on the horizon, a sentinel standing guard on a cliff high above the river. He admired the ingenuity of those who decided to build a fortress there. From a distance, the crenelated castle wall facing the valley appeared to be an impenetrable extension of the limestone cliff.

He pondered the human propensity to fight, conquer, and enslave. Evidence of the pernicious trait to seek dominion presented itself all around him in the castles and fortresses, and in the very fact that he had to flee Dartford for expressing his thoughts. Did the simple act of holding an opinion harm anyone? He gazed up at the steep castle walls. How many souls had perished trying to get in? How many more had lost their lives after leaving the safety of the walls? And what was the fighting all for, in the end? Eventually everyone ended up in the same place—those who built the castle, those who fought over the land—all ended up in Purgatory. His loose jumble of questions almost congealed into an answer, but then dissipated like a bird that lights on a branch and flutters away.

His thoughts shifted to his truffle cargo. This run would net him enough money to buy new clothes in Bordeaux before he called on Isabelle again, but a constant concern plagued him: the more he ventured out, the greater his risk of being caught for his crimes in England. What if an English merchant, on the lookout for a Dartford fugitive, spotted him in Bordeaux? What if one of the king's men, in Bordeaux to purchase wine for King Henry, saw him selling truffles? No matter where he traveled, a black panther of fear prowled the dark corners of his mind.

He contemplated visiting a priest to confess. Getting his misdeeds off his chest and paying penitence would bring sweet relief, but it was also fraught with risk. All information shared in a confessional was supposed to be confidential, but everyone knew stories of priests with loose lips, leaking bits of juicy confessions. *Here we go again*, he sighed. *Enslaved by walls. Enslaved by deeds. Enslaved by kings. Enslaved by one's fellowmen. Enslaved by conscience.* Life was a prison with only one escape.

His canoe sliced through the castle's reflection upon the water as he continued past the 400-year-old structure. *Where was I?* he thought. *Oh, yes. Clothing. Isabelle. Ah, Isabelle.* He could tell by her smile that she was impressed when he picked up the scattered truffles and recompensed the merchant. *To have a beautiful woman in my life…marry…get away from Bonner.*

It would be two weeks, under the best of circumstances, before he could see her again: at least five more days on the river, lodging in various villages along the route to Bordeaux, a day or two to do business, and a week's return to Sarlat on horseback. *Imagine father's surprise if I returned home with a French bride*, he mused, his thoughts drifting lazily like the river current.

November, 1539

—

Pacing behind the church, Christopher checked the sun's position every few seconds. Where was she? Sunlight struggled to penetrate a low-lying blanket of clouds trapping chimney smoke and making the air unpleasant and heavy. He blew warm breath into his hands and pulled his cloak closer around him to fend off the damp chill before venturing around the corner of the church to peer down High Street.

Richard Crispe, engaged in his end-of-the day routine, placed unsold pickled artichokes in a basket to carry home, while Abby Wellington stacked the empty baskets that carried her taffaty tarts to market. Many vendors had already closed and returned to their homes. He figured it to be near three o'clock in the afternoon.

Unusual activity from Simon Nix caught his eye. Simon picked up a small souvenir from his display. William Wade stood with his back turned, a few feet away from the linen cart, showing an embroidered tablecloth to a newly married young woman in the village. Simon strolled next to the cart and squatted, feigning a search for something on the ground. He slipped the object in his hand between folded layers of cloth and scurried back to The Pilgrim Hat. At first Christopher thought his father noticed, as William briefly glanced sideways. However, William continued to converse with the customer, paying Simon no heed.

By God's teeth, what was the sly fox up to? Christopher fought the impulse to run to his father and report what he saw, but he was supposed to be on an errand to fetch some cloves for Elizabeth's toothache. He willed Anne to appear around the corner from the Shambles. He'd grown accustomed to their weekly ritual of meeting behind the church and sneaking up East Hill to the Saint Edmunds churchyard. Time was running out. He needed to get back to the cart to help pack up for the trek home.

"Looking for someone?" Christopher almost jumped out of his skin. He turned around to see Father Garrett a few feet behind him, hugging a box of candles.

"Good day, Father. I was just looking for a couple of pence I dropped near here. Have you seen any coins on the ground?"

"No, but I'll help you look." Father Garrett set the box on a stone walkway, knelt down and ran his nimble fingers along the grass.

"'Tis no use," Christopher said, guilty to see the priest on hands and knees. "I've already looked. Someone probably picked them up."

"Ol' Harry got his hands on them, perhaps, as much time as he spends around here. A penny or two would be at least twice what he begs for." Garrett stood and dusted off his cassock.

With a crooked grin, Christopher shrugged his shoulders. "Perhaps. Well, I must be going. Father needs my help."

"Could you spare a moment to help me carry these candles to the vicarage?" Father Garrett pointed to the box on the ground. "You're young and spry. I'm…" he rolled his neck stiffly, "well, not spry."

"Why are you ridding yourself of them, Father?"

"They're no longer permitted, per…"

"I know," Christopher interrupted. "Per the injunctions."

"The new rules permit only light from the windows. No popish candles." Garrett rolled his eyes.

"I would like to help, but Father will be wondering where I am."

"'Tis only a hop, skip and a jump past the church. Surely, a few extra minutes won't matter?"

Christopher looked toward the linen cart. The customer ran her fingers across the embroidery, still chattering. William bore a look of feigned politeness.

"I thought I would retrace my steps and look for my coins one last time before we pack up the cart." Christopher tipped his cap, slipped into the nearby apple orchard before the priest could protest, and waited a few minutes before sneaking back behind the church. Peering around the corner he had a good view of Market Square and High Street. A quick scope of the horizon, up one side of the street and down the other, revealed no sign of Anne, but he saw Simon Nix speaking with his father. Simon appeared agitated.

"Looking for your coins again?"

Christopher spun around to face Father Garrett, making his way back to the church from the vicarage. "I was just on my way," Christopher stammered. He trudged to the cart, feeling Father Garrett's penetrating glare on his back.

"A deceiver," the priest muttered under his breath. "Just like his father."

೮೮

Elizabeth's heavy sigh sliced through the silence around the supper table as poignantly as if she'd screamed. Rubbing Dart's silky belly under the table with his toe, Christopher chewed a stale piece of rye bread, avoiding eye contact with either parent.

After swallowing a spoonful of eel stew, William cleared his throat. "Christopher, I need to speak with you."

His heart skipping a beat, Christopher rubbed Dart's belly faster and responded, "Yes, sir?"

"Simon Nix spoke with me at the market this afternoon. He claims to be missing a lover's badge. Said someone saw you around his stand at the market. Is this true?"

Christopher's breathing shallowed. "Why would I go anywhere near Mister Nix? He wants nothing to do with me."

"You need not have spoken to him. He claims to have a witness who saw you take the badge and hide it on our cart."

"I have no need for a lover's badge. Who would lie about me?"

"I want to believe you, but he suggested I go through the fabric. Sure enough, I found this lover's badge between two pieces of sheet cloth." William held up a pewter badge, featuring a gloved hand extending quatrefoil flowers.

Christopher's heart sank. "By Mary's blood, by God's teeth, by whatever I can swear, I took nothing from Simon, nor would I."

Elizabeth stared into her bread trencher, shaking the table with her foot.

"Swearing is not necessary. But can you see why I find your story troubling?"

His voice rising, Christopher protested, "Father, when I went to fetch clove oil, I saw Mister Nix put something on the cart when your back was turned. Have you ever known me to steal?"

"No, but what do you suggest I tell Simon? He's already convinced we're heretics. Now he has fodder to believe we are thieves."

Elizabeth watched her son's face redden, fighting her instinct to jump to his defense.

95

"Would you like me to say I took it, when I didn't? I have no idea why he would accuse me of such a thing."

William pressed. "Every week, you have a different excuse for your disappearances. I know you fancy the Cooper girl. Did you think I wouldn't notice? A lover's badge would make a fine gift."

"I was nowhere near his stand today." Christopher glared into his stew.

Tapping his fingers on the table, William demanded, "Can you prove that?"

"I can't prove it. I simply wasn't at his stand. You would have seen me there. From a distance, I saw Simon put something on the cart."

William and Elizabeth cast each other dubious glances before William continued. "Unless you can prove where you were, you'll have to pay for this badge and stay at the stand from now on to help me. You were gone when the badge went missing, and you refuse to tell me where you disappeared this afternoon. You leave me no choice."

"Very well, Father. Believe Simon Nix over your own son." Christopher pushed away from the table and stormed out the door. Dart trotted behind, scratching and whining to be let out.

William rushed to the door and threw it open. "Come back here!" he demanded. "I'll not have you tarnishing my reputation with thievery!"

Christopher ran toward the Brent as fast as his legs would carry him, with Dart galloping behind to catch up.

Gironde Estuary near Bordeaux, France

A glance at the sun's sinking position on the western horizon filled Thomas with angst. Signs of Bordeaux—a vineyard, a ship coming or going—should have been in sight by now. *Please, Saint Thomas, send me a sign*, he begged. Weary from battling the estuary's relentless tidal currents, he propped his oars against the boat rail, leaned his head back and closed his eyes.

His thoughts drifted to what Bonner must be thinking. Thomas should have returned to Sarlat with the profits from his truffle sale two weeks earlier but, near Bergerac, about halfway to Bordeaux, a large boulder beneath the river's surface gashed a hole in his boat. The snail's pace at which the repairman worked set him back considerably.

A strong tidal current lifted the canoe and spun it like a top. Thomas' first panicked thought was for the truffles, wrapped in burlap and tucked into the stern. He grabbed the oars just as something below the water's surface flipped the canoe and spit him into the Garonne. Seconds too late, he stretched a hand toward the stern. The capsized boat spun several feet from reach. Kicking and waving frantically, he watched helplessly as the prized truffles popped to the surface and bobbed away, still attached to the boat with a rope.

He sucked in one last greedy gulp of air before a strong undercurrent yanked him below the water's surface.

Dartford

"Anne! I need to talk to you." John stood outside the fence surrounding Anne's cottage, breathless.

"I'm busy, John. I must finish the wash and get supper fixed." Steam curled up from the washbasin. She heaved a sigh without looking up. The excitement she once felt about John's attention had long since evaporated. He spoke endlessly of his acceptance to Cambridge, and had the audacity to ask her if she thought a fishmonger's daughter had ever been courted by a gentleman's son.

Undaunted, he persisted. "'Tis important, Anne. I beg you, please, just give me a few minutes of your time." She continued to scrub the clothes in the tub, silent. "I have some information you might find pertinent," he added.

With chapped hands and fingers red from the cold, she dipped her father's nightshirt into the basin and squinted up at John against the midday sun. "If you came with news about Christopher, I've already heard everything you have to say." She wrung the water from the nightshirt with a firm twist on both ends and dropped it in a basket with other freshly washed items. Next, she plunged Nathan's shirt into the murky wash water.

"I don't believe you have," he replied, miffed by her indifference. "I have your best interests at heart. I can save you from needless heartache."

Anne sighed. "Very well." She stood up, leaving the garment to soak in the basin, and pushed a few stray hair strands away from her eyes. "Pray tell, what is this important news?"

"How do I tell you this?" He hesitated for several seconds. "'Tis about Christopher."

Frowning, she folded her arms. "Of course."

"Please don't doubt my sincerity. You know how I feel about you. Mister Nix and I were outside the Bull's Head a fortnight ago, when along came Christopher, hand in hand with Margaret Foxe—you know, the daughter of that knave who works in the chalk pits. They continued past us as if no one else in the world existed, and stopped shortly after. Christopher bid Margaret to close her eyes, and presented her with a lover's badge. But that's not the worst of it. It turns out Simon saw Christopher steal a lover's badge the week before. As if it weren't bad enough for him to be a Lollard, he's also a thief! A thief, Anne. You deserve better. It pains me to be the bearer of bad news. I just don't want you to be hurt."

Her eyebrows lifted. "Are you quite sure it was him?"

He raised his right hand. "As God is my witness. Simon saw it as well."

Anne knelt at the wash tub and dunked Nathan's shirt up and down as if she were trying to drown a demon, yanked it out of the water and tossed it, soaked, on top of the clean clothing pile. With an icy glance at John she jumped up, lifted the hem of her skirt and ran into the cottage without a word.

He waited for several minutes before descending the pathway to the cottage with a bounce in his step.

◌

Anne hurried along Spyttal Street with a small basket of poppy seed cakes purchased at Bartholomew's bakery. She had just reached the lime quarry when she felt a tug on the back of her cloak.

"Please," Christopher pleaded. "Speak to me!"

Spinning around, she slapped his hand away. "Let me alone." Her eyes were red and swollen. She turned and pressed forward, wishing she had somewhere to escape besides a dreary cottage with an intolerable father.

With a lunge forward, he grabbed her arm. "Stop! I pray you, let me speak with you."

She shook off his hand. "My father will whip me if he sees me with you. Besides, perhaps you should talk to Margaret Foxe," she snapped.

Christopher's heart caught in his throat. "Margaret Foxe? What are you talking about?"

"Walking hand in hand with her? Giving her a lover's badge? How dare you pretend not to know what I'm talking about. I have it on good word."

"Whose word? 'Tis nonsense."

"Someone saw you. Don't deny it."

"How could anyone see me when nothing of the sort happened? Do you want to be rid of me? Tell me to my face."

"I refuse to speak with you anymore. Let me be." She lurched forward.

Running in front of her he turned, planted his hands on his hips and demanded, "Listen! You owe it to me. Margaret Foxe? Where is this lie coming from?"

"Mister Nix saw you! He saw you with Margaret Foxe, walking hand in hand."

"Simon Nix?"

Anne's bottom lip quivered.

"Simon Nix? Surely, you jest. What would he know? I would sooner trust Amy Coppinger."

"I refuse to talk to you anymore! Now, leave me be!" She pushed past him.

Choking on bitterness, Christopher watched her pass the lime kiln and hurry up West Hill until she was out of sight. He kicked a stone the size of a hen's egg into the heel of an elderly man walking several paces in front of him. The man turned and scolded him with slanted eyes. Christopher glowered back and spun around, jogged through the village, across the stone bridge, past the fulling mill, and up East Hill to the grounds of St. Edmunds.

His mood matched the cold drizzle and thick fog socked into the valley. Sitting on wet grass at the hill's edge, he surveyed the wretched village wishing he could run away from Lollards, from fire-breathing dragon-fathers with pretty daughters, from slandering souvenir salesmen, and from taunting peers whose wealthy fathers could afford a fancy education. He picked up a rock and threw it at a tombstone.

"I hate everyone," he shouted. "I hate Father Garrett. I hate Matthew Cooper. I hate Simon Nix. I hate William Wade." He exhaled a frustrated groan, stood, and trudged home.

"Christopher, is that you?" Elizabeth had her back turned while she poked the fire.

"Yes. I came to take Dart for a walk." He took the leather leash from its hook and called, "Here, boy." Dart jumped up from his resting place before the fire, his tail wagging. Christopher secured the leash around the dog's neck and left without another word.

Bordeaux, France

Squinting against sunlight cascading through an eastern window, Thomas discovered himself lying on a pallet, face to face with a man who had beady brown eyes and a beak of a nose. To his right, across a stylish salon, a row of wine caskets stood against an oak wall intricately carved with grapes and vines. To his left, a painting of the Blessed Virgin hung beside an expansive brick fireplace. Upon the mantle, numerous wood and ivory carvings of saints brought comfort to Thomas' weary soul. The room began to spin. His eyes fluttered closed.

"Put a few more drops of cider in his mouth, Jean-Louis."

Jean-Louis DuBois hovered over Thomas with a teaspoon. His brother, François, paced back and forth rubbing his own head, which was as smooth as a polished river stone. Based on appearance, no one would guess the two were brothers.

"Do you think we'll be able to save him, Papa?" Twelve-year-old Marcel DuBois fiddled with a partially whittled block of birch wood while he stared at the stranger, wide-eyed.

"I can't say, Marcel," François responded. "When we pulled him out of the estuary, I thought he was already dead. He's trying to open his eyes. That's a good sign. He hasn't yet given up the ghost."

"I wonder where he's from." Scratching the side of his beak, Jean-Louis looked Thomas up and down with a sneer. "He doesn't look like he's from around here. What do you think, François?"

"He smells like dead fish, but I suppose he can't help it. From the looks of him, I would guess he's English."

"He has a bird's legs." Marcel pointed at Thomas' pale, bare legs and giggled.

"*Chut*," François scolded. "Don't make fun of our visitor. He might hear you."

A pleasant female voice called from the kitchen adjacent to the salon. "François? The broth is finished. Are you ready for it?"

"Bring the broth, Jeanette. Make sure it's cooled so we don't burn his mouth."

Jeanette DuBois emerged, carrying a teacup half-filled with thin vegetable broth. "Have you gotten any cider down him? No? Perhaps this will help him better." She traded Jean-Louis the cup for a rag with which he was dabbing Thomas' forehead. A petite woman of Spanish descent with black hair and fair skin, Jeanette's family teased her that what nature withheld from her in stature was made up for in spunk.

Jean-Louis coaxed Thomas' lips open and trickled a few drops of broth into his mouth with the spoon. Thomas accepted with a groggy moan.

Clasping a wooden donkey her uncle Jean-Louis had carved and painted for her, six-year-old Colette asked, "Maman, will the man stay with us?"

"I have no idea, Colette. He will probably need to stay with us to regain his strength. Perhaps we can make a place in the stable for him. What do you think?"

"Yes, Maman! I like his moustache."

"Silly Colette! It is rather amusing." Jeanette smiled at a clump of hair under Thomas' nose that looked like a dark brown field mouse.

"It makes me want to laugh!" Colette tiptoed to Thomas' side and inched her fingers toward his moustache. He flinched. She jerked her hand back as if she'd been stung.

As his eyes sprung open, Thomas groaned, "*Mon Dieu!*" Five astonished faces gazed down at him.

"He speaks French!" Marcel exclaimed.

"Don't hurt me!" Thomas rolled to his side.

"We're trying to help you." Jean-Louis held up the teacup as proof. "You nearly drowned in the estuary. Here, you must get more liquid down. François, prop up his head."

François knelt behind Thomas and lifted him to a sitting position, while Jean-Louis touched a spoonful of broth to the stranger's lips. Accidentally inhaling the liquid, Thomas flew into a coughing fit. François patted his back until the spasms calmed.

"It went down wrong. Now, here you go." Jean-Louis dipped the spoon in the teacup. "Take some more."

Thomas drank several spoons full, whispered "*merci*," and rested his head against the pallet.

"I suppose you're not up to answering many questions right now." François patted Thomas on the arm. "But we have many things to ask you when you're ready. First, I must know if you have somewhere to stay here in Bordeaux."

Straining his neck muscles, Thomas lifted his head. "Where am I?"

"Bordeaux."

His eyes wide, Thomas exclaimed, "Bordeaux?"

"We found you in the estuary," François explained. "You don't remember?" Thomas shook his head.

"You must get some nourishment and rest. Marcel, take Colette and fix the man a place to sleep in the stable. Get some wool blankets and a pillow from the guest chamber."

"Yes, Papa. Come, Colette."

"He gets to stay?" Colette jumped up and down and clapped her hands.

"For tonight. Now, be a good girl and help your brother make a place for the stranger."

"Yes, Papa."

CB

Outside the stable, a rooster crowed. A spongy object brushed against Thomas' arm. His eyes flew open. He found himself face to face with a stocky, grey Bazadais cow. The bovine blinked. With a loud *aïe!* he rushed his fingers to his thigh to remove an embedded piece of straw. Tamping down the straw around him with his hand, his fingers landed on a solid object. He picked it up and smiled. Colette's wooden donkey. She must have left it to keep him company.

He folded back the thick wool blanket covering him and sat up, shocked by the sting of damp, icy air on his skin. Hit by a wave of vertigo, he laid back down and focused on his breathing. The Bazadais watched his every move, chomping sideways on sweet straw.

"What? Am I in your bedchamber?" he demanded. She swished her tail and lowed.

With a quick catch-breath, he propped himself up on his elbows and waited. No dizziness. After pushing himself to a sitting position, he held his breath. A few steps away, on a nail embedded in a post, hung his clothes, his purse, and an unfamiliar wool cloak that he assumed someone put there for his use. A final push brought him upright. He stumbled to the post and steadied himself against an empty wine casket.

"Stop staring at me!" he shouted. The inquisitive bovine blinked. Clinging to the pole for balance, Thomas picked up a stick near his feet and tossed it at the cow. It bounced off her neck and fell back down to the straw. She walked several paces before casting a backwards glance.

He let go of the post to slip on his breeches and stumbled backwards onto a sharp pebble. "A pox on this place!" he muttered, easing himself to a sitting position. Just as he stretched to remove the pebble from his heel, he heard voices outside the stable.

"Charlotte, he is an odd man." It was Marcel's voice. "I wonder where he comes from."

"Perhaps he's dangerous. I can't believe Papa let him stay here."

"He came with no weapon, no dagger, nothing. How could he be dangerous?"

"Is he strong? Perhaps he'll overpower us. I don't want to go in there."

Thomas recognized Marcel's voice, but the other voice, that of a young woman, he hadn't heard before.

"Papa wouldn't put us in harm's way," Marcel said. "Come, let's check on him as Papa asked."

Two silhouettes darkened the stable door. Thomas reached for the blanket to cover himself.

January, 1540

—

Dartford

"Methinks these fingers will have a hard time spinning again." Elizabeth grimaced, opening and closing her fingers stiffly. "Too much time away from the wheel these past twelve days." Christopher had never before paid much attention to his mother's hands, with their bony knuckles and prominent veins protruding just below the skin. He contemplated all the work those leathery hands had done along the course of her thirty-eight years. Across the room, the spinning wheel sat idle for the holy days, adorned with ribbons.

"Mother, would you be happier if you could keep spinning?" Christopher couldn't understand why anyone would complain about a break from work. The twelve days of Christmas were one of his favorite times of year, a period of food and festivity, rest and regale. Spinning was specifically forbidden. She should be happy about that, especially since so many other feast days had become regular work days after the injunctions.

"'Tis not the rest I mind. 'Tis the startin' up again." She laid a damp linen dishtowel on the kitchen table and hung the copper pot she'd just finished drying next to the fireplace, then dipped her forefinger in a small pot of beeswax salve she concocted herself. The soft aroma of lavender wafted past his nose as she rubbed a pea-sized dab of salve into her hands and asked, "Are you goin' wassailin' this evening?"

"Yes, Nicholas should be here any minute." He looked out the window. A light snow began to fall. "By the way, what does wassail have to do with the three kings?"

"They brought the baby Jesus frankincense and myrrh, and wassail is brewed with spices."

Christopher nodded, still gazing out the window.

"Mind yourself out there, you hear?" Elizabeth continued. "I'll have no stories about my son vandalizin' the neighbors."

Christopher rolled his eyes.

"Who'll be bringin' the wassail bowl?" She crossed the room to scold Dart off the bed.

"Someone always does. I don't concern myself with it."

"Have some minced pie before you leave. It needs to be finished off." The pie's thirteen ingredients represented Christ and the twelve apostles, and included dried fruits, spices, and chopped mutton in remembrance of the shepherds.

"Do we have nothing else to eat?" Christopher felt like a prisoner having the same food slipped under his door day in and day out without any respite, but the slightest intimation of ingratitude would set Elizabeth off on a lecture about being thankful for everything the good Lord gave them. By the end of the Nativity season, Christopher didn't want to even look at minced pie. Elizabeth always baked more than enough to share with neighbors and friends, leaving him and William to choke down the leftovers. All he could think of was how delicious a taffaty tart would taste about now.

"When I was your age, I would be grateful to have a morsel of bread. Why, young folks these days have no appreciation. Off, I said!" Dart looked at her and slinked off the bed to curl up in front of the fireplace.

Nicholas' distinct three raps at the door came none too soon.

"Godspeed, Mother." Christopher threw his cloak around his shoulders and grabbed his cap and gloves.

"Behave yourself like a good Christian man out there."

"Of course." Christopher slipped outside, relieved to escape.

"I thought you would never get here," he whispered to Nicholas.

Nicholas shook his head. "Between my father warning me about the seven deadly sins, and my mother lecturing me about the company I keep, I thought I would be stuck at home all night."

"Good thing the seven deadly sins don't mention turning Coppinger's cow loose in Twisden's orchard." Christopher let out a hoot.

"Or throwing eggs at doors!" Nicholas chimed in.

"When will our parents realize we're almost men in our own right?" Christopher huffed. "We're nearly sixteen."

Alarmed to see Christopher empty-handed, Nicholas asked, "Did you bring a disguise?"

"I forgot," Christopher moaned. "Now what?"

"Sneak back and get something."

"Mother wouldn't let me hear the end of it. We must think of something else."

They stood in silence for several moments. Nicholas tightened his cloak about him to create a snug barrier against the biting January chill, while sounds of merry-making wafted up the snow-dusted hill.

"I've got it!" Christopher clasped his hands together. "The chalk pits. I'll pat my face and hair white. No one will recognize me then."

Nicholas opened his hand to reveal a large lump of coal. "I brought coal to blacken my face. I have enough for both of us."

"We can blacken our faces, and chalk our hair and ears."

Nicholas raised his eyebrows. "You whiten your face, and I'll blacken mine. You blacken your hair and ears, and I'll whiten mine. They won't know what to think."

"We'll look like buffoons."

"Well, we want to be disguised."

"I suppose," Christopher agreed, "But not to be the laughing stock of the village." After brooding for a moment he added, "I guess 'tis better than nothing."

"We must hurry," Nicholas tugged on Christopher's elbow. "They'll be waiting for us."

They raced down the hill, hooting, hollering and leaving skid marks in the snow.

༰

"Did you hear something?" Mark Whitfield cast his wife, Margaret, a quizzical look.

"What did it sound like?" She cocked her head.

Tap. Tap.

"There it is again—something tapping on the door. Methinks I heard voices, as well." Whitfield rose from his chair next to the fireplace and crossed the room. At the lift of the door latch, a dozen adolescents, disguised in as many ways, broke into a song more reminiscent of honking geese than a chorus.

A wassail, a wassail throughout our town,
Our cup it is white and our ale it is brown.
Our wassail is made of the good ale and true,
Some nutmeg and ginger, 'tis the best we can brew

"Let us in," Nicholas pleaded. "'Tis frightfully cold out here." He cupped his hands over his mouth and blew. The boys broke into another verse.

There's a master and a mistress sitting down by the fire
While we poor wassail boys do wait in the mire,
And so pretty maid with your silver-headed pin,
Please open the door and let us come in.

"What have we here? A group of Dartford rogues wreaking havoc upon unsuspecting townsfolk? Come in for some minced pie." Master Whitfield threw the front door open. A fire blazing in his parlor drew them into its warm embrace.

"If it please you, share our wassail bowl." Nicholas extended a black clay vessel. Mark Whitfield took a polite sip, while Margaret shuffled from lad to lad with a tray of pre-cut minced pie. When the offering reached him, Christopher grimaced.

"Who is it, Father?" John peeked around the corner. At the sight of Christopher and Nicholas, he smirked. The pair resembled Holstein calves. Christopher's face—including eyebrows and eyelashes—was whitened with chalk. His hair, ears and neck were blackened with coal. Christopher avoided eye contact, fixing his gaze on a soot stain that clung to the plaster above the fireplace.

"You should have joined us," Edwin Taylor scolded in response to John's question. "'Tis a perfect night for wassailing."

"I've too much to do to prepare for Cambridge," John countered.

Christopher wanted to roll his eyes, but refrained. He held back near the door with the excuse that his stomach ached, while the other wassailers shared pleasantries and pie.

Spying his prey alone, John moved in. In a low voice he taunted, "Is Farmer Cox missing his calves?" Christopher kept his eyes fixed on the soot stain, bristling. John moved his lips close to Christopher's ear and mooed. Christopher flinched. "Moooooo," John repeated, leaning forward on his tiptoes.

No longer able to resist, Christopher elbowed him in the side.

John stumbled sideways. All eyes, including those belonging to the family bulldog, turned to him. Thinking quickly, he quipped, "Ho, where is the wassail?"

A lad disguised as a court jester brought the wassail to him and hurried back to the group to hear Master Whitfield recount the tale of his great-great-great grandfather's fight in Wat Tyler's rebellion against the poll tax. Tyler's army of angry rebels passed through Dartford, Whitfield claimed, and even stopped for ale at the Crown & Anchor.

John took a sip of wassail and passed it to Christopher. Just as Christopher lifted the bowl to his lips, John tapped the underside and watched Christopher squirm while the liquid trickled down his chest, across his belly, and down his left thigh.

"Pardon my clumsiness," John snipped. Enthralled with Master Whitfield's tale, no one noticed the drama playing out near the front door. Finally, Nicholas thanked Master and Mistress Whitfield for their hospitality. The wassailers swarmed to the front door.

"Just you wait," John growled.

Christopher responded the only way he could think of: he stuck out his tongue.

Bordeaux

"Come, everyone. It's time for the galette." Jeanette summoned her family and Thomas to her long oak kitchen table. Thomas set the Saint Thomas figurine he was whittling for Colette on the cabinet, along with a carving knife Jean-Louis loaned him.

"Come, Monsieur Archer," Jeanette smiled. "You will cut the galette. One piece for each of us, plus one for the poor."

Thomas protested. "I can't take the place of François. It's your tradition."

"You're our guest of honor, and we insist." Jeanette handed him the knife. "You'll be leaving us for Sarlat in the morning, so it is fitting."

"You'll never win an argument with Jeanette. And don't forget to count two pieces for me," François teased.

Thomas took stock of the group. "Let me see. François, Jeanette, Jean-Louis, Charlotte, Marcel and Colette. Six pieces."

"And yourself," twenty-year-old Charlotte blushed. She pushed a strand of auburn hair away from her hazel eyes that sparkled with mischief, like her father's. She possessed a mixture of her father's affability and her mother's spunk, along with a measure of stubborn strength that François insisted came from her mother's side of the family.

"Seven." Thomas nodded.

"And one for the poor," Charlotte added.

"Eight pieces," Thomas said.

"But they'll be tiny." Marcel folded his arms with a frown.

"Don't worry, Marcel," his mother warned, her eyes slanted. "You've had so many treats over the course of the holy days that a small piece of galette won't hurt you."

Marcel persisted, "But galette is my favorite."

"You may have my piece," Thomas offered.

Marcel's face lit up. "May I, Maman?"

"*Mais, non*! Shame on you. Perhaps Harold would enjoy being king for the day. What if he has the fève? I won't hear of you taking his piece of cake."

"If he gets the fève he'll have to buy us all drinks!" Jean-Louis clapped.

"We have our own wine, of course. So Harold will be king for the day, nothing more." Jeanette spoke with finality.

Thomas shrugged his shoulders and cast Marcel a look that said, *I tried.* Marcel shrugged his shoulders in return. Secretly, Thomas hoped he wouldn't get the fève, a small trinket baked into the pastry. He worried about choking on it.

"Like this?" Thomas laid the knife across the center of the cake.

"Yes, cut it crossways, like so." She modeled four cross-cuts with the side of her hand. "And we'll have our eight pieces. Perfect."

"Do you have to go back to Sarlat? I want you to stay." Colette wiggled on her stool. "You could marry Charlotte! She wants to find a husband."

The faces of both Thomas and Charlotte raced from pink to crimson.

"Colette!" Jeanette frowned.

"Oh, no!" François thrust his arms upward and paced beside the table, his face flushed.

"I can't believe you said that." Jeanette shook her head. "Please, Harold, pay her no mind. She's young and hasn't learned how to control her tongue. I'll have a talk with her later." Jeanette cast a stern warning glance at Colette. "Harold must get back to his work running truffles, Colette. Many depend upon him." Jeanette smiled at him with a nod.

"But Charlotte does want to find a husband," Colette insisted. "It's all she talks about. And she thinks you are handsome."

Charlotte cast an icy glare at her sister.

"Colette, you must say nothing more, or you will march to the salon and miss the galette." Colette responded to her mother with folded arms and a crinkled brow.

"We're so happy you could celebrate Three Kings' Day with us before you go," Jean-Louis remarked.

109

"I'm grateful as well." Thomas made eye contact with the folks surrounding the table as he cut the galette. "Back in Dartford, the king was abolishing feast days faster than Marcel wolfs down sweets. Since I left last November, I've often wondered if there are any holy days left in England." Jean-Louis' startled expression confused him. "What is it, Jean-Louis? Did I say something?"

"Dartford? Where is this Dartford? Aren't you from Calais?"

All color drained from Thomas' face. Jeanette backed away from the table. Tension-infused silence saturated the room, broken only by a hen clucking outside. Thomas averted his gaze to the floor, then slowly lifted it to the back door a few steps away.

François kept a steady eye on the kitchen knife in Thomas' right hand. "You're not from Calais? Where is this Dartford?"

Jeanette signaled with her hand for the children to gather behind her. Marcel obeyed, while Colette frowned and shook her head no. Jeanette cast François a warning glance. He grabbed Colette's arm and pulled her to his side.

"Yes, Harold, tell us the truth," Jeanette pleaded. "And please, put the knife down."

Thomas blinked and took a deep breath. After surveying the kindly faces surrounding him, he laid the knife on the table and exhaled slowly. "Madame and Monsieur DuBois, Jean-Louis," he sighed, "I don't know how to tell you this."

"Start at the beginning," Jeanette said weakly.

Mustering his courage, Thomas began. "Very well. First of all, my name is not Harold Archer. I'm not from Calais. I'm Thomas Nix, from Dartford, England."

Dartford

"Anne, come inside."

Her heart stopped. Anne threw one last handful of scratch to the chickens and looked over her shoulder to see Matthew leaning against the door frame, tightening and releasing his facial muscles while he rolled the birch switch between his hands. She closed the chicken coop door and dragged her feet uphill, feeling like a heretic about to face an inquisition. Matthew arched his arm across the doorway and bid her to walk under it.

A kettle of pease pottage simmering in the fireplace infused the tense atmosphere with pleasant aromas of mint and sage. Her inquisitor directed her to a stool next to the fireplace and commanded her to sit. She did as she was told, staring at the floor.

"I have a reputation in this village," he began. "And you're putting a stain on it. That sly fox, Christopher Wade, is taking advantage of you with John off at Cambridge. Don't you realize folks gossip? Have you no concern for the good name I've given you?"

Her fingers fondled the tie on her apron while she kept her head lowered. He leaned forward, white-knuckling the switch in his right hand. "Answer me," he demanded.

With her heart in her throat, she looked him squarely in the eyes and asked, "What are they saying now?"

"Folks have seen you walking with him."

"Who saw me?"

"Your brother, for one. 'Tis no matter who else saw you. I have it on good word that you were seen with him at Saint Edmunds' churchyard and the Brent."

Anne swallowed hard. "I haven't spoken with him for weeks—at least since he was seen with Margaret Foxe."

She fell for it, he thought, knowing full well he concocted the Margaret Foxe story with John Whitfield to get her away from the knave. Suppressing a smug smile, Matthew began to pace, his voice rising with each pass in front of her.

"As I thought. Playing one maiden after another. You would think his father, who claims to be a godly man, would do a better job raising his son. Everyone in town knows the boy is going rogue. He's been spotted outside the tavern numerous times with the Hall lad, waiting for Harry to sneak them liquor."

"Who told you these things?"

"'Tis no matter who told me. I have news for you, and I fancy you won't be happy about it."

She stated matter-of-factly, "You're sending me away. That's it, isn't it?"

He stopped pacing and waited for her to cry, to stomp, to shout—anything—but she simply stared at him, unruffled.

"Well, yes. You're becoming a woman in your own right, and 'tis beyond me to teach you the arts of women. I've corresponded with Aunt Victoria. She's happy to take you under her wing. We'll start for London in the morning, and be there by tomorrow eve. Pack your belongings tonight so I can load the wagon. We'll leave at daybreak."

"Who will care for the children?"

"They'll stay with Amy Coppinger while we're away."

111

"I mean after I leave, who will take care of them?"

"I intend to hire help."

"Very well, Father. Would you like me to pack now, or get supper on?" At the sizzle of pottage boiling over onto the coals, she jumped up from her stool. Smoke billowed into the room.

"Supper," he choked. Covering his mouth and nose with the hem of his tunic, he leaned the birch switch against the wall and grunted, "I'm glad to see you've come by some sense." Without another word, he ventured outside.

Anne lifted the kettle from its tripod and set it on the hearth to cool, her mind racing. Would she ever see Christopher again? Did she even care? She had given the matter much thought. The benefits of going to London far outweighed those of staying in Dartford.

A joyful realization hit her: this was the last dinner she would have to cook for her father. Dancing and humming, she arranged five wooden bowls on the table and followed up with five pewter spoons. "London," she whispered, wishing she could climb atop her thatched rooftop and shout it across the Darent Valley. "I'm going to London!"

April, 1540

—

John nodded at the stocky, grey-haired waiter, known to patrons simply as Jolly. The joyful exuberance with which Jolly bounced about the tavern gave the impression he met his life's highest purpose serving ale and mingling with customers.

Jolly crossed the candlelit room and laid a hand on John's shoulder. "Can I get you something else, lad?"

"Another ale, please."

"Aye, sorry I can't," Jolly replied, his expression somber. "You've surpassed your limit." In response to the astonished look on John's face, he broke into laughter and slapped John's back. "I jest, lad. Drink to your heart's content. You can pay for it tomorrow, if you make it there."

"You'll barely be able to stagger home as it is." Geoffrey Brown, John's roommate, uttered his rebuke from the other side of the table. "One more makes five. Don't you know that drunkenness is one of the seven deadly sins?"

"You're wrong on that one. 'Tis gluttony that is one of the deadly sins."

"You're a glutton for ale."

"According to Saint Thomas Aquinas, 'tis an obsession with food that constitutes gluttony. I'm simply enjoying a few cups of ale." John perused the crowded White Horse tavern. It was brimming with university students, many recognizable from his classes. A palpable energy expanded to fill the room as young men loosened up from their Cambridge studies. "Furthermore," John continued, "Saint Thomas specifically outlined six ways of committing gluttony. *Praepropere*, eating too soon. *Laute*, eating too expensively…"

"Let me interrupt you before you waste more breath." Geoffrey took a sip of ale and continued. "You could apply those six things to ale. Drinking too soon. Drinking too expensively. Drinking too much. Drinking too eagerly. Drinking too daintily. And drinking too wildly. You're guilty of all."

113

"I hate to contradict you again, but you leave me no choice. First, I waited until after class to drink; therefore, I'm not drinking too soon. Second, the ale here at the White Horse is reasonable in price; therefore, I'm not drinking too expensively. I've not yet drunk too much, and I'm not drinking daintily, but rather like a man." He flexed his arm in a mock show of muscular strength, then lifted his mug and guzzled it without pausing. After a loud burp, he continued. "I'm not drinking wildly, though that may be about to change. If I do have a sin, it would be drinking too eagerly, as I'm all too eager to start on my next mug." He slammed his mug on the table. "There." He smacked his lips. "Drag me to the confession booth."

"John, let's be earnest for a moment."

"I am being earnest. I earnestly desire another pint."

"Listen, John. Do you see those folks over there?" Geoffrey pointed with his nose to a group of men heartily engaged in discussion in the corner of the tavern.

"Of course. They're at that table almost every night."

"They come here regularly to speak of heretical ideas, following in the footsteps of Luther, Tyndale and their ilk. Sometimes I sit closer so I can eavesdrop."

"Why would you want to listen to them?" John scanned the room, his mind elsewhere.

"Their discussions intrigue me. I don't altogether agree, but they challenge my thinking. It's like sitting in a room with open windows and a breeze wafting through—their ideas are refreshing."

"If I were soused, I might find them interesting."

"I find them interesting when I'm sober."

"Geoffrey, you sound quite taken with them. My father warned me to stay away from heretics when I came here, and I intend to heed his advice. My life is too precious to expend it in pursuit of fleeting opinions."

"No ill will come to you for simply listening. You'll hear ideas that challenge your thinking. Isn't that why one attends university, after all? To expand his mind? You should join me one evening. How about tomorrow? If nothing else, you'll enjoy a good cup of ale."

"Tomorrow is Friday. I'm going to Dartford to see Anne. Perhaps another time."

"Ah, the maiden back home. Out with the old, in with the new, I say. Look around the town of Cambridge—the maidens are clamoring for university men. Beautiful flowers in the Cambridge garden, begging to be plucked." He winked.

114

"Don't think I haven't noticed."

"Anne needn't know. You're not betrothed, are you? You're missing out on the university life, man. Drink from the fountains! The fountains of knowledge, the fountains of love, they're all here, and they're passing you by while you hold on to a fishmonger's daughter. She's beneath your station. At least take a sip! You've nothing to lose."

"You make a convincing argument. 'Almost thou hast persuaded me,' said Caesar." John set down his mug with a wobbly hand. "How about we take a walk about town?"

"Are you sure you can walk? Because I'll be damned if I'm dragging you back to the chamber."

"Do you doubt my abilities?" John fished through his pouch and dropped several coins on the table without bothering to count them.

"Never, my friend. I'm doubting mine."

John stood and stumbled sideways. Geoffrey jumped to his side, linking elbows to escort him outside. They had taken only a few steps down King's Lane when three attractive young women chatting on the street corner caught John's eye. He howled and moved in their direction until Geoffrey grabbed the back of his cape and pulled him back.

"Do yourself a favor. Wait until you're sober before you approach them, or you'll play such a fool tonight they'll never speak to you again."

"Let go! You're spoiling my pleasure." John wriggled loose. Stumbling sideways, he tripped over a rock and tumbled to the ground with a loud grunt. The maidens—two brunettes and a blonde—pointed and giggled.

Extending a hand, Geoffrey helped John to his feet. "Trust me, you'll thank me tomorrow." He hopped backwards. "Your face looks putrid."

"Help me to the room, will you?" John doubled over. "I think I'm going to puke."

෮

"I've had a night to sleep on it." John shielded his eyes from the morning sun while stopping to watch the parade of students and teachers crisscrossing Queens' College court. "Pray, tell me more about this group that meets at the White Horse."

"We're almost to class," Geoffrey replied. "'Twould take more time than we have now. Besides, far better than me telling you about them, why don't you come tonight and listen for yourself? I feel to warn you, though, you might find yourself rethinking the meaning of heresy."

"My last lecture lets out at four this afternoon," John replied. "What time do they show up at the tavern?"

Geoffrey thought for a moment. "They're usually at the table when I arrive. Shall we plan on six?"

"Six it is. I feel a strange curiosity about them—I suppose because this 'new learning' swirls everywhere about us. Besides, can I consider myself truly educated if I don't consider a variety of views?"

"That's what I was trying to tell you last night. No trip to Dartford, then?"

"What were you saying about flowers in the Cambridge garden?" John winked.

"Your eyes are opening already. Here we are." Geoffrey held the door. "Did you study for the Greek exam?"

John crossed his fingers. "I'm hoping Doctor Clark will forego an exam today."

"Don't get your hopes up." Geoffrey took his seat. John plopped down next to him.

A slender, nervous man, his hair greying at the temples, entered and cleared his throat. "I trust you've all prepared for the exam. You were to memorize the rules for past verb tenses in Greek. When I call out a verb, your task is to give me the conjugation. Put all notes away."

Geoffrey leaned over and whispered, "I'd rather be at the White Horse." With raised eyebrows, Doctor Clark shuffled to Geoffrey's side.

"Mister Brown?"

"Yes, Sir."

"You will receive a zero mark."

"But Sir, I was only…" It was no use arguing. Geoffrey folded his arms and bowed his head, fuming. John snickered.

The professor moved to John's side. "Mister Whitfield?"

"Yes, Sir?"

"Your mark will be zero as well."

John bit his tongue, glaring at the professor's shoes.

July, 1540

—

Bordeaux

"Thomas, do you have a minute? I'd like you to meet a friend."

Upon hearing François DuBois' voice, Thomas paused in his task of dusting a wine cask to shout "Coming!" Wiping his hands on his apron, he ascended a narrow spiral staircase and emerged into the main room of one of many stone outbuildings dotting the DuBois estate.

François greeted him, standing next to a stocky, black-haired man about Thomas' height who projected an air of self-assurance. The stranger eyed Thomas with a look of familiarity and extended his hand. "Monsieur Nix, is it?"

"Yes, Thomas Nix." Thomas studied him for a moment before snapping his fingers. "I met you at the Mardi Gras carnival. You were selling souvenirs, weren't you?"

A look of recognition flashed in the man's eyes. "That's right. I'm Jacques Rosier." At the sight of Thomas' soiled apron, Rosier elbowed François. "I see you have Monsieur Nix doing your dirty work."

"Room and board, and all the wine I can drink. I can't complain," Thomas patted his belly with a grin.

"I suppose my offer will have to be very attractive, then. Let me get straight to the point. You carved a statue for little Colette DuBois—of Thomas Becket, was it?" Thomas nodded. "I'm always looking for talented people to create items to sell." Thomas' heart leaped. "Do you have any other work you might show me?"

"To tell you the truth, I haven't had much time for carving."

François raised a hand to interject. "What about the Saint Vincent statue you've been working on?"

"Well, I barely started—it's not finished."

"Show him what you have so far. It's good. I'll have Charlotte fetch it." François burst out the door and shouted across the yard to Charlotte before

Thomas could protest. She was hanging freshly washed clothing on a line near the stable. He re-entered with a mischievous glint in his eye. "She's on her way."

"Where did you learn to carve?" Monsieur Rosier asked. François watched the two men converse, thinking they could easily be mistaken for brothers.

"From my father. We sold souvenirs in England, until the king's reforms ended it."

"Such a pity, with talent like yours."

"Are you saying his talents are going to waste here?" François scolded.

"Of course. Look at him. The man is wiping barrels in a cellar when he could be carving works of art. Let him out of his cage, François."

Charlotte burst in, out of breath, and handed a partially carved statue of Saint Vincent, patron saint of wine, to Rosier. François watched Thomas' pupils enlarge when Charlotte entered the cottage. He winked at Rosier. Rosier turned the carving back and forth in his hands with a satisfied smile.

"Charlotte," François inquired, "don't you think Thomas would be an asset to Monsieur Rosier?"

"Why—yes, Papa," she stammered. "Thomas is a good carver."

"He's a hard worker. I would hate to lose him, but I don't want to hold him hostage—as Jacques accuses me of doing."

After extending the statue to Thomas, Rosier turned to François. "Could you spare him tomorrow?"

"It's his decision, of course." François waited for Thomas' response.

"This is unexpected." Thomas shrugged his shoulders. "I would love to go."

"I'll send Charlotte and Marcel to accompany you." A twinkle brightened François' eyes. "She knows her way to Monsieur Rosier's shop, and can pick up some things at the market while Thomas is occupied." Charlotte and Thomas blushed simultaneously.

Rosier clapped his hands together. "I'll look forward to it. On the morrow then?"

Thomas nodded.

"Charlotte?" François cocked his head sideways with a look that demanded compliance.

"I planned on helping Maman with—"

"Charlotte would love to go," François interrupted. She folded her arms and glowered at him.

Anne aimed her spade at a dandelion root and gave it a hard *whack*, wondering whether Christopher, at that very moment, might be weeding his mother's garden and thinking about her. She wiped beads of perspiration from her temples with her sleeve hem. A glance at the sun suggested the time to be near noon.

For the most part, she was relieved to be in London helping Victoria keep the gardens and do housekeeping for Master McMillan, a grocer, in exchange for room and board. If she were presented a choice between London and Dartford—not that she had a choice—she would lean toward London. It was better than a life of fishmongering with her father hovering over her.

From the open cottage door, the aroma of ham and onion wafted past her nose, making her mouth water. She wished she could get Christopher off her mind. Did he really like Margaret Foxe? Did he even care that Anne went to London? The low vibration of McMillan's voice opposite a tall, vine-covered trellis in the courtyard interrupted her musings. She rested against the spade to listen.

"…from Amherst. How would you like me to deliver them?" The male voice was not familiar to her.

"Will you be using the chest—the one with the false bottom—to transport them?" McMillan inquired.

"If that is what you prefer."

"Yes. Fill the chest with spices and deliver it to my shop. I'll sort things out and get it back to you." McMillan paused. "Are you concerned that Lord Cromwell is to be executed next week?"

"Terribly concerned, I am. The king is unstable, and what will become of Cromwell's reforms?"

Church bells erupted across the city, drowning out the men's voices. Anne's hands began to perspire. Delivering something in a false-bottomed chest? The king executing his chief minister? She aimed the spade at another dandelion when Victoria called her name. After resting the tool against an iron fence, she stepped inside the cottage, relieved to feel cool air against her clammy skin.

"The stew smells delicious," Anne remarked, washing her hands in a basin and patting them dry on a towel.

"I hope you like ham and pea porridge. Have a seat." Victoria motioned to a bench that ran the length of the table. "Would you like a slice of bannock?"

"Yes, thank you."

Victoria seated herself and said grace.

Anne cleared her throat to speak, but froze.

Victoria dabbed at a corner of her mouth with a serviette and asked, "Is something wrong?"

Tapping her fingers on the table, Anne responded, "Call me lunatic, but I think Master McMillan might be a thief. I just overheard him speaking with a man about delivering something in the secret compartment of a chest."

Victoria bowed her head and slurped her porridge, her breathing shallow.

Perplexed, Anne waited several seconds and demanded, "Doesn't it bother you that our landlord might be a scoundrel?"

Victoria leaned forward on her elbows and, in a low voice, warned, "'Tis better to look the other way. Our rector, Thomas Gerard, was ordered to recant for preaching heresy at St. Paul's Cross. Trouble follows him like flies to dung. Years ago, he secretly distributed Tyndale Bibles. Such are the folks Master McMillan mixes with. Trust me—you must mind your own affairs and pretend not to notice anything."

Anne's heart skipped a beat. "Master McMillan is a smuggler?" Victoria shrugged her shoulders. "What would Father think?" Anne continued. "He sent me here to get me away from such things."

"If he thought sending you to London would keep you away from the new learning, he was sorely mistaken. Those ideas breed here."

"Why didn't you warn him?"

"I go about my life and don't pay any heed to such nonsense, and I figured you would do the same. At least here in London you're not around that—what was his name? The one who was thieving and sneaking around with another maiden?"

Victoria's description of Christopher struck Anne like a slap in the face. "I don't know if those things were true," she objected. "And his name is Christopher Wade."

"At any rate, you're better off here. My brother has been a mess since your mother passed away." Anne ate her porridge in silence, contemplating her aunt's stern warning.

"Charlotte Nix! Charlotte Nix!" Marcel jumped sideways to dodge a swat from his sister.

"Chut! Stop, Marcel. I'm not his wife."

"You don't think Papa sent you on this trip just so you could give Thomas directions, Madame Nix? I see the way he looks at you."

Charlotte felt heat spread across her chest. *Charlotte Nix*—she liked the sound of it. Marcel wasn't the only one who noticed the way Thomas looked at her, but she wasn't about to let on and give her brother more ammunition to tease her. They passed through the city gate. She breathed a sigh of relief. She could finally be rid of him.

"Stop being a pest. Maman gave me a list for you. Go get two rounds of chèvre, a crock of olives, and two loaves of bread. Meet me in fifteen minutes at the fountain." Charlotte slipped Marcel a small pouch filled with coins and watched him wander off through the maze of market stands. Certain he would become distracted with market entertainers, she figured she had at least a half an hour before he showed up at the fountain.

As soon as Marcel disappeared into the crowd, she backtracked to a narrow side street they passed coming into Market Square. Hurrying along the cobblestone, she stopped to tap the back of an elderly man busy arranging books on a table. He turned. His eyes widened at the sight of a beautiful young woman.

"Pardon, Monsieur," she said. "I'm looking for the writings of John Calvin."

Color drained from the man's face. He glanced in all directions. Leaning close to her he whispered, "Mademoiselle, you mustn't even say that name unless you want to attract trouble." Noting her bewildered expression, he explained, "King Francis issued an edict last month. Anyone involved in activities contrary to the Holy Mother Church is guilty of high treason against God and mankind."

Charlotte protested, "But I only want to find out for myself what the heretics are saying, so I can refute them."

"You might as well drink poison. After the placard affair, the king won't tolerate any—and I do mean any—rebellion from his subjects."

Frowning, she countered, "Then how will I recognize their lies?"

He fumbled through a stack of books. "I have other books here—poetry by Jean Molinet, perhaps? Or a primer?" He extended a small book toward her. She made no effort to accept it.

"Do you have any French Bibles?" she asked.

A heavy-set woman in front of a bakery two doors down cocked her head like a bird, wondering why the bookseller was speaking with a younger woman.

"Bonjour, Madame Fournier," he shouted. She nodded and retreated into her shop. Lowering his voice, the bookseller said, "You've come to the wrong place. I would never risk my life to carry heretical books. You shouldn't risk your life to read them."

Disappointed, she made her way back to Market Square. As expected, Marcel hadn't arrived. She zigzagged through the market, searching for a bookseller, when she saw Marcel in line at a pastry shop.

"Do you have any money left?" she asked, nudging his side with her elbow. He startled. "What are you getting?" she inquired.

"A crêpe with sugar."

"Get me one, too," she demanded. He handed her a sack containing the items he was tasked to purchase and ordered a second crêpe. "Get one for Monsieur Nix, also," Charlotte added.

Marcel rolled his eyes. "Of course, Madame Nix. I thought I would have some money left over. Thank you for making me spend it all."

"Thomas will thank you," she smiled sweetly. He rolled his eyes again and traded her the bag of merchandise for two sweet, steaming crêpes.

November, 1540

——

Bordeaux

Gazing into Thomas' eyes, Charlotte blotted a trickle of moisture from her cheek with a white kerchief. Providence showered her with everything she could ask for—a man loyal to God, talented, hard-working, beloved of her parents, and—she blinked profusely—a tall, dark, handsome Englishman.

Taking her hands in his, Thomas proclaimed, "I Thomas Nix, take thee, Charlotte DuBois, to be my wedded wife, to have and to hold from this day forward, for better, for worse, for richer, for poorer, in sickness, and in health, till death do us part, if the holy church will ordain it: And thereto I plight thee my troth." His hand trembling, he slipped a ring on his bride's finger. Charlotte glanced sideways to see her mother, Jeanette, dab at her eyes with an embroidered kerchief. A lump formed in Charlotte's throat.

After the nuptial mass, guests emerged from the rural gothic church into blinding afternoon sun. Jubilant, François scrambled atop a large boulder and shouted, "I've arranged for covered wagons to take you all to our estate for the feast." Excited murmurs animated the guests. François DuBois did nothing halfway. François continued, "Madame and Monsieur Nix, you'll lead the party." He pointed to a dirt road beside the church where two white Percherons stood ready to transport the bride and groom. Charlotte gasped. The horses' trappings glistened in the sunshine—light blue silk collars embroidered with black fleur-de-lis, trimmed in gold fringe.

Thomas squeezed Charlotte's hand and, loud enough for only her to hear, he said, "To a lifetime of adventure."

"To a lifetime of adventure," she whispered.

May, 1541

―

Momentous events swirled in London. Just days after McMillan's secret conversation behind the trellis the previous summer, Thomas Lord Cromwell was executed at the Tower of London, and his head placed on a pike on London Bridge. On the day of Cromwell's execution, King Henry married his fifth wife, Catherine Howard, more than thirty years his junior. Two days later, Thomas Gerard, rector of All Hallows Honey Lane parish, was burnt at the stake with two others. Anne recalled the thunderous jeers when a raucous crowd passed with the three men, drawn on a sled, to Smithfield. On the same day, three priests who refused to acknowledge the king as Supreme Head of the Church were hung for treason.

Through it all, folks whispered that the king had gone mad.

Determined to coax Victoria into breaking her silence, Anne set the table with a white linen tablecloth she purchased on Cheapside and pulled a pan of freshly baked lemon cakes from the fireplace coals. She placed a basket of the lemon cakes and two cups of hot chamomile tea on the table and, in her most pleasant voice, called to Victoria in the adjacent sitting room.

"I poured some tea and put on some cakes. Would you like to join me?"

"It smells wonderful. I'll join you in just a moment," came the reply. Victoria finished a running stitch, knotted the black silk thread, and cut it with a small knife. She held up a girl's chemise at arm's length, admiring the contrast of her intricate black zigzag embroidery pattern against the ivory linen. The chair squeaked as she stood to make her way to the table. "What do you think?" she asked, emerging into the dining area with the garment.

Fingering Victoria's blackwork along the sleeve's edge, Anne gushed, "If I were Alice, I would feel like the prettiest girl in all of London." A satisfied smile brightened Victoria's usually somber expression. She'd grown close to Master McMillan's seven-year-old daughter, Alice, caring for the girl while Mistress McMillan battled scarlet fever.

Anne invited her aunt to sit across from her. Victoria laid the chemise over a wooden chair back, and took a seat.

After a long sip of tea, Victoria inquired, "What are you up to?"

"What do you mean?" Anne replied, blowing on a hot cake.

"You've been with me almost a year and a half. This is the first time you've invited me to sit for tea and cakes. You're up to something."

Anne bit into the cake, taking her time to chew and swallow while calculating a reply. "I wish you would tell me more about you, Master McMillan, my father, and why you're so afraid of…"

Victoria cut her short. "I understand. You want answers. You're seventeen. I was seventeen once—twenty years ago, but it seems like yesterday."

"Where were you at my age?" Anne took another bite of cake, pleased that Victoria seemed ready to open up.

"At Delapré Abbey in Northampton, preparing to take my vows."

"At my age, you were a nun?" Victoria nodded. "What brought you to London?" Anne pressed.

"I'll give you the simple answer. A few years ago, Lord Cromwell hired preachers to cross the realm and spew hatred from pulpits and village squares against those of us who chose to follow vocations as monks or nuns. At the same time, commissioners undertook to visit religious houses, pretending to look for corruption. We knew better; they were taking inventory of our precious things to prepare for the king's seizure of church properties. Cromwell's agents accused us of vile activities, things I won't even utter out loud, and painted us as a burden to the common folk—said we were living off their hard work. Folks were told that once the king seized the wealth of the monasteries, they would no longer have to pay taxes to the Crown. Lies." She paused to take a sip of tea and a bite of cake.

Anne realized she'd been holding her breath and inhaled deeply, anxious for Victoria to continue.

"When King Henry dissolved the monasteries three years ago, Sister Stock, the abbess at Delapré, surrendered the abbey. She had no choice. Those who resisted were sometimes—" Victoria's complexion grew ashen as her voice trailed off. "I had friends who were put to death." She toyed with a bright flowered serviette next to her plate, somber. "Houses that refused to surrender risked being razed to the ground. Sister Stock wouldn't abide such a fate for the abbey, to have four hundred years of devotion to God erased that way." Victoria's eyes moistened.

"How did you end up here, with Master McMillan?"

125

"He and your father grew up together in Tonbridge. Matthew made arrangements for me to come here. Your father's not a bad man, by the way. The loss of your mother changed him. Life's sorrows can harden even the gentlest of souls. Perhaps someday, he'll move past the grief. I'm sorry if you shouldered the brunt of his anger at life's harshness."

Anne stared into her teacup, digesting the information. Until that moment, she hadn't much considered life from another's perspective. "Thank you for telling me," she whispered. She hesitated. "I do have another question—about Master McMillan's secrecy, and why you won't speak of him."

Victoria's jaw stiffened.

"Victoria?" Anne persisted.

She met Anne's gaze. "I don't intend to be rude, but I won't speak of the king's reforms, or of those who work for or against them. That is something you'll have to find out for yourself—if you dare."

Anne hoped Victoria didn't notice her disappointed sigh.

November, 1541

—

William dabbed at the corners of his eyes with a kerchief, his chin quivering. Three years had passed since Father Garrett announced the placement of an English Bible in the parish. It had seemed the day would never arrive.

"'Tis beautiful," he sniffed. Caressing the cover, he allowed his fingertips to linger over the words "Holy Bible." As if he were handling a butterfly, he opened to the title page, greeted by an image of King Henry extending the Bible to bishops and clergy on his right hand, and to Cromwell and members of the laity on his left.

William turned the pages until he came to the preface, written by Thomas Cranmer, Archbishop of Canterbury. "Godly men and women have given their lives for this book," his voice cracked. "I never thought I would see the English Bible in the parish, out in the open for all to read. With the king's blessing, to boot."

Elizabeth kept her head low. Most folks were too busy chatting with those around them to notice her husband's embarrassing display, except for a wide-eyed young boy just behind them who had never seen a grown man cry. "I wish Thomas Hitton were here to witness this," William lamented. "But surely he's smiling from heaven." With his head bowed, William whispered, "'Twas not in vain, Thomas. Your sacrifice was not in vain."

"Papa, stop weeping. Folks will see you!" Christopher whispered loudly so anyone in earshot would know he disapproved of his father's blubbering.

"Christopher!" Elizabeth pinched her son's elbow. "Leave him be to have this moment."

The Great Bible, measuring sixteen and a half by eleven inches, lay chained to a podium where all could flip through its pages. A line of folks waiting their turn snaked all the way outside the front door of Holy Trinity, past the Crown & Anchor.

Sunshine poured through Holy Trinity's stained glass windows, projecting multicolored specks of light across the Bible's pages. The significance tugged at William's heart. "No more will common folk have to rely on windows to be their scripture. Today light is shining through those very windows, illuminating the word of God in our own tongue. Think of it, Elizabeth!" His eyes glistened. "God heard his people's prayers. No more hiding to read the Bible. No more arrests. No more burnings." Elizabeth nodded halfheartedly.

"Do you think chaining it down was necessary?" Christopher ran his fingers along the chain that secured the Bible to the podium. "Who would want to carry that beast out, anyway?"

"Beast?" William's eyes narrowed. Christopher rolled his eyes, careful not to cross the line and incur his father's wrath. "But not five years ago, King Henry burned Master Tyndale for translating the word of God into English. Now he orders it to be placed in the parish churches. I'm only making a point. I wouldn't dare get overly excited. His Majesty could wake up in bad humor one day and yank it from all the parishes."

"You must watch the way you speak of His Majesty," Elizabeth shushed.

"I know, I know. Don't speak of this. Don't say that. I'm going outside." Christopher turned to make his way past the line and out the front door, which had been propped open to accommodate the crowd.

"Something's gotten into that boy," Elizabeth lamented. Preoccupied with reading the Archbishop's preface to the Bible, William failed to notice the exchange between Christopher and his mother.

"What does it say?" Elizabeth prodded.

"It speaks of two sorts of people—those who refuse to read the words, and those who treat them carelessly." He continued to read, using his finger to guide his eyes along each line. Suddenly, he stopped.

"What does it say? Don't stop."

Dabbing his nose with his kerchief, William continued. "Here in the preface, Cranmer writes,

'I would marvel that any man should be so mad, as to refuse in darkness, light; in hunger, food; in cold, fire. For the word of God is light: *Thy word is a lantern unto my feet*. It is food: *Man shall not live by bread only, but by every word of God*. It is fire: *I am come to send fire on the earth, and what is my desire but that it be kindled?*'"

William blinked up at the church windows. "Light. Food. Fire. At last, the king has provided his subjects with God's word. I shall never forget this day, as long as I live." He intertwined his fingers with Elizabeth's. "I'll tell it to my son, and my grandchildren, and my great grandchildren, if I live that long."

"Let's hope it lasts." Elizabeth felt an inexplicable melancholy. "Christopher has a point. The king may change his mind again."

"Perhaps. But something significant is happening. I feel it in my marrow. God is doing a mighty work. The king will never be able to take away the light of God's word once it has illuminated the minds of the people." He closed the Bible reverently.

Edward Bartholomew stood next in line with his family. William extended his hand, beaming.

"'Tis a fine day in England, my good friend," Edward smiled, opening his arms in an embrace. Elizabeth noted a light in Edward's countenance. Even his red hair looked aglow. *Like the burning bush*, she mused.

"A very fine day," William agreed. "Will I see you at Bible study Sunday afternoon—here at Saint Mary's Chapel, four o'clock?"

Edward nodded. "Wouldn't miss it."

As William and Elizabeth made their way out, a familiar voice stopped them.

"Mister Wade, did I hear you say something about Bible study?" It was fifteen-year-old Willie Malden. An intense lad who spoke only when he had something thoughtful to say, he appeared positively giddy, like a puppy about to be taken for a walk.

"Yes, it's official. We'll start Bible readings here on Sunday at four in the afternoon. You're welcome to join us."

Running his fingers through his wavy blonde hair, the boy flashed a grin. "I'll be there."

"I'll be there as well." Thomas Jeffrey, an apprentice to Willie's father, stood next to Willie in line.

"I look forward to seeing you lads there." William shook their hands, noting the absence of Willie's parents.

"I've been studying my English primer every Sunday to learn to read," Willie beamed. "I want to be able to read the Bible for myself."

"Keep it up." William Wade patted the lad's arm. Malden's dark blue eyes danced at the encouragement.

Humming, William emerged from the church into the brisk November afternoon air with Elizabeth's hand in his. "The enthusiasm of those lads does my heart good," he said.

Elizabeth sighed. "But don't you wish our son was among them?"

Swallowing his disappointment, he replied, "The lad will come to his senses."

They walked home in silence, each lost in thought about the momentous events taking place.

If only Christopher understood, William mused.

Bordeaux

"Look for some truffles, would you? We can afford them, and roasted duck with truffles will impress this evening's dinner guests. If all goes well tonight, I'll have a new client for my carvings. You want me to pick you up at the clock tower after I meet with Monsieur Rosier, correct?"

Thomas slipped off Bijou's back and offered his clasped fingers as a stirrup for Charlotte to dismount. The dappled grey palfrey was a wedding gift from Charlotte's parents.

"It depends." Charlotte dismounted the horse with a grunt and brushed Bijou's coarse hair from her green wool skirt. Tightening her cloak around her shoulders, she asked, "How long will you be with Jacques?"

"Two hours, at most. Does that give you time to finish your errands and make it to the tower?" He untied her shopping basket from the panier and handed it to her.

Charlotte eyed the clock tower, calculating the time needed to make her circuit. She nodded. Thomas kissed her and mounted Bijou. "See you in a couple hours," he shouted, blowing her a kiss as he rode away. Her heart fluttered.

Slipping her hood over her head to block out a frigid wind, she turned toward the village square, mentally checking her list: white beans, sausage, bread, truffles, and a book that she learned had recently been translated from Latin into French: Calvin's *Institutes of the Christian Religion*. What little she knew of the French reformer, whom some compared to Luther, came from Thomas' friends in the souvenir business. They called Calvin a coward for fleeing France five years earlier, after King Francis issued an edict allowing reformers six months to reconcile with the Holy Mother Church.

Following her nose to the nearest bakery, she purchased a loaf of coarse wheat bread before moving on for beans and sausage. As she pulled coins from her purse to pay for two garlic salamis, she heard the cry, "Truffles! Fresh Sarlat truffles! Best of the season." Turning, she saw a man with salt-and-pepper hair and friendly brown eyes standing next to a basket. She arranged her purchases in the basket on her arm and hurried toward him.

"Bonjour, Monsieur," she nodded.

"Madame." He rubbed his nose, pink from the cold. "What may I do for you?"

"Two truffles, if you please."

"My pleasure." He weighed two black truffles on a scale and, with one in each hand, offered them to her. She laid them in her basket and reached into her coin purse when, on a table behind him, what appeared to be a stack of books tightly wrapped in linen caught her eye. "Something else for you, Madame?" he inquired.

She shook her head and thanked him. He moved on to his next customer.

Charlotte scanned the busy market and spotted a bearded man across the square with a large, open leather sack beside him on the cobblestone. He stood on a wood crate, waving in the air what appeared to be a book. She hurried across the square, only to discover the object in his hand was an elaborate wood box.

Disappointed, she turned and watched the truffle merchant. An inexplicable urge compelled her to speak with him. She pushed her way back through the busy crowd.

"Madame," he greeted her with smile and a tip of his cap. "More truffles?"

She pointed at the linen bundle. "I don't mean to be nosy, but might those be books?"

He nodded.

"Do you happen to know of a bookseller in Bordeaux?"

"May I ask what sort of books you're seeking?" She hesitated. Sensing her reticence, he repeated, "I know several booksellers, but it would help to know what sort of books you're looking for."

They held one another's gaze for several seconds. His eyes were clear, trustworthy. Sensing that she had nothing to fear, she leaned close and whispered, "I don't wish to betray the king's edicts, but I would like to learn more of Calvin. To refute the heretics, of course."

With a thoughtful nod, he uttered the words she longed to hear. "I may be able to help you."

February, 1542

—

Christopher drew back his arm, aiming for Nicholas' shutter, when a rustle in the bushes next to him nearly sent him jumping out of his skin. He dropped the snowball and ran. Nicholas emerged from the bush, calling his name.

His heart still racing, Christopher stopped and turned. "Zounds! Nicholas! What are you doing in the bush?"

"The constable passed by, going toward town, just as I was coming out to meet you. It's past curfew. I didn't want to rouse his suspicions, so I hid." Nicholas dusted snow from his cloak.

"He wouldn't suspect you. 'Tis me he keeps his eye on."

"What did you do to bring such a curse upon yourself? Did you walk under a ladder? Cross paths with a black cat?"

"I was born to William Wade, Lollard." Christopher kicked at the snow with his toe.

"You had no choice in the matter. Why should anyone be after you?"

"Like father, like son. That's what they think, I suppose." Christopher packed a handful of wet snow into a ball and drew his arm back.

"Oh no you don't!" Nicholas took a couple steps backward and lobbed a snowball at Christopher's chest.

"I'll show you how to throw a snowball." Christopher scooped up a handful of snow and pointed to a nearby walnut tree. "See those folks right there?" Nicholas looked at the tree, wondering if Christopher had gone mad. He saw nothing but a trunk and bare branches. "Right there, Simon Nix and Matthew Cooper." Christopher squared his legs, drew back his arm, and let the snowball fly. It hit the tree and spattered in all directions. "Take that, sons of the devil," he said, dusting the snow off his hands.

"They have their teeth in your heel, eh?"

"I can't shake them off."

"At least Anne fancied you."

"Why do you say that?"

"At church, at the market, anywhere you were near, her eyes followed your every move."

"Lucky me." Christopher hurled another snowball at the tree. "What difference does it make? She's gone. Her fire-breathing father had to guard his lair."

"You mustn't give up," Nicholas encouraged. "A prince never stops fighting for his lady."

"Pauper's more like it. Besides, I'm quite sure no prince ever had a Lollard father."

Nicholas patted a scoop of snow back and forth in his hands with a mischievous glint in his eye. "Let's throw snowballs at folks," he said.

"'Tis past curfew. Are you mad? Besides, no one will be out."

"No one need know it's us. And someone is always out. Let's race!" Nicholas bolted forward, waving his arm for Christopher to join him.

"Where are you going?" Christopher called.

"To the edge of the hill, to see if anyone is walking on the pathway below."

Christopher hurried to catch up. They sprinted as fast as the slick ground would allow to the edge of East Hill. Skidding to a stop, Nicholas slipped and landed on his back. Christopher came up a couple seconds behind, huffing and puffing breaths of steam in the cold night air. They peered through heavily falling snow to the street below.

"I can't see anything," Christopher lamented. "'Tis a waste of time."

"Let's stay at least a few minutes. What will your parents do if they discover you coming in after curfew?"

"Send me to the dunking stool? Put me in the stocks? I don't know. I've never broken curfew before. Besides, I've already been branded a Lollard. I might as well have an L on my forehead. And you?"

"They trust me."

"Lucky you."

"Shh! Look!" Christopher peered down the steep hill. Two flickering lights snaked slowly past the church along St. Edmunds' Way.

"They're coming in this direction."

"The constable, perhaps? Let's sneak closer. We might get a good shot!"

Christopher balked. "I've enough troubles already. Do I want to add 'disturber of the peace' to my list of crimes?"

"Don't be a coward." Nicholas slid down the hill on his buttocks. Christopher followed reluctantly, bristling at the insult. They crouched behind a cluster of juniper bushes at the bottom.

"I hear them," Nicholas whispered.

Christopher cocked his ear. "I'm soaked," he whispered, his teeth chattering. "The breeze doesn't help."

"Shh, they're coming."

They held their breath. The passersby stopped a few feet away.

"Did you hear something?" The male voice sounded familiar.

"No. What did it sound like?" The woman's voice—Christopher was sure he'd heard it somewhere, but he couldn't place it.

"I thought I heard a voice," the man's tenor voice quivered. "It must have been my imagination."

"Perhaps it's my heart, Laine. 'Tis beating so hard in my chest, I fancy it must be loud enough for others to hear." The woman spoke just above a whisper.

Taking his companion by the hands the man gushed, "Oh, wretched beast that I am. To feel such desire I want to inhale you." He pulled her to his chest, nibbled her cheek and worked his way to her lips. "Teresa—oh, what shall I do?" He stopped for a moment. "I'm a man of God. But I can't help myself. Am I so wrong to want to drink in your beauty? 'Tis God who made you beautiful."

"You're a man, after all," she cooed.

With a gasp, Christopher threw his elbow into Nicholas' side. Nicholas lost his balance and grabbed the bush in front of him.

"Who's there?" Father Garrett stiffened and let Teresa Willoughby slip from his embrace.

"Who is it, Laine?" the widow whispered.

Nicholas lifted his hand to throw the snowball. Christopher slapped it down.

"Are you lunatic?" he growled. The snowball fell to the ground with a soft crunch.

Scanning the hillside, Father Garrett demanded, "Show yourself!"

Christopher rose to one knee. Nicholas gripped the back of his cloak.

"I know you're there. Make yourself known." Father Garrett's eyes darted frantically back and forth, up and down the hill.

Christopher worked his way to a standing position, his legs wobbling like a newborn foal's.

Frowning, Father Garrett lifted his lantern high. "The Wade lad. I should have known." He surveyed the area around Christopher. "I don't suppose you're alone?"

Nicholas stood.

Garrett nodded. "Nicholas Hall. What are you lads doing out after curfew?"

"We were looking for Dart," Nicholas lied.

"A dog can fend well enough for himself." Father Garrett slicked back his disheveled hair with his free hand. "But two lads out past curfew—you risk being branded as rascals, you know." Christopher almost choked on the irony of Father Garrett's comment. The priest took a step back. "This is not as it might appear. A widow needs comfort. Widow Willoughby has suffered frightfully since her husband passed away. I reckon you lads are too young to understand."

Christopher and Nicholas stared at him, mute.

"None of us need tarry any longer," Garrett continued. "The snow is picking up, and you lads are soaked. Take my lamp and run along home. Tell your folks, or anyone who might inquire, that you were assisting me, and time got away from us. No one need know a thing. Yes?"

Their faces pale, the boys nodded in unison.

"Run along, then." Father Garrett's voice quivered. "All is well."

℘

Father Garrett stood at his lectern, dabbing at beads of perspiration with a kerchief. Violet crescent moons cradled his hollow eyes. Looking over his parishioners' heads he began, "We shall recite the tenth commandment. 'Thou shalt not covet thy neighbor's house, thou shalt not covet thy neighbor's wife, nor his manservant, nor his maidservant, nor his ox, nor his ass, nor any thing that is thy neighbor's.'" He waited for the congregation to repeat the words before continuing, "The bishop advised me that you must have all Ten Commandments memorized in order to partake of the host when Eastertide arrives. Of course, you must recite the Creed and the Pater Noster as well. Please see me if you have concerns."

Christopher glanced sideways at Teresa Willoughby. She was staring at the floor. Garrett's probing gaze locked on Christopher. Christopher looked away.

When the service was over, William felt a tap on his shoulder. He turned to see Simon Nix, arms folded, wearing a scowl. "Was that your son I saw up on the hill last night?" Simon demanded.

135

William nodded. "He was helping Father Garrett. Came home with the Father's own lamp, since it was past curfew."

"That's not what it looked like to me." Nix scratched at the floor with his toe, reminding William of a chicken. "He was with the Hall lad, probably out doing some sort of knavery. Tell me, what does a lad need to be out doing after curfew? I've a mind to tell the constable."

"Go right ahead, Simon. Father Garrett will vouch for the lads. And pray tell, what were *you* doing out after curfew?"

Simon looked down at his feet and chicken-scratched the floor again. "That is none of your affair, Wade." He glared into William's eyes. "I have my reasons."

"I would commend the Master's teaching to behold the mote in your own eye before trying to cast the beam out of another's."

"Motes and beams, is it?" Simon mocked. "Making up your own Bible stories now, are you? That Lollard learning will be your downfall yet. Mark my words: the tide is in your favor now, but 'twill not end well for you."

"My end is in hands greater than yours or anyone else's."

"Whose hands might you be speaking of? Methinks your heretical learnings are making you mad."

"Think what you wish." William wrestled with a number of clever retorts, but bit his tongue. "A group of us will be having Bible study this evening at the back of the nave. Won't you join us?"

Simon twisted his face in contempt and stormed away.

April, 1542

―

Dartford

Morning sunlight cast a bright glare on the table at the Bull's Head pub, where Kenneth Malden sat over breakfast porridge with Father Garrett. Movement on High Street caught Malden's eye. He pushed back a green damask curtain and watched William Wade enter Bartholomew's bakery across the street. Malden's expression soured.

"Those filthy whoresons have their claws in my son," he growled. "They meet in Saint Mary's Chapel to discuss scripture in the vulgar tongue. What will His Majesty allow next? Pigs in the nave?"

Father Garrett fiddled with a bread crumb left on the table by a previous patron, then crushed it with his thumb and flicked it.

"Haven't you something to say, Father?" If there was one thing Kenneth couldn't tolerate, it was awkward silence.

Staring blankly at his mug, the priest responded, "God's ways are mysterious and impossible to understand. I can't pretend to speak for the pope or king, much less God." He reached for his mug and took a hearty sip of cider.

"Pardon me, Father, but surely you have an opinion. Rare is the man who hasn't taken a side."

"Every day I pray for the wisdom of Solomon," Father Garrett answered. "Opinions are dangerous things. They can get a man killed."

"But you're our shepherd. If your parishioners can't come to you for answers, to whom can we go?"

"Do as the reformers do. Turn to Luther and Tyndale." Garrett rolled his eyes.

"They're polluting the Bible, throwing pearls to the swine. The entire kingdom is a giant tavern, brawling on the right hand and on the left over God's word. Does His Majesty have any idea of the tempest he unleashed?"

137

"Of course he does, but 'tis too late. The dam has already burst. He continues to change his directives, today this, tomorrow that. We Englishmen are dogs on the leash of an insufferable master, dragged one way and then another."

Kenneth scowled at his mug. "Perhaps the king is too busy trying to produce an heir. The demons of hell are unleashed upon us, while the king goes about his merry mission of propagation."

"A merry mission it is." Father Garrett lifted his mug and drew a long, slow sip. He set the mug down and tapped his fingers on the table. "Let us wish him success."

With raised eyebrows, Kenneth studied Garrett's unusually flippant demeanor. "Is that the best you can do, Father? The church is under attack, and all you can do is wish the king merry propagation?"

"What do you wish me to say, Kenneth? That the king is wrong, or that the reformers are wrong? Perhaps we are all wrong together, or all right together. 'Tis my duty to care for the flock—to visit the sick, the fatherless, the widows. I'll carry out those tasks regardless of which direction the wind is blowing."

"But Father, the sacraments, the feasts, the liturgies—they change in the very hour. Does it matter whether Thomas Becket was a saint or a villain? Are holy things to be bantered about in taverns by vulgar men? By my troth, these things matter. They're the very essence of our faith."

"Answer me this, Kenneth. Does the sun come up every morning?"

"Yes."

"Does it set again in the eve?"

"Yes. But what is your point?"

"Regardless of my opinion, the sun will rise and set every day. The king will do as he wishes. 'Tis beyond my reach, so I'll go my way and leave it for others to resolve."

"But surely God isn't pleased with an entire kingdom contending over his church."

"This discussion is going in circles. We simply won't solve this problem, you and I, across the table. Be merry, enjoy your ale, and keep your views to yourself. And I shall keep mine as well. That is my advice to you."

The priest's words were not intended as a reprimand, but Kenneth took them that way. In spite, he blurted, "Father, are you aware that some in the village are gossiping about you?"

Garrett sat up straight, his face reddening. "Gossiping about me? What do you mean?"

"It concerns Widow Willoughby. 'Tis rumored you've been seen with her. Why would anyone speak such dribble? Do you have enemies in the ranks of the townsfolk?"

His heart racing, the priest forced a calm response. "Who are the culprits?"

"I'm not at liberty to divulge them. But if I were you, I would certainly not give them any fodder."

"There will always be folks who find fodder where there is none." Father Garrett tapped his fingers on the table and changed the subject. "Do you have anywhere to be this morning?"

Grateful for an escape, Malden picked up his cap from the table. "As a matter of fact, I do. My wife asked me to fix the butter churn." He stood and made his way to the door. With a farewell nod, he exited.

Father Garrett stared out the window, wondering if Christopher Wade and Nicholas Hall had betrayed him.

London

Is His Majesty mad? Anne contemplated the question as she strolled hand in hand with Alice along Cheapside toward Poultry Lane. Anne needed to drop Alice off with Master McMillan at the Grocer's Hall, and purchase cloves and mace for Mistress McMillan.

At the cheerful *chirr-up, chirr-up* of a redbreast, Alice gazed skyward to watch the bird preen on a branch atop a beech tree up ahead.

"Do you know the legend of robin redbreast?" Anne asked.

"No. What is it?" Alice opened her inquisitive blue eyes wide. Cascading blonde curls framed her cherubic face.

"When our Lord was dying on the cross, a solid brown robin came to his side and sang in his ear to him to comfort him. Blood from Christ's wounds dripped onto the bird's breast. From then on, all robins had a red breast."

"Our Lord must love them, then," Alice replied, watching the bird flit from branch to branch.

"I'm quite sure he does. We must move along." Anne tugged the girl's hand. "Your father is waiting." Alice skipped ahead of Anne all the way to the Grocer's Hall.

On her way home, Anne stopped to purchase cloves and mace from Mistress McMillan's favorite spice vendor on Cheapside. She stopped several times on her way home to breathe deeply of their perfume.

Yes, His Majesty is mad. The definitive answer popped into her mind just as she turned the corner onto Honey Lane. He'd recently had his fifth wife, Catherine Howard, executed at the Tower for alleged infidelity. Executions. Ransacked churches. Tempestuous marriages. *King Henry is a dragon, wreaking destruction on the hapless victims of his kingdom and stealing their riches for his lair.* She understood why Victoria guarded her opinions.

Anne passed a linen cart, when it struck her: weeks had passed since she last thought of Christopher.

July, 1542

—

John Whitfield grasped the iron handle of Holy Trinity's heavy oak door and tugged, when a wave of self-doubt swept over him. He eased the portal to a close, rested his forehead against it, and wondered if they would accept him. Why would anyone in Dartford want his company after the arrogant way he behaved before going off to Cambridge two years earlier?

There was no way around it. If he wanted to join them, he would have to face them sooner or later. Summoning his courage, he took a deep breath and slipped inside the door. Upon hearing a male voice in Saint Mary's Chapel, he took a few steps forward and stopped behind a stone pillar in the nave to listen.

"'If ye were of the world, the world would love his own. Howbeit because ye are not of the world but I have chosen you out of the world, therefore hateth you the world.' This comes from the gospel of John, fifteenth chapter."

"Mister Wade, what does that mean?" Willie Malden asked.

John tiptoed a few steps closer and rested behind another stone pillar, wondering whether he dared to join them, when the screech of the front door gave him a start.

A lightning bolt in the form of Kenneth Malden stormed inside, pointed his finger at John and barked, "Are you with the scoundrels who study the Bible?" The Bible study group fell silent. "Heretics!" Kenneth shouted. "Those whoresons have their claws in Willie. I'm putting an end to it."

John stepped forward and rested a hand on Malden's shoulder. "Mister—Malden is it?" Malden scowled. "I don't wish to speak out of place, but surely you've better things to do than get upset with a few folks reading God's word."

Kenneth thrust John aside and lurched in the direction of the voices. When he reached the group—some standing, some on stools, and others sitting on the cold floor—Malden crossed his arms, glowering at William Wade.

141

Undeterred, William continued, "Many hated the Son of God, because his teachings put them ill at ease."

"But why?" With a fearful glance at his father, Willie fidgeted on his stool. "He taught them to love one another. He was kind to folks, and did only good to them."

"There's another side to it, Willie. He also chided folks who only pretended to goodness to impress others. He taught us to be pure in our hearts. 'Tis not an easy message to accept. Folks whose hearts are cankered with pride aren't happy to be told they need to change." He glanced at Kenneth Malden.

Malden strode to Willie's side, placed his forefinger and thumb over his son's collarbone and squeezed, his teeth clenched. Willie writhed while the color drained from his face.

"What are you doing here, boy?" Kenneth demanded. Willie closed his eyes.

William rose from his stool and with slow, deliberate steps approached Kenneth Malden. Stopping within arm's reach of the angry father, William stated matter-of-factly, "Get your hands off him."

Kenneth snarled, "How dare you turn a lad against his upbringing. If I had my way, you'd be chased clean out of town." He released his grip from Willie and turned to Jeffrey. "Does your father know you're coming to these meetings?" Jeffrey shook his head. "As I thought. I can't be housing heretics."

Willie rose from his stool, straightened his tunic, and faced his father. "We're not heretics." Working to control the quiver in his voice he continued, "The king's injunctions encouraged us to learn the Bible. And Mister Wade isn't forcing me to be here. I came of my own accord. We're doing nothing wrong."

Kenneth Malden cast a threatening glare at William Wade and shouted, "A pox on all of you." He stormed out.

Through pursed lips, William blew out a heavy sigh. "I'm sorry, lads. What will he do to you when you get home?"

"He'll most likely take a switch to me," Willie replied. "But I'm not afraid of him."

"Then I wager you're experiencing just what Christ said. Let me find it." William licked his thumb and flipped to the book of Matthew. "Here it is: 'Blessed are ye when men revile you, and persecute you, and shall falsely say all manner of evil sayings against you for my sake. Rejoice and be glad for great is your reward in heaven.'"

"Rejoice in being persecuted? How is that possible?" Willie massaged the sore spot on his shoulder.

John stepped forward from behind the pillar, rousing a collective gasp from the group. "If I might interject?" he said.

After a few seconds' hesitation, William extended his hand. "John Whitfield? When did you get back in town?"

"Last night. My father said you've been holding Bible study here."

"Pray, share your thoughts with us." William invited John to be seated on his stool.

John opted to stand, while he studied the eager expressions of folks gathered in the chapel. "It hasn't been my lot to suffer for Jesus' sake, but at Cambridge, I brushed shoulders with some who have. My thought is this: that through proving—through persecutions—we discover what we are made of, as fire refines the gold and separates the dross. Do we wish to remain as dross, or will we endure hardship, as good soldiers? To share in the sufferings of Christ is an honor. Think: should Christ suffer persecution on this earth, and we escape? Would we consider ourselves worthy to be with him, were we not also tested in the fire of affliction? And yet, in our hour of greatest affliction God draws us nearest to his bosom. In all these things we may rejoice, for we become conquerors, as the Apostle Paul wrote." A reverent silence distilled upon the group.

William broke the silence first. "Cambridge has served you well, lad. I, for one, am glad you were here this evening." Several nodded in agreement. William concluded, "Let's give some thought to the verses we discussed tonight. When we meet next Sunday, we'll take up where we left off."

October, 1542

—

"Charlotte! By God's teeth, what is this?"

She bolted upright in bed to see Thomas hovering over her, his face crimson. He shook Calvin's *Institutes* in his right hand as if he were wringing a chicken's neck. Beads of perspiration formed around her hairline. She cowered in silence.

"Yes, you should be afraid," he ranted, his eyes wild. "How long have you been deceiving me?" With clenched teeth, he shook the book in her face. "Inviting the demons of hell into our midst. How dare you! I've a mind to—" He drew back the hand holding the book and aimed it at her cheek.

"Thomas, no!" she cried. "I only wanted to…"

The force of the book against her face knocked her back against the silk bedsheets. Her head spinning, she buried her face in her pillow to muffle her sobs.

"If I ever catch you with such trash again, so help me—" He stormed out of the chamber in his nightshirt, mumbling expletives. She heard the fireplace grate screech across the stone hearth, and a *poof* when the book burst into flames. Three-month-old Gabrielle let out a high-pitched wail from her bassinet in a small room adjacent to the chamber. Charlotte hurried to pick her up.

Thomas stormed back into the chamber. "Where are you? Are you hiding?"

With a knot in her stomach, Charlotte emerged cradling Gabrielle against her chest. "Chut," she whispered. "You upset her."

"How long has that book been in this house?" he demanded.

"Not long," she sniffed, wiping her eyes on her chemise sleeve. "I only wanted to read the writings so I would know how to refute them. I wanted to impress you with my learning. You're always discussing these things with your friends." She swayed back and forth to lull Gabrielle back to sleep. A glance at the window told her the sun had not yet risen.

144

"My wife, studying Calvin under my nose." He plopped on the bed, massaging his temples. "Do you realize what would happen to my business if folks were to find out?"

"I didn't think of it that way," she said, sincere. She glanced down at Gabrielle. The infant's eyes were closed.

"Folks who buy my wares are devoted to the Mother Church. Don't forget that." Thomas looked up at the ceiling as if pleading for help.

"But Thomas, listen. Calvin raised a question I haven't been able to get off my mind. Does it take faith to understand nothing, and simply let the Church determine our convictions? Is it so wrong to seek understanding? Calvin studied the Bible. I wish I could do so."

Wringing his hands through his hair, Thomas groaned. He stood and paced back and forth across the oriental carpet in their chamber when, in a sudden fit of rage, he spun around and shook his finger at her.

"My work has provided you with this beautiful cottage on the outskirts of Bordeaux, with fine furnishings and a few acres to roam, to garden, to ride our horses. You wear fine dresses and have your own housemaid. I can give you practically anything you want. Many women would love to be in your shoes. Why would you risk it all to chase after doctrines of devils?"

She stared at him, tight-lipped.

With daggers in his eyes, he decreed, "I forbid you to read from Calvin, from the Bible, or any other heretical writings. Do you understand?"

She held his menacing gaze for several seconds, silent, until he slipped between the bedsheets and turned on his side with an exaggerated sigh. Choking back a sob, she tiptoed to the bassinet and tucked in Gabrielle, her body trembling.

Dartford

"Ho, Christopher." Christopher stopped in his tracks and turned, miffed to see Willie Malden almost standing in his shadow.

"I'm already late. What is it?" he barked.

"Are you coming to Bible study tonight?" Willie acted as if the question were as natural as asking whether Christopher planned to eat supper that eve.

"Do I ever come to Bible study? I've got more important things to do." Christopher hurried up Spyttal Street, bound for the king's manor house construction site where Nicholas laid brick with his father.

"More important?" Willie followed at Christopher's heels like a pet dog. "But your father leads the discussions. You're lucky. I wish my father was like yours."

"Fortunate, indeed." Christopher turned and put his hands on his hips. "Leave me be, Willie. And thank you for taking my place at Bible study. You can play the son my father wishes he had."

"I don't understand." Willie's shoulders slumped.

"Just be on your way, and don't pester me again." Christopher pursued his course, hoping Nicholas would arrive on the scene to help him escape the pest.

Not to be deterred, Willie caught up alongside Christopher, jogging to keep pace. "I'm hoping your father will help me get my own Bible. I've been saving."

"You'll have to ask him that." Christopher kept his eyes on the street ahead. "He seems to be well-connected with all the heretics around here."

"Heretics? Your father is no heretic. I would give anything for my father to be like yours. Look at this." With a groan, Christopher stopped. Willie pulled up his sleeve to reveal a green and purple bruise, four inches across. "My father threw me across the room because I went to Bible study. Your father would never do that."

"And I would never want to buy a Bible or go to a Bible study meeting."

"Doesn't your father care? Doesn't he want you to come?"

Christopher bristled. "Listen, Willie. 'Tis none of your affair what my father thinks. If you want to talk to my father about a Bible, you'll need to find him yourself." Spying Nicholas in the distance, Christopher waved. Nicholas waved back.

Willie persisted. "Anyway, he already said he would get me a Bible. Do you know where he is now?" Christopher ignored the question and continued forward until Willie grabbed the back of his tunic. "Christopher, wait. I have to speak to your father without mine around." Christopher flicked Willie away as if he were a fly. One last time, the lad demanded, "Christopher! Please, listen."

Before he had time to react, Willie discovered himself sprawled on the ground with Christopher on top of him. Clenching a fistful of Willie's jerkin Christopher growled, "Listen to me. I want nothing to do with you or your Bible. Leave me alone and don't bother me again. Do you understand?" Willie gulped. Christopher slammed him into the ground and stormed off to meet Nicholas.

"You shouldn't be so mean!" Willie shouted after him.

Christopher dipped a spoonful of pork pottage from his bowl and slurped the broth. Three bite-sized pieces of pork remained on the spoon. He sucked one into his mouth and chewed, then chewed some more, tiring his jaw. Finally, he spit the wad of pork on his spoon and plopped the utensil in his bowl with a huff.

Uncharacteristically distant, Elizabeth didn't realize how loud she was smacking when she chewed. Lost in thought, William wheezed between slurps. Dart was snoring next to the fireplace. Annoyed, Christopher broke the noisy silence.

"Where did you get the pork? 'Tis tougher than Sheriff Wakefield's boots."

William's eyebrows slanted inward, almost touching in the middle. "'Tis better to say nothing than to speak such rubbish. Apologize to your mother."

Elizabeth rushed to her son's defense. "No, 'tis altogether true. 'Tis a shame Miss Piggle gave her life for a rank kettle of pottage." She glared at her husband. "You should have spared her. We could have gotten by. I told you I would sell more towels or thread. You didn't listen. You never listen." She turned her head to hide the tears pooling in her eyes, then stood up from the table and ran to the fireplace. With her back turned, she pulled a handkerchief from her bosom.

"You slaughtered Miss Piggle?" Christopher's comment proved to be the apple that tipped the cart.

"I'll have no more of this carrying on!" William slammed his fist on the table. Elizabeth choked out a sob.

Christopher crossed the room and patted Elizabeth's shoulder. "We'll manage, Mother. Please, stop crying." She buried her head in her hands. Christopher returned to the table and sat down with a plop.

William *tap-tap, tap-tapped* his fingers on the table for several seconds, when out of his mouth flew a one-word indictment: "Christopher."

Christopher swallowed. "Yes, Father."

"I have word that you harassed Willie Malden."

His throat tight, Christopher retorted, "Did the worm tattle? Are spies following me now?" He waited a few seconds before uncorking the poison he'd kept bottled inside. "Perhaps 'tis you they should be after."

William felt his chest tighten. He sucked in slowly and exhaled deliberately several times before continuing. "Is it true Willie asked you about getting a Bible, and you were outright rude to the lad?"

147

"He was bothering me, that's all." Christopher knew his terse answer would not suffice, but he could think of nothing else to say.

"Did you throw him to the ground?"

Christopher rolled his eyes and looked at Dart. "'Throw' would be an exaggeration."

"Don't roll your eyes at me, do you hear? Did he ask you where he could get a Bible?"

Off in the corner, Elizabeth broke into another sobbing fit. "Please, Elizabeth," William pleaded, massaging his neck with one hand. "I'm trying to have a conversation with Christopher. As for the other, we'll get through it."

"What will we get through?" Christopher searched William's eyes.

"Nothing. We're facing some hardships."

"Things must be desperate if you slaughtered Miss Piggle." Christopher pried a string of pork from between his teeth with a fingernail.

A tortured look came over William. "You'll learn soon enough. They're threatening to tear down our cottage and turn the land to sheep pasture."

"Who is? What do you mean, take our cottage?"

"The land owners. They're threatening to tear down the cottages in this area to fence the land off for sheep pasture. Wool is profitable."

"They can remove people from their dwellings that way?" From news of Miss Piggle to the prospect of being booted from their home, Christopher couldn't remember a worse day in all his eighteen years.

Elizabeth turned to face them, still dabbing at her nose. "Cornmeal prices are up, because corn farmers are being put under by the sheep grazers. The wool merchants will put Father clean out of business." She hesitated and glanced at William. "That, and your reputation as a Lollard."

Without uttering a word, William rose, pulled his cloak from a hook, slipped out quietly, and eased the door closed.

For what seemed to Christopher an eternity, Elizabeth sat with her back turned, sniffling and dabbing at her eyes. Finally, satisfied that William would be away for a safe spell, she returned to the table and cradled her head in her hands.

"What will become of us?" she moaned.

"What do you mean, Father's reputation as a Lollard could put us out of business?"

She looked up, her eyes red and swollen. "I shouldn't have spoken those words. Your father and I agreed to never argue about such matters in front of you."

"I won't say anything to him."

She poked the handkerchief at the inside corners of her eyes and explained, "The villagers talk. Amy Coppinger overheard some men at the tavern talking about a campaign to get buyers to stop comin' to the linen cart. Folks don't have dealings with heretics. 'Twould be the end of us. The end! We could lose what little we have and end up worse than old ha'penny Harry. Can you imagine beggin' for bread? I couldn't stand the shame of it!" She snorted.

Christopher strode to the fireplace and scratched Dart's head, struggling to digest her words.

"I shouldn't have opened my mouth; truly, I shouldn't have," she sniffled.

"No, I think you should have." Christopher contemplated his miserable lot— Anne in London, false accusations, his parents at odds, and William's reputation as a Lollard staining the family name. A wave of melancholy crashed over him.

February, 1543

—

"How much have you got, Willie?" Thomas Jeffrey sat on the edge of his bed in the attic chamber he and Willie shared, giddy with anticipation. He moved to the floor, taking care not to hit his head on a rough wood beam, and held a candle close to Willie. "Here, you'll see better to count."

Willie dumped an assortment of coins from his pouch onto the warped oak floor. "I haven't counted my earnings for a few days." He licked his fingers and started sorting. "Exactly how much do we need?"

"Four shillings," Thomas replied, scratching his thigh through his nightshirt.

Willie sorted his coins into two piles: groats and pence. "Two, four, six, eight, ten pence plus two groats. That makes a shilling and six pence." He slipped the coins back into his pouch.

Thomas retrieved a drawstring leather pouch from under his pillow and turned its contents onto his bed. "Four groats, and—let me see." He separated the pennies. "All together, I have one shilling and eight pence." He sighed. "We lack ten pence. One would think a shilling a day would add up faster, but I spend most of my earnings to help my family buy food. I think I could save five more pence by summer. How soon could you have your portion?"

Scratching his chin, Willie responded, "I should be able to have five by then, too. We're almost there! Just think, our own copy of Tyndale's Bible. Father will tan my hide if he finds out."

"We must make sure he never finds out, then."

"I'll count the Bible a treasure greater than all the gold in England." Willie squeezed his coin pouch as if it were a pet.

"Why does your father hate the Bible so?" Thomas asked.

"He fancies Bible-reading is tearing apart the whole of England, and that if it hadn't gotten into folks' hands, they wouldn't have it in their heads to stand up against the Romish church. Says the king is looting the whole realm because of that book."

"Do you suppose there's some truth to it?" Thomas watched candlelight flicker on the soot-stained attic walls. "King Henry did tear down Dartford Priory to build his manor house. I feel sorry for the nuns."

"My father calls the king's actions treasonous." Willie put his pouch into a rough wood box under his bed, and slid between the bed covers.

Slipping his pouch under his pillow, Thomas commented, "How can His Majesty be guilty of treason? The laws are for his subjects."

"When you're the king, you can do as you wish, I suppose." Willie watched a cobweb dance between beams in the candlelight. "Do you think it will always be this way?"

"What way?" Thomas yawned and eased between his cold bed sheets with a moan.

"We can freely read the Bible chained in the parish, but we fear reading it in our own cottages. Why should reading the word of God be allowed in one place and not in another?"

"Because His Majesty says so, I suppose," Thomas replied, his teeth chattering.

"But things are changing beyond anyone's wildest imaginations. The king broke with Rome. We're getting an English Bible."

"Yes, and we've come full circle to the question, how will we get it?" Thomas rolled onto his side.

"We'll ask Mister Wade next time we see him."

"Good idea."

At the sound of the front door latch rattling downstairs, Willie blew the candle out and pulled his covers to his chin. A few seconds later, Kenneth Malden appeared at the top of the ladder. He sniffed melted wax and smoke, saw two lads who appeared to be asleep, and descended the ladder.

July, 1543

"Perhaps you'd like to lead our next meeting? With your learning of Hebrew and Greek, I reckon you could shed light on a good many topics."

John Whitfield seized William's offer. "I'll plan on it."

Turning to Thomas and Willie, William asked, "Do you lads have a moment?"

In response to their eager nods, he ushered them into a corner of the chapel and whispered, "I wanted to wait until folks cleared out."

Thomas clasped his hands together. "Did you get it?"

William grinned. "It wasn't easy to come by, but you're now the owners of your very own English Bible." He pulled the book from his bag and caressed the cover, pleased to see the greed in Thomas' eyes.

The two lads reached for the book at the same time. Thomas got his hands on it first. He squeezed the Bible to his chest and offered it to Willie. Willie tucked it under his arm, scanning the empty church building.

"Guard it carefully," William admonished. "Many consider the Bible a greater threat to the realm than the armies of Spain or France."

"We will, Mister Wade." Willie thrust the book to Thomas.

William frowned. "Willie, you're not responding to your long-awaited treasure as I would have expected."

His eyes downcast, Willie tugged at his left sleeve. "'Tis nothing, Mister Wade."

"Are you hiding something? Pray, tell."

Willie shook his head.

"Show your arm, lad." Willie inched his sleeve up to expose a scarlet and lime-green bruise across his forearm. William's eyes widened. "I wouldn't call that nothing. How did you come by it?"

With pursed lips, Willie looked past William to the church's front door.

"'Tis as I figured." William wagged his head.

Like steam bursting from a boiling kettle, Willie's emotions exploded. "Father forbade me to come to Bible study. Said if he catches me again, I might not live to tell about it. He grabbed me by the arm and threw me against the wall."

"Is that so?" William's cheeks flushed. "The man is possessed of a demon," he muttered under his breath. "Very well, son. Perhaps you should heed your heathen–I mean to say, heed your father. For your own safety."

"No!" Willie squared his shoulders. "He won't keep me from the word of God. 'Tis not right!"

A side door to the nave creaked open. Thomas and Willie stiffened at the sound of footsteps thumping in their direction. Father Garrett peeked into the chapel.

"Did I hear shouting?" the priest inquired.

"We were just leaving." William ushered Willie and Thomas toward the front door.

With an icy glare at William, the priest asked, "Does Mister Malden know they're here?"

"I can't answer for Kenneth Malden."

At the sight of something in Thomas' arms, Garrett's pupils dilated. "What is that?" he probed. Thomas tightened his grip.

"As I said," William repeated, "we were just leaving."

When the door closed behind his three parishioners, Father Garrett gazed up at the crucifix on the wall. "Tell me Lord," he whispered. "What shall I do with the heretics?"

CB

Jacques Rosier watched with a sense of reverence as Thomas' hands carved life into a dead block of birch wood. "Your talent is remarkable," he said. "I was lucky to find you."

With a lackluster nod, Thomas lifted the woodblock to his lips and blew shavings in all directions. He had every tool he could wish for at his fingertips—knives, awls rifflers, files. He enjoyed an ideal place to work on the outskirts of Bordeaux, a convenient fifteen-minute horseback ride from his own cottage, through beautiful countryside dotted with vineyards. He couldn't complain. Actually, he *shouldn't* complain—but dissatisfaction consumed him.

153

Using more force than necessary, he poked an awl into the eye socket of the face he was carving. The tool slipped and cut a one-inch gash in his wrist. He dropped the block of wood and rushed the wound to his mouth.

Grabbing a clean rag, Jacques sprinted to Thomas' side. Thomas pressed the cloth against his wound. "I should have been more careful," he stated flatly.

"Is it serious?" Jacques asked.

Lifting the cloth to examine the damage, Thomas replied, "It's not deep. I'll be fine."

Jacques tied a piece of twine around the cloth to hold it in place, then leaned back against a table and folded his arms, studying Thomas' expression. "Is something bothering you today?" he asked.

Thomas stared at the floor for several seconds before offering a measured response. "Are you happy with my work these past two years?"

"Of course. My sales are the best they've been in fifteen years. Your stuff is in demand. Why do you ask?"

"Much of what you sell is trinkets—cheap pewter badges and such. My work is of a higher quality, I think."

"Of course it is. Your work is art. Those trinkets are junk." He pointed to a table full of scallop shells. "What are you getting at?"

They locked eyes. "I want a greater share of the profits."

Jacques glanced at a shelf where a row of Saint James statues stood side by side, painted and ready to go to market. Thomas strode to the shelf and picked up a statue, then moved to a table covered with pewter scallop shells. With a statue in his right hand and a scallop in his left, he demanded, "Which is making you more money?"

His expression sheepish, Jacques inquired, "What are you asking for?"

Without hesitation, Thomas replied, "My own stand near the cathedral and sixty percent of the profits of my carvings. I'm not asking for a percentage of your other merchandise. I only want to profit from my own work." He held his breath, fearing a negative reaction.

Jacques massaged the inside of his cheek with his tongue. Several tense seconds passed. "Sixty percent? That's twenty percent more than you make now."

Thomas nodded, his chest tight. "I have a growing family. I need sixty percent, or I'll have to break out on my own."

"Become my competitor?" Jacques' face turned red. "You caught me off guard. Can you give me a day or two to think about it?"

154

Taking a deep breath, Thomas shook his head. "I need to know by the day's end."

Frowning, Jacques turned his back and began straightening tools on the wall, feeling Thomas' penetrating gaze on his back. Thomas sat on a stool and returned to work on the unfinished statue, biting his lower lip.

After several minutes, Jacques turned and blurted, "I made you. You'd be nowhere without me."

With his eyes fixed on the block of wood in his hand, Thomas retorted, "I was thinking it to be the other way around. You've grown wealthy from my work." He watched Jacques' shoulders slump, and smiled inside. He had Jacques cornered.

"Very well. Your own stand and fifty percent of the profits. You benefit from my reputation and connections. It's only fair that I get half."

"My own stand and fifty-five percent of the profits of my own work. You can sell your other merchandise at my stand."

The muscles around Jacques' mouth relaxed. "You're a sly devil," he quipped. "Let's hope folks pushing the new religion don't put us both out of business."

Thomas' eyes narrowed. "I lost my livelihood once. I won't let it happen again."

August, 1543

Dartford

"How would you like to accompany me to the fair in London?" William swatted at a fly with the linseed-oil soaked rag he was using to condition the loom. "Blasted pests."

"Bartholomew's Fair?" Skimming a cake of beeswax along the loom's tie cords, Christopher cast his father a sideways glance. What father would wish to spend several days in close quarters with his wayward son, at an event rumored for its debauchery? Besides, whether or not his father wished to spend time with him, he definitely had no desire to spend a single hour, much less a week or more, hopelessly captive to his father's lectures. Yet, against his will, images of Bartholomew's Fair teased their way into his thoughts—visions of tight-rope walkers, exotic caged beasts, and England's best jugglers. And, perchance, Anne.

"Yes, Bartholomew's." William studied Christopher's reaction while massaging oil into the wood. "Methinks it a good idea for us to explore markets beyond Dartford. Cloth merchants from across the realm will be in London for the Cloth Fair. We'll take as much linen to sell as we can produce, and see what other weavers are doing. Heard tell there is likely to be a juggler or two performing there." He stopped inspecting the loom's bolts to offer Christopher a smile and a wink.

Christopher glowered at his father. Making mention of jugglers to entice him might have been appropriate when he was a child. He plucked the handkerchief from his belt and wiped rivulets of sweat from his brow. "I'm not a child, Father."

William sighed. Everything he said these days seemed to strike a sour chord.

Tucking his handkerchief into his belt, Christopher challenged, "What will we do at the fair? Read the Bible while cut-purses mill about us? You wouldn't want me surrounded by such debauchery, would you?"

Doing his best to brush aside the sting of his son's sardonic attitude, William tightened a loose bolt on one of the loom legs and persisted. "'Tis the grandest cloth fair in England. I reckon we can tolerate some debauchery in exchange for what we stand to gain. What say you?" He watched Christopher grapple with the question. "Take some time to think about it. The fair's in three weeks. 'Twould be a good opportunity to introduce your work outside of Dartford. Mother is anxious to pitch in some of her blackwork as well. Goodness knows, her coin crock could use a few deposits."

Still clutching the wax cake, Christopher paused. "Would I get a share of the profits, seeing as I'm pitching in my work?"

"Of course. I don't expect you to work for nothing."

"Where will we lodge?"

"I thought to ask Uncle Nathan if he might accommodate us for three nights. If not, we'll camp outside the city wall."

A plethora of possibilities entertained Christopher's thoughts, foremost among them, the chance of encountering the hazel-eyed girl he'd spent three years pining over. In a city populated by more than 100,000 folks from all over the world, chances were slim. Even if their paths crossed, would they recognize one another? A boy when Anne left, he was now almost twenty and just shy of six feet tall. His physique had hardened into that of a young man. Maidens looked twice when he passed by. To someone who hadn't seen him in three years, the difference would be stark.

"It sounds enticing," he replied. "When must you know?"

"On the morrow. 'Twill give you time to think, and me time to plan. We'll have to put in extra hours to produce enough cloth to make it worth our while. We must weave our very best linen."

"I'll consider it." Christopher returned the beeswax cake to the table where Elizabeth kept her spinning supplies, feigning disinterest while his heart spun cartwheels. He couldn't wait to tell Nicholas the news; Nicholas would be beside himself with envy.

"Is there anything else you need me to do, Father?"

"No, take some time to consider the opportunity, while I tweak the loom. Tomorrow I aim to start up as soon as the crock crows, and continue until sunset."

With a nod, Christopher ventured outside and strolled past Miss Piggle's empty sty to the apple tree. Gazing skyward through the branches, hope surged in his breast. For the first time in months, he had something to look forward to.

A cacophony of sights, smells, and sounds competed for Christopher's attention. Traversing the last few steps on Cloth Street before emerging into West Smithfield, he gazed up at three-, four- and five-story timber-framed buildings crowded together like trees growing side-by-side in a thick forest. Curious faces peered out here and there behind the latticed windows of taverns and shops, eager to get a glimpse of the curiosities swarming in the streets.

To Christopher's left, a rowdy crowd cheered a fire-eater introducing a long torch down his throat. The enticing aroma of roast pork wafted through the air, teasing Christopher's taste buds. His stomach growled, crying out for solid sustenance after the meager diet of hard rolls and last year's dried apples they ate on their trek from Dartford. He searched in all directions for the source of the pork.

"Fine Bartholomew babies!" a gruff voice echoed in the distance. "'Ere's yer toys for yer girls and boys!" As Christopher continued walking, he saw that the call came from a portly man standing next to a cart full of carved wooden dolls, clothed in various fashions of the day. The vendor made eye contact with Christopher and approached.

"You, lad." The man pointed to him and held up a doll dressed like a courtier. "Ye got younger brothers or sisters, do ye?" Christopher shook his head. "Is yer mother here with you?" Christopher shook his head again. "Get the good woman a Bartholomew baby. Let me see here." He rummaged through the collection. "Anne Boleyn. Yes. Lookie there, dressed like the ill-fated queen, she is. This one is sure to make yer mother smile. Don't go home empty-handed!

"You there!" The man quickly changed his focus from Christopher to a woman with two children in tow, deeming it imperative to catch her before she scurried away with potential double profits. "You there, the gentlewoman," he shouted louder, pointing a finger at her. The startled woman looked in the vendor's direction. "Yes, you there. Bartholomew babies for the urchins. Guaranteed to keep 'em pleased for hours while ye go about yer affairs." He extended a doll toward the woman's daughter, a pretty young imp with rosy cheeks, freckles and curly red hair.

"Please, Mother! Could I have one?" The girl, who looked to be about six, relinquished her hold on her mother's hand and reached for the doll. After the vendor placed it in her eager fingers, she held it up to her cheek. "I so want her. Please, Mother, buy her for me."

"How much?" the woman asked, feeling under her sleeve for a beaded pouch attached to her wrist with a gold cord. The young girl smiled, revealing two missing front teeth.

"Ha'-penny is all. Best deal at the fair, 'tis." He leaned forward and pressed his face close to the girl's. "What might be yer name, pretty young lady?"

"Tillie," she replied, batting her eyelashes.

"Lovely name, Miss. Enjoy yer baby, now." He smiled at the girl's mother. "She's a nymph, she is." The toddler in tow started to scream. Christopher watched the scene unfold, relieved that the vendor's attention was no longer directed at him.

"Better to get the imp something as well, or you'll be in for an unpleasant time of it," the vendor stated matter-of-factly. "I do happen to have something for yer young lad, best price anywhere." He rummaged in a bin situated next to his cart and pulled out a wooden paddle with a cup and ball. "'Twill keep the lad busy for hours, it will. Just a ha'-penny; small price to pay to keep the urchin happy." He tried to demonstrate how to toss the ball into the cup, but kept missing. "Very well. Methinks I could use some practice. But 'tis easy enough for the urchins."

"I'll take it." The harried woman shushed her crying toddler and handed the vendor two pence. He extended the cup and ball to the toddler. The young boy waved it erratically before throwing it in frustration.

"Tillie, run and fetch it, please." The young mother exhaled in exasperation. Tillie retrieved the ball and cup and handed it to her brother. He pulled on the ball, broke the string, and threw the ball in a tantrum. It bounced away and disappeared in the crowd. The harried woman continued on her way, forgetting to collect her change, while her son's screams tapered off in the distance.

"Hot mutton pies, hot!" A woman's voice beckoned ahead. "Hot mutton pies! Best at the fair!"

"Do we have enough for a mutton pie?" Christopher asked William, forgetting about the roast pork.

"Let's see how much they cost. Are you as hungry as I am?"

Christopher nodded. "Famished."

They picked their way through the crowd, following the calls for mutton pie until they saw the cart a stone's throw from Saint Bartholomew church. Christopher's heart nearly stopped. The young woman selling mutton pies looked to be about twenty, with chestnut hair swept up and tucked under a white coif.

As they approached, he noticed a smattering of freckles across the bridge of her nose. He fought the urge to bolt to the front of the queue.

"The pie must be fine, judging from size of the line," William remarked. Christopher was too mesmerized with the maiden at the cart to pay his father any heed. As he watched her interact with customers, his certainty grew that fortune had carried him straight to Anne. When he and William finally reached the front of the line, Christopher removed his hat with a slight bow.

She scrunched her brow. "I'm vexed, I am. Have I made your acquaintance?"

"'Tis me, Christopher."

"Begging your pardon, I don't know anyone by the name of Christopher."

As if manipulated by a puppeteer, Christopher's eyes and mouth suddenly drooped. Moved by sympathy, William stepped forward. "You share the likeness of a maiden from Dartford. 'Tis a compliment my son has paid you; she's a lovely young lady. We'll have two mutton pies. Here's an extra ha'penny for your trouble."

She flashed a smile. "'Tis no trouble, Goodman. I was simply caught off guard, I was. Don't recognize the likes of either of you, and I've lived in London all my life." The young lady selected two mutton pies and handed them to William.

Regaining his wits, Christopher said, "I do beg your pardon. She moved to London three years past, and you bear a striking resemblance to her."

"S'pose I've got a twin then. Are you searching for this maiden?" She stuck her bottom lip out to blow away a few stray hairs tickling her eyes.

"Yes, I thought perchance I might encounter her in London while we attend the fair."

"I wish you well." She nodded politely, looking past them to the next folks in line.

"Enough of the chatter," a short, sweaty man behind William and Christopher bellowed. "We came to get mutton pie, not to listen to you and the wench."

The maiden frowned. "I do wish you well," she said politely. Christopher nodded.

As he and William turned back into the throng, Christopher bit into the pie. His taste buds swooned. *Abby's taffaty tarts have met their match*, he thought. Glancing over his shoulder at the young vendor, he mused, *I could live in London. London is most definitely a fine place to be.*

Sinking his teeth into the pie, William exclaimed, "Oh my!" He wiped a crumb from the corner of his mouth. "Abby has met her match."

Christopher smiled. "My thoughts exactly." He surveyed all directions, enticed by too many wonders to focus on anything in particular.

"We need to make our way to Nathan's. I'm thankful he offered us three nights' lodging. After we set up in the morning, you can take a look around. Sound fair?" William hesitated before adding, "No pun intended."

"Fair." Happy he made the decision to tolerate his intolerable father and come to London, Christopher mused, *I can't wait to see what the morrow brings.*

ↂ

A large crowd gathered on the corner of Watling and Bread Street drew Anne's attention. She tugged on Victoria's elbow. "Let's see what the commotion is."

Victoria balked, fanning her face with a day-old Bartholomew Fair handbill she picked up from the street. "In my experience, a crowd gathered on a London street almost always spells trouble. You go ahead. I'll wait here."

Anne worked her way to the mob's edge and raised to her tiptoes, unable to see what was attracting folks' attention. Zigzagging her way to an opening on the other side of the crowd, she heard a woman's voice above the noise of the busy street.

"They claim their god is in a piece of bread. The true God doesn't dwell in the works of man's hands."

Anne's heart skipped a beat. Did the woman know that to deny one of Six Articles—Christ's real presence in the bread and wine—could invite a death sentence? Victoria's warnings about the reformers' teachings raced through her mind—*you'll have to find out for yourself, if you dare.* Surely, no harm could come of just listening. She worked her way closer, annoyed by a tall man in front of her wearing a hat that blocked her view.

"I would rather read five lines in the Bible than hear five masses in the temple," the woman shouted above the throng.

Anne marveled. A woman street preacher? Had the world turned upside down? She squeezed past the tall man and caught a glimpse of a pretty young woman who looked to be about her own age, holding a Bible in her left hand. The courage it took for a young woman to preach against the king's religion on a London street corner made Anne feel suddenly small in comparison. She backed

161

away and searched for Victoria. Her aunt stood a few paces from the crowd, watching boats on the river.

"'Tis a woman street preacher," Anne reported, breathless. "They allow women to preach in London?"

"Not to my knowledge," Victoria responded. "Shall we start for home?"

"Yes," Anne replied. As they traversed central London in the afternoon heat, she mulled over the shocking spectacle of a woman preacher.

Dartford

Elizabeth beamed as Father Garrett adjusted the amice on his shoulders, shuffled a few papers on the podium, and cleared his throat.

"As you are most certainly aware," he stopped to sneeze, "Parliament recently passed an act restricting Bible reading. Might I jog your memory as to the provisions of the Act." Edward Bartholomew let his head fall back, folded his arms, and stared at the vaulted ceiling. Father Garrett focused on Elizabeth, where he knew he would find sympathy, occasionally glancing down at a paper upon which he had scribbled a few notes.

"The king requires that Bible reading shall be allowed only by clerics, noblemen, gentry and well-off merchants. Women of gentry or nobility may read it in private. To all others," he glared at Willie Malden, "Bible reading is forbidden."

Willie stared him squarely in the eyes without blinking.

"I would further add," the priest sneezed again, "that the true meaning of Scripture is easily corrupted by those who aren't trained or educated in its understanding. We must not take the things of God and cast them to the swine." Kenneth Malden offered an appreciative nod.

Returning his eyes to the paper from which he was reading, Garrett used his finger to find the place where he left off. "This includes all manner of printed stuffs purporting to instruct the people—and most especially the youth—of the word of God. I quote directly: 'His Majesty considers it most requisite to purge his realm of all such books, ballads, rhymes, and songs, as be pestiferous and noisome.'"

I wish my husband were here, Elizabeth thought. *Why is he always absent when the message is tailored to him? 'Twould be no use. He's an obstinate man.* She smiled her approval at Father Garrett.

162

Amy Coppinger waddled to Elizabeth's side after the service. "'Tis just what you've been waiting for!" she clucked. "'Tis a shame William wasn't here to listen. Putting your family in danger the way he keeps that Bible in your home, he should be pilloried. Or worse."

Elizabeth recoiled at the thought of William in the pillory, but she agreed with the rest of Amy's comment. "He would sooner go to the Clink than give up his Bible. 'Tis impossible to speak sense to him."

"I feel for you, Elizabeth. I'm happy my husband doesn't bring heretical writings into my home."

Elizabeth pictured herself slapping Amy's cheek.

ᘉ

"What else did you and Christopher do in London?" Elizabeth prodded. "Did you see any caged lions?" She tapped her fingers on her knee, waiting for an answer.

William had seemed a world away since he returned from the fair, and Christopher uttered barely two words since their return. Her son spent his days weaving in silence, and his nights with Nicholas doing Lord only knew what.

William ran a sharpening stone along the blade of Elizabeth's best kitchen knife. "Lions, monkeys, tightrope walkers…" His answer trailed off as he retreated into whatever mysterious world of thought possessed him these days. Suddenly, seized by a fit of righteous indignation, he tightened his grip on the knife handle and growled, "What kind of monster would do that to a boy? Willie's only crime is reading God's word."

Elizabeth shrugged her shoulders. "He disobeyed his king. Surely you hold that such behavior should be punished? We'd have nothin' but trouble if subjects went about doin' as they pleased, latchin' onto any and all pestiferous ideas floatin' about. The king is our protector." She ran a strand of black embroidery thread across her cake of beeswax, squinting as she poked the thread at a needle's eye.

"Protector? A father beats his son black and blue for reading the Bible, while every day boys engage in revelry and destruction with nary a consequence. Where was Willie's protector when that happened?" William dropped the knife and jerked his right foot away just in time.

Her eyes opened wide. "You barely missed your toe!"

163

He picked up the knife as if nothing happened, continuing his tirade. "Did you see the lad's bruises? Did you?" She shook her head and inhaled deeply, determined to speak her piece.

"No, I didn't see the marks on him, but have you forgotten? 'Tis forbidden to folks like us to read the Bible, for good reason. Your eyes aren't blind to the brawls in the taverns and churches. Poor priests and nuns have to search for a place to lay their head, while the king dissolves God's houses, one after the other. Mobs are runnin' loose like wolves, tearin' apart churches and ruinin' holy things. You see all this, yet you keep that Bible hidden in our home and put us all at risk. You willfully defy the injunctions. Father Garrett spoke at length about the evils of Bible readin' while you were in London. 'Tis a shame you weren't there to hear it."

"'Tis a shame you were there." William clenched his teeth and pressed hard against the knife with the sharpening stone.

Undaunted, Elizabeth continued, her voice elevating with each phrase. "Is it Kenneth's fault that his son disobeyed and snuck a Bible into his house? Who would provide a boy with that book, anyway? 'Tis criminal to give a boy a Bible, jeopardizin' his safety." William's face flushed. "Would that the book were out of here. I've a mind to throw that thing in the fire, by God's teeth."

"Oh, no you don't." William stopped sharpening and narrowed his eyes. "'Tis not your book to dispose of. I'll not have my wife disobeying my authority in this home."

"Yet you disobey His Majesty, which is akin to disobeyin' God." She fell silent, calculating the risk of what she wanted to say next. Her words were measured and deliberate. "Word is, Father Garrett is thinkin' of writin' to the bishop about the problems in our parish. I think you should know the risk you are takin'."

Burning with anger, William felt as if his heart would combust in his chest. He set the knife and stone on a small table next to him and cocked his head forward. "What 'problems' would that be?" She shook her head, lips taught, and finished a running stitch in her towel. He inched his nose close to hers. "So help me, I will give my last breath fighting for a man's right to read the words of God in the English tongue. So help me, Elizabeth." He shook his fist in her face and pulled back, lowering his arm with his fingers still clenched.

She shuddered. William had never lifted a hand to her, yet lately his hair-trigger temper made her uneasy. Who could predict what a man driven to despair might do? Willing herself to stay calm, she took a deep breath and lowered her voice. "What happened to you in London? You've been broodin' since your return. You're angry, sullen, far away."

Deflating like a punctured football, he slumped his shoulders and bowed his head. "I don't think you would understand, being of the king's persuasion."

"I don't always agree with you, but you're my husband. I'll stand with you as best I can."

"But you're standing against me. Jesus said a man's foes would be those of his own household. He could have been speaking of us."

She wove her needle into the towel, set the fabric on her lap and whispered, "I'm sorry. It pierces my heart that you consider me a foe. I don't embrace the new learnin' as you do. It's tearin' apart all I hold dear." Burying her face in her hands she choked, "I hate this. I want it to end."

Softened by her emotion, William approached his wife, intertwined his fingers in hers, and pulled her to his bosom. "Somehow, by God's grace, we'll get through this. Young boys beaten, churches torn apart, beheadings and burnings—I don't know how, but we'll make it. We must pull together. For you, for me, and for our son, we must put aside our differences and work together."

She nestled her head between his neck and shoulder and sniffed, "What happened to you in London?" Her tears moistened his neck.

Tipping her chin up with his forefinger, he searched the fear and fatigue in her eyes. "Where do I start?" He shook his head. "The debauchery in London excited Christopher's interest. He would have happily stayed in Smithfield. One thing you and I can agree on, the place is a chamber pot of unsavory folks and activities. I fear losing my son, and I fear the king is clamping down on reformers. I learned Nathan's parish has been under watch for years."

"Which parish is that?"

"All Hallows Honey Lane."

She sighed. "The king won't tolerate rebellion on any front. That's why I fear for you, for Willie, for all who persist in defyin' him."

"But if we don't stand, who will? I refuse to cower. The Lord's apostles stood with their master, except for one who betrayed him for thirty pieces of silver. I refuse to be a Judas. I believe God is bringing forth his holy word for a purpose. I believe a better day is dawning, when folks will read the Bible without fear, and worship without punishment. But it won't come about if we refuse to stand. You should read the book, Elizabeth. Read our Lord's words for yourself."

Pulling back, she glared at him. "You ask me to risk my very life? I won't disobey those who rule over us."

He let his arms slip from her neck and paced back and forth in front of the fireplace. "But they're keeping us in darkness. Folks' minds are full of superstitions and fables. Read the Bible with me, Elizabeth. Or I shall read it to you."

"No." She sat down and picked up her embroidery. "I won't put my life in danger to read a forbidden book. Why can't you see?"

"I'll never give up reading the Bible. 'Tis the word of God to man."

She pulled the needle from the fabric with a heavy sigh. "Very well. The curse you bring upon us will fall upon your own head."

June, 1544

—

Dartford

Leaning back at his desk in the rectory with a satisfied smile, Father Garrett pictured the goats among his flock—specifically Edward Bartholomew and William Wade—with ropes around their necks, being led to a stall and tied up.

The priest took a deep breath and blew it out slowly, tapping his fingers on the desktop while his mind tallied a list of encouraging events of late. For starters, King Henry's injunction against Bible reading the previous year stopped Wade's Bible study group in its tracks—at least in the church building. As a result, Kenneth Malden hadn't pestered him for months.

Another providential development occurred just before Palm Sunday, when Teresa Willoughby moved to Canterbury to live with her family. It was a bittersweet parting, but he'd lived long enough to know doors sometimes had to be closed before new ones could open. Now he could work to salvage his reputation and move forward.

Scratching a tickle under his thin moustache, he contemplated one unresolved matter needing swift attention. He retrieved a sheet of parchment from the desk drawer and, with plume in hand, scribbled furiously.

August, 1544

——

Rochester, England

Bishop Henry Holbeach reached forward and picked up a folded piece of parchment on his desk. Flipping it over, he identified its origin—Dartford Parish, June, 1544—and broke the wax seal. A hornet buzzing around his face landed on the paper. He flicked it away and leaned back in his chair to read the message, written in impeccable calligraphy. After scanning it he folded it closed, opened his desk drawer, and set the letter on a stack of similar correspondence from all over the Rochester diocese.

He closed the drawer and fiddled with a paperweight for several seconds. With a weary sigh, he stood and walked out of the Bishop's Palace into the bright sunlight, wishing he could shed his heavy cassock for something less stilting. Still, he preferred the insufferably hot and humid August air outdoors to the dank air inside the palace.

Rochester had been his home the few months since he received his election as bishop. He'd spent a majority of his years in Worcester serving in numerous ecclesiastical positions, starting out as a monk, then Prior of Worcester, Suffragen Bishop of Bristol, and Dean of Worcester. Tending the flock was easier before the dissolution, he thought, back when most questions were black and white.

The sense that he lived in both dangerous and momentous times weighed heavily upon him. Could Bishop John Fisher, his predecessor just nine years earlier, have anticipated his own beheading on the Tower green for standing loyal to the Mother Church? Fisher had been one of the king's favorites. Holbeach shuddered.

As he walked across the green, contemplating the letter from Dartford, he heard a voice calling for him and smiled to see a young boy skipping in his direction.

"Father! I'm over here!"

"Thomas!" Bishop Holbeach opened his arms wide to receive the light of his life. They spun in a circle, Thomas giggling with joy. "And where is Mother?" the bishop asked, setting Thomas down on the grass and looking in the direction from whence he came.

"She's coming. Can you walk home with us?"

Holbeach surveyed his surroundings. "Is she close behind you? I haven't much time."

"She was right behind me." Thomas looked over his shoulder. "There she is! Picking some flowers." He pointed downhill to a slender brunette in a green gown, who looked in their direction and waved.

"Let's go meet her." Thomas tugged his father's hand. Henry chuckled as the lad practically dragged him downhill. Upon reaching his wife, Henry glanced in all directions before leaning down to give her a peck on the cheek. She repaid him with a warm smile.

"Joan, what a nice surprise. What brings you and Thomas this way?" the bishop inquired.

"We were out for a stroll to get some fresh air, but this dreadful heat is giving me second thoughts." She held up to her nose a handful of roses, some peach-colored and some pink. Inhaling deeply, she gushed, "Aren't they lovely?"

"Lovely like you, my rose," he replied, with an affectionate squeeze of her arm.

"Oh, you …" she giggled. "What occupies you today at the palace?"

"Letters from priests."

"More letters? And did you respond?"

"Would that I had the wisdom of Solomon. I'm not sure quite how to respond to the steady stream of charges." A perplexed tone betrayed his usual confidence. "The Dartford priest requests a meeting with me to discuss Bible-readers in his parish."

"God will guide you." She stroked his arm.

"Whose god?" he replied. "The god of King Henry, the god of Rome, or the god of Luther? Perhaps Zeus will come to my aid!"

Joan squeezed his elbow. "Your god, Henry. The true god."

"God could have chosen a better man for this position. Was I truly born for these times? I'm perplexed. I have no answers."

"Of course you were born for these times. Look at you. Bishop of Rochester. Does God err?"

"No, but his feeble servants do."

"You're where God has placed you. He'll grant you his wisdom. I'm sure of it." She sniffed the roses again.

"Your encouragement is balm to my soul. Now, if only you could give me the words I need to answer the letters."

"Would that I could. I don't envy you."

"Oh, that the shifting sand upon which we stumble would become a firm foundation." He let out a troubled sigh.

"Mother! Father!"

The couple turned to see their son kneeling next to a puppy that was smothering his face with sloppy licks. "Look at the puppy! Can I have him?" The Talbot wagged his backside while Thomas scratched his neck. "Please? I'll take good care of him. I promise I will!"

Chuckling, Bishop Holbeach and Joan strode to Thomas' side. "Surely he belongs to someone who lives near here," Joan said, kneeling down to tickle the puppy's head.

"Maybe he's lost," Thomas insisted. "Look how he wags his tail. He fancies me. Oh please, let me take him home." The hound wiggled and spun around, then put his front paws on the boy's knees, wagging his tail and barking with such vigor the pup lost his balance.

"Speaking of wagging," the bishop said, scanning the green, "tongues will be wagging if we linger much longer."

Joan's countenance clouded. "When will we see you again? Will you come home tonight?"

"It depends on how things go," Holbeach answered. "For the time being, I must return to my insufferable palace cell and formulate a plan for dealing with the priests. I would much rather be with you." He planted his lips on hers. "Godspeed."

She reached for his hand and held tight. "Do hurry home. The house is empty without you. Our son needs his father. He desperately wants you to play with him."

"Are you trying to make me feel guilty? If so, you're wildly succeeding."

"Goodness, no. I'm only saying we love and miss you. We need you."

"And I you." He squeezed her hand, then reluctantly released his grip. "But I must be discreet, so as not to rouse the cacklers."

"Don't folks know? Surely our marriage is no secret."

"Perhaps not to some, but many disapprove. Most look the other way for now, but in times like these, I can ill afford to draw undue attention to our union." He kissed her earlobe. "I'll come home as soon as I can."

"Very well." Thomas beckoned to his mother from down the hill. "I'm coming, Thomas," she shouted. "Say good-bye to the puppy."

With a final, lingering gaze, Bishop Holbeach and Joan parted in opposite directions.

October, 1544

"I understand you harbor concerns about some of your parishioners?"

Father Garrett squirmed, feeling as if he'd shrunk several sizes in the bishop's presence. Instead of looking in the bishop's eyes, he gazed past his superior at a dirty window streaming sheets of cold rain. "Yes," he replied. "I have some who insist upon keeping and reading English Bibles, in direct rebellion to the injunctions—a punishable offense, as you know."

The bishop nodded. "Do they have other crimes?"

"I suspect they would deny the holy presence if pressed, but I have no proof, nor have I pursued the issue." Garrett studied a crack in the cold stone wall. A shiver ran up his spine. He found the ambiance in the decrepit Bishop's Palace unwelcoming.

Holbeach leaned forward on his elbows, his brow furrowed. "We can't convict folks without evidence. Do you have proof against those you accuse of holding Bibles?"

The priest pursed his lips. "Several months ago, I saw a lad clutching a Bible that was secretly secured for him and another lad by an older member of my parish, a man by the name of William Wade. I walked in on the very transaction in the rear of the nave one evening, after the other parishioners had gone home. The lad tried to shield it from my eyes, but there was no mistaking what I saw. Furthermore, this Wade is widely known to hold Lollard sympathies and to possess a Tyndale Bible. He led Bible study in the church before the injunctions forbade it, and drew these particular lads into his lair. The father of one of the lads is distraught about Wade's influence on his son and his apprentice. An informer insisting on secrecy told me Wade continues to hold secret Bible meetings."

"I see. And how do you propose going after these individuals?"

"I could have my justice of the peace keep an eye on their activities, although these foxes are adept at staying in the shadows. I could also recruit a parishioner to feign sympathy and gain Wade's trust. In fact, one comes to mind at this very moment. I could trap Wade at one of his secret Bible meetings, and have Luke Tisdale—he's my justice of the peace—ready to arrest him. I don't so much hold the lads responsible; 'tis this Wade spreading the seeds of heresy. Please understand, Your Excellency, I take enforcing obedience to the injunctions with utmost sobriety."

Bishop Holbeach tapped his fingers together, contemplating the priest's words. His response was measured.

"Father Garrett, I understand you consider obedience to the injunctions to be a matter of great import."

"Yes, Bishop, I consider it my utmost duty to obey my superiors in enforcing the will of our rulers."

"And you know the injunctions well, I take it? You've been enforcing them in Dartford?"

"Yes. My congregation has memorized—in the English tongue—the Pater Noster and Creed, and I believe all have come close to memorizing the Ten Commandments. We've dutifully removed the candles, abolished the required feast days, and removed the altar of Saint Thomas…"

Bishop Holbeach raised a hand to interrupt. "It sounds as if your obedience in those things is impeccable. Are you aware of what the Six Articles say about priests, celibacy, and chastity?"

Garrett stiffened. "Why do you ask me this, Your Excellency?"

"You're not the first to come to me from Dartford with concerns about the conduct of individuals in your parish."

"What do you mean?"

"You're attentive to your flock, as you should be. But some in your flock are mindful of your behavior as well. If you value your appointment, you would do well to examine your own conduct with regard to the Injunctions and Articles."

The priest's jaw dropped.

Bishop Holbeach pushed his chair back and stood. "Would you like to join me for supper?"

Fanning his face with a piece of paper upon which he'd scribbled notes to prepare for his meeting with the bishop, the priest stood. "Thank you, Your Excellency. I have other matters to attend to."

After wishing Garrett well, the bishop watched him slink out of the room.

March, 1545

—

Fie on Lollards! Wallowing in resentment, Christopher glared at the diaper weave cloth expanding on the loom in front of him. He'd had enough of the ugly word *Lollard*. It had gotten him mercilessly teased and tormented from the time he was too young to understand why. It was whispered behind his back. It led Matthew Cooper to hate him, even though Christopher had no opinion about the popish religion or the new learning. *Lollard* got Anne sent away to London. It had townsfolk lying about his character and spreading false rumors. One simple, terrible word: *Lollard*.

He never wanted to hear the word again. He never wanted to listen to folks argue about the English Bible, or about the real presence in the Eucharist. He never wanted to sit through another announcement about the king's injunctions while parishioners murmured, quarreled, and butted heads. He wanted to distance himself as far as he could from his father and the man's heretical notions. As long as he lived in Dartford, folks would brand him William Wade's son, Lollard.

I might as well have the letter L *branded on my cheek*, he stewed. *We brand murderers with an* M. *Thieves with a* V. *Lollards' sons with an invisible* L. *Some sons are at least lucky enough to inherit a good name. Thank you, Father, for bringing shame upon me. Perhaps 'tis time to pursue the life of a juggler.* He snickered. At least he still had a sense of humor.

Weary of Christopher's brooding, William spoke up. "You've said nary a word all morning. Is something wrong, son?" Since Christopher's return from the fair in London, the lad had infused the home atmosphere with tension. William almost wished him gone.

His lips taut, Christopher worked on a repeating pattern of small diamonds. Weaving, once a source of pride and fulfillment, now represented strangling threads binding him tighter and tighter, rendering him unable to escape. He was a caged falcon, longing to soar and hunt for something exciting, something of his own choosing.

William and Elizabeth had always tried to provide a good enough life for him. Their humble but comely surroundings represented the industry of William's hands and heart, his life's tapestry of struggle and triumph, joy and pain. William saw a great deal of himself in Christopher: quiet but with rock-hard determination, independent of mind, contemplative. William wondered whether independence of thought was a blessing or a curse. Following the throng would be so much easier.

"Christopher," William prodded, "'tis unlike you to be so tight-lipped. Do you care to reveal what is troubling you?"

Christopher muttered a terse, "I would rather not discuss it."

William wrapped his right hand around the breast beam and shook the loom. "You will discuss this!" he shouted. "Your preoccupation of late is affecting your work. I fear our reputation for quality will suffer. I've spent my life building this industry, and I won't have you tearing it down."

Christopher smirked, thinking, *me, harm your reputation? Odd that you should speak of reputation, you, who gave me a Lollard's brand to hamper my every effort in life.* He inspected the fabric on the loom. His father was right: the tension was inconsistent and the diamond pattern uneven.

"Hmm," he replied, his tone pickled with sarcasm, "I suppose you're right."

Willing himself to calm down, William paced in front of the door before positioning himself next to Christopher. Fingering the fabric, he said softly, "It's not like you to produce flawed work." He intended the comment as a compliment, but it was not taken that way.

"Not like me?" Christopher stood, his face and neck reddening. "What do you know about me?"

"I just meant—you take after me. You take pride in your work." He hopped sideways, his eyes wide. The shuttle flew past, just missing his face. The tool bounced off the front door and landed a few inches from William's feet.

"I'm not you, Father!" Christopher shouted, his fists clenched. He pushed his face into William's. "I want nothing to do with you, your God-forsaken religion, your cursed weaving, or this intolerable village! This is your life, not mine."

William stepped back, his shock giving way to rage. "How dare you speak to me this way! Is Nicholas planting these seeds of rebellion in your mind? The two of you spend too much time at the alehouse, bantering foolish ideas about." His voice quivered with adrenaline.

Looking William squarely in the eyes, Christopher replied, "Weaving day in and day out is torment. I fear I'll strangle the next person who uses the word *Lollard* in my presence. I want nothing to do with the King's religion, the Pope's, Luther's, or any other." Stomping across the room to a stack of cloth in the corner, he picked up a sample of diaper cloth. "You say my work is suffering, and perhaps it is. I can't pretend any longer." He crumpled the fabric, crossed the room and tossed it into the fire, watching it dance, shrink, and shrivel into ash. "That's how I feel about my life as the son of a Lollard linen weaver." He wiped his trembling hands on his breeches and heaved out a sigh.

William raced to the fireplace, his heart pounding. "How dare you!" He shook his forefinger at Christopher. "When I was your age, I would have been grateful to have a father who provided a path for me to follow. I had no father at all."

"You want my gratitude? Thanks for nothing, Father. What have you provided me? Do you hear what people say about us, about Lollards? They whisper behind our backs. They call us heretics. Do you know what happens to heretics?"

William bowed his head. He knew all too well.

Christopher continued. "All my life, I've been called a Lollard because of you. Well, I'm not a Lollard, and I never will be. I've already made arrangements. Nicholas and I are leaving in the morning."

"Leaving?" William peered out the window and watched a sparrow flutter its wings on a yew tree branch. He turned to face his son. "I intend to leave all of this to you. 'Tis what you've trained for, worked for. You can't just up and throw it away."

"'Tis what you planned, not me."

"You haven't thought this through. You have no idea what you're doing."

"I've thought about it plenty, and I know exactly what I'm doing. I'm a man in my own right. You won't change my mind."

"Does your mother know about this?"

"Nothing she says will change my mind, either."

"How could you do this to her? What happened to you?" William crumpled onto a stool at the kitchen table and buried his face in his hands, not bothering to look up when the door slammed shut.

CS

A resplendent rose, gold and light blue glow crowned the morning horizon with possibility. As he and Christopher trekked along Watling Street, London-bound, Nicholas broke the silence first.

"How did your father react?"

Christopher chuckled. "You should have seen his face. I feel a bit sorry for the old man. All of his ambitions for me, up in smoke."

Nicholas switched his knapsack from the left shoulder to the right. "'Twas much the same with my father. When I told him I would be better off shoveling stables in London than laying bricks in Dartford, he insisted I was making a mistake. His last words to me were, 'You'll soon learn better.' He'll see, eh?"

"Yes. We're men now, not boys under our father's thumbs. We're free!" They slapped each other on the back.

Nicholas swallowed hard. "How did your mother take the news?"

"I tried to sneak out this morning, but my stirrings woke her. She pleaded with me not to leave. Said London is a dangerous place."

"Breaking my mother's heart—that was the hard part."

"For me as well. She ran to catch up with me just after I left. Gave me a loaf of bread and the crock full of money she saved from her sales at the market. I told her I would fare well enough on my own, but she insisted." Christopher reached into his leather pouch, suspended from a belt around his waist. "She gave me this for luck—an old pilgrim badge she got before she married father."

Nicholas turned the badge back and forth in his hand. "Thomas Becket. Did your mother make a pilgrimage to Canterbury?"

"She never told me about one. Perhaps she doesn't like to speak of it in front of my father, or she may have kept the badge hidden because of the injunctions."

Returning it to Christopher, Nicholas asked, "Do you ever miss pilgrims stopping in Dartford?"

"It kept Dartford interesting, so many folks passing through. I can't believe it's been six years since they were banned. I feel sorry for the families who had their livings yanked out from under them. Drove Thomas Nix clean out of Dartford."

"I wonder what became of him. Poor Simon Nix, lost his son and his living all at the same time."

Talk of father and son left Christopher wondering how William would fare without his help. He pushed the thought out of his mind.

177

"Christopher, do you ever wish folks still went on pilgrimages? Not to lick the feet of images, or seek a cure from relics, but for the sake of adventure? Think of all the pilgrims who've traveled this very road, back and forth, for centuries."

"If you think about it, you and I are on a pilgrimage, of sorts."

"I like that idea." Nicholas smiled.

"I hope we find work in London. I don't want to end up a beggar, like ol' Harry. He told me that to win Anne's affection, I needed to pretend I was a knight. Tried to help me list my knightly qualities and gave up in frustration."

"I wouldn't exactly look to a vagabond for advice on wooing. What if Anne met another in London?"

Christopher picked up a stone the size of a robin's egg and launched it ahead. "I try not to think about it."

"What if you could be like King Henry, with his wandering eye? I suppose having your pick of the ladies is a perk of being king."

"'Tis more than his eyes that wander," Christopher smirked.

"You got that right." Nicholas kicked the same stone Christopher had thrown a few seconds earlier. "How would you like to have your marriage arranged, like the nobles?"

"It spelled disaster for Anne of Cleves. The face that could stop a horse in its tracks was more than the king could take." Christopher whinnied.

Nicholas blustered. "At least she got the king's manor house in Dartford for her trouble. Every time I passed by there, looking at the bricks I laid, I wondered how she felt being shunned by His Majesty. She fared better than his other wives—at least she lived to tell her story. Anyway, I hear the king isn't much to look at. Perhaps she got the better of the deal." He paused. "Back to Anne— perhaps you'll see her in London."

"I'm hoping for a bit of divine providence, but feel unworthy to ask for it."

"I thought you were doubting God's very existence?"

"I'm not sure what I believe, but I know what I don't believe. I don't believe in a God who allows men and women to suffer for following him. Isn't he supposed to be a god of love? How could a god who loves us watch us suffer, and do nothing to stop it?"

"His ways are beyond my understanding, but he did say a sparrow can't fall to the ground without his notice. If that's true, can we go to London without his providence?"

"You missed your calling. You should have been a priest."

"Not so. I happen to like the maidenfolk too much for that."

"Who says priests don't like maidens?" Christopher pretended to twirl a piece of hair around his finger and cooed, 'Oh, Laine! Can you hear my heartbeat? You're a man, after all'."

Nicholas snorted. "Christopher Wade! With comments like that, how dare you ask heaven for favor?"

"Everyone thinks it. I simply dare to voice it."

ॐ

Sitting on a boulder to rest, Christopher gawked at the diverse assortment of folks traveling the busy road in and out of the city.

With his back against an oak, Nicholas pointed skyward with his chin. "That cloud looks like a falcon in flight."

"Which cloud?"

"That one, right there." Using his forefinger, he guided Christopher's gaze to a raptor-shaped white puff.

"By Jove, it does. Let that be a good omen. Like falcons, we come hunting good fortune." Christopher pulled half of a loaf of bread from his knapsack and offered some to Nicholas.

"Thank you—I'm famished. I have a bit of cheese to share, if you'd like." He unwrapped a wedge of cheddar from a cloth and broke off a chunk for himself before offering it to Christopher. They ate in silence, contemplating the adventure ahead.

"I could use a bit of ale to wash it all down with." Nicholas swallowed hard.

"All the ale you could want, right there." Christopher referred to the city of London, spread out before them on the horizon. A smoky haze hovered above the rooftops. "What else awaits us?"

"Riches, maidens, adventure—name your pleasure."

"My pleasure is streets paved with gold, fountains running with ale, Anne Cooper on my arm, and no Lollards to disturb the peace." Christopher stood and stretched his fingers to his toes with a groan.

"And if we can't find work, end up begging on the streets, you never see Anne, and we encounter Lollards preaching on every street corner?"

"Only one way to find out." Christopher picked up his knapsack and nudged Nicholas in the thigh with his foot. "Let's get on with it. I can't wait to sink my teeth into London."

179

"Zounds! Some welcome the city provides." Nicholas stared, open-mouthed, at severed heads towering precipitously on pikes high above him on the bridge gate. "Do you think His Majesty is sending a message?"

"He doesn't take kindly to traitors." Christopher glanced up, but quickly averted his eyes from the grisly scene.

"I'll do my best to stay in his good favor." Nicholas felt a morbid fascination with the heads. They were dipped in tar for preservation, giving them an otherworldly appearance. A mob of carts, people and animals waited to cross the bridge from Southwark into London.

Tightening his cloak about him, Nicholas gazed up and down Borough High Street, the main route in and out of Southwark, lined with two- and three-story carriage inns. "We passed several inns. I saw signs for the George and the Tabard. Shall we find a place to lodge for the night?"

Lazy puffs of smoke loitered above brick chimneys in the stagnant air. Courtyards bustled with carriage horses swishing their tails and stamping their legs, while drivers unbridled and foddered the animals. A Babel-like cacophony of languages swirled about. The bustling town of Southwark appeared to have sprung into existence expressly for the accommodation and entertainment of revelers outside of London's bounds.

To their left, out of view, a robust shout rose from a crowd cheering what sounded like a bear-baiting. To their right, the heavy oak door of Boar's Head Tavern screeched open and spit out a swarm of ruffians not much older than they. Like hornets, the lads flitted back and forth in the street laughing loudly and bouncing off of one another. One of them ogled a maiden strolling arm-in-arm with a stately gentleman dressed in slashed German clothing. She avoided eye contact with the ruffian and locked elbows with her beau for security. The suitor escorted her to the porch of a candle shop and instructed her to wait. He rolled up his sleeves, marched over to the soused young man, and pushed the offender's chest with both hands. The intoxicated lad put up no resistance, but stumbled and toppled over like a rotten tree. The rest of the swarm flew away, looking back occasionally to make sure no one followed them.

On an adjacent street corner, a juggler caught Christopher's eye. He wore a red, green and blue tunic over mismatched stockings, shoes with pointed toes curled upward, and a traditional headpiece with three long, conical projections jutting outward, embellished at the tips with tiny bells. Passers-by lingered to enjoy his antics and bawdy humor, and rewarded him by tossing coins in a slouched leather bag nearby. The juggler kept one eye on the pouch and one eye on his audience.

"Did you say something?" Christopher's eyes remained fixed on the juggler.

"The sun is setting. We might have trouble finding a room if we don't hurry."

"The activity around here looks to be just getting started. Let's refresh ourselves at a tavern first. You wanted a cup of ale."

"Look at these crowds. I fear we won't find a room if we wait."

Christopher looked up and down the street. "There are inns in both directions. Relax. We'll have no trouble finding lodging. Let's refresh ourselves first."

With a sigh and a shrug of his shoulders, Nicholas consented. "As you wish. But if we end up sleeping on the street, may the cut-throats get you first."

"Since you were kind enough to go along with me, you pick an ale house."

After perusing inns and taverns within view, Nicholas settled on the one closest to where they stood. He pointed to a colorful sign suspended from a wrought iron hook. "The White Knight. Are you buying, since you're dragging me there against my will?"

"Sure. Your drink is on me." The two adventurers entered the candlelit tavern and quickly discovered they were the center of attention.

"They're sizing us up," Nicholas whispered.

"Perhaps they're not accustomed to seeing such dapper lads." Christopher stood tall, stuck his chest out and straightened his cap. The oak floor squeaked beneath their feet as a tapster led them to a table in a dark corner of the room.

"What'll it be?" he growled, the flickering lamplight accentuating pockmarks on his face.

"A flagon of sack, please." Christopher licked his lips.

"Make that two." Nicholas scanned the congested room, grateful they found a table.

"Ya willin' to pay a pretty penny for it?" The tapster's gaze crawled from Christopher's head to his torso and back up, until their eyes met.

"Why?" Christopher watched the waiter pinch the tip of a bushy, salt-and-pepper beard that extended to the top of his protruding belly. A soiled apron failed miserably at the task of covering his paunch.

"The Spaniards don't take kindly to the king divorcin' Catherine and thumbin' 'is nose at the Pope. They jailed our sack merchant for not denoucin'

181

King Henry. The stuff is in short supply. Not to mention they no longer want our coins."

"The Spanish don't want English coins?" The comment struck Nicholas as ludicrous.

"Oh, they'll accept 'em if they have no choice. But the king is debasin' our coins faster than he can marry and discard wives. Other realms want nothin' to do with our money. It's not worth the metal it's stamped on." The tapster wiped his nose with the back of his hand, leaving behind a shiny streak. "We have to keep raisin' our prices, and sack is sky high. So, sack it is?"

At the dismal report, Christopher reached into his bag and pulled out a groat, squinting in the dark to examine King Henry's head on the face. A copper hue shone beneath the silver veneer, prominently highlighting the king's nose.

"See there?" The waiter pointed to King Henry's nose. "Folks are callin' him 'Old Coppernose because he's addin' so much copper to our silver coins. Silver's so thin, the copper shows clean through. I heard tell he's makin' more and more coins, because they're so cheap." The waiter shook his head. "The price of bread has lately more 'n doubled."

"At first glance, it appears the entire town is celebrating a fair, but you paint a different picture." Christopher looked around the tavern. Folks appeared cheerful and well enough off.

"Don't let appearances deceive you, lad. Nothin' like strong ale and bear-baiting to dull the senses. At least half the population is too soused to care about the king's scandals. What'll it be then?"

"Perry will do." Christopher looked to Nicholas for a nod of approval, which was quick in coming. "And what do you recommend for supper?"

"Perry? 'Tis a rich man's drink. Country lads out to find your fortune in London like all the others, are you? Bet it's your first time in the city."

"I wouldn't say we're like all the others." Christopher bristled at the insult.

"Our peasecod pie is easy on the belly and the purse. I've eaten a few myself, if you couldn't tell." The waiter patted his belly. "And our ale will satisfy you and leave you a few coins to spare."

"Ale and peasecod then?" Christopher waited for Nicholas' response.

"Ale and peasecod it is." Nicholas rested his elbows on the table, looking forward to his first meal and drink in London.

"Pray, carry me out on your back." Nicholas pushed his wooden trencher away. "I can hardly breathe."

Christopher stood, wobbled precipitously, regained his balance, and extended his hand. "Come. Our adventure is just beginning." He pulled Nicholas up, almost tumbling over himself.

"The ale was fine, eh?" Nicholas stammered. "Must have been a bit stronger than Amy Coppinger's."

"Something I could get used to. We'll have to come back often."

"My head feels foggy." Nicholas rubbed his eyes.

"The cool night air will clear you up." Christopher held the door while Nicholas ventured onto the bustling city street. A heavy fog had settled over Southwark, trapping in smoke and bringing a biting chill that cut through their heavy wool cloaks.

"Which direction? Your choice." Christopher glanced up and down the street.

"I would prefer lodging closer to the bridge, so we might be among the first to cross into London in the morning."

"As you wish."

They turned left onto Borough High Street. An attractive young woman standing a few yards away on the corner of High Street and Tooley caught Christopher's eye. Wavy red locks tumbled past her shoulders, reaching to the low-cut bodice of her emerald gown. He planted himself in front of Nicholas, wiped the sweat and oil from his face with his cloak, removed his cap to smooth his hair and asked, "Do I look presentable?"

"A mongrel like you?" Nicholas watched the woman study them through the fog.

Christopher strolled across the street, sidestepped a steaming pile of horse manure, and positioned himself by her side. "Good evening," he flirted, sweeping off his cap with a slight bow.

The redhead offered a curtsy and a crooked grin in return. "It is a fine evening, at that, if a bit foggy."

"Would you happen to know where a traveler might find suitable lodging?"

Her face was powdered white and her lips stained with a deep shade of red, a look Christopher found both confusing and enticing.

"You look a bit impish, lad. How old are you, if I may ask?"

"Old enough to be on my own in Southwark," came his retort.

After a final once-over, she let her guard down. "Over near Bankside, there's a street lined with many fine rooms." She pointed in the direction of the Thames. "Would you like me to show you there?"

Feeling positively giddy, Christopher glanced across the street to see if Nicholas was taking note of the conquest. Nicholas mouthed something. Christopher scrunched his face, quizzical. Nicholas mouthed his message again. Christopher shrugged his shoulders.

"Are you with someone?" She glanced at Nicholas.

"I have a traveling companion." Nicholas waved. Christopher beckoned him to cross the street.

"Nicholas, this is—"

"Betsy," came the reply.

"Betsy, I present Nicholas Hall."

"Pleased, to be sure." Betsy curtsied.

Placing a hand on Nicholas' shoulder, Christopher explained, "Betsy is going to take us to a place where we can find lodging and taverns. She says it borders the river."

"Might it border the *stew-ponds*?" Nicholas pinched Christopher's elbow. Christopher swatted the hand away. Betsy raised her eyebrows.

"Bankside lies near the Bishop of Winchester's fish ponds, where they raise pike," Betsy explained, sweeping her right hand in the direction of the ponds.

"Yes, the *stew-ponds*." Nicholas cast Christopher a warning glance. His love-struck friend was too distracted notice.

"Do they sell the pike at market?" Christopher stared at Betsy's red lips, waiting for a response.

"Yes, they do. They use some for those who live on the estate, and give the surplus away to the poor. Follow me. I'll show you." The three made their way along High Street, when a crowd of people flooding onto the passage from the west side nearly blocked the street.

"Where are all these folks coming from?" Christopher gawked.

"A bear-baiting just let out. The arenas lie just over there, by the river." Betsy pointed in a westerly direction.

"Your manner of speech is a bit different, if you don't mind me saying so." Christopher continued to stare at her lips. "Are you from here?"

"My uncle brought me here from Flanders to work as a housekeeper for a wool merchant, a friend of his."

184

"You're a housekeeper?"

Nicholas poked his elbow into Christopher's side.

Betsy adjusted her bodice. "Enough about me. What brings you to Southwark?"

Christopher jumped at the chance to talk about himself. "We came to seek our fortune. I understand London is a city filled with possibilities—even for a linen weaver, I hope."

"A weaver, are you? And you?" She smiled at Nicholas.

Weak-kneed, Nicholas pointed his thumb at Christopher. "He dragged me here."

"Betsy!" A beastly, Nordic man a few paces up the street commanded Betsy's attention.

"Prithee, a moment's pardon." She lifted her skirt hem and trotted in his direction.

As soon as she was out of earshot, Nicholas spit in disgust and scolded, "Snap out of it! Do you really not know Betsy's line of labor?"

"Do I look like an imbecile? She's a housekeeper in Southwark. Probably works for the man who called her name."

"How could you be such a dolt?" Nicholas placed his hands on his hips. "The painted face? She's a strumpet, yet you're drooling and wagging your tail like a hound."

"A beauty like her, a strumpet? You're envious because she took to me and not you. Come on, admit she's a beauty."

"Hers is not the sort of beauty I fancy. What if you encounter Anne in London? Would you risk her for a common…"

Christopher cut him off. "I see no harm in enjoying a little sport. I thought the ale relaxed you a bit. Loosen up, already."

Nicholas wagged his head with a disgusted sigh. "I'm going to find a room on High Street near the bridge. Are you coming?"

"My plans have changed. Hiding in a room our first night in the city would be madness."

"You can find your own lodging, then." Nicholas adjusted the strap of his bag over his shoulder, and looked to see which direction he wanted to go.

"Here she comes." Christopher watched Betsy approach. "I'll meet you at the White Knight for breakfast. And I'm not paying."

"As you wish." Nicholas disappeared into the fog.

185

Thirty-six inches across an oak table separated Christopher and Nicholas, but an icy silence placed them worlds apart.

"Rough night, was it?" Nicholas took a sip of ale, smirking.

Christopher cast a death stare across the table, leaned forward on his elbows and massaged his temples. Morning sun streamed in through the leadlight glass window of the tavern, casting a latticed pattern across Nicholas and the wall behind him.

"Your doublet is torn," Nicholas snipped.

Christopher checked his left armpit. The seam was torn all the way to the hem.

"Your hose are shredded," Nicholas continued. Christopher stuck his right leg out from under the table. His knee protruded from the hose, revealing a fresh scab and a trickle of dried blood. "You're sporting a good-sized gash on your left cheek. And judging from your bloodshot eyes, I would think you had missed several nights' sleep."

"No, only one," Christopher groaned.

"When you sat down at the table, an odor wafted past my nose that I would describe as the stench of a wet dog dunked in a barrel of ale."

The two glared at each other. Christopher's frown and bloodshot eyes gave him the appearance of a bulldog. Nicholas burst into laughter. An elderly couple at the table next to them smiled, warmed at the spectacle of what appeared to be two lads enjoying themselves.

"A fine friend you are," Christopher snarled.

"I tried to stop you, but you wouldn't listen. Dare I ask what happened last night?"

"If you'll stop mocking me." Christopher cradled his head in his hands.

"I can hardly believe my eyes. I've never seen you this way."

"'Tis me, indeed," Christopher mumbled. "I've the headache to prove it. After you left last night, I accompanied Betsy from High Street to Bankside, thinking I would find comfortable lodging with a view across the river, something we couldn't get from High Street. I was out to best you."

"Did you find lodging?"

"Oh, I found lodging, I did. The bank is lined with brothel houses, neatly whitewashed and in a row. It turns out their names are painted flat on the walls rather than hung perpendicular in the regular manner, so customers approaching from the river will know where to disembark for their recreation. The Bear's Head, The Cross Keys, The Castle, The Cardinal's Hat—I counted upwards of eighteen names, thinking I would have an easy pick of rooms, and that I had outsmarted you." Christopher took a sip of ale and stared at the table, his eyes puffy.

"What happened next?" Nicholas leaned forward, eager for details.

"Betsy approached Bankside as if she were very comfortable there. I found her behavior unusual, since a respectable maiden would never be seen in such an area. I said, 'You seem quite familiar with Bankside. Are you a housekeeper here?' to which she giggled and replied, 'Why, yes, this is where I live and work.' 'Which inn would you recommend for a newcomer to the area?' I inquired. She asked me how much money I carried in my purse, to which I replied that I had enough for my needs. 'Do let me see how much money you have in your purse,' she teased. 'The rooms aren't free.' Then she grabbed my purse."

"I tried to warn you." Nicholas shook his head.

"What do you mean, you tried to warn me?"

"About the stews. I tried to warn you about the stews. The Southwark brothels are legendary."

"I was too smitten to heed your warnings."

"I hope you'll be the wiser now. Then what happened?"

"She wrapped the strap of my purse around her wrist and led me toward The Cardinal's Hat while folks loitered about, leaning against walls, boarding and deboarding boats—'twas frightful. Then I realized…"

"What took you so long?" Nicholas interrupted. "I recognized what she was at the very beginning."

"The ale? Her feminine wiles? I don't know. But listen, when I realized what she was, I demanded my purse. She refused to give it to me. Imagine my dilemma. If I were too forceful with her, who knows what manner of riffraff would come to her rescue? So I reached for it, and she pulled back. She looked across the street to the blonde beast who called out to her last night. I warned her to return my purse, or I would be forced to do something unseemly.'"

"What did she do?"

"She held up my purse to show the man across the street, and he raced toward us. Panicked, I grabbed for my purse. Would you believe she scratched at my face?"

The corners of Nicholas' mouth turned up into a crooked smile. "How quickly she changed from maid of your dreams to angry feline."

187

Christopher rubbed his eyes. "I got hold of the purse strap and tried to yank it away from her, just as the blonde beast approached and grabbed my doublet. While she scratched at me, he threw me down and got away with my knapsack. The two of them disappeared down an alleyway. What a team. God pity unsuspecting travelers."

"You lost your purse and knapsack?"

"They got away with everything. I saw ruffians about, so I fled. To top it off, I realized I forgot my mother's crock here at the tavern. I came by to see if perchance it was still here, and the place was closed. I had no money for a room, so I slept on the street last night—if you could call it sleep. Let's just say I slept with one eye open."

"That explains everything." Nicholas tore a piece of bread from a small loaf and stuffed it in his mouth.

"How could I be such an idiot?" Christopher slammed the table with his fist, rattling the dishes. The couple next to them stared. He glowered until they turned away.

"Perhaps we should go home. Already you're penniless, and I don't have enough for both of us."

"Nonsense. I'll ask if the crock is here and, regardless, I'll find work in London. My uncle lives here. He can help us."

"But you don't want anything to do with Lollards. Your uncle is Lollard from head to toe, isn't he?"

"Do you have to look for obstacles? We arrived just last night, and you're ready to turn and run. Let's not forget why we came here." Christopher yawned.

"Not forget why we came here? You forgot the first night! What will you do for money?"

"First, I'll inquire about the crock. Then we can call upon Uncle Nathan. He might have work to offer, or know of someone who does."

"I don't know. This is going to be more challenging that we thought."

"Look. If you turn back now, you'll never know what might have been. This is our chance. Think of our fathers. Mine will be weaving, and yours will be bricklaying until they're too old and stiff to move. Is that what you want? My father will never leave Dartford. Every day is the same for him. We're here. Let's not squander our chance."

"Ask about the crock. I'll decide from there."

Christopher waited for the tapster to pass by and tugged on the young man's arm. "I left a crock here last night just before closing time. Are you aware of anything of the sort?"

The tapster plunked a tray full of soiled dishes on the table and wiped his hands on his apron. "Crock? Off the top of my head, I know of nothing. Let me check." He disappeared through the kitchen to the rubbish bin behind the restaurant and pushed the crock he'd hidden the night before as far to the bottom as he could. After making sure it was well-hidden, he hurried back to the table.

"No one reported anything of the sort. Last night, it was?"

Christopher nodded. "I left it sitting on the table over there." He pointed to the table where he and Nicholas sat the night before.

"Check back later, if you wish. I'll keep an eye out for it." The tapster shrugged his shoulders, picked up the tray and disappeared into the kitchen.

"Now what?" Nicholas sighed. "How will you survive in London with no money?"

"I'll speak with my uncle."

"And if he can't help?"

"We'll go from there."

"I suppose I can help you for a day or two." Nicholas breathed out an annoyed sigh. "But beyond that, we'll both go under."

"Things will work to our favor." Christopher spoke to convince himself as much as Nicholas. "They have to."

Bordeaux

Thomas rolled the Virgin Mary statue he was carving back and forth between his hands, the words of Saint Francis of Assisi illuminating his thoughts: *Start by doing what's necessary; then do what's possible; and suddenly you are doing the impossible.* He had grown to love Saint Francis as he loved Saint Thomas Becket. By God's grace, he was doing the impossible, from fleeing England, to hunting truffles, to carving high-quality souvenirs, to running his own stand in Bordeaux along the Way of Saint James. *Take that, King Henry*, he thought. *God shall always have the last word.*

If only his father could know that what had seemed like a tragedy had turned into a blessing. Thomas bowed his head to thank Saint Thomas for bringing him this far. Ah, but life had an interesting way of unfolding. In the midst of turmoil he might have said life had an interesting way of unraveling—but today, he saw life unfolding in all its glory. He smiled and shook his head. Nothing could circumvent God's providence. How easily one forgot God's goodness, doubted the divine power, and became angry at the harshness of life when one did not know the good things the future held. To top it off, God placed Charlotte in his path when he was not even looking for a wife. He eased his knife into the soft wood. The mysteries of God surpassed man's understanding.

"What do you think, Charlotte? Is she ready to be painted?" He lifted up the statue so Charlotte, nursing their infant son across the room, could see it.

"I think she needs a bit more definition on the mouth. She looks sad. I think she would be happy to have a son. I know how happy I am to have ours." She gazed into the face of the infant at her bosom, stroking his cheek with her forefinger and rocking him gently. "Yes, my little angel. I am so happy to have you." The baby cooed and smiled. "You will be a good brother for Gabrielle."

"But the virgin is never shown smiling. Perhaps customers will think it unbecoming, and not buy the statue." He held the statue in front of him to study her facial expression.

"Don't you think she would be happy to be a chosen vessel in the hands of God?"

"She's unhappy because she knows what her son will suffer."

"But she knows the ending. He will be resurrected, never to suffer again." She kissed her babe on the cheek.

"To suffer is to suffocate, *ma chère*, and to see a loved one suffer is no less painful. Pain can asphyxiate the soul. When one is suffocating, one thinks of nothing but the need for air, not of picking flowers."

"I suppose you're right. Why doesn't God skip the suffering, and offer us only happy times, if that is where we will end up anyway?"

"If I had never struggled for breath, I would not appreciate being able to breathe." Thomas studied the statue's expression.

Charlotte sat in silent contemplation for several seconds. "Say what you will, I think the Blessed Mother should look happier. She rejoiced at the angel Gabriel's news that God chose her to be the mother of God. What greater joy could anyone have than to hold the son of God in her arms, to see God's promise fulfilled?"

Thomas picked up a whittling tool and carved around the mouth of his figurine, working the lips into a slight smile while Charlotte continued to nurse their son. After a few minutes he blew away the shavings and held it up triumphantly.

"There," he said. "What do you think?"

"Much better," she responded. "And you, my little man," she teased, tickling Anatole's stomach. "What lies ahead for you?" The baby smiled. "Look at him. He has your smile."

"And he has your good humor." Thomas polished the statue with a cloth, deep in thought. "I think it is better not to know what lies ahead. If we knew what we must pass through, we might live in constant dread."

"Thomas, listen to you. You like to remind me how God guided your pathway to Bordeaux, to me, and to making souvenirs. If you hadn't passed through your hardships, you wouldn't be here now."

"Yes, but sometimes the hardships tempt me to fear what may yet lie ahead." He sighed. "And Anatole…I don't want him to suffer. But I know he will, as we all do."

Gazing into the babe's eyes, she sighed, "I don't want to think about that. Let us enjoy him today, and we'll put his tomorrows in God's hands. Anatole— his name means *daybreak*. We must teach him to always raise his eyes to the light."

She had a way of saying just the right thing, the words of comfort Thomas needed. She was right. He would enjoy this moment, and remember God's miracles.

London

In the silver light of dusk, Christopher rapped on the door of a three-story tenement just off Cheapside in central London. The man who cracked it open squinted, able to distinguish only his visitors' silhouettes in the darkness. He bore a strong resemblance to William Wade.

"Prithee, what can I do for you lads? If you're here to inquire about Bible study, I must tell you we no longer hold Bible study here."

"Why, 'tis you we're looking for." Christopher removed his cap.

"And who might you be, lad?" Nathan stretched his neck forward.

"'Tis Christopher. Father and I were here when we attended Bartholomew Fair."

"Let me fetch a candle. Prithee, wait one moment." Nathan locked the door. A woman inside could be heard inquiring as to who was outside. Christopher heard Nathan say he didn't know.

Nicholas leaned to Christopher's ear and whispered, "I thought you knew this man."

The door inched open. No sooner did Nathan hold up the candle than his face brightened. "Oh, my heavens, yes! I beg your pardon. You caught me off my guard. Please, come in." He pushed aside a spool of thread on the kitchen table and invited the visitors to be seated at a bench. After setting the candle on the table, he leaned against the wall and wiped his brow with a handkerchief. The woman was nowhere in sight.

"Forgive me, lads. I believe the pressure is getting to me. Ever since they caught our rector preaching Lutheranism, they keep a watchful eye on us. The streets have ears, I tell you."

"Spies?" Christopher and Nicholas glanced sideways at one another.

"The first commandment declares that our God is a jealous God, but let me tell you, King Henry has him beat. Doesn't want a subject putting God above him. I've already said too much, lads. Prithee, pretend you didn't hear that. Enough of the—what shall I call it?—unpleasantries. You survived the fair, I see? Are you here with your father?"

Christopher shook his head. "My friend Nicholas and I came to find work in London."

As his probing gaze worked its way downward from Nicholas' soiled felt cap to his worn leather shoes, Nathan determined the lad appeared respectable enough. "I see. Methought you were weaving with your father?"

Fidgeting his cap between his fingers, Christopher confessed, "I thought it best to strike out on my own."

"Oh?" Nathan's brows sunk downward.

"We arrived yesterday, and spent last night in Southwark. I thought you might know of someone who could use our skills. I can weave, of course, and Nicholas is a bricklayer. He worked on the king's manor house in Dartford after the priory was torn down."

"Weaving and brickwork. Let me think." He tapped his fingers on his thigh. "I know many in the Clothworker's Guild; in fact, some of the best cloth markets are located here in Honey Lane Parish. I may be able to find something for you, but I can't make any assurances. As for brickwork, I'll have to inquire, as nothing comes immediately to mind. Are you lads willing to do anything? I don't mean to discourage you, but London is overrun with young lads seeking a living."

Christopher and Nicholas looked at each other and nodded.

Christopher continued, "Do you know where we might find affordable lodging while we're seeking work?"

192

Nathan scratched his head. "There again, lads, London is overrun with vagrants and folks who can't find work in the countryside. Do you have much money?"

"A few pounds." Nicholas patted the pouch around his waist to make sure it was still in place. "Given London's size, we fancied finding work would be an easy task."

"Not so, I'm afraid." Nathan glanced at the meager knapsack on the floor next to Nicholas, his eyes shifting back and forth from one lad to another. "Have you brought any provisions with you—blankets and such?"

Christopher nodded. "Nicholas has some money and a few possessions. An unsavory sort of maiden in Southwark robbed me of my few things. I left a crock of money my mother gave me at a tavern, and had no luck when I went back for it." Hearing himself explain, Christopher felt nakedly irresponsible.

Nathan crossed his arms. With a grimace, he responded, "Very unfortunate indeed. In Southwark one expects to encounter ruffians of all sorts, but London also has its share. We'll see what we can round up." He took a deep breath, as if summoning his resolve. "You're welcome to lodge a few days with Lucy and me."

Christopher shook his head. "We don't wish to take advantage of your kindness. We're willing to work for our keep." Nathan appeared relieved.

At the sound of his stomach rumbling, Nicholas blushed.

"Hungry, lads?" Nathan chuckled. "Lucy has a fresh kettle of pottage in the kitchen. Come along to the back." He picked up his candlestick. Christopher and Nicholas hesitated, not wanting to appear overeager to take advantage of Nathan's generosity. "Don't be bashful, now. Lucy loves to fatten folks up. Follow me."

Nathan led them through a narrow corridor, out a back door and along a stone walkway, to a small brick kitchen behind the main dwelling. A garden plot lined the walkway.

"Lucy!" Nathan called out while approaching the building.

A petite woman, her auburn hair tucked under a white bonnet, peeked her head out the door. Perspiration on her face reflected the candlelight. "By my faith, what is it?"

"We have visitors. Do you recall Christopher, my nephew who visited during the fair?"

"Of course," she replied. "Prithee, come in. 'Tis a bit hot and smoky in here, but I trust it to be better than standing in the damp cold."

Inside the kitchen, the familiar aromas of rosemary and thyme permeated the steamy air, transporting Christopher home to Elizabeth dipping up hot pottage while he and William sat at the table. A crackling fire bathed the room in a comforting glow. Homesickness tugged at him. He pushed the forlorn feeling away.

"Have a seat, lads. Let me fetch some bowls." Lucy scurried to a handmade cupboard about her height to retrieve four wooden bowls and four pewter soup spoons. A round table just ample enough to seat the four of them stood in a corner by the fireplace. "Nathan, pull the table out, would you? If I'd known we were to be expecting company I would have been better prepared." She cast her husband a scolding glance.

"The lads arrived in the city just tonight." Nathan pulled out the table, cringing when its legs screeched across the wood floor planks. "Said they spent last night in Southwark. Christopher stumbled upon a cutpurse in Bankside who took his knapsack, and someone stole his crock. The lads are nearly penniless now. Looking for work, they are."

She frowned at the pottage while stirring. "Well that's no way to arrive, I tell you. You lads are finished before you've begun." Although intended to offer empathy, her comment struck a discouraging note with Christopher. She ladled steaming soup into the bowls and delivered them to the table one by one. "Would anyone be wanting oatcakes with his pottage?" Several round flatbreads showed up in a basket on the table before anyone could answer, joining a pitcher of ale drawn before the men arrived. "Oh me, I almost forgot the butter," she lamented. She retrieved her butter crock from the windowsill, and set it on the table before taking her place on a stool across from her husband. With a sigh, she tucked a loose strand of hair under her bonnet.

"The lads are wondering if I know of anyone who needs laborers." Nathan blew on a spoonful of pottage. Lazy curls of steam floated toward the ceiling. "Can you think of anyone?"

Nicholas appeared to be lost in his bowl of pottage. Lucy nudged the basket of cakes in his direction. "Our children all presently work as apprentices, save for Natalia; she's a housemaid for James Fitzgibbon, a draper on Fleet Street. Next time I see her I'll inquire as to whether her employer needs able-bodied young laborers."

"When do you expect you shall see her next?" Christopher took a sip of pottage.

"She has a day off next week. I plan to meet her to do some shopping."

194

At the prospect of waiting a week before learning of any job prospects, Christopher's heart sank.

"I supply linen to several cloth merchants in the city," Nathan offered. "I'll inquire about laborer needs at our next guild meeting." Sensing Christopher and Nicholas' anxiety, he added, "Our next meeting is tomorrow afternoon. You're welcome to join me if you'd like. Then the men can meet you personally." Their faces brightened. "Until then, you lads are welcome to sleep on pallets here in the kitchen. 'Tis a bit drafty, but I reckon it better than sleeping among cutpurses in Southwark. I regret not being able to offer you better accommodations."

"Don't think of it." Christopher savored a tender morsel of pork. "We're grateful for your hospitality."

As an afterthought, Nathan added, "Say, after the guild meeting, I'll be going to hear the Fair Gospeler speak. Have you heard of her?"

"Nary a word," Nicholas replied. His curiosity piqued, he added, "Fair Gospeler?"

"Her fame is quite established here in London. Lady Askew is lovely to look upon—hence the nickname. Close to you lads in age, as well. You might find her intriguing."

Wishing to garner favor, Christopher feared turning down the offer, but the mention of a religious gathering rendered him mute. Nicholas accepted for them both.

Lucy shook her head. "I know why you men go. 'Tis not so much to hear the Bible expounded, as to look upon a pretty face."

A sheepish grin crossed Nathan's face. "I suppose some might be guilty of that. You should come, Lucy. Join us tomorrow."

"You'll never catch me at such a meeting. Not a chance." Lucy pushed the butter toward Christopher. "Not a chance," she repeated, her lips pursed.

ଓ

Christopher studied the boisterous crowd gathered in front of Saint Mary le Bow church. Most in attendance were simple folk—laborers, apprentices. Two men in front of him conversed loudly, apparently unconcerned that others could hear.

"Marry!" one of them quipped, running his fat fingers through the thin black beard dangling from his chin. "A woman preacher. I had to see it to believe it." Twitching his lips, he adjusted his red feathered flat cap.

"She preaches against the king's religion. Won't last long, by my faith," the other replied. He tugged up on his tights, twisted his moustache and scanned the crowd, judging himself superior in comparison. His gaze came to rest on a comely, twenty-something brunette atop the stairs whose dress and manners identified her as a lady of means.

Christopher watched the captivating brunette about his age prepare to address the gathering. At the sound of her voice, the crowd fell silent.

"Good folk, the papists would have you believe bread blessed by the priest becomes the very real body of Christ. Yet if that same bread were left on the table, within a few weeks' time it would be moldy. Would Christ's body mold? Reason tells us not. Indeed, the bread and wine are but a symbol of Christ's body and blood, nothing more or less."

Murmurs rippled through the audience. From the back of the crowd, a greying man with bushy sideburns lifted his chin and shouted, "You contradict the king's doctrine."

Lady Anne Askew elevated her voice above the throng, raising Tyndale's Bible in her right hand. "Read it here, Sir, in God's own word."

He backed away as if she were offering poison. "Heresy!" he cried.

She ignored the detractor and continued, "God spoke in symbols, yet plainly. He called himself the living vine, the door, the lamb. He wasn't in very deed these things; they're but representations of qualities embodied in him. When he took the bread and said, 'This is my body, eat in remembrance of me,' he meant it as a symbol of his sacrifice."

"I wouldn't touch that book!" the heckler shrieked. "'Tis for God's anointed to teach God's word. A pox upon you!" He hobbled away.

Christopher and Nicholas looked sideways at one another before returning their attention to Lady Askew. Elbowing his friend Nicholas whispered, "Are you thinking what I'm thinking?"

"What are you thinking?" Christopher kept his eyes on the beautiful creature in front of him.

"She looks to be near our age. Why would she risk her life to preach against the Six Articles?"

Christopher whispered, "Only a fool would speak against the king's doctrine. But she doesn't appear to be a fool. If more heretics looked like her, I might be tempted to believe."

"You lads have noticed." Nathan grinned, amused.

"Shh." Christopher put a finger to his lips.

"If a mouse were to eat the bread," Lady Askew continued, "would the mouse find salvation? No, the bread is but a symbol of our Lord's body. 'Twould be sacrilege for a mouse to sup from our Lord's flesh."

Christopher leaned toward Nathan. "What prompts her to speak out so boldly?"

"Some—mostly papists—say she is mad. Her love of the gospel drives her to preach fearlessly, despite some who say women shouldn't preach at all."

Christopher took a moment to digest his uncle's words. "How can she be so sure she speaks the truth? Is it the king's truth, the pope's, or the Lollards' truth?"

"Her message comes straight from God's holy word." Nathan kept his eyes upon her when he spoke, his countenance radiant.

Turning to Nathan, Christopher whispered, "My guess is the menfolk listen because she's beautiful. I thought most Lollards were men like my father. She's pleasantly proved me wrong."

Nathan corrected him. "She's no Lollard, as you call it."

"A heretic in any skin is still a heretic. I came to London to get away from them."

"You won't escape the new ideas here," Nathan retorted. "Come to a meeting with me tomorrow night. You might be surprised at who you meet among these so-called heretics."

"What sort of meeting?"

"A group of us meets to discuss the new learning. The tired old views of the papists will soon be a thing of the past. 'Tis the dawn of a new day."

"I have no desire to watch folks fight over the ways of God. I wash my hands of it all."

"Fighting over the ways of God? Hardly! We discuss ideas of the great thinkers of antiquity, the Greeks and Romans, Paul the apostle, Christ himself."

Will she be there?" Christopher glanced at Askew.

"I can't promise anything, but she will most likely be."

"Where and wh—?"

A booming male voice cried, "Make way for the sheriff!" interrupting Christopher's question.

Folks parted right and left. Silence fell over the multitude, accentuating the heavy clip-clop of boots on cobble. Lady Askew paused in her conversation with a hunchbacked elderly woman to face the law enforcer.

"By orders of His Majesty," the sheriff decreed, "I place you under arrest."

197

Askew fixed her gaze on his wide-set brown eyes. "For what crime do you arrest me? I've done nothing but speak truth from this book, the very words our Lord spoke when he was on the earth." A small pocket of applause broke out.

"Heresy and sedition," he replied, his jaw stiff.

"God bless you, Lady Askew." The voice belonged to a cordwainer in his mid-twenties. Christopher had passed him many times on Cheapside.

"Thank you, good lad," Lady Askew replied, waving. As the sheriff placed shackles on her wrists, she cried, "If it is a crime to speak against falsehood, I'm guilty. I can't but speak the truth. 'Tis an honor to suffer for my Lord."

"If it is suffering you seek, you've found it." The sheriff glanced over his shoulder. "Where are your friends?" The multitude had dispersed, leaving only a few curious lingerers.

Lady Askew raised her shackled hands and pointed at Christopher. "There." A gentle smile warmed her face. His heart sank.

"Are you a follower of this heretic?" The sheriff sized him up.

His face pale, Christopher stammered, "I never met this woman. I only came to see what the hurly-burly is about." The disappointment in Askew's eyes racked him with guilt.

"If you know what's good for you," the sheriff warned, "you'll stay away from heretic gatherings. If I see you at another, I'll have to conclude you're one of them. And who is this?" The sheriff pointed his nose at Nicholas.

Nicholas blinked, his heart catching in his throat. "Mister Hall, Sir. We're visiting from Dartford. We were told of Lady Askew, and simply wanted to see her for ourselves."

"You made a long trek to join up with Lutherans. Do yourselves a favor. Stay as far away as you can. London offers less dangerous merriment. Now, be on your way."

"Yes, Sir."

Christopher, Nicholas and Nathan were strolling along Cheapside toward Nathan's home, when a tap on Christopher's shoulder stole his breath.

"Bread Street, is it?" It was the cordwainer.

Christopher looked at the young man blankly. Nathan stepped forward. "Yes," he whispered. "My place, nine o'clock, tomorrow eve."

"I'll be there." The lad disappeared down an alley way.

"But they arrested her," Christopher said, searching Nathan's eyes. "What is the point?"

"They've arrested Lady Askew, but the truth is grander than one person. Look what they did to Luther, Tyndale and the others, hoping to silence the truth tellers. Truth can't be extinguished; it will only smolder until it reignites even brighter. The persecution of Christ's followers fans the flames of a fire that can't be stopped. I hope they'll question and release her, and we'll have her to preach to us again."

Nicholas stopped to face Nathan. "I don't know what I think about all of this. Could we discuss it more?" A light danced in Nathan's eyes.

"Oh, no you don't!" Christopher objected. "I came to London to escape such nonsense."

"Then go on ahead," Nicholas retorted, "while your uncle and I talk."

"I hope spies aren't following you." Christopher accelerated his pace.

Nicholas and Nathan strolled along Cheapside at a leisurely pace. "He's very bitter," Nicholas explained. "In Dartford, the label of Lollard's son hardened him. He felt unfairly branded because of his father. The desire for a new start brought him here, and now he finds his hopes threatened."

Nathan scratched his chin. "'Tis unfortunate. My brother is a good man. He would never intend for Christopher to suffer. I suppose Christopher will have to make his way through the thorns strewn in his path, as we all do."

"I worry about him." Nicholas stooped down to pick up a ha'-penny on the street, tucked it in his pouch and continued. "There's a maiden he fancies here in London, whose father sent her away from Dartford, all because of Mister Wade's reputation as a Lollard. 'Twas the final straw. I hope he finds her here, and luck will go his way this time."

Nathan smiled. "Ah, a maiden can drive a young man to madness."

"Indeed." Nicholas continued in silence.

 egg

"Are these the lads you told us about at the guild meeting?"

Nathan nodded. "They're staying with me until they can find work and lodging."

A stocky, muscular man extended a hand, first to Christopher and then to Nathan. Christopher found the man's presence intimidating, though if asked to explain why he would struggle to do so. Perhaps it had to do with the man's sheer size, but there was also a stiffness in the way he carried himself that lent him an air of inflexibility.

199

"Name's Johnson. Barnard Johnson. I need able hands in the meat market. Not pleasant work, to be frank, but 'twill give you a start. I have a tenement you can stay in, with a fair wage and some scrap meat. Can you come with me for a look?"

They nodded in unison.

"Follow me."

Ten minutes into the fifteen-minute walk from Bread Street to Smithfield, the stench of animal excrement greeted Christopher's nostrils.

"You've been here before?" Johnson stretched his hand toward the market, noting the grimace on Christopher's face. "Then you know a bit about the tasks necessary—shoveling manure, dumping entrails, cleaning counters, draining blood. Not dainty work, as I said, but necessary to the workings of the market. Does it interest you?"

They shrugged their shoulders. Christopher fought the urge to retch while he watched a boy of about thirteen dump a bucket of blood in a shallow ditch.

"You're hired, then. Be here tomorrow at three o'clock."

Christopher raised his eyebrows. "In the morning?" Nicholas jabbed an elbow in his side.

Barnard frowned. "Will that pose a problem?"

"To tell you the…"

"Of course not," Nicholas interceded.

"The tenement is this way." They tagged along behind Master Johnson down a dingy, narrow street, where neglected buildings scowled at them as they passed by. A section of structures tilted precipitously, defying a strong wind to topple them. Nicholas cast a sideways glance at Christopher.

They passed two urchins, a girl and boy who looked to have bathed in dirt, scolding a Bartholomew baby in front of a mud-splattered tenement door. The children stared at the trespassers as if they'd never seen another human. The boy stopped playing and asked, "Who are you?" Johnson ignored him and continued a few doors further.

After selecting a key from his voluminous key ring, he brushed a large spider web away from the knob. The displaced spider raced for dear life up the splintered door frame. Turning the key in the lock, Johnson pushed the door open with his toe. Rotting wood at the bottom of the door crumbled under the pressure. "There you go." He ushered them in.

Christopher gulped.

May, 1545

—

Nicholas drew back his right arm and closed his left eye. A ball made from the tip of a stocking, filled with dirt and knotted closed, flew past Christopher and hit its target: a one-inch cockroach racing across the base of the wall. The vermin landed upside-down on the floor with its legs up, joining a score of others that had already met the same fate.

"Got it," he said proudly, waving the ball. "Cockroach cannon." He jumped up to retrieve his handmade weapon, crossed the room, and sat back down on the floor to continue his sport.

"I've had it," he declared. "I'm heading back to Dartford."

Christopher feared Nicholas meant it this time. "But we came here to find our fortune," he argued. "I intend to keep my part of our agreement."

"Bad luck has plagued us since we arrived. You're perpetually penniless, and I want to get back home while I have the means. Besides, London isn't what I expected."

"What did you expect? We've been here only two months. How can you give up so soon?"

"There's nothing here for me. I'd rather return home and lay bricks with my father than shovel manure and stain my hands in bloody entrails. I desperately need a better wage. Yesterday I stopped to buy a bag of cornmeal, and it cost me twice what I last paid. The king's debasement is taking a toll. Look at us."

Putrid air from the street outside seeped in through a large gap in the door frame, a morbid complement to the odor of mildew clinging to the tenement walls. Despite regular sweepings, rat droppings stubbornly reappeared in one corner. Circular ceiling stains marked spots that leaked during the almost daily downpours.

Christopher held his ground. "I won't go back. I would regret your leaving, but do what you must. Good fortune lies ahead of me yet. I feel it in my bones.

I met a dockworker at The Anchor last night who said he could get me hired on a Dutch galley to Bordeaux. 'Twill be several weeks' work, with room and board included. The adventure will be even better than the wages. Think of it, getting paid to travel to France and back! Ship work will get us out of this rat-infested tenement. Or would you rather go back to Dartford and be a measly bricklayer? France?" He held his left palm open in front of him. "Or Dartford?" He held out his right palm and moved his hands up and down, weighing the options. "Which will it be?"

With a chuckle, Nicholas tossed the ball in the air and caught it. "You never give up, do you? I honestly don't know whether to admire your importunity, or detest it." He aimed the ball at Christopher's chest.

Christopher ducked just in time. He picked up the ball and lobbed it back.

"Relations between England and France are frigid at the moment," Nicholas said, tossing the makeshift ball back and forth in his hands. "Are you sure you want to venture over dangerous seas to a hostile land? Besides," he smirked, "I hear French men dress like maids."

Christopher snickered. "I'll see for myself, and report back to you. Could labor on a merchant ship be any more hostile than the rats, cut-throats, and heretic hunters that surround us now? Besides—'tis a Dutch ship. They're not involved in the king's war with France."

"Have you thought about pirates or shipwrecks? What if they seize you and hold you in France, like English merchants in Spain? Any number of misfortunes could befall you. But if you return to Dartford, you'll soon take over the weaving and have a good living. Your father told you when you left that he intended to turn it all over to you. Are you willing to trade security for an unknown future?"

"I doubt my father would even speak to me after the way I left. Besides, the future is never truly secure. We could be robbed and murdered on our way back to Dartford."

"Anyone who robs you will be worse off than he started."

"Thank you for reminding me." Christopher reflected on his sparse possessions: a cloak, a threadbare blanket, and a couple changes of clothing. "I never fancied this would be easy. I'm not going back to Dartford. Circumstances could take a turn for the better any day. And besides, how will your new heretic friends abide without you?"

Although a couple of clever retorts coursed through his mind, Nicholas bit his tongue and stared at the dirt floor. Several icy seconds later he lifted his head, waited for Christopher's eyes to meet his and demanded, "Does seeking the truth make me a heretic?"

Disarmed by the penetrating look in Nicholas' eyes, Christopher stammered, "I was only kidding. But since you brought it up, whose truth do you seek? Seems to me, folks have different ideas about it all. His Majesty is happy to snuff out anyone who disagrees, so why waste your time with heretics? Eat, drink and be merry, for tomorrow we die."

"I can't forget the fire in Lady Askew's eyes, or the light of her countenance. What makes a young maid willing to risk her life to proclaim her convictions?"

"Lunacy? Intelligent folks shun heretics for a reason. They're lunatics, can't you see? Their fervor defies reason. They're zealous to spout off about a god they've never seen—that no one has ever seen. They bring shame upon their families, ruin their own reputations, and risk their livelihoods with blind allegiance to fables. 'Tis lunacy, pure and simple. Get that through your skull. Why else would folks be willing to go to prison for an invisible being that fails to rescue them or protect them from harm? They claim this being is all-powerful, all-loving, yet he sits silently by in their hour of need, while they go to their death praising his name. Lunacy." Satisfied that his words struck a chord, Christopher folded his arms over his chest and leaned back against the wall.

Nicholas reached into his purse and pulled out a small cloth sack. From it, he retrieved two candied figs. "Have you tried these?" he extended one to Christopher. "I got them at the market yesterday." Tearing a fig in half between his teeth, Nicholas continued, "I've inquired about Anne Askew. Her husband cast her out, upon her priest's advice, for adhering to Luther's ideas. Time on the streets was supposed to cure her. Instead, she came to London seeking a divorce, and preached to anyone who would listen. What would motivate a woman to do such?" With wonder in his eyes, he mused, "A married maid in London, preaching. Think of it! How did she eat? Where did she stay? Most maids would crawl back to their husbands. Not this one."

Christopher bit off half a fig and held the other half up for examination. "Delicious," he commented, popping it in his mouth. He reached for another one and continued. "Look at you. We came to London for a new start, yet the heretics have their claws in you already. What did they tell you at that meeting?"

"Things I'd never considered, from the faults of the Romish church to a man's right to reason for himself." He put the second half of the fig in his mouth and rolled it between his cheek and gums.

"To the king, your words are heresy. If you voiced these things to a priest or bishop, 'twould be the end of you."

"Not so. Many good priests, bishops and monks agree, and would give their lives for the new learning. In fact, many already have. Yet Christ never had anyone put to death for his beliefs. If God himself allows a man free thought, who is man to take it away?"

"The king is God's representative on earth."

"What of unjust kings? Does God ordain wickedness? Think of it. Few dare voice these things out loud."

"These folks you met with are dangerous. They preach sedition. Listen to yourself. They're challenging the very foundations of empires. If these notions you speak of were to gain hold, the world would be turned on its head."

Nicholas rose and paced in the small space. "Christ himself spoke of making men free. 'Tis no wonder popes and kings are threatened when God's word is put into the hands of everyday folks. Imagine! Such ideas threaten their very existence."

Shaking his head, Christopher responded, "I fear being caught in your company, the way you're spouting these heretical notions. If you value your life, stay away from those meetings."

Nicholas stopped pacing and lowered his voice. "Consider this. If a king rules in wickedness, would a just God oblige His subjects to support him?" He paused to pick up his ball and launched it at a cockroach in the corner. The bug fell to the floor and wiggled for a few seconds, then lay perfectly still on its back with its legs in the air. "Why would God keep the very book that contains his laws from the people he intends to have them? Such a notion defies reason, and makes the popish religion a lie."

Christopher's eyes narrowed. "Challenging the king's right to rule his subjects? Are you ready to take your place at the stake along with all the other heretics? Come with me to Bordeaux. Earn some money, see new places. 'Twill give you a whole new outlook."

Nicholas shook his head. "Count me out. But I'll stay here with you until you're on your way to France. Then I'm returning to Dartford."

Dartford

William inspected the loom's faulty heddle and cursed under his breath. As he pulled his hand away, his middle finger skimmed a sliver on the cross beam. A drop of blood landed on the satin weave in the loom before he could get his finger to his mouth.

"By God's teeth," he snarled.

"What's the matter?" Elizabeth looked up from her spinning wheel.

"A heddle broke yesterday, and I need to buy a replacement. I can ill afford a day with the loom down. And I just caught my finger on a splinter."

"Tinker with the heddle. You're able to fix things when you've a mind to."

"No, I've done all I can. There's just no way around it. I need to borrow some money from your crock. I'll replace it after Market Day."

Elizabeth flinched, keeping her eyes fixed on the spinning wheel. "I'll need to look for it, dear."

"It's on the mantle, isn't it? Where you always keep it? I need the money now. My production will be halted until I can get the heddle fixed." William glanced up at the mantle. The money crock was missing. In its stead stood a prized clay jug painted with vines from Saintonge, France, passed down by Elizabeth's mother. He rushed to the fireplace and shuffled a carved wooden sheep, several candles, a vase with sprigs of dried lavender, and the French jug.

Spinning around, he demanded, "Where is it?"

With her eyes fixed on the wheel, she muttered, "You'll scold me if I tell you."

He shuffled toward her. "Elizabeth, what did you do with the crock?"

After several seconds' hesitation she admitted, "I gave it to Christopher when he left."

With a heavy sigh of disapproval, he wrung his hands together and paced in front of the fireplace. "Supporting the lad in his debauchery, you are. What were you thinking? He probably squandered the money at the first tavern he passed. I thought we agreed, he would have to find his way. He chose the thorny path; now let him experience it."

She let go of the thread she was spinning and watched him until he stopped pacing. A proper woman obeyed her husband, but she could no longer hold her thoughts inside. Her eyes met his. "I told you not to take him to the tavern when he was a young lad. Then you carted him off to London and exposed him to all manner of debauchery at the fair." Her voice faltering, she bit her bottom lip and continued. "Look at him. He got a taste for the knave life and now he's run off. It's not his fault. I couldn't send him off empty-handed. What would he eat? Where would he stay? Does it hurt to help him get off with a few coins to his name?"

205

"Are you blaming me for the lad's debauchery? No, that's not the trouble. You never let that lad learn from his foolery. How will I fix the loom now? If I can't get it fixed, we'll have almost nothing to sell at market this week. I've spent all day tinkering with it. Tomorrow is Wednesday, and once I have the proper parts it will take me some time to fix it. That puts me into Friday before I can start weaving, assuming I can get the part."

William sat at the loom and tapped his fingers on the breast beam, while Elizabeth continued the argument in her mind. Who could fault a mother for helping her own son? She shuffled to the fireplace to stir the turnip stew simmering on the coals for supper.

With her back turned, she chided, "It was just a wee bit of money. Not enough to trouble yourself with. Besides, what is the story of the prodigal? The father welcomed him with a fatted calf."

He glared at the back of her head. "That was after the boy came to his senses, not before. You don't understand. Since Christopher left, I can't keep up as before. I had to borrow money to rent a booth at Saint Bartholomew's Fair, and I used the loom as collateral. Mr. Tunsdale is demanding payment by Friday, or he's going to take the loom. With no loom, we have no livelihood."

She dropped her stirring spoon in the kettle and jerked her hand away from the boiling liquid. "You used the loom as collateral and didn't tell me?"

"I felt I had no choice. I was backed into a corner."

Peering into the kettle, Elizabeth demanded, "Why does Mister Tunsdale insist on havin' payment now? Why can't he give you more time?"

William tinkered with the heddle, biting his lower lip. "I'm not sure, but I have my suspicions. He knows I led a Bible study group, and I once overheard him saying he would take down every last Lollard."

"You're an honest man. You haven't harmed anyone."

"We're a threat to the papists' livelihood. They live in palaces while humble folk labor to support them. They deny the saving ordinances of God to folks who can't pay their fees. You must understand their hatred. They want us gone. Gone."

Elizabeth retrieved the submerged spoon and laid it on the hearth before crossing the room to her bed. She stretched out atop the coverlet on her side, her back to William.

At her first sniffle, he made his way to the door. "I'm going out for some fresh air," he mumbled.

She didn't bother to turn around.

June, 1545

—

"The antichrists wish to silence us!" Watching heads bob in agreement, Nicholas judged the tunic-clad blacksmith who made the statement to be near thirty. The blacksmith raised a calloused hand and continued, "What are we to do? For the sake of peace, would it be better to go along with the king's edicts?"

"Methinks we must stand our ground." In the congested room, Nicholas couldn't determine to whom the female voice belonged.

"By God's blood, we stand!" cried a well-dressed, middle-aged scrivener leaning against the wall. Thunderous applause rewarded his statement.

They all speak with the same passion, Nicholas mused, thinking it a shame that Christopher chose to waste the pleasant summer evening at The Anchor tavern in Southwark. Many of the faces in the room were familiar patrons of Smithfield meat market and alehouses about London. The host, a wool merchant by the name of Master Pembroke, leaned in a doorway, arms folded, nodding in agreement.

"I pray you, bear with me a moment," the blacksmith announced abruptly. "I'm told we have a visitor. Feel free to chat while I sort this out." He stepped aside to converse with a grocer whom Nicholas once saw unloading books from a chest at a home on Honey Lane.

As Nicholas scanned the crowd, a face with an air of familiarity stopped him. While she watched the goings-on at the front of the room, he studied her features—nutmeg hair, sage-colored eyes, and a light sprinkling of freckles that danced across the bridge of her nose. Over a linen chemise, she wore a yellow kirtle that laced up in the front. His heart skipped a beat. He pressed his way through the crowd. She turned toward him before he reached her and gasped, a wave of recognition brightening her eyes.

"Anne Cooper? It is still Cooper?" He extended his hand.

"Still Cooper. Are you still Nicholas Hall?" she teased, giving his hand a soft squeeze. She looked up into his eyes. The last time she saw him in Dartford they stood eye-to-eye, his clothing hanging on him like a tent. Before her now stood a well-built young man.

"What are you doing here?" he stammered, mesmerized at the woman who had replaced the maiden from Dartford.

"I could ask you the same." Her eyes smiled. "You've changed."

He tugged at the hem of his doublet and glanced down at his shoes, horrified to see a small hole in the left toe. Red-faced, he replied, "To tell you the truth, I'm wondering whether I should be here or not. If a man is judged by the company he keeps, this could be dubious company indeed."

"I came to hear Lady Askew. I find her spellbinding."

"Have you come to such gatherings before?"

"Yes, many." After an awkward pause, she asked, "What brings you to London?"

"I came with Christopher this spring. We wanted to spread our wings, I suppose. The notion sounded good at the time."

"Christopher is here?"

"Well, not *here*, here. But here in London. He had other plans tonight that didn't include—how did he put it—heretic baitings."

"I hardly think of our meetings as heretic baitings." Anne looked to the front of the room. Reassured that she wasn't missing anything, she returned her attention to Nicholas. "Why would you leave Dartford? You both had a good livelihood waiting."

He wagged his head. "You would scarcely recognize the place. After the injunctions abolished pilgrimages and the priory closed, folks had their livings destroyed, just like that." He snapped his fingers. "A sense of fear about what would come next poisoned the air. To be sure, Christopher and I had opportunities for bricklaying and weaving, but we found the suspicion, confusion and contention among townsfolk too much to bear. 'Tis miserable to live always looking over one's shoulder."

"You fancied the atmosphere would be different in London? The new learning is spreading everywhere—here even more than in Dartford."

Searching her face, he experienced a pleasant fluttering of his heart. "What about you? How are you faring?" Looking her up and down he gushed, "Life appears to be treating you well?"

208

"'Tis a bit warm in here." She loosened the tie on her coif. "Shall we move to the back of the room?"

They worked their way to the back wall. It was decorated with ornate, gold-framed paintings of ships and important English battles that Nicholas knew nothing about.

"My Aunt Victoria has been exceptionally good to me," she said, keeping her voice low. "In exchange for lodging, we keep the gardens and home on Honey Lane for a grocer—Master McMillan."

"A grocer, eh? The one who showed up a few minutes ago?" Nicholas wondered how many times he and Christopher had passed by Anne's residence. Was she there the first time they heard Anne Askew speak?

"I didn't see Master McMillan here, so I can't answer. As for Christopher? Is he well?"

Scratching his chin, he replied, "I'm not sure how to answer. Christopher has—how shall I say this—coarsened since you left Dartford."

"Is that why he didn't accompany you tonight?"

"He has no interest in these things. He's gotten a taste for taverns and bear-baitings. Tonight he went to The Anchor in Southwark with a group of dockworkers. Ruffians, if you ask me. I couldn't convince him otherwise."

Disappointment darkened her countenance. "But Christopher admired his father. I fancied Christopher would follow in Mister Wade's footsteps."

"Not even close. He's floating about like a dandelion seed in the wind."

"I'm sorry to hear that." Her comment trailed off weakly.

"He's leaving for France at the end of the week. He found work on a Dutch merchant ship from London to Bordeaux."

"Leaving?" Her brows furrowed. "How long will he be gone?"

"A month, if all goes well. I warned him about working on a foreign vessel, but he wouldn't listen. Barring unforeseen calamities, he'll be back in August."

"August?" She kicked her toe at the floor.

A shuffle in front of the room rescued Nicholas from the topic of Christopher. The blacksmith raised his voice.

"Most of you came hoping to hear Lady Askew. As you likely know, the king's officers arrested her in March and put her on trial after several days in Newgate. They ordered Sir Askew to take her home, though she had come to London seeking a divorce. If anyone should know the frustration of being unable to secure a divorce, 'tis His Majesty, but did she find sympathy?"

Murmurs of "no!" swept across the crowd.

209

"I have good news. She escaped, and is here with us!" Thunderous applause drowned out the rest of his introduction.

Voices hushed as Lady Askew stepped forward. Nicholas found himself mesmerized by something intangible in her demeanor.

"My cherished friends in the kingdom of God," she began, "for as the Bible says, we're no more strangers, but fellow citizens…"

"How did you escape, Lady Askew?" a man called out.

"The good Lord set me free," she declared. "He is my strength and my hiding place. Be of good cheer, dear friends, and don't fear, for he'll never leave us or forsake us. Let us be about his work, sharing his word, for that is what he taught—to go into all the world and preach the gospel to every creature."

A stout young tallow chandler, from whom Nicholas regularly purchased candles on Cheapside, piped up, "But the king outlawed Bible reading for folks like us." The crowd hissed.

With a wry smile she replied, "Good sir, we must be bold as serpents, but harmless as doves. God's early disciples followed their master at all costs, and so must we if we wish to inherit his glory."

After Lady Askew finished her discourse, the blacksmith invited her to favor the gathering with a prayer. Nicholas bowed his head, keeping an eye on Anne Cooper.

"Almighty God, strengthen us in the cause of truth. Grant that we not fear man, for thou art with us forever." A ripple of *amens* followed. Immediately, the throng pressed around her.

"May I walk you home?" Anne Cooper hadn't yet lifted her head before Nicholas startled her with the request.

"Why—why, I suppose," she stammered.

"To Honey Lane?" he inquired. She nodded. They pressed through the raucous crowd along Fenchurch Street, finally breaking into open walkway, when he again caught her off guard. "May I ask you something personal?"

Her heart racing, she replied, "Yes, go ahead."

"You must be fighting off suitors?"

"I've had a few, but I'm certainly not fighting them off. And you? London is teeming with young maidens anxious to make a catch."

"If only I had time. I spend my days either working or seeking work."

"Like most of those here, I suppose. 'Tis a shame. London has much to enjoy." They engaged in small talk until they reached her cottage.

210

Fighting the urge to take her hands in his, he said politely, "When might I see you again?"

Feeling like a butterfly cornered with a net, she lifted an eyebrow and stuttered, "You're, uh—you can…" She stopped, flustered.

"Forgive my forthrightness. I'm a bit embarrassed, actually."

She looked down for a moment, contemplative, before lifting her eyes to meet his. Her heart skipped a beat. "I suppose you could join me next time Lady Askew speaks."

"I was hoping for something a bit more festive," he objected. "The day after tomorrow is Midsummer's Eve. May I call on you to accompany me to the bonfire?"

"Perhaps Christopher would like to join us?" She watched the corners of his mouth droop.

"I'll extend the invitation, but I can't make any guarantees. Shall I be by for you at seven o'clock?"

"Yes, seven will work."

He removed his cap with a slight nod. "'Twas a pleasure to see you tonight."

"My pleasure as well." She smiled and watched him walk away.

Dartford

William closed his Bible, blew out the candle, and gazed across the moonlit room. Elizabeth was snoring loudly. To keep the peace, he read when she wasn't around or awake to henpeck him for it. *I've already lost a son. I don't need to lose a husband too,* she'd say.

Moonlight filtered into the room around cracks in the window and door. With Bible in hand, he tiptoed toward the front door. Elizabeth stopped snoring and smacked her lips. He stiffened. She rolled over and mumbled something unintelligible. After waiting several seconds, he tiptoed to the door. It creaked when he pulled the handle. He stopped and looked across the room. She didn't budge. Once outside he eased the door closed, breathing a sigh of relief.

Circling around the house, he tensed with every cracking twig under his feet. How he needed some quiet time alone to contemplate events of the past few months. His life seemed a constant crisis. Pushing himself to weave enough linen to sell at market. Frantically trying to get the loom fixed, and working day and night to come up with the money to pay Johnson. Arguing with Elizabeth. Fretting about Christopher. Fearing the king's reforms would leave him stranded

211

on the wrong side of current opinion. Just thinking about it all made his chest tighten.

He sat on a stump near the empty pig sty and laid the Bible on his lap. Gazing up at the stars, he wondered how far heaven's expanse reached. The moon peeked intermittently from behind the clouds and bathed the trees, fields and rooftops across the valley in a heavenly glow. His heart flooded with tenderness toward the town and countryside that had nurtured him, provided his livelihood, and cradled him his entire adult life. But then he considered the accusations. The dissention. The confrontations. The sideways glances. The rumors that damaged his livelihood. It wasn't fair. He had done nothing to his accusers.

He could just make out Watling Street in the distance. If only the old Roman road could talk, what stories it would tell. It would speak of pilgrims, of kings and rebellions, of Roman rulers, of barbarian invaders and conquering tribes. Another image came to mind. His eyes moistened. It would also tell a tale of two prodigals rejecting everything their fathers wanted to give them.

How was Christopher faring in London, if he had even made it to London? For all William knew, rogues had robbed the two naïve travelers before they even made it to the city. He longed for news that Christopher and Nicholas were safe and getting along well. More than anything, William's heart ached for the camaraderie he and his son had once enjoyed.

He longed for his prodigal son to return home, a longing so deep he felt it as a physical ache. He thought of cradling his infant son in his arms, and of Elizabeth's jealousy when Christopher uttered his first word, *papa*. He pictured Christopher learning to walk, and Elizabeth running to pick him up when he fell, while William scolded that the boy needed to learn to pick himself up. He pondered the days when Christopher followed him everywhere, wanting to imitate everything he did. Later, as a young lad, Christopher couldn't wait to learn how to weave, and then he took pride in wanting to excel above his father.

But somewhere along the way, something went terribly wrong. Christopher began to crave the ruffian life above his future, his family. What turned his sweet boy so bitter, so angry? *Was it my fault?* he asked himself. *Did I chase the boy away?* Had he truly been too harsh, as Elizabeth claimed? Or had Elizabeth been too soft, as he sometimes believed? Did the conflict between them sour the boy, or was Christopher simply born with a disposition to test things, to go his own way, and nothing William or Elizabeth could have done or not done would have made a difference? The self-recrimination and *what ifs* tormented him.

212

William bowed his head and whispered, "Father, please bring my son to his senses. Please send something, someone, to touch his heart." From deep within him, a crushing primal pain rose up, filling his entire being until he felt anguish oozing from his pores. The pain was there all along, festering, but he held it in. Year after year, he pushed the pain back, telling himself it was a man's job to remain strong, come what may. But there, huddled on a stump bathed in moonlight, he felt the culmination of a lifetime of disappointment and sorrow crash over him like one giant ocean wave, threatening to suck his life's breath out of him. He tried to push the grief back, like a beast too hideous and ugly to be let out of a cage, but it refused to be held in. Losing his father as a young lad; his friend Thomas burning at the stake; his son's rejection; conflicts with Elizabeth; struggling to make a livelihood; the scorn of those in his community and endless accusations of being a Lollard; persecution for simply possessing an English Bible.

He studied his hands in the moonlight, opening and closing his fingers stiffly. Using his hands to support his family all these years had taken a toll on him. He wasn't sure how much longer he could fight through the aches and pains and continue weaving alone. Elizabeth helped some, but minding the household and spinning flax thread kept her occupied. The wear and tear of worrying about her son was taking a toll on her as well.

Should he wait for Christopher to come home, or begin training an apprentice? Or, should he keep going on his own for as long as his body held out, and then try to find something else to do? To whom would he leave the business, if Christopher never turned around? These were the weighty matters that kept him awake in the wee hours of the night, long after Elizabeth had drifted off to sleep.

"Why?" The word choked from his soul, surprising him, as if it were uttered by someone else. "What have I done to earn your wrath?" he demanded, his pounding heart lacerated into a thousand pieces by cut after painful cut of circumstances. The anger, hurt, rejection, false accusations, guilt, confusion, weariness, feeling of betrayal by God, all melted into a nameless cavern of despair. "Why!" he demanded again, clenching his fists. Hot tears flowed down his cheeks. He leaned his head in his hands and sobbed.

"I can take no more," he choked, hoping the invisible being to whom he spoke would hear, and have mercy on him. He waited for the whisper of an answer, but heard only the usual sounds of night—a faint breeze rustling the leaves, the far off bleating of a sheep, a dog barking. He wasn't asking for much, not even a whole piece of bread, but merely a crumb from heaven—a sign that the higher power in which he believed sympathized with his plight. "Where are you?" he demanded. "Why are you letting this happen to me?" He waited again, for a mere whisper of peace, a thought, an impression—anything that would speak comfort to his distress. "What have I done wrong? Have I failed you? Have I failed my son?"

He fancied the circumstances of his life as dozens of threads tangled into a knot so twisted that it could never be unraveled. Ah, the irony—a weaver with a life of threads tangled beyond repair. What an unsightly fabric his life would make! Some weaver he was!

He looked to heaven. "Please comfort Elizabeth and me, and help us know what to do. I pray thee, help me keep up with the weaving. Should I hire an apprentice, or wait for Christopher to return home? If I make the wrong decision, it could spell the end of my livelihood. And Father..."

A cracking sound coming from the front of the cottage interrupted his plea. His muscles tensed. He jumped up to face the sound and croaked, "Who's there?" Unnerving silence mocked his question. "Who is it? Who's there?" He heard a rustle again, followed by the faint tap of footsteps on grass. The hair on his arms stood up.

"Ho! Make yourself known," William shouted. Whoever it was broke into a run. How long had the person been there? Was he being watched? He picked up a large stone and tiptoed around the side of the cottage. The pound of footsteps grew further away, finally evaporating into the darkness. He ran to the front door and discovered fresh footprints in the dirt near the doorstep.

With trepidation, he pulled the door open and saw straw strewn about the room. The bedspread and sheets lay in a heap on the floor. Elizabeth knelt in a corner near the fireplace, her hair disheveled and her eyes wide with fear. He ran, knelt beside her and put an arm around her shoulder.

"Oh, William," she choked. "Two men wearing masks—they were after your Bible."

London

Victoria busied herself gathering flowers and herbs for the Midsummer's Eve and Saint John's Day festivities. The celebrations took a close second to Christmastide as her favorite time of year. Thank goodness, she thought, the king did not do away with Saint John's feast day when striking saints' days from the calendar.

First, to collect herbs. 'Twas kind of Master McMillan to offer her a small plot of garden space where she could grow what she wished. She ventured outside, her first stop the Saint John's wort patch. The herb's bright yellow flowers opened near June 24th, the day celebrated as Saint John the Baptist's birthday. Plucking one flower, she contemplated the five petals' resemblance of a halo, and the cut stems' crimson red liquid, reminiscent of Saint John's blood. She cut three thick fists full to weave into a door wreath for keeping evil away. The surplus would be dried to use in a tea to rid its user of demons tormenting the imagination. Harvesting it on Saint John's Day ensured its maximum potency. Next, she cut several white lilies to include in the wreath. After she finished her cuttings in the herb garden, all that remained was to fetch birch leaves.

An enlivening fragrance wafted about her as she passed by her rose patch. She imagined the roses, with their warm palette of red, pink and yellow blossoms, boasting of their beauty to the other flowers in the garden. When she was a young girl, her mother taught her that a rose picked on Midsummer's Eve would stay fresh until Christmas. She cut several roses of different colors with the intention to give some petals to Anne. A girl's true love would appear the next day if, on Midsummer's Eve, she laid rose petals in front of her while reciting the poem,

Rose leaves, rose leaves, rose leaves I strew.
He that will love me come after me now.

Anne could use help divining her true love. She had reached marriageable age and, although plenty of suitors took an interest in her over the years, Anne found fault with all of them. Victoria noted a change in Anne the past couple of days. Absent-minded and distracted, Anne denied that anything was bothering her, but when she descended the stairs that morning with her nightshirt on backwards, Victoria knew something was wrong. The girl must be having trouble with a lad; why else would she act that way? Victoria hoped the rose ritual would help. She plucked a few sprigs of goldenrod as well, for if a girl wore goldenrod during the waxing of the moon on Midsummer's Eve, she would glimpse her true love the next day.

After harvesting the other plants she needed, Victoria gathered the entire bundle in her arms and deposited them on the kitchen table. She sat down and proceeded to sort through them, dreading the day Anne would leave to establish a home of her own. After her vocation as a nun had been so cruelly stolen by the injunctions, Victoria floundered for a purpose in life. Having Anne to care for filled the void.

An attractive woman in her own right, Victoria drew a fair amount of male attention. Sometimes, like a bather dipping the tip of a finger into the bath water to check the temperature, she let her thoughts skim the realm of what might happen if she responded. She kept her thoughts private, and never plunged too deeply into these uncharted waters. Perhaps she should set aside a few of those rose petals and goldenrod sprigs for herself. She smiled at the thought.

When Anne started attending Lutheran meetings after seeing Lady Askew preach on the street, Victoria struggled with whether to put her foot down or turn a blind eye. Was her niece caught up in a youthful diversion, or jeopardizing her own life with the new religion? Having been expelled from her priory, Victoria knew all too well the tumult that resulted from taking the wrong side of religious reform.

Brushing her worries aside, she focused on crafting the front door wreath. A new suitor would be knocking on the door in a few hours, and she wanted to be ready.

❣

Anne kept an eye on the door, the rocking of her foot vibrating the kitchen table.

After taking a sip of Saint John's Wort tea, Victoria set her cup next to the goldenrod sprigs and small bowl of rose petals set aside for Anne. Aiming to diffuse the nervous tension, she inquired, "What sort of lad is this Nicholas Hall?"

Cracking her knuckles, Anne muttered, "He worked as a bricklayer apprentice with his father before coming to London with a friend recently."

"He came with a friend?" She noticed that Anne avoided eye contact.

"Yes, someone he grew up with in Dartford. No one of any importance."

Two young men from Dartford, one whom Anne didn't seem to want to name?

Her curiosity piqued, Victoria pressed. "Is the friend someone you know?"

"Yes, but I don't know that I would recognize him now, even if I saw him on the street."

"Who is this lad?" Victoria blew on her tea and took another sip.

Anne met Victoria's gaze. "A weaver's son."

216

Raising her eyebrows, Victoria probed, "A weaver's son? Didn't you fancy a weaver's son in Dartford?"

"For a time."

Extracting information about the lad was like coaxing a timid puppy out of hiding after a thunder clap. "Does this lad have a name?"

"Yes. If you must know, it's Christopher Wade."

Frowning, Victoria scolded, "Anne! That lad is the very reason your father sent you here. The Wade lad is in London? Your father would go mad if he knew."

"I just found out, and I've yet to see him. Apparently he's taken up with questionable company."

"As if his company were not questionable enough already. 'Twas Matthew's concern about that lad's father that got you sent here. Rightly so, I might add."

"It appears he rejected his father's traditions. According to Nicholas, he calls our meetings heretic baitings."

"He may not be far from the truth. You never know who might be in attendance at those meetings. What if the king has spies there? Lady Askew has been arrested more than once. They take note of her activities. I have a hunch they track those who attend as well." She picked up a handful of rose petals and inhaled before extending her hand toward Anne.

Anne took a deep whiff. "Lovely."

Victoria continued, "This other lad, Nicholas. Where do his religious sympathies lie?"

"I met him at a meeting night before last. I don't know if curiosity brought him there, or genuine sympathy for the new learning."

Victoria shook her head. "For your sake, I hope this Nicholas holds with the king's religion." A flash in Anne's eyes told Victoria she had struck a nerve.

Biting her lower lip, Anne countered, "Should we turn a blind eye when wolves lead God's flock? Do you fancy our Lord would prevent folks from having his word in their own tongue?"

A knot tightened in Victoria's stomach. "'Tis the heart that matters. God knows your heart, and he will reward you for it." She busied herself gathering the flowers on the table.

A robust *rap-rap-rap* on the door sent Anne's heart racing. Springing to her feet, she smoothed her blue wool skirt and fussed with the white linen coif atop her head. Her hair was parted in the middle and pulled into a chignon at the nape

217

of her neck. A small, filigreed pomander hung from a chain around her waist, filled with fragrant lavender and rose petals—a gift from Victoria.

Pinching her cheeks, Anne whispered, "Do I look presentable?"

"You look lovely, dear." Starting toward the door, Victoria added, "I fear he will find you irresistible, and whisk you away from me."

The eager-looking lad at the door removed his wool flat cap, smoothed his thick, brown hair and offered a slight bow. "You must be Victoria?"

"Yes. Pleased to meet you. Come in."

Anne peered past Nicholas, disappointed to see him alone. Hand extended, she stepped forward with a halfhearted smile. "Nicholas. How nice to see you again." The three exchanged pleasantries until Nicholas began to fiddle with his hat.

"I noticed, as I passed through the city, that the festivities have already begun." Addressing Victoria, Nicholas continued, "Do you trust me to return her at a respectable hour?"

"I don't know that I can trust a Dartford lad," Victoria teased. Anne rolled her eyes. Resting her hand on Anne's shoulder, Victoria smiled. "I don't think it necessary for me to give two folks your age a curfew. Enjoy yourselves."

Relieved to be leaving, Nicholas held the door for Anne. Victoria found the lad quite charming.

ઈ

"'Ave ye 'ad enough to drink, lad? Methinks ye have." The bartender sized Christopher up with a smirk.

After a loud burp, Christopher held up his mug and stammered, "Nay, Goodman, fill me up again."

"Aye, the lad cannot even hold the mug upright." The bartender addressed a bemused alehouse crowd. "Take a look at this. Thinks he needs more to drink, yet he can't even steady his mug." Holding the pitcher directly above Christopher's mug, the bartender poured a trickle. It cleanly missed.

A dock worker stood up from his table, walked the few paces to Christopher, and grabbed the jerkin at the scruff of his neck. "Come, lad, let's see if you can walk as steady as you hold your mug. Up! Up!" He yanked the startled young man upwards off his stool. Christopher swung a fist at him, hitting nothing but air. Laughter exploded throughout the tavern.

"Throw him out to the cutpurses, Harry. The lad is soused." The bartender, relieved to have help with the intoxicated patron, wiped his hands on his apron and leaned against the counter to enjoy the spectacle. Harry pushed Christopher away while releasing his grip. Christopher stumbled backwards and fell to the floor.

"Keep your hands off me, you louse," Christopher snarled.

"Ah, did you hear that, goodmen? This urchin called me a louse."

His egg-yolk colored teeth glowing in the darkened room, the bartender shouted, "Throw him out, Harry. Let the devil have him. 'Tis Midsummer's Eve—the spirits will be looking for unsuspecting victims."

"Throw him out!" A couple of patrons began to chant, joined by one more, then two, until all the patrons in the alehouse united in chanting, "Throw him out! Throw him out!"

"I shall go out on my own accord." Christopher placed his hands flat on the floor to push himself up. His legs refused to cooperate.

"The lad needs help." Harry turned to the bartender.

"Throw him in the Thames!" The growled suggestion drifted from a dimly lit corner of the tavern.

Harry looked to the corner. "'Twould be cruel, Will. 'Twould shock the poor lad. He's probably too soused to swim. 'Twould be to his death."

"Serves 'im right for calling you a louse," Will persisted.

"Leave me be!" Christopher hissed. He crawled to the nearest table and tried to pull himself up, laughter exploding around him.

"He wobbles like a newly birthed calf." Laughter and applause erupted at Will's observation.

Harry watched Christopher's legs, amused. "Perhaps it would teach the lad a lesson. Give me a hand." Will slammed his ale down and trotted to Christopher's side.

"Grab 'is feet while I get 'is hands." Too inebriated to fend off his tormentors, Christopher nevertheless thrashed while Harry held his hands. Will grabbed at Christopher's ankles, knocking off one of his shoes. The two men hoisted Christopher off the floor and charged for the door like they were carrying a battering ram. A boy who appeared too young to have any business at the alehouse jumped up, ran to the door and threw it open.

"Where are you taking him?" someone piped up.

"Shall we throw him in the Thames?" Harry surveyed the patrons for a reaction.

"In the Thames! In the Thames!" The chorus of voices calling for Christopher's fate drowned out his weak protests.

As they emerged from the tavern, the cool night air awakened Christopher's senses. Wriggling and twisting, he shouted, "Let me go! Release me!"

"Oh, we'll release you all right," Harry quipped. "I hope ye can swim, lad, or else your bloated corpse'll be floating somewhere in the North Sea a fortnight from now."

Sobered by the gravity of his situation, Christopher fought with a newfound ferocity. Will lost his grip on one ankle, leaving one of Christopher's legs free. The panicked captive thrust his leg straight out, hitting Will's kneecap.

"Ouch!" Will stumbled. "He fights like a rabid dog. I lost his ankle."

"Grab hold," Harry grunted. "We're almost there." Will got a grip on Christopher's breeches, holding so tight his knuckles turned white. "Down this street." Harry pointed with his chin. The river came into view. Struggling against their feisty prey, they made their way to the muddy bank. Harry lost his footing and slipped, but managed to hold tight to Christopher's hands.

"You got his ankles?" Harry cast a steely glance at Will.

"An ankle and his breeches, but my hands are getting numb."

"Ready. On the count of three." Christopher took a panicked look at the dank, muddy water. He wriggled again, to no avail. "One. Two. Three!" With a heave, Harry and Will sent Christopher airborne. A loud splash told them their mission was successful.

"Harry! I got his breeches." Will waved Christopher's breeches in his left hand with a hoot. "They slipped off when we let go."

"Ho!" Harry chuckled. "That'll teach him."

For several seconds the two men watched Christopher's head bob up and down in the water. Then it was gone.

⟡

Fiery streaks of orange and yellow emblazoned the western sky, as the sun slipped behind London's steepled horizon. All eyes were on Father Tonbridge.

"I'll now set the watch," he announced to a large gathering. Holding a lighted torch to the tall pile of sticks and branches, he waited for the fire to catch. With the blaze burning brightly, he shouted, "Our help is in the name of the Lord."

"Who made heaven and earth," the onlookers responded in chorus.

"The Lord be with you."

"May He also be with you."

Father Tonbridge bowed his head. "Let us pray. Lord God, almighty Father, the light that never fails and the source of all light, sanctify this new fire, and grant that after the darkness of this life we may come unsullied to Thee, Who art light eternal, through Christ our Lord." Nicholas and Anne offered their *amens* in unison with the others.

Next, Tonbridge sprinkled the fire with holy water while the crowd broke into a song in praise of Saint John. At the song's conclusion, the priest proclaimed, "There was a man sent from God."

"Whose name was John," came the reply.

Tonbridge concluded, "God, who by reason of the birth of blessed John made this day praiseworthy, give Thy people the grace of spiritual joy, and keep the hearts of thy faithful fixed on the way that leads to everlasting salvation through Christ our Lord."

A chorus of voices shouted, "Amen."

Folks young and old circled the bonfire clockwise, the devout reciting prayers on their rosaries. A grey-haired woman, participating in a time-honored tradition, squeezed past Anne and placed several worn out objects of religious devotion in the fire. Anne watched a rosary and a small statue of the Virgin Mary melt in the flames. Nearly ten years had passed since the injunctions abolished relics. *So much for Cromwell's injunctions*, Anne mused.

As prayers around the fire dwindled, the atmosphere exploded. Loud horns, shouts, and laughter brought the streets to life. Two boys streaked past Anne, one chasing the other, screeching in delight. The aroma of roast pork wafted past Nicholas' nose and activated his salivary glands, while thick smoke in the air tickled his throat.

After covering a cough, he reached for Anne's hand. "Jump over the fire with me!"

"But…" She protested, but couldn't think of an excuse.

"Come, let's jump!" He tightened his grip. "'Twill bring us good fortune."

She balked. "Do you really believe in those silly superstitions?"

"Come. 'Tis all in good fun." He pulled Anne to the fire's edge. "Watch. I'll go first." Nicholas positioned himself at the edge of the fire, backed up several steps, ran and vaulted over the flames. From the opposite side he beckoned to Anne, the flames casting eerie shadows over his face.

"'Twill singe my dress!"

A teenaged lad nearby stopped beating on a pot to shout encouragement. "You'll be fine, wench. Jump! Join your lover on the other side of the fire. 'Twill bring you both luck."

Anne blushed. Lover? She saw Nicholas as nothing more than a friend, but protesting the lad's comment would serve no purpose.

"Very well. Here goes." She backed up, lifted her skirt above her ankles and ran toward the fire. In an instant, she found herself safely on the other side. Nicholas reached for her hand. A sensation of warmth filled her bosom.

"See there, luck is with us already. We made it over the fire without getting singed." He gave her a gentle tug. "Come, let's see what else is going on."

Excitement bubbled within her, lifting her spirit and quickening her pace. "I've always wanted to see what Cheapside is like on a busy night," she confessed, "but never dared to venture out alone."

"Nor should you, but here's your chance. Tonight I'll escort you wherever your heart desires. Perhaps we'll see a midsummer's eve sprite or two." His eyes danced. "Are you hungry?"

She sniffed the air. "Something smells delicious, now that you mention it."

"Choose your fancy. On my way here, I passed a number of food carts. Spice cakes, eel jelly, pease pudding…"

An older gentleman with his eye on a voluptuous maid selling roasted oysters bumped into Anne, pressing her into Nicholas' side. Her closeness sent a thrill through his body.

Embarrassed, she straightened up and cleared her throat. "Why, I expected the streets to be busy, but not this crowded."

"Do you enjoy the hustle and bustle of London?"

"I sometimes miss Dartford, but London has its good points."

"Pray tell?" He listened while his eyes scanned the vendors.

"I enjoy merchants selling goods from every corner of the world, and folks from faraway places in their native costume, speaking foreign tongues. I like living in the center of things, where change and new ideas are taking root. And I'm especially thankful folks here aren't watching my every move and reporting to my father, as in Dartford."

"It must be difficult, though, to be so far away from your family?"

She shrugged her shoulders. "Father grew stern after mother's death, and so terribly afraid I would reject his faith."

"By all appearances, you've embraced the new learning despite his best efforts to prevent it. Does your father have any inkling of what you've been up to?"

"Not as far as I know. I don't see him often. He comes to London only once or twice a year, for a day or two at a time."

"What about your aunt—would she tell your father?"

"I doubt it. She's not overly fond of him, and takes it upon herself to be my protector."

"What of your attendance at the meetings?"

"I've invited her to come, but she says she has no interest. Methinks she fears the authorities."

"With good reason. England is well-fertilized with the ashes of martyrs."

Anne shuddered.

"Are you chilled?"

"No. Perhaps we should speak of happier things."

"Yes. Such as pease pudding." Nicholas stopped in front of a cart. "What is your pleasure, Madame?" He took off his hat and bowed.

She giggled. "Why, I feel as if I'm in the royal court. Do they have any spice cakes?"

"Thpice cake, indeed," a silver-haired man replied with his back turned. Hobbling toward them in a stooped-over position, he continued, "But don't thop with just one. Get thome extras to take home. Best thpice cakes in town, they are. How many'll it be, then? A dozen?" His grin revealed a space where his two top front teeth should have been. Without waiting for a reply, he began to count a dozen cakes.

"I certainly can't eat more than one or two." She glanced at Nicholas. "Pushy fellow," she murmured.

"A dozen it is." Nicholas opened his purse and pulled out four pence and a clean kerchief. He exchanged his coins for the spice cakes and wrapped them in the cloth before turning to Anne. "Shall we find a place to sit?"

As they walked away, she fumed, "Why did you buy a dozen, and pay him more than you needed to? He was taking advantage of you."

"His wife died of the pox not long ago, along with two of his children." Nicholas pointed to a dark ribbon winding between Southwark and London. "I know a fine place with a view of the river."

At the prospect of seeing the river at night, she lit up. "I would like that."

223

They worked their way through raucous mobs and turned down a narrow dirt street toward the church of Saint James, stopping to catch a glimpse of the Thames between buildings. Light from the full moon danced across the water. Hand in hand, they continued to the church grounds.

"Here?" Nicholas asked.

"'Tis quite pleasant." She looked for a place to sit.

Leading her to a low stone wall, Nicholas seated himself next to her, set the spice cakes on the wall and offered her one. A gentle breeze rustled the churchyard grass, carrying with it the fragrance of roses and honeysuckle from a trellis against the church wall. The soft moonlight accentuated her beauty. She pressed her index finger to a crumb of spice cake clinging to the corner of her mouth and licked it off, drawing his attention to her lips. Surging with longing to press his lips against hers, he settled instead for a bite of cake.

Wistful, he quipped, "The cake would be delicious with a bit of honey."

She took another bite and, licking the crumbs from her lips, remarked, "Yes, but it is quite good plain."

"Speaking of honey," he pointed to gentle ripples on the river's surface, "the honey moon is beautiful, the way it casts its light across the river."

"I love the moonlight," she agreed, shifting her weight on the hard, uneven surface. "Tell me, Nicholas, what do you truly think of these traditions, such as Midsummer's Eve? Do you believe in luck, spells, fairies, and such?"

"I think of it as innocent mirth. And you?"

"I can't decide. Is it just merriment, or do folks' traditions blind them to truth? Can we consider it mirth when folks persecute—even put to death—those who question their traditions?"

Nicholas sighed, thinking perhaps she had attended too many Lutheran meetings. "You have a very earnest side about you. Have you always pondered such things?"

She popped the rest of her cake in her mouth, taking time to chew and swallow before replying. "I suppose it began with my father trying to keep me away from Christopher. He harbored so much hatred toward William Wade. It never seemed to me that one who claims to defend God's true religion should be filled with hate."

"I never gave the matter much thought." Nicholas yawned and stretched his legs in front of him. "I suppose lots of folks go through the motions so the authorities will leave them alone, or because they never considered an alternative."

Taking his yawn as a sign of boredom, she changed the subject. "At any rate, we came to enjoy the festivities. Please, forgive me."

Nicholas picked up another cake and bit it in half. "'Twould be difficult to celebrate when you question the very reason for the celebration."

Anne sighed. "Yes, that's where I find myself."

Shouting broke out in the direction of the river. A dog started barking frantically. Anne and Nicholas looked at each other, eyebrows raised.

"Let's go see what the commotion is." Nicholas stuffed the rest of the cake in his mouth.

"Is it safe? Victoria warned me about the river at night."

"The streets are busy and lit by fires. I'll keep you safe. Come on." He tugged her hand. She balked.

"Come," he insisted. "Don't let fear keep you from adventure." She gave in and trotted behind him, along Upper Thames Street toward the river.

Ↄ

A bull mastiff with its legs planted in the mud tugged on a wet heap on the riverbank, letting go to bark and growl, then latching on again, tossing its head back and forth.

"'Tis a monster." A boy about nine years old stared at the lump with fear in his eyes. "Look, it's covered in smelly slime." He tapped it with his toe and jumped back as if he'd been bitten.

"'Tis hideous," mumbled a peasant woman, her eyes wide. "I can barely look at it."

"The smell is far worse." A balding man of slight build, with tufts of grey hair at his temples, stood plugging his nose. "Smells like a week-old chamber pot."

"A mermaid!" A young boy pranced about while tugging up on his breeches, excited at the rare spectacle. "It has only one leg."

"'Twould be a merman, if indeed there were such a creature," said the boy's mother. "To think, such nasty creatures are swimming right here in the river."

"Perhaps it swam upriver from the sea." The man with tufts on his temples leaned forward with his hands on his waist to study the mysterious object.

The bull mastiff pulled off a large chunk of slime wrapped around the figure's lower half. A mother gasped and rushed her hand over her daughter's eyes.

A moan escaped from deep within the slime-covered creature as he rolled from his stomach onto his back. Upon viewing the audience gathered around

225

him, he threw his hands over the area that should have been covered with breeches. "Leave me be!" he snarled at the crowd gazing down upon him.

"It has no clothes!" shrieked the mother.

"Mama, let me see!" The little girl tried to push her way forward.

"No, Molly, we must go. This is no scene for respectable womenfolk." The mother grabbed the little girl's hand and hustled her away from the crowd, looking back occasionally to verify that her eyes had not tricked her.

Nicholas watched from the outer edge of the melee, waiting for Anne to catch up. As she approached he barked, "Cover your eyes."

"Why?" Anne responded. Just then, a break in the crowd gave her a view of the figure lying in the street. She gasped.

Dartford

Cradling Elizabeth's face between his hands, William cried, "Did they harm you?"

She shook her head and lifted her eyes to meet his. "I can't live like this anymore, William," she whispered, wiping a clump of disheveled hair from her perspiration-soaked forehead.

"What did you say?" He pulled his hands back and stood up slowly.

"I can no longer live like this," she moaned. "I won't live like this. I refuse to go on this way." She buried her face in her hands.

"What do you mean? There is nothing to be done; 'tis simply the way things are." He wrung his hands. "Do you mean to blame me for this?" He turned and walked a few paces away, then spun around to face her. "I'm but a common man. I have no power. Do I tell His Majesty what laws to enact? Do I counsel the pope on matters of doctrine? I'm nothing more than a pawn. A pawn! Do you hear me?"

She wiped her eyes with the backs of her hands. "It doesn't have to be this way. You could stop bein' so stubborn, so set on your rebellious ways." Her icy glare bored through him. "When King Henry abolished Bible readin' by the commons, you could have gotten rid of yours. With all your Bible study, you can practically quote the whole book anyway. Why do you keep it here? You know the law, yet defy it. Did you expect to go on your merry way, in defiance of His Majesty?"

"I don't think of it as defying His Majesty, but rather obeying my Lord."

226

She pushed herself to a standing position and shook her forefinger at him. "That book is nothin' but trouble. It's torn apart the kingdom, brought good men and women to their deaths, chased away our son. That book makes people mad, William. Completely mad! 'Tis a cursed book!"

He glared at her. "Are you blaming me that Christopher ran away? You must stop such dribble." He took a shallow gasp for breath and continued. "Don't you dare blame the Bible for the ills around us. 'Tis men who cause the evils you complain of. The Bible never harmed a soul. It teaches of love—even of loving our enemies—not hate and killing. The world needs more of His word, not less. How could you say such a thing?"

"No one has to know your views; you could keep 'em to yourself. We don't have to live this way."

He strode to the window and peered outside, looking but not seeing. "You don't know what you're asking of me," he said, somber. "To give up the word of God for popish idolatry or the king's folly? I would rather give up food. I would rather give up breath." He massaged the knot in his abdomen.

"You're not hearin' me. I won't live this way anymore!" Elizabeth shouted. "Curse you, and that damned book with you!" As soon as the words left her lips, she wished she hadn't uttered them. She watched him jolt, as if she'd punched him in the gut. "I only mean…" She moved behind him and massaged his shoulders, feeling him cringe. "Listen to you. You would rather give up food and breath than the book. And from the appearance of it, you would rather give up your family, too. That book is more important to you than our son. I fear it is more important to you than our marriage vows. I can't live this way anymore—the sideways glances, the whispers…." She laid her cheek against his back and sniffed. "I'm weary of the humiliation."

William continued to stare out the window, at a loss for words. Was it true? Did he put the Bible above his family? On the one hand, holy writ taught that a man must cleave to his spouse and care for his family; on the other, it taught loyalty to God at all costs. He felt like a carcass torn apart by a pack of wolves—a skeleton from which the bones had been stripped of every trace of meat. *The wolves will have to leave me alone at last*, he thought. *They have torn every bit of flesh from me.*

Christopher looked about, muddy rivulets of river water trickling from his hair down his face. His hecklers had gone their separate ways. Only he, Nicholas, and Anne remained. An uncomfortable silence permeated the air, broken only by the sound of the river sloshing against the bank. Christopher pulled Nicholas' cloak tightly around his loins, wishing he could disappear.

"I thought I would meet my death out there," he confessed, his teeth chattering. "If the rower of that small vessel crossing back from the Southwark stews hadn't pitied me, my corpse would be halfway out to sea by now."

Nicholas and Anne exchanged uncomfortable glances.

"How did the two of you happen to come together on this Midsummer's Eve?" Christopher demanded, his tone sharp.

"'Twas coincidence, really," Nicholas stated matter-of-factly. "We bumped into one another at a cottage meeting a few days ago—remember, the one I invited you to, but you declined?

"Mm-hmm." Christopher avoided eye contact with Anne, mortified about the pathetic state in which he stood before her.

"Anne and I thought we might enjoy catching up while taking in tonight's festivities."

Christopher kicked a rock toward the Thames and spit to expel the taste of river water. Glaring at Nicholas, he snipped, "Some friend you are." With a quick glance at Anne he added, "After all these years, fancy discovering you with my best friend."

Shaking his head, Nicholas protested, "You speak to us as if we did something wrong. You've become nothing but a bitter, drunken, irresponsible louse. It's all I can do to tolerate sharing a room with you."

"Is that so? Well, I'm leaving for Bordeaux in the morning, and you're free to head back to your precious Dartford."

"I was doing you a favor by staying until you leave," Nicholas countered.

"I see what sort of favors you're up to." Christopher cast a derisive glance at Anne.

Shifting her weight nervously from right foot to left, Anne asked, "You're leaving in the morning?" Her voice dripped with disappointment.

Christopher spit again and kicked at the wet, hard-packed dirt. "We're setting sail a couple of days earlier than planned in hopes of beating a storm. Believe me, tomorrow isn't soon enough. Sweet Anne, sneaking around under my nose. You remind me of Betsy, a mongrel I met in Southwark."

The pained look on Anne's face launched Nicholas into action. Charging like a wild boar, he thrust Christopher backwards. As Christopher threw his hands behind himself to break the fall, he lost his grip on the cloak and landed on his buttocks with a thud. Anne gasped and averted her attention to the moon, while Nicholas retrieved the cloak. He threw it over Christopher, straddled him, and demanded, "Apologize to her." A spray of warm saliva landed on Nicholas' cheek and oozed downward. "You brute!" he shouted. He pinned Christopher's arms to the ground with his knees and pummeled until Christopher lay limp and moaning.

Digging her fingers into Nicholas' shoulders, Anne pulled back with all the strength she could muster. "Stop. Both of you. Please, stop," she cried. Seeing that they paid her no heed, she stepped back, fearful of being caught in the middle.

"Let me tell you something," Nicholas hissed, so close Christopher smelled the spice cake on his breath. "You and I came to London to find our fortunes. I found nothing but miserable, day-to-day subsistence, and you've sunk to the bottom, living like a sewer rat. You drift from tavern to tavern, come home every night soused, and keep company with the dregs of London. Yet, you have the audacity to speak to Anne and me as if we did something wrong. You don't deserve her. Find someone else to drag down with you. I'm through with you."

"I don't need you or anyone else," Christopher growled. "Ho, Anne," he called, bucking against Nicholas' hold on him. "I never imagined when I saw you again, it would be like this." The ridiculous irony of his statement almost choked her.

Nicholas eased his way to a standing position and brushed himself off. "Someday, I trust you'll come to your senses."

Christopher struggled first to his knees and then to his feet, clenching the cloak around him. "My senses are fine—except they failed to warn me about what was going on right under my nose."

At the sight of a night watchman approaching, Nicholas warned, "You have five seconds to be on your way. Understood?"

"I'm going of my own accord, not because you're telling me to."

Nicholas counted, "One. Two…"

Christopher turned and dragged himself uphill toward the Tower without a backwards glance. Nicholas and Anne watched his silhouette grow distant and finally disappear.

Light from a torch suddenly illuminated the area immediately around them. The watchman—an imposing figure—approached and asked, "Did I hear a fight?"

"A friend and I had a scuffle, but 'tis resolved," Nicholas responded.

Holding his torch high, the watchman surveyed the area. "You'd best get back to the crowd. I don't recommend being alone on the riverbank."

"We were just on our way," Nicholas replied. The watchman nodded. They watched his torch bob up and down as he continued along the riverbank.

As Anne and Nicholas made their way back to central London, Nicholas massaged his hands together, sore from the pummeling.

"What happened to Christopher?" Anne's voice shook.

"He's sowing his wild oats, with nary a thought about what he's reaping in return."

"How long has he been like this?"

"I saw hints of it in Dartford, but from the moment we arrived in London something in him broke. He's deeply embittered. Talking to him about it is of no use."

"Have you any idea what he is fighting against?"

"His father? The church? God himself? Everyone and everything? I honestly can't say for certain. I pray he'll come to his senses. I'm sorry it turned out this way. But then again …" He trailed off.

"What is it?"

"Oh, 'tis nothing."

"Please, share your thought with me."

He took her left hand in his. "The truth is, if Christopher were not in the state he is in, I might not be here with you now."

With a pained smile, she eased her hand away. "I pray you, don't take this the wrong way. I just don't know if I'm quite ready for this."

"I'm sorry." He stepped back. "I'm a fool for thinking you might accept me as a suitor."

"No, it's—I haven't sorted through my thoughts since I discovered that you and Christopher were here. It's all happening so quickly."

With a shrug of acceptance, he moved the conversation forward. "Shall we try to redeem this evening, or may I arrange to call on you again for a fresh attempt—or both?"

She giggled. There was something indomitable in Nicholas' spirit that she liked. Twirling a strand of hair around her finger, she replied, "Aunt Victoria will be anxious if I'm out too much longer."

"I wouldn't want to make a bad impression on our first outing. I should at least wait until the third or fourth." He winked. "We can at least enjoy our spice cakes on the walk back."

"Goodman, I would like a thpice cake, if you please."

"What will you give me for these top-of-the-line delicacies?" Nicholas teased.

"The pleasure of my company?" She extended her elbow.

He patted his purse and threw back his head with a moan. "In my haste to get here, I forgot them at the churchyard."

☙

Anne cupped the rose petals that Victoria gave her, inhaled deeply, and laid them gently, one by one, in a line in front of her. Closing her eyes, she recited,

Rose leaves, rose leaves, rose leaves I strew,
He that will love me come after me now.

She picked up a looking glass on the armoire in her chamber and studied herself with new eyes, thinking, *he fancies me.* Closer inspection revealed a crumb of cake stuck between her front teeth. With a gasp, she reached for her ivory toothpick on the armoire. A knock on the door jarred her out of her fantasies.

"Coming." Mirror in hand, she tugged on the door handle. Victoria slipped in, her face pale.

"Victoria, pray tell, what is it?"

"How was your evening?"

"Quite good, actually."

A faint smile brightened Victoria's face at the sight of the rose petals, but it was quickly overshadowed with a frown. "I have difficult news. Master McMillan informed me spies are watching your cottage meetings."

231

Christopher leaned over the ship rail to retch, cursing the insult to his aching abdominal muscles. His legs wobbled, barely able to support his weight. A ten-foot wave reeled the boat, throwing him off balance. He clutched the rail as the swell lurched him upward and downward, causing his knees to buckle. Crumpling to the deck, he curled up and moaned.

"Judgin' from yer appearance, lad, I'd say ye got a worse case than Jove himself ever saw, and he's looked over a lot of sailors." The voice belonged to Patrick, the ship bosun. He was a man born for the sea, and Christopher took an instant liking to him. Carrot-colored hair dusted with grey tumbled in waves from the top of Patrick's head to his chin. A bushy beard of the same color descended from his chin to the top of his chest. The wild mane atop and below framed his ruddy face, leathered from decades of sun and saltwater. He was a wisp of a man, a sack of loose skin, veins and wrinkles, and Christopher guessed that with a full stomach he might weigh one hundred forty pounds. Fully upright, he reached only to Christopher's chin, but what he lacked in stature he made up for in spirit. Like a guardian angel, Patrick had an uncanny ability to show up just when Christopher needed an encouraging word.

"Am I going to die?" Christopher groaned.

"That would be the easy way out." Patrick knelt down beside the tormented young sailor. "A case of seasickness as bad as yers will make ye wish ye was dead, but I wager you'll get better." Reaching into a small leather pouch that hung from his waist, Patrick retrieved a penny-sized disk. "Chew on this. It might help, and it sure won't hurt."

Still drooling from dry heaves, Christopher whimpered, "I don't think I can keep anything down."

"Open up, lad. It'll cure what ails ye." Patrick pushed the dried ginger disk into Christopher's mouth. "Suck on it. If it don't help, nothing will."

Christopher choked. "Horrid."

"If ye refuse help, I can't do nothin' for ye. Now up, up. We need to get ye to the fo'c'sle so ye don't take up space on the deck like a wet mop." Surveying the deck for other sailors, Patrick warned, "Men are startin' to complain about ye, not the least of which is the capt'n. I don't speak Dutch, but those who do tell me he's not happy." He placed his hands under Christopher's armpits and tugged, to no avail.

"The lad's been useless from day one." The gravelly voice gave Patrick a start. "We oughta throw him overboard. 'Twould be good for the men's spirits."

"He just needs to find 'is sea legs, John. Give me a hand and we'll get 'im to 'is hammock."

"It's been a week already. We're more than halfway to Bordeaux. All he does is take up space. Hasn't done an ounce of work around here, and I'm tired of moppin' up 'is puke." When Christopher glanced at him, John made a threatening fist.

"Go ahead, throw me over. Put me out of my misery." Christopher's face sagged like loose chicken skin.

"We need to extract some work from ye, lad. Can't throw ye overboard yet. But that don't mean it won't happen." John lifted Christopher under the armpits. Patrick carried his feet.

"Now this is yer last chance, lad," Patrick warned. "Rest up a tad, and if ye know what's good for ye chew on that piece of ginger. I repeat, it'll likely help you, and it sure won't hurt. What will hurt is stayin' the way ye are. The men are gettin' angry, tired of pulling yer weight. Hired to work ye were, and work ye must, or the mates'll toss you to the sharks. It's a long swim to France, lad, and further back to England. Did ye spit it out?"

Christopher rolled the disk in his mouth and held it between his teeth. The two men stuffed him into his hammock, bumping his head on a wood beam and eliciting a pained cry. The smell of vomit on his bedding activated Christopher's gag reflex. John hopped backwards.

"Don't worry; he's dry as a bone. Hasn't eaten a bite since yesterday morn," Patrick said.

"I'm not takin' any chances," John snipped.

A violent rock of the ship hurled John and Patrick sideways.

"If this keeps up, I'll be laying up sick in me own hammock," Patrick complained. "Godspeed, son. Time's running out—better start prayin'." Patrick tucked a damp wool blanket around Christopher's sides.

Rolling to his side Christopher closed his eyes, willing the vertigo to stop. For a few seconds, he chewed on the ginger before tucking the disk between his teeth and cheek. Soaked with seawater, he shivered uncontrollably. His thoughts drifted to the last conversation he had with his father before setting out for London. *There's no easy pathway, son. God told Adam the ground would produce thorns and thistles. A man has to earn his bread by his own toil. If you think you'll have an easier time of it in London, you're sorely mistaken.*

233

I wasn't looking for an easy path, Christopher thought. *Just my own path. I want to chart my own way, not have someone else chart it for me.* He wondered why some folks seemed content to accept their allotment in life while others, like him, chafed against their circumstances. But blind acceptance wasn't in his nature, plain and simple. His thoughts drifted to Anne and Nicholas keeping company in London, attending heretic meetings, strolling home hand-in-hand, and enjoying lingering goodnight kisses. It was too much to take.

"God, if you're really there…" he whispered. The wood door to the forecastle screeched and hammered against its frame. He whipped his head around to see if someone had entered. A floor board creaked. His muscles tensed. "Who's there?" he croaked. A couple of tense minutes later, he continued, "God, I need help. I know I don't deserve it, but if you're there, please help me get better. If I don't, the men will punish me."

A wave of nausea activated his salivary glands. *Not again*, he mumbled. *Help me if you're there. Please.* Counting backwards from ten, he waited for something supernatural to happen. Eight. The door creaked. Six. The ship rocked. Three. Two. One. *Please, God. I need help. I need it now.*

A nine-foot wave rocked the ship. His stomach cartwheeled. He held his knees to his chest until a wave of nausea forced him from his hammock, through the door and across the deck. A few feet short of the rail he keeled over, spewing slimy yellow and green bile onto the wet deck in front of him.

Is this the way you answer prayers? A loud *crack!* from the forecastle door sent spasms of fear through his body. Above the creaking and heaving of the ship he made out voices, barely discernible above the angry ocean roar.

"He hasn't done a single blasted watch yet. I've 'ad enough of doing the work of two men, 'is and mine. Didn't come here to do someone else's job. I got enough as it is, without 'is piling on top of me. Me hands is raw and me feet blistered doing the scrubbing for two. Had to clean the privy area in his stead twice already. If he can't do the work, he shouldn't be here. I spoke my mind to the capt'n." It was John.

"Why was he brought on? No one can tell. The urchin hasn't spent a day at sea in his life before now. Word among the crew is he ran away from home. I know his kind; as soon as the going gets tough they grab a knapsack and run. Never amount to nothin', his kind. We need to get rid of him. The whole crew wants him gone." The second voice belonged to Ol' Barb, the ship's barber.

Christopher eavesdropped, silently protesting. Was it his fault seasickness rendered him useless? He wanted to lash out in self-defense, but bit his tongue

234

and laid still until Lucky, the ship's furry black and white mouser, emerged from below deck and rubbed against his leg. *Please, please don't mew*, he thought. She purred loudly. He pushed her away with his toe. Undaunted, she trotted to his side with her tail straight up, still purring. "Shh! Lucky!" he whispered. *Meow*, she replied, kneading the deck.

"By Jove's teeth, who is Lucky talkin' to?" John looked in the direction of the sound. "She don't mew unless someone is around." Christopher saw the tops of the men's heads bobbing in his direction and scrambled toward an ale barrel. He was too late.

"Ah, there's the scoundrel." John strode to Christopher and pushed his boot into the miserable lad's side. "Time ye pulled yer weight around 'ere, lad." Lucky scurried away.

"Dead weight is what you are," the barber chimed in. "And you know what happens to dead weight on a ship, don't you, lad?" Ol' Barb smiled wide, exposing a tangled mix of empty gums and twisted teeth.

With his sea- and vomit-drenched sleeve, Christopher wiped a pool of saliva from the corner of his mouth and gagged.

"Ye worried, lad?" John flashed a wicked grin. Christopher returned a meek nod. "Ye should be," John taunted. "If we do throw ye over, ye won't be the first. And ye sure won't be the last." They howled in unison. John continued, "Thinks he's going to his death out there in that deep, dark, churning sea." He opened his eyes as wide as they would go, stretching out the words *deep…dark…* and *churning*. Pointing in the direction of the water with his nose, he mocked, "Water's so rough it could turn cream into butter in a minute or two, I wager." Christopher's face turned pale green. "The last one to go over was near yer age, if I recall. Running from something, just like yerself. Didn't want no one tellin' him what to do, not on land or sea. 'Tis a shame. Wasn't a bad lad, I wager, just wasn't pulling his weight and refused to cooperate. A deadly mistake, it was."

"Got 'is life cut off too short, he did." Ol' Barb shook his head. "Maybe a watch at the mast-head'll cure what ails this urchin." The barber lifted his eyes to the top of the mast, when a strong gust of wind ripped the cap from his head and slammed it to the white-capped waves.

Warm liquid trickled down Christopher's right leg. "Please, no," he pleaded. "Don't make me go up there."

John sniffed and looked around. He sniffed again, looking up and down Christopher's pant leg. "I think he pissed 'is pants." He put his face close to Christopher's. "Are ye scared, little miss?"

Christopher grimaced.

"You're not pullin' your weight around the ship," Ol' Barb growled. "We'll string you up where you'll at least be out of the way."

"Rotten idea that is. The lad'll be puking all over the deck." John grabbed hold of a line to steady himself. "Think yer doin' extra work now? Wait'll the wind blows 'is puke in all directions."

"Puke, shmuke," Ol' Barb retorted. "Let's get 'im by the breeches and string 'im up like a sail as high as he'll go. Let the wind whip 'im into shape. Come 'ere, lad."

Curling into a fetal position, Christopher pleaded, "I beg of you, please. Don't do this."

"I'll have nothing to do with yer shenanigans, ye miscreant." John addressed the comment to Ol' Barb. "If that shriveled up ol' prune Patrick gets a whiff of this, you'll be the one overboard. Looks out for the lad for some reason. For the life of me I can't tell why, useless as he is." John turned to Christopher. "I had nothin' to do with this, ye hear? So hold yer tongue when it comes to me, and I won't cause ye no harm." John turned and disappeared behind the forecastle door.

"'Tis just you and me, lad. Tattle and you won't live to see England again. 'Ere we go, upsy, up." Ol' Barb poked his dagger into Christopher's side. "Up, up, lad." With enormous effort, Christopher pulled himself to his feet. "To the mast we go. Move along, lad." Christopher shuffled along, leaning upon ropes and barrels to stay upright. He arrived at the mast and looked up, the howling wind whipping his hair. Filled with dread, he mouthed a silent prayer: *God, if you are there, please have pity on me...* He felt Ol' Barb's hands around his torso.

ॐ

Christopher blinked his eyes to fight back the burning saltwater. His fingers and hands ached from holding to the riggings. Ocean spray trickled down his face and slipped between his chattering teeth. The repulsive taste of sea water punished his impulse to lick his cracked lips.

From his vantage point below the crow's nest, he saw nothing but bone-chilling darkness, a vast, terrifying coffin of churning water eager to swallow him up. Damn the storm! Damn the sea! Curse the sailors! Curse his wretched life! If he survived, he intended to kill the man who put him on the masthead.

236

I'm letting go, he decided. *I can no longer hold on.* Hoping the fall would put him out of his misery once and for all, he tried to release his grip. His fingers wouldn't budge. Summoning the power of mind over flesh, he commanded his hands to open. They clung stubbornly to the rigging. *Curse my hands!*

A whimper of despair turned to weeping. How long he wept, he didn't know, when a quiet but piercing voice whispered within him, *Be still. Don't let go. All will be well.* A sensation of warmth bathed his soul with assurance that the ordeal would pass, that he would survive, that he had a reason to live. He didn't know how he knew, but he knew. He closed his eyes and surrendered.

He awoke to discover his head on Patrick's lap, the sailor's piercing blue eyes staring into his own. "'Ad a rough go of it, 'aven't ye, lad? Look yonder." Patrick pointed eastward. Rays of light peeked above a cloudless horizon. "Who put ye up on the masthead? They'll be hearing from me." Christopher's eyes fluttered closed. "There'll be time enough to hear yer story. Fer now, ye need to rest up. How's yer belly doing, lad?"

Christopher took a deep breath and opened his eyes. "Better, I think."

"By my faith, let's get ye to a hammock so ye can rest. I've ordered the surgeon to keep watch so those rogues can't bother ye further." Patrick put an arm around Christopher's waist and helped him to a hammock near the captain's quarters. After tucking his own dry wool blanket around the exhausted sailor, Patrick patted Christopher's head. "I'll be back by and by to check on ye, lad."

"Thank you." Christopher's voice cracked. He settled into the hammock and watched Patrick walk away, then called after him. Patrick didn't hear. Mustering his last ounce of energy Christopher croaked, "Patrick!"

Patrick turned, eyebrows raised, and shuffled a few steps toward Christopher. "Yea, lad?"

"Why are you doing this? Why are you looking after me?"

Patrick stuck his little finger in his ear to swipe out some wax, looked cross-eyed at the yellow residue, and contemplated for a moment while he wiped it on his cloak. "'Tis my Christian duty, lad." Taking a few steps closer, he put his lips next to Christopher's ear. "And by my faith, if the strangest thing didn't occur last night. I awoke from a dream, and ye were on my mind. Heard a voice whisper, 'Look out for the lad.' So strong it was, I looked about me to see if it was a sprite. 'Spose it was in me head, but whatever it was, I couldn't shake it. You've a work to do, although I won't pretend to know what it is. Scrawny lad though ye be, unknown to anyone of merit, yet ye got somethin' in your future. 'Tis not yer time to meet yer maker. So get well, and let us get on with the work at hand. After we leave Bordeaux, I'll be expecting ye to labor with all yer might. Just 'cause I have sprites talking to me about ye don't mean yer off the hook." He smiled and lowered his voice to a whisper. "And don't tell the mates, lad, but see me before ye debark. I've got some coins to slip ye. Only part wages, since ye haven't labored as ye were s'posed to. They'll be irate if they find out—don't think ye deserve a penny, and I reckon they're right."

Christopher offered a faint smile, and mulled over Patrick's words. A work to do? What did he mean? Patrick walked away, his footsteps echoing on the deck.

Secure in the assurance that he would safely reach his destination, Christopher closed his eyes and drifted into a deep slumber.

July, 1545

—

"Lizzie, time to go." William feigned cheerfulness despite her tardiness. He was in no mood to start his Sabbath Day with a marital squabble. They were, and always would be, late. On the bright side, her tardiness vexed him a bit less these days, as standing in the rear of the nave meant fewer icy stares at the back of his head.

"I'm coming." Her comb clinked when she set it on the butter churn, a sound that signaled the final step in a routine she followed with precision every Sunday morning. He blew out a sigh of relief. The day started off peacefully. His effort to not prod her paid off.

Joyful chatter from a goldfinch in the apple tree beckoned him outside. He opened the door and stepped over the threshold to get a glimpse of the bird, when his foot tapped against a solid object. Looking down, he discovered a wad of wool butted against the cottage. Using his forefinger and thumb he picked up the bundle, jumping backwards when a blood-soaked, black rat plummeted to the ground. He shook the cloth open and read the word *heretic,* scribbled in blood. A chill crawled up his spine.

Searching for a culprit, he saw only five-year-old Margaret in her yard a couple houses away, chattering to a calico cat dressed like a doll. In haste, he crossed the yard to pick up a rag he'd hung on a shovel to dry and used it to scoop up the rat and the blood-stained cloth. He tucked the wad into a root cavity in the apple tree, intending to dispose of it after church.

Elizabeth peeked her head out the door and watched him approach the cottage. "I'm ready. What were you doing over there?"

"I heard a goldfinch singing and wanted to get a look at it." He felt no guilt for leaving out the details. To add yet another incident to the mounting repertoire of harassments plaguing them would only make matters worse. She already had trouble sleeping at night, and feared being home alone.

239

A few heads turned to see who entered ten minutes late for mass. Father Garrett glanced over his spectacles at the two latecomers without breaking his chant. William and Elizabeth found a place in the rear of the nave. Elizabeth fixed her eyes on the priest, while William set about to study the men in attendance. *They persecute me because I read the same words the priest speaks to the congregation*, he thought. *Perhaps if they would read God's word, they would see their hypocrisy.*

He found guilty pleasure in taking mental stock of his accusers' sins. The priest himself provided fruitful fodder for gossip. Everyone knew about Father Garrett's "secret" liaisons with widow Willoughby. As her abdomen expanded, she claimed to be suffering from an illness and moved to live with her family in Canterbury. Rumors flowed through the village like sewage along the gutters. *Speaking of hypocrites*, William thought, Simon Nix stood several rows in front of him. It was common knowledge Simon misrepresented the value of the metal in some of his trinkets, charging far more than they were worth. Six days per week he conducted business with a smile and a handshake. On the seventh, he recited the commandment "Thou shalt not steal" without batting an eye.

Who among them wished him ill? He'd done nothing that he could think of to harm anyone. Was it Simon Nix, who never forgave him for Thomas' middle-of-the-night flight? Or Matthew Cooper, who blamed him for having to send Anne away? Or Father Garrett—was he trying to root dissenters from his flock? Or Mark Whitfield?

A dead rat, a blood-stained cloth and the word *heretic. I must keep it from Elizabeth*, he thought, *but what will they do next?*

Bordeaux

Thomas plucked three-year-old Gabrielle from the ground and set her on a table to keep her from wandering off into the busy crowd. She grasped at a neatly arranged stack of shell-shaped pilgrim badges. He intervened just before she knocked them from the table. Before he could stop her, she wrapped her fingers around a candle and cooed, *"Bougie."* As he pried it from her fingers she kicked and screamed in protest, *"Bougie! I want the bougie!"*

"Gabrielle, my petite octopus, you must not touch the merchandise. It is for the buyers," he scolded.

Her cheeks puffed up as she kicked and cried, "I want the *bougie*!"

He picked up a small statue of a courtly lady he had carved and painted for her, and placed it in her hands. She waved it up and down in the air for several seconds before dropping it to reach for a whistle. The statue hit the stone pavement with a thud.

With an exasperated sigh he muttered, "Where is Maman when I need her?" Prying the whistle from Gabrielle's greedy fingers he continued, "I must be able to focus on the customers this morning, while it is busy."

From clanging ships' bells to banging barrels and crates; from the screech of gulls to the shouts of workers loading and unloading goods from around the world—noise from the busy port drifted over the city's walls and through its turreted gate, Port Cailhau, to Thomas' market stall in front of the Church of Saint Peter. The sounds of commerce were music to Thomas' ear.

A man wearing an English-style cap and a puzzled look slowed down as he walked past the stall.

"I'm still setting up, Monsieur, but please take a look. We have candles and holders, badges, Saint James pilgrim shells, ivory carvings, bells," he swept his hand past an assortment of items on the left side of the table, then continued with others on the right, "and here, some wood carvings I did myself." He held up a statue of the virgin with child, then set it down and picked up a statue of Saint Thomas. Leaning over a wood crate he had not yet unloaded, he retrieved a few leather bags.

"Over here, I have knapsacks and pouches. What is your fancy?"

"If you please, I'm only lookin'." The man offered Thomas a gruff nod.

"Let me know. If I have it, I will get it for you. If I don't, I will find it for you."

Turning a Saint Thomas statue back and forth in his hands, the customer remarked, "Beautiful work. Can't find the likes of Becket in England anymore. The king ran him clean out of the realm, he did. Rather nice to see 'is likeness again."

"You know about Becket in England?" Thomas' eyes lit up.

"By God's teeth, I do. I'm an Englishman, by Jove."

"A pleasant surprise." Thomas emerged from behind his table to shake the stranger's hand. "What brings you to Bordeaux?"

"Pickin' up tuns of wine and dropping off kersey cloth. Work on a Dutch ship, I do," he replied. "She sailed out of London a couple fortnights ago. Stormy weather snagged us. We docked just this mornin'. I'm lookin' for souvenirs to take back to England, not to mention comin' ashore for fresh air. Had a young lad was seasick the whole time, and spent my days cleanin' 'is puke. Lad never made a sea voyage in 'is life. The crewmates and I wagered a bet he's runnin' from home."

Running from home? That was a topic Thomas understood well. "Where is the unfortunate lad from?"

"Boarded the ship in London, but he says he's from Dartford."

Thomas' heart skipped a beat. "Dartford, is it? I have family there. Do you know the lad's name?"

"Let me think. Starts with a C, last name's Ward—no, Wade."

Could it be? Thomas felt a burning sensation in his chest. "Wade. Yes, I was acquainted with some Wades from Dartford. 'Tis a shame you can't remember the lad's first name."

"Let me think…Conrad, Christian, no—I remember, it's Christopher. Christopher Wade, that's it."

"Christopher Wade." Thomas massaged his chin while shifting his gaze toward the city gate, where a cluster of pilgrims passed into the city. "Did the lad come ashore with you?"

"Not with me. Got a bit crossways with the lad when I threatened to mastheaded 'im, but he might've come on his own." John studied the Becket statue.

Mastheading. Thomas smiled. "How long are you in port?"

"Another day at best, two at worst. S'posed to leave on the morrow at dawn." John put the statue back in its place. "Pray tell, where might a man get a good drink of claret? I wish to discover what King Henry sees in the stuff."

Thomas pointed to a cluster of stone buildings across the square. "Cross to the tavern there on the corner." He waited for a look of recognition in John's eyes. "See the sign, 'L'Aquitaine'?"

John nodded. "I'll take yer recommendation." He took a step back.

"Before you leave, pray tell," Thomas stopped him, "how are affairs in England?"

"What affairs might ye be referencin'?"

"The king's affairs. The abolishing of feasts, the closing of monasteries, the…"

John interrupted. "Ah, yes. Don't know how long ye been gone, so I don't know how much has changed since ye left."

"The king had just sacked Canterbury when I came here."

"By God's teeth, ye wouldn't know yer own country. He shut the monasteries, abolished most feasts, and even put the English Bible in the churches until folks were brawlin' so much, he turned around and banned the readin' of it by the common folk."

"An English Bible in the churches?" Thomas intertwined his fingers and rested his hands atop his head. "But why should anything surprise me?"

"'Tis not the half of it, lad, but I can tell ye, possession of that Becket statue there would land ye in the stocks or worse. Becket was clean abolished, ordered to be erased from calendars and prayer books, and removed from churches. The king would've beheaded, drawn and quartered, and burned Becket at the stake—all three, if he could of. Heard tell, Ol' Coppernose dug up Becket's remains and burned 'em, just to have the last word in the matter."

"You don't say." Thomas got a faraway look in his eyes. "I miss merry England, but at least this realm is true to the Holy Mother Church."

"I wouldn't trade England for France, but at least ye don't have the Lollards here to turn the kingdom upside down, I'm guessin'?"

"No Lollards. By the way, name's Thomas Nix." He tipped his cap. "And you?"

"John Wyatt. Obliged."

Thomas took a deep breath. "A different sort of Lollard has sprung up in this land, the réformées they're called. Stirred up by a heretic named Calvin, but he fled to Geneva. Glad this realm had the sense to chase him out. I suppose a man can't escape heretics these days, but at least this kingdom doesn't tolerate them."

John picked up a mahogany carving of the Virgin Mary and ran his fingers across the smooth surface, as if he were caressing a loved one. "The king abolished such statues, calling it idolatry. Folks are havin' to hide their stuff. If I weren't goin' back, I would purchase one. Ye carve souvenirs, then?"

"Yes, and sell them to pilgrims passing through on the Way of Saint James. Following in my father's footsteps, I suppose. He sold souvenirs in Dartford, mostly to pilgrims on their way to Canterbury. The injunctions wiped clean our very means of living, they did."

"Just wait 'til I tell my wife back home, the king chasin' English folks all the way to the Aquitaine. I wish you well, lad, indeed I do."

"Kind of you. Remember, L'Aquitaine tavern, right down the way there. Fine claret. You'll never forget it. The cassoulet is equally good."

"Perhaps ye'd like to meet up there later? I suspect a good many Englishmen'll be there, if ye've a mind to gather with us. Might do ye good to spend a bit of time with your countrymen. 'Tis no one more lonely than a man without a country."

Thomas nodded. "I may do that. Thanks, indeed." He watched Wyatt stop at a fruit and vegetable stand while, nearby, a boy with black, curly hair performed with a monkey. Perhaps Wade would be at the tavern. The time for revenge had arrived. He smiled. Yes, his time had come.

೮೪

Christopher scanned the crescent shoreline of the Garonne River along the city wall, amazed at the variety of vessels from around the world. An uncomfortable pinch in his stomach reminded him he needed nourishment. Beckoning him like the open arms of a friend, the aroma of fresh bread wafted through the city gate. He made his way to Port Cailhau.

"*Saucisson! Fromage!*" A short man with a bald crown atop his head, the first in a long thread of vendors inside the gate, repeated the cry over and over. As Christopher passed, the gentleman rattled off a lengthy description of his offerings.

With a shrug of the shoulders Christopher muttered, "I don't understand." The vendor shrugged his shoulders in return. Christopher's mouth watered at the appetizing assortment of sausages, cheeses, breads, and grapes. Feeling wealthy with undeserved pay padding his purse, he retrieved two testons and pointed to a string of sausages divided into equal portions about the size of his thumb. The vendor rattled something off again. Christopher shook his head in bewilderment.

Picking up the sausage string, the man patted his belly with a satisfied smile and said, "*Saucisson.*"

Christopher nodded. The gentleman pointed to an assortment of cheeses. Christopher selected a fist-sized round of *chèvre*—goat cheese—and a small loaf of bread.

Patting his belly again, the vendor quipped, "*Fromage, c'est bon.*"

"Formaj?"

"*Fromage.* Cheese." Assessing the lad's blank look, the vendor accepted the futility of trying to communicate and requested payment. "*Huit sols, s'il vous plaît.*" He held up eight fingers.

244

Christopher held out his two testons, trusting the salesman to take the proper amount.

"Englich?" the man inquired. Christopher nodded. The vendor took one teston and returned two sols, sending Christopher on his way with a polite, "*Bon appétit.*"

After slipping the change into his pouch, Christopher tore into the sweet bread with his teeth, gnawed off a morsel of sausage and bit into the pungent chèvre. The melding of flavors brought a smile to his lips.

His head spun at the swirl of vendors and patrons bargaining around him in a language he didn't comprehend. Aromas pleasant and pungent—perspiration, animal manure, spices, roasting meats—hung heavily in the summer air.

An adolescent boy, in a hurry to get somewhere, scuttled by carrying a chicken upside down by its legs. The chicken squawked and flapped its wings in a frenzied effort to free itself. As the boy struggled with the bird, his foot slipped in something gooey. "By the mass!" he cried, stopping to wipe the side of his shoe against the ground to scrape off as much chicken dung as he could. An elderly woman selling fruits, vegetables and eggs averted her eyes, but her guilty grin betrayed her witness to the boy's misfortune.

Taking into consideration that he might never again set foot in Bordeaux, Christopher stopped to determine what he most wanted to experience. A grand clock tower in the distance piqued his curiosity, but he decided to first find a gift for Anne. If only winning her heart were as easy as buying her a gift. He kicked himself for acting so stupidly in London. After years of longing, he finally had her under his nose. What a terrible impression he must have left.

He wove past purses and pouches, lace and belts, carved wood and ivory, artisan loaves and cheeses, spices, candles and perfumes. A pigeon landed on the stone walkway in front of him, looking sideways at him as if he should know what was expected. He tossed a chunk of his bread to the ground. The bird hopped down and pinched it in his beak, then skipped a few steps and lit into flight as several other pigeons swooped in. Christopher threw a few more pieces to the gathering flock before deciding to reserve some for himself.

Up ahead, four pilgrims decked in robes and wide-brimmed hats were huddled around a table adorned with wood and ivory carvings, overseen by a striking woman with twinkling hazel eyes and dark brown hair.

"*Bonjour, monsieur,*" she nodded cordially as Christopher approached.

"Uh, *bunjer.*"

"You are Englich?"

Taken aback, he replied, "How did you know?"

"My husband is Englich. I know your accent. Do you look for a carving? We have here some Saint Thomases, some little animals for children, here is a box for a nice gift…"

"The box is lovely. May I pick it up?"

"Of course." His interest pleased her.

He examined the wooden box, intricately carved with a unicorn and vines. "'Tis lovely." He set it down and continued looking.

"Thank you. My husband makes most of them." Christopher felt something brush against his toe. There it was again. Startled, he peeked under the table. A mischievous imp with large brown eyes smiled up at him. Her olive skin and curly, black locks gave her an exotic appearance.

The woman peeked under the table and nudged the child with her toe. "Gabrielle! Come out right now. It is not nice to bother the man."

"She's not bothering me. She reminds me of my sister. Died when she was four."

"I'm very sorry." The woman crossed herself. "May the Blessed Virgin watch over her." She bit her lip and straightened her apron.

"Thank you." He spent several moments admiring the carvings. "Your husband is very skilled. Does he make combs?"

"He doesn't make them, but we do carry some. Over here." She glided to a separate display table, where he saw an assortment of boxwood and ivory combs arranged from simple to ornate. "How do you like this one?" She held up an H-shaped ivory comb, the center cross section carved with birds, flowers and leaves, and painted with navy blue and gold. It had wide teeth on one side for smoothing the hair, and narrow teeth on the other for picking nits from the hair and scalp. She held it out to him.

Christopher flipped it back and forth between his hands. "'Tis lovely." He pictured Anne's face lighting up upon opening such a beautiful gift and asked, "Would you fancy receiving this as a gift?"

She nodded. "Of course. It is fit for a lord to give his lady."

"How much are you asking for it?" he inquired.

She looked him up and down, entertaining second thoughts upon examining his soiled frock and tattered felt cap. "I regret, Monsieur. Few could afford that one. Here we go." She picked up a plain oval boxwood comb. Christopher's expression soured. Anne probably already owned something nicer. Reading his disappointment, she inquired, "It is for a demoiselle?"

"Yes. It needs to be something special."

"We have these, here." She directed him to several double-sided boxwood combs of different shapes and sizes, with simple carvings in the crossbar.

"*Maman*!" Gabrielle shouted.

"I must attend to my daughter. *Pardon.*"

Relieved to peruse the combs without the woman hovering over him, he turned one after another in his hands, when a comb with hearts carved into the crosspiece caught his eye. He pictured Anne pulling it through her silky hair.

Occupied with getting her daughter a snack, the woman glanced up and saw the comb in his hand. "Did you find one?"

"Yes." He held it up. "I can pay ten sols for it."

She frowned. "You ask me to give it to you, Monsieur. Non, I must have fifteen sols, no less." Her tone was sharp.

Unsure how much money he had, Christopher set the comb down. "I'll continue to look around. Perhaps I'll be back."

"Fourteen sols," she said matter-of-factly. "You won't find a prettier comb at a better price in Bordeaux."

"Thank you. I may be back."

"Yes, of course." With a melodic "*Bonne journée,*" she wished him good day.

He stammered "bun journey" and scuttled along, pretending to browse other vendors' displays. Glancing over his shoulder, he saw her attention occupied with the group of pilgrims, who were *ooh-ing* and *ah-ing* over statues of the Virgin with Child. Darting between the Aquitaine tavern and the last market stand along the edge of the square, he counted fifteen sols, unaware that he was being closely watched. If he could talk her down to twelve, he would have three for a claret. He put the coins in his purse and stopped by another merchant to look at combs, waiting for her to notice she had competition before he returned to her stand.

"You decide to buy, Monsieur?"

"Twelve sols are all I can offer. The man over there offers many fine combs as well." He pointed with his chin.

She studied him for several seconds, pensive. "*Bon.* For your lady, I will do it."

Christopher fished a teston and two sols from his pouch and placed the coins in her hand. She extended the heart-engraved comb with a smile.

"I hope she will like it."

"Thank you." Gleeful, he slipped the purchase into his pouch. Thoughts of Anne's face lighting up at the sight of the comb propelled him, almost skipping, toward the Aquitaine. Outside the tavern door, he double checked the coins in his pouch. A fervent search produced only one sol. He retraced his steps, but found no lost coins. With a sigh, he realized he would have to skip the claret.

August, 1545

―

London

Anne rubbed her eyes. Dark circles betrayed a stream of nights spent tossing and turning. Gazing across Tower Hill to the Tower of London, its somber grey walls luminescent in the midday sun, she recalled the days when she thought a trip to London would offer an escape from her stifling lot in Dartford. How wrong she'd been. Lately, she felt like she was bobbing in a cauldron of angst.

She stopped pacing to face Nicholas, who was reclined on the grass. "I don't dare attend the meetings anymore. Why should we put our lives at risk?"

Nicholas rose to a sitting position and popped the last bite of a venison pie in his mouth. Still chewing, he responded, "You don't believe anything bad will happen, do you? No one suspects Victoria. She was a nun, after all. Methinks God placed you under her wing for your protection."

"Master McMillan warned her. He knows of the wolves prowling about in London. Victoria told me he's on the inside circle of a group of well-placed men—merchants, aldermen, and others—that helps reformers escape. He also helps smuggle Bibles and writings of the reformers into London. They call themselves the Christian Brethren. If the king's men were to discover Master McMillan housing a so-called heretic while he engages in such activities, Master McMillan himself would certainly be charged with heresy. And what would happen to me?"

"A group in London that helps reformers escape England? I had no idea!" Nicholas scanned the Tower's crenelated ramparts while contemplating the gory end of folks imprisoned within those walls for sedition. "How do the Brethren conceal their work? And how did your aunt learn of them?"

"I don't know how they conceal their work. As for where Victoria came by her information, I don't know that either. 'Tis the most she's ever shared with me; I didn't dare press her for more. Master McMillan himself told her, I wager."

"I understand your fear, but how can you simply abandon your convictions?"

She put her hands on her hips and cocked her head sideways. "I'm not abandoning my convictions. I only intend to hold them close, so as not to put myself or others in danger. Surely you understand?"

He thought for a moment. "But aren't we supposed to let our light shine?"

Plopping down on the grass next to him with a defeated sigh, she whispered, "I don't know." She wiped her eyes with her sleeve.

"Are you crying?"

"Perhaps," she sniffled.

Nicholas scooted beside her and put a hand on her shoulder. "I'm sorry. I didn't mean to upset you."

"'Tis not your fault. Nearly everything is upsetting these days." She buried her face in her knees. "I wish there were somewhere to escape." She looked sideways at him, her eyes clouded with angst.

"I wish there were such a place as well." Taking her hand in his, he stroked the petal-soft skin on the back of her hand.

Intertwining her fingers with his, she sat up straight and declared, "God led Israel out of Egypt, to the promised land. He could lead us out of peril, if he had a mind to."

"Of course. He is God; he can do anything. But if he had a mind to lead us somewhere, don't you think he would have done so by now?"

"I suppose. So many terrible things have already happened, surely he would have intervened to prevent them, if he intended to."

Nicholas looked downhill to the murky Thames. Vessels large and small glided up and down the busy waterway. He brightened. "Have you heard of Amerigo Vespucci, the explorer?"

Eyeing him as if he were mad, she blurted, "Ameri-who?"

"Amerigo Vespucci. A Spanish merchant selling books in London told a group of us at the market about him. This Vespucci explored a new land, peopled with a non-Christian race entirely different from our own. In writing of his adventures, he described a naked, red-skinned folk who embed stones and bones in their flesh and actually eat other humans. Imagine! Such are the tribes who populate the New World across the sea. King Ferdinand of Spain financed Vespucci's journeys, as he did those of Christopher Columbus."

At the mention of a people eating human flesh, her arms erupted in goosebumps. "*The* King Ferdinand, married to Queen Isabella, parents of King Henry's first wife?"

"Yes, parents of Queen Catherine, she whom His Majesty turned the world upside down to divorce."

"Does this Vespucci still live?"

"No, he died a few years after King Henry was born."

Her eyebrows slanted. "Why are you telling me this now?"

"You mentioned wishing there were somewhere to flee. Perhaps one day, the English will have more interest in exploring the New World. This merchant who told of Vespucci said the Spanish intend to Christianize the natives. Perhaps if the New World were to become Christianized, it would be suitable for living."

"It seems utter folly to me for any Englishman to voyage to a savage land across the sea. We can't even solve our troubles at home."

"I suppose I hadn't considered it from that angle." He thought for a moment. "Come to think of it, King Henry's father financed John Cabot's explorations. It seems Englishmen have some interest in exploration, after all."

"Pray tell, what did Cabot find?"

"A land he called 'Newfoundland.' Folks call this land across the sea the New World, or America."

"America. I don't recall hearing of it. How do you learn of these things?"

"Foreign merchants tell the tales, and the stories spread like ripples in a pond. As I mentioned, Vespucci's adventures are also in print. It turns out they're quite well known among folks who read."

"Would you journey across the sea, if the opportunity presented itself?"

"I don't know that I have the courage of an explorer."

Anne sighed. "You had the courage to come to London. I don't even have the courage to attend the meetings anymore."

Snuggling close to her, he whispered, "Let me take care of you." He cradled her face in his hands and pulled her toward him, kissing her softly at first, then with a hunger that frightened her. "Marry me," he pleaded. "I want to protect you."

She abruptly stood and stumbled backwards, breathless. "I don't know what to say. This comes as a surprise."

Jumping to his feet, he brushed the grass off his trousers and declared, "Surely it's no surprise that I care for you. Spending the past few weeks in your company has made me sure. I want to make you my wife." He pulled her close to him.

A wave of confusion crashed through her mind. She laid her head against his chest and heard his heart thumping loudly. "I care for you—truly, I do. But marriage? I don't know." She took a step back, feeling a twinge of guilt upon seeing him look as if she'd just pierced his heart with a hot iron.

He stepped forward. She backed further away. Thrusting his hands upward, he complained, "What holds you back? What must I do to win your heart?"

Looking down at her toes, she whispered, "I don't know. I need some time alone." She turned and trotted up the grassy hill, leaving Nicholas to question the wisdom of bearing his heart.

September, 1545

——

Christopher dropped his travel bag on the ground, taking care to avoid landing it in a mud puddle. The coins he'd earned on *The Wayfair* jingled merrily upon impact. He knocked on the door and shouted, "Nicholas!" No one answered. A hound the color and size of a fawn bounded toward him, sniffed his legs and started barking. He pushed the mutt away with his knee and tapped on the door again. "Nicholas!"

Out of sight, a man's voice stammered, "Enough of the racket, eh? I'm trying to get some sleep here." Peeking around the corner, Christopher saw a vagrant slumped against the building like a half-empty barley sack. The man looked up at him, one eye swollen and half closed, and several days' stubble on his cheeks and chin.

Christopher slipped his forearm over his nose and mouth to block the stench of urine and choked out the words, "Have you seen someone about my age coming and going from this tenement?"

"Do I look like yer watchdog, lad?" After a loud burp, the vagrant closed his eyes.

With your jiggling jowls and bloodshot eyes, I rather think you do, Christopher thought to himself. He gave the man a once-over and decided that trying to extract information from him would be a waste of time. Once again, he rattled the door handle. No luck. Throwing his bag over his shoulder, he gazed across the river to Southwark, deciding upon his next move.

A screech behind him gave him a start. The door next to his former tenement cracked open. Two crystal blue eyes, belonging to a small face topped by a thick tuft of blonde hair, peered up at him.

"Good day," Christopher nodded.

The boy stared, stone-faced, his freckles smudged with dirt, his cheeks and eye sockets sunken in. Upon Christopher's approach, the boy hastily closed the door.

Christopher swallowed his frustration and knocked. The door latch wiggled ever so slightly.

"Away from the door." A shrill female voice inside the tenement penetrated the thin walls. Christopher wondered whether the warning was directed at him or the child. "Away," the voice screeched. "I warned ye not to open the door, or I'll take the switch to yer behind." The latch stopped moving.

Shadows fell across the alleyway as the sun sank below the horizon. Christopher started toward the bridge, intending to traverse into Southwark. He stopped to admire Saint Paul's lofty steeple, glowing in the setting sun, and thought of nearby Honey Lane, where in all likelihood his former best friend spent a good deal of time courting the maiden he loved. Lodging in London would keep him closer to Anne.

A brisk walk took him to Bishopsgate, to a cluster of inns just inside the city wall. He ducked into The Four Swans and discovered himself face-to-face with a sallow-skinned woman too careworn to smile.

"May I help you?" She spoke with a thick Flemish accent.

"Have you any rooms available?"

As if his question were a burden, she sighed, "We're full tonight. You'd have better luck in Southwark. Down that way and across the bridge."

"Yes, I know the area. Thank you."

He stepped outside. Darkness cloaked the city, filling him with malaise. Perhaps Nathan would allow him lodging for a night. He didn't want to take advantage of his uncle, but he needed to save everything he could. If he were careful with his ship's wages, he figured he could sustain himself for a couple months while he looked for work. He patted his pouch. It felt good to have money.

A scruffy, middle-aged man who materialized from nowhere tottered toward him. His muscles tensing, Christopher scoped all directions for an escape. The man picked up speed.

"Pardon me," the stranger called in a thick Flemish accent, his breath reeking of whiskey. "I start a job day after da morrow. A penny or two vould help." Afraid to say no, Christopher pulled a penny from his purse and handed it to the supplicant.

"'Tis all I can spare." He took a couple steps backward.

The drunkard's eyes locked on Christopher's bag. "I zee you have full purse. Don't be zelfish." Just as the stranger reached for his arm, Christopher spun around. Clutching a handful of Christopher's cloak the man hissed, "Not so fast. Da English dogs kill my vife and you vill pay for it. Hand it over."

"Let me go!" Writhing to shake the stranger off, Christopher shouted, "I have no idea what you're talking about."

After he released the cloak to swipe at the bag, the beggar latched on to Christopher's arm. "He burn Margareta, my poor vife," he howled. "Dis English king burn her, do you hear me?" Pulling and pushing, he reduced Christopher to a rag doll.

Impelled by a rush of adrenaline, Christopher thrust his knee to the man's groin. Shouting out a string of expletives, the menace crumpled to the street. As fast as his legs could carry him, Christopher ran past the Aldgate pump before he slowed down to look over his shoulder. The stranger was nowhere in sight. Newly spooked of the dangers lurking in London's alleys and streets after dark, he decided to swallow his pride and drop in on Nathan unannounced.

Fifteen minutes later, he knocked. No one answered, He knocked again, relieved when he heard the sound of footsteps approaching the door. The door cracked open only far enough for one eye to peer through the opening.

"Christopher?" Inch by inch Nathan opened the door, until he knew it was Christopher on the other side. "You're back from France, are you?"

Removing his cap, Christopher nodded. "Yes, safe and sound."

"Please, come in." Christopher stepped inside, wondering why Nathan seemed in a rush to close the door. "Set your bag down there, by the barrel. When did you return?"

"Just this eve. Pardon me for dropping in at this hour. I stopped at the tenement where Nicholas and I lodged before I left, but he wasn't there. Then I thought to rent a room near Bishopsgate, but the inns were full. After an encounter with a vagabond intent on robbing me, I decided to solicit your kindness instead—just for tonight."

"Don't think of it. Get that cloak off." He hung Christopher's cloak on a peg next to a bouquet of goldenrod hanging upside down to dry. "How was your journey? You must tell me everything."

"'Twas more than I can recount after a tiresome day. But it was most definitely an adventure."

"Have you had any vittles?"

"Some pork pottage at a tavern across the bridge. And how are you and Lucy?"

"Well enough off. Our daughter gave birth two weeks ago to a lovely little imp—a girl, it is. We almost lost them both to a fever, but by God's grace they made it. Lucy is there now to tend to them."

"A new granddaughter. Congratulations."

"Yes, 'tis our first. Marie's the name."

With the pleasantries expended, Nathan sat unusually quiet, tapping his fingers on the table.

"The cutpurse that almost got my bag," Christopher piped up, "he said something about the king killing his wife. He had a Flemish accent."

"Oh, God bless you. The poor Flemish brethren. They've been clean chased from their homeland, only to be persecuted in ours. Said his wife was killed, did he?"

"Yes, said she was burned by the king."

Nathan shook his head. "She must have been an Anabaptist. They've been burned and buried alive in their homeland by the thousands. Many of them aren't faring much better here."

"Perhaps I should have given him an extra penny or two. You might be interested to know I met an Englishman in France. He told me the land is still loyal to the pope, save for followers of a man named John Calvin stirring up dissent. 'Tis not just England and Germany that are at war with Rome."

"Is that so? Folks are raising their voices against Nero everywhere. Calvin—yes, I've heard of him."

Christopher searched his mind for another topic, but came up empty.

Nathan twiddled his thumbs while his eyes shifted about the room. Finally, he took a deep breath and broke the silence. "I don't know if now is the best time to tell you, but I suppose there won't be a better."

Christopher leaned forward. "What is it?"

"'Tis your father."

Bordeaux

"I can't believe my ill fortune." Thomas slammed his fist on the padded arm of his chair, sending a small cloud of dust airborne. Pushing himself to a standing position, he paced before the chair for several seconds and sat back down with a *humph*. "How did I miss him?"

"He seemed very concerned about money. He must not have gone to L'Aquitaine."

"His shipmates said he was a sluggard. They wanted to throw him overboard, and were rooting for me to finish him off so they wouldn't have to endure a return voyage with the louse. I watched him walk straight toward the tavern, then stop and turn away. He was so close! I came here to get away from heretics, and the son of that detestable Lollard, Wade, shows up in this village! How can it be?"

Charlotte massaged the back of his neck. "Don't worry. He has returned to his home. He'll never bother you again. It was a strange twist of fate."

He leaned forward. Her touch was grating on him. "But now that he knows where I am, he might notify the authorities. After all these years, I had finally let my guard down." He stood and slammed the wall with his fist. A statue of Saint Christopher wobbled and toppled from a shelf onto the floor. Taking long steps he strode to the statue, wrapped his fingers around it, and hurled it across the room. Charlotte's jaw dropped.

"Thomas!" she scolded. "You must calm down. I don't want our children to see their father act this way."

He spun around, his face scrunched up and scarlet like a child having a tantrum. Charlotte backed away. "What do you know of these things?" he shouted. "You've lived in this land your entire life. You'll never know what it means to be without a homeland, to never see your father or friends again. I've given up everything I hold dear. Everything! A heretic's son roams free, while I live in exile."

She took a deep breath to calm herself. "I thought you were happy here with me, with Gabrielle and Anatole. You consider life here with us exile? Why didn't you say you were so unhappy? Perhaps we could go to your homeland, visit your father."

"You don't understand. I spoke ill of the king's reforms."

"Someday you'll have a new king, and he'll make changes, no? New rulers always do. You'll return to your homeland. I'll go with you. I'll stay by your side."

Her expression of loyalty softened his heart. "I suppose such changes are possible. I just don't know." He sat down and buried his face in his hands.

Charlotte sat in a chair across from him, her face pale. "Something will work out. You'll see. Look how things are changing in France. Just last week, I discussed the Bible with some of Calvin's followers." She rushed her hand over her mouth, wishing to inhale the words that had just escaped.

257

The darkness in his eyes could have turned a wolf in its tracks. She held his gaze, hoping her fear didn't show.

London

Victoria looked up from her needlework. "Did I hear someone tapping at the door?"

"I didn't hear it." Anne neither glanced up nor broke stride as her hand glided an embroidery needle up and down along a pillow case edge.

Victoria cocked her head. "There it is again. You didn't hear anything?" Anne shook her head. After folding the linen tablecloth she was stitching with blackwork, Victoria set it on the arm of her chair. "I'll get it." She stood up and smoothed her apron, puzzled by her niece's evasive behavior.

Anne's body quaked as she strained to hear the goings-on in the next room. The door creaked open. With a lump in her throat, she thought of a neighbor arrested the week before for attending Bible study meetings. She heard Victoria say, "Yes, she is. Let me fetch her for you. Please, come in." Her body stiffened. A man cleared his throat.

"Anne, you have a visitor," her aunt called.

Struggling to steady her voice, Anne responded, "Coming." She wove her needle into the linen and folded the fabric, taking her time to precisely match the edges and corners, and set the piece on a small table near her chair. Placing the palms of her hands against her cheeks, she felt heat radiating from her face. She tucked a few stray hairs inside her coif and steeled herself.

"'Tis impolite to keep a visitor waiting," Victoria called. "'Tis not like her," Anne heard Victoria tell the stranger. The man uttered something unintelligible.

With a sudden surge of determination to face her fate with courage, Anne took a deep breath, tightened the bow on her apron, straightened her back and crossed the kitchen to the front room. When she saw the visitor, her heart stopped.

He removed his cap. "Anne."

Slipping her hands behind her back to hide the trembling, she offered a polite nod and stated the obvious. "You're back from your voyage."

Fiddling with his hat, Christopher replied, "We docked last night, just before sunset."

"W...w...welcome back," she stammered. Silence lingered as they stood, paralyzed.

Watching the awkward ordeal, Victoria stepped forward and offered to take his cloak. "Please, have a seat. You must tell us about your travels."

"I can stay but a few minutes," he explained, declining her offer. "I've an appointment with a butcher in Smithfield—Barnard Johnson. Are you acquainted with him?"

Anne nodded. "We buy our meat from him on occasion." Her tone was terse, her mind reeling with images of their last encounter—Christopher drunk, saturated with foul water from the Thames, spitting curses at her and Nicholas.

Sensing the tension, Victoria excused herself.

"How was your voyage?" Anne strained to be polite.

"It ended well enough, but it got off to a rough start. I fought a terrible bout of seasickness that lasted almost all the way to Bordeaux. A kindly ship's mate told me 'twas the worst case he'd ever seen."

"'Tis fortunate that you overcame it and returned safely, I suppose."

He found her detached air disconcerting, but continued, "Yes, 'twas frightful. By the time I arrived in Bordeaux, I was in a very weakened state." He stared at his hat while they struggled for words to bridge the uncomfortable silence. After several seconds, he sighed. "I see that my coming caught you off guard. I won't tarry." Her heart skipped a beat when his eyes locked on hers. "I wished to apologize for my behavior when you saw me last, and the impression I must have left with you while I ran about London like a knave. I wish I could erase the months after Nicholas and I first arrived in London, and have them to live over. While I was out on the ship, I saw the error of my ways. I…"

Lifting a hand, she interrupted, "Please—what's past is past. I bear you no ill will. Nicholas told me some of what you were enduring when you left Dartford—the accusations and suchlike. It must have been intolerable, to be falsely branded."

Fighting the urge to ask her how much time she and Nicholas spent together, he bit his bottom lip and searched in vain to find a flicker of warmth in the hazel eyes he had fallen in love with on an autumn day seven years earlier. A glint near her breast caught his eye. It was a penny suspended on a ribbon around her neck, smoothed of its original design, bent into an S shape, and carved with the letters *AC*—Anne Cooper. A lover's token.

"I mustn't keep Master Barnard waiting," he said. Feeling like his arms were made of lead, he slapped on his hat and, with a knot in his stomach, turned to leave. At the sound of his name he turned, hoping for a kind word to assuage the sinking feeling in his gut. She fiddled with the penny between the forefinger and thumb on her left hand, stalling.

"What is it?" he asked, hopeful.

"This isn't easy. It's that Nicholas and I are…we're betrothed to be married. I don't want you to waste time thinking about me."

"I see." He swallowed hard, his discomfort growing with each heartbeat. "I don't know what to say. Godspeed." After tipping his hat, let himself out the door and disappeared into the fog.

"Godspeed," she whispered, watching him walk away.

Once out of sight he quickened his pace to a trot, then broke into a full-speed sprint toward the river. Upon reaching the bank of the Thames he fished through his purse for the comb he purchased in Bordeaux, and lifted his arm toward the churning water.

☘

A clap of thunder shook the ground, rousing Christopher from a fitful sleep. He rubbed his temples to relieve the pressure in his head, wondering if life would ever offer a reprieve from its vexations. He had decisions to make, none of the answers evident. Nathan urged Christopher to visit his father immediately, for William was being harassed in Dartford and Nathan feared for his brother's life. Christopher worried that if he left London to see his father, he would forever lose the opportunity to win Anne back.

The words, "Nicholas and I are betrothed to be married" clawed at his thoughts like a frantic, caged badger. She might as well have tied an anchor around his neck and thrown him into the English Sea.

Alack, alack, what shall I do?
For care is cast into my heart,
And true love locked thereto.

They were King Henry's words, and they were fitting—the words of a man endlessly embroiled in tempestuous love affairs. Another clap of thunder jolted Christopher's frayed nerves. He had feared the possibility of Anne and Nicholas coming together, but nothing prepared him to hear the words from her own mouth—*betrothed to Nicholas. 'Tis no use*, he muttered out loud, punching his pillow.

No sooner had he uttered the words than a voice rebuked him. It wasn't an audible voice, nor was it his own voice. It was a voice from his past, that of a beggar who had admonished him on the Darent riverbank nearly six years earlier. The folly of it almost made him laugh in the midst of his agony.

"*What do you mean, 'tis no use?*" the voice said. "*Has she run away on a pilgrimage? Does she want to be a nun? Has she married the Oxford lad? Has she taken up housekeeping with a vicar?*"

His response now, as then, was no. No, she didn't run away on a pilgrimage; no, she didn't want to be a nun; and no, she didn't take up housekeeping with a vicar. But the answer to the fourth question was not so simple. No, she wasn't married to the Oxford lad, but her betrothal to his best friend was no better. "*Then ye have hope, lad. Ye got to fight for what ye want. Fight for the maiden! 'Tis all about chivalry—the maids fancy the chivalrous sort.*"

Chivalry. Why did Harry's words come to him as nearly an answer to prayer as the reassuring voice on the masthead? Christopher had her at arm's length. If he lost her now, he would lose her forever.

Ye got to fight for what ye want. Fight for the maiden! Yes, he would. He would fight for Anne. Even if it meant fighting against his best friend.

He slept little that night, busy devising ways to win the heart of his lady.

Dartford

"Elizabeth! Elizabeth!"

In no mood to waste her precious time as an audience for Amy's wagging tongue, Elizabeth pretended not to hear. The beleaguered wife of William Wade picked up her pace and continued on Watling Street, eager to reach the privacy of her cottage away from probing stares and sideways glances.

"Elizabeth!"

Feeling a tap on her shoulder, Elizabeth turned. "Amy! Why, what do you know?"

"Give me just a moment." Amy inhaled deeply and exhaled slowly. "By my faith, 'tis becoming more and more challenging to keep up these days." Elizabeth smiled at Amy's growing girth, wickedly satisfied that Amy was fatter than herself. The gossip waddled like a duck on legs that resembled tree stumps. *Must be sneaking too much food at the tavern*, Elizabeth mused.

Impatience churning inside her, Elizabeth replied, "Amy, by my troth I must hasten home. William isn't feelin' well and needs my attention. I've been to the wise woman and…"

"Don't you wish to know what Luke Tisdale said at the tavern last night?"

After Elizabeth learned that Amy spread rumors she and William were to blame for Christopher's prodigal turn, Elizabeth couldn't find it within herself to forgive. Amy's children were far from perfect. William rightly suggested a gossip's bridle to cure the woman.

"I've only a minute. What did Luke say?" Elizabeth fought back a grimace.

"They're laying a snare for your husband. Luke and his accomplices have been watching your cottage, trying to lure William outside so they can enter in and seize his Bible. I overheard when I was serving them at the tavern last night."

"By God's teeth, those men are evil." Elizabeth bristled. "Did you learn anythin' else? Have they any other plans?"

"They'll do anything they can to get William away from the cottage so they can search without him in the way. Hounds on a blood trail, they are."

Elizabeth rubbed her fingertips over the goosebumps on her arms. "And if I'm home when they come? Do they have plans for me as well?"

"They made no mention of you. I wager you're nothing but a gnat that they'll swat out of the way. Be on your guard."

Elizabeth felt her legs go weak. "We need your prayers, Amy. Will you pray for us?"

"Of course. No one wishes you well more than I." With a sweet smile, Amy clasped Elizabeth's hands in hers. Bowing her head she prayed, "Sacred Virgin, give this good woman strength against her enemies."

"Thank you. I beg you, continue to pray for us."

"I will." Amy squeezed her hand. "Godspeed."

Elizabeth walked a few paces when the call of her name stopped her.

"Oh, Elizabeth!" It was Amy.

Elizabeth sighed and turned. "Yes?"

"What seems to be ailing William? Something that a bit of pottage from the tavern might help with?"

"He was taken with a fever this morn, chills and such. 'Tisn't like him to stay in bed, but he couldn't get himself up and about."

"Hope he doesn't have the ague," Amy said. "If you have a moment, I'll send you home with a crock of my fresh leek pottage."

262

Impatient to be on her way, but not wanting to be rude, Elizabeth accepted. "'Twould be kind of you. Would you mind if I waited here?"

"Of course not. I'll be right back."

Elizabeth watched Amy waddle toward the Crown & Anchor. Just as Amy reached for the tavern door, Luke Tisdale emerged. Anger seized Elizabeth's breast. *How dare he! I've a mind to tell him what I think about him this very minute.* Tisdale chatted briefly with Amy until he saw Simon Nix wheel a cart of goods from the street into The Pilgrim Hat. The two men disappeared into the store.

They're likely plannin' a trap for my William this very minute, she thought, frustrated at the helplessness she felt. As impulse overruled reason, she stormed toward The Pilgrim Hat, ruminating on what to say when she entered. Her hand just touched the door handle when Amy emerged from the tavern with a hot crock of pottage wrapped in towels. The aroma of onion and sage seeped through their cloth barrier and teased Elizabeth's nose.

Looking Elizabeth up and down, Amy asked, "What are you doing?"

"Well, I…" The shop door opened, pushing Elizabeth backwards.

"Why, Luke," she exclaimed, steadying herself.

Luke tipped his hat. "Elizabeth. In town this evening, are you?"

"I came to fetch a potion for William. He's taken ill."

"Nothing grave, I hope?"

"'Tis too early to tell. Perhaps Amy's pottage will help."

"I've heard no reports of sweating sickness. Let's hope he suffers from nothing of the sort."

"I believe his fever would be worse if sweatin' sickness were the problem, but he's ill enough to be laid up."

"Sorry to hear it. Wish him well for me."

"Thank you. I'll tell him." She adjusted the towels around the crock and started on her way, fuming at Luke's hypocrisy.

As soon as he knew Elizabeth was out of earshot, Luke turned to Amy. "Is William truly ill?"

"Has chills, she says, and can't get himself out of bed."

"I see." His lips twisted into a wry grin. "Unfortunate, indeed."

"I feel sympathy for the poor woman." Amy watched Elizabeth amble up East Hill. "Plagued with trouble, she is. Don't know how she holds up."

"A lesser woman would have broken by now," Luke replied. "Perhaps I should call on William to offer my help."

263

Male and female, young and old, rich and poor filed into the church for evening mass. A wild-eyed elderly man with wiry grey hair, cradling a small terrier-mix, shuffled past and squeezed into a line four rows in front of Christopher before settling the dog on his lap. Christopher had seen the man begging at various city gates.

On his tiptoes, Christopher searched frantically across the heads of those seated close to the front. A hush fell over the congregation as the priest entered with a deacon close behind. After kissing the altar, the priest chanted, "In the name of the Father, and the Son, and the Holy Ghost."

Christopher made the sign of the cross, along with the rest of the congregation.

"Have mercy on us, Lord," the priest chanted loudly.

"For we have sinned against you," came the response.

"Show us, O Lord, your mercy," the priest sang.

"And grant us your salvation." Christopher's lips moved, but no sound came out.

"May almighty God have mercy on us, forgive us our sins, and bring us to everlasting life."

The priest has a rather pleasant voice, Christopher thought. In his distraction, he said *amen* after everyone else. A freckle-faced, redheaded boy beside him snickered. Christopher stuck out his tongue. The wide-eyed boy elbowed his father. Christopher focused on the priest as if nothing had happened.

"Behold the Lamb of God," the priest continued. "Behold him who takes away the sins of the world." At the ringing of the Sanctus bell the priest elevated the bread for all to see. A second later, the man who brought the terrier into the church lifted the dog above the heads of the congregation. A collective gasp rippled across the room.

"He's mad." A tunic-clad chandler stood and made the announcement. The priest's jaw dropped. "I mean no disrespect, speaking during communion," the chandler looked about, "but, in earnest, Collins there—he with the dog—is lunatic. He means no ill, raising his dog as the host." Folks rose from their knees, mumbling one to another.

"Remove him." An elderly man, whose head shone like it was polished with wax, pointed his cane at Collins and cried, "He blasphemes the host." Two officers rushed forward, each taking Collins by an arm, and dragged him out of the nave while the terrier nipped at one of the officers' feet. A swift kick from the officer sent the animal sprawling. The congregation parted to avoid the furry projectile.

"Let me alone!" Collins protested, kicking with all his might. "Lucy! Lucy!" he shouted after his dog. The terrier's high-pitched bark ricocheted off the church's stone walls. Another officer scooped up the animal and rushed out of the nave with the dog writhing under his arm.

Once the commotion left the building the priest directed all to kneel, and resumed as if nothing had happened. Christopher scanned the crowd for Anne, this time spying Nicholas and Anne kneeling side-by-side, several rows ahead and to his left. His heart stopped. He took a deep breath and exhaled slowly, steeling himself. Chivalry. He would practice chivalry, if it killed him.

ಣ

At the sight of Christopher waiting next to the open church doors, Nicholas' countenance fell. *Perfect*, Christopher thought. The element of the unexpected would work in his favor. *Knights are cunning.* Christopher smiled and extended his hand. Nicholas crossed his arms with an icy glare.

"What are you doing here?" Anne whispered, her heart racing.

Giddy at having the wherewithal to insert himself into their evening, Christopher chirped, "Do you two have plans for the rest of the evening?"

"We planned—the two of us—to find something to eat." Nicholas kicked at the floor while a young couple pushed past, looking daggers at the three folks blocking the exit.

"Mind if I join you? I could tell you about my adventures at sea and in France, and the two of you could tell me about events in London of late. I see much has happened in my absence." Without waiting for an answer, Christopher descended the church steps in lockstep with Nicholas while the street flooded with churchgoers leaving evening mass.

A light breeze chilled the air. Anne rubbed her arms vigorously with the palms of her hands.

"It's a bit brisk." Christopher offered her his cloak while Nicholas frowned. "You must think it odd of me to ask to join you. I assure you, I've no intention of making trouble."

Why would he even think he could? Nicholas fumed.

265

"I wouldn't blame you for not wanting my company," Christopher continued. "I behaved shamefully before I left."

"I won't argue with you on that," Nicholas snipped.

Up ahead, a costermonger with a basket on her head screeched, "Hot pudding pies! Hot! Hot pudding pies! Hot!" Hungry patrons flocked around her.

"May I buy us all a pudding pie?" With a quick glance at both of them, Christopher opened his purse.

Nicholas shook his head. "I've lost my appetite."

Ignoring Nicholas, Christopher stepped into a queue forming around the vendor and winked at Anne while Nicholas' head was turned. She scrunched her eyebrows in stern rebuke, while her heart fluttered.

Nicholas stepped forward, fumbling through his purse. "Let me get them. It was to be our evening, after all." He winked at Anne, getting only a blank look in return. Christopher spied a break in the line and worked himself into a position close to the front, while Nicholas glowered.

A knight must be generous. Christopher laughed inside. Harry would be proud of him. After he paid for and distributed the pies, he looked left and right and asked, "Where shall we go?"

"Saint Paul's?" Sinking her teeth into her pudding pie, Anne pointed in the direction of the church with her elbow.

Nicholas licked crumbs from his mouth and the tips of his fingers and added, "We can eavesdrop on the newsmongers. Perhaps we'll learn something of the king's twelve mistresses."

"His Majesty has twelve mistresses?" Anne studied Nicholas, perplexed.

"Not that I know of, but that doesn't mean you won't hear it on Paul's Walk." Reaching for Anne's free hand, Nicholas laced his fingers between hers.

Chivalry, Christopher thought, his heart sinking at the sight of their clasped hands. *If chivalry doesn't work, nothing will.* He took a bite of his pudding pie and swallowed hard. "If you hear it on Paul's Walk, it must be believed. Is that how the news in London works?"

To spite Christopher, Nicholas offered a passing hound the remainder of his pie. The dog choked it down, wagged his tail, and waited to see if more was forthcoming before it trotted off.

Ignoring the gesture, Christopher commented, "Paul's Walk is a part of London life with which I'm not acquainted." He nibbled at the crust of his pie, despite a marked decline in appetite.

As they ambled along the street to Saint Paul's, Anne begged, "Tell us about your voyage."

"Where do I begin?" Christopher replied, relieved that she asked. "The experience left me a changed man."

Her eyes lit up. "Start with the voyage. What was the sea crossing like? Did you see any sea creatures?"

He stuffed the last bit of pie into his mouth and wiped his fingers on his trousers. "The water was rough from the moment we entered the English Sea. I spent the entire journey battling a horrible case of seasickness and wished to die, by my faith. A good man by the name of Patrick helped me through it. I saw no sea creatures—I barely saw the light of day."

"Oh, my." Her sympathies roused, Anne remarked, "I did think you looked a bit thin upon your return." Nicholas cast her a sideways glance.

"Did the other sailors get angry?" Anne pressed. Nicholas hoped the answer was yes. "You were hired to do a job, after all."

"I should say so. One of them mastheaded me. By then I not only wanted to die, but I was sure dying would be my fate out on the churning waves." They stopped in front of the cathedral. "I suppose I should end my tale here," Christopher offered, "so we can listen in on the newsmongers."

"No, don't stop," Anne pleaded. "Let's find a place to sit, and you can finish your story."

"The two of you have other affairs. I won't bother you any further."

"By my faith, Christopher, don't leave us hanging. We want to hear your story, don't we?" She elbowed Nicholas. "Here's a good place to sit." She pointed to a stone bench.

"Very well," Christopher obliged. "But I'll be brief so you can get along with your evening."

"Don't be silly. We have nowhere to go," Anne insisted. She settled next to Christopher, eager for him to continue.

"We promised Victoria we would be back by dusk," Nicholas complained, peering across the river through a gap in the buildings. A golden glow haloed the horizon. "'Tis almost dusk, in fact." Anne ignored him, her eyes riveted on Christopher. Fighting a crushing sensation in his chest, Nicholas watched a group of young men in a scuffle across the street, determined to deny Christopher the satisfaction of his attention.

"Something curious happened while I was on the masthead," Christopher continued. "I tried to let go. I hoped to end my misery once and for all, but my fingers wouldn't open. I truly could not open my hands to let go."

"You tried to let go and couldn't? How strange!" Anne's eyes searched his.

"Yes, by my troth, I willed them to open, and they absolutely wouldn't budge." He demonstrated with a clenched fist.

Nicholas picked at a loose thread on his jerkin hem and let out a loud yawn.

"What do you make of it?" Anne asked, holding onto every word.

"I can't explain it. Something came over me, a sensation the likes of which—well, 'twas as if a voice spoke to me."

Anne covered a gasp. "Out loud? What did the voice say?"

An unruly mob approached the cathedral from Watling Street, drowning out Christopher's voice. Shackled, Collins—the madman who lifted up his dog during the mass—stumbled past, accompanied by an officer and a group of hecklers. A second officer followed, with the terrier tucked under his arm.

Grateful for the distraction, Nicholas stood for a better view. "They've arrested him," he reported. An onlooker threw a stone at the lunatic, while Collins hissed at the crowd.

"What will they do with him?" Genuine concern filled Anne's voice.

Standing on his tiptoes, Nicholas replied, "They'll find him guilty of heresy for mocking the host. And you know what that means."

"The stake?" she cried. "But he's mad. He didn't know what he was doing."

As he watched the mob work its way down the street, Nicholas agreed. "Pity the poor man, for he'll find no mercy." He reached for Anne's elbow and helped her to her feet. "We must be on our way if I'm to have you home by dusk."

She protested. "But I must hear the rest of Christopher's tale."

Christopher's heart swelled. He had her eating from the palm of his hand. He stood and said cheerfully, "I look forward to seeing you both again." Nicholas ignored the comment and tugged Anne's hand.

As Anne and Nicholas ventured toward Honey Lane, Anne stole a glance over her shoulder. Her eyes met Christopher's. He smiled. Her heart skipped a beat.

ఴ

Christopher swatted at his shoulder to chase away the insect tickling him, but it persisted. He turned his head.

"Could we speak?"

It was Anne. He dropped the pork entrails he was transferring from a trough to a wheelbarrow, surveying all directions to see if Barnard was anywhere in sight.

At the sight of the wheelbarrow's contents, she gagged. "Could you step away for a moment?" she choked, covering her mouth with one hand.

Christopher checked his surroundings again before stepping sideways.

"I know this is unexpected, and you're at work. I simply felt I *must* come."

The cacophony of protesting animals held hostage in Smithfield's stalls drowned out her voice. He cocked an ear closer. She spoke louder, with urgency. "About your tale last night. You told of being on the masthead, but you weren't able to finish. I want to hear the rest."

"I'm happy that you found the evening worth your time, as occupied as you are with planning a wedding." The comment wasn't intended to sound sarcastic. He turned back to his work, glancing up every few seconds to see if his boss was watching.

Desperate for his attention, she moved beside him and tapped his arm. "I pray you. I must know what happened to you on that ship. While you were speaking, something pricked my heart. I need to know more."

"I can't talk here." He didn't stop to look up. "By my faith, Barnard keeps one eye on me at all times. May I call on you this evening, after work?"

"Nicholas will be calling on me."

From the corner of his eye, Christopher spied Barnard standing near a sheep pen. Plunging his hands into the trough, he spoke in a low voice. "I'm off at seven. Can you meet me at the gate? Even for a few moments?"

"I'll try, but I can't promise."

"Tell Nicholas you need to fetch something." Christopher searched her eyes. "Some fresh cakes." She shrugged her shoulders. "I'll look for you," he said matter-of-factly.

Anne nodded and walked away with butterflies in her stomach.

⁊

Forty-five minutes had passed. The western horizon donned hues of rose and light blue, while the bells of Saint Bartholomew signaled the eight o'clock hour. Christopher found himself hoping she wouldn't show; London's streets were no place for a woman at night. Like roaches that wait until dark to come out

269

of hiding, unsavory characters began to emerge from the shadows along the perimeter of West Smithfield.

He slung his purse over his shoulder and breathed out a disappointed sigh, contemplating the best route to take home—Rennerstrete through Newgate, or Duklane through Aldersgate. An aggressive beggar had recently taken to menacing passersby outside Aldersgate in front of Saint Botolph's churchyard, and Christopher was in no mood to be accosted. The vagabond needed a good whipping at the post.

Indigents posed a growing problem all about London. Just days earlier, a wool merchant dumping his rubbish at City Ditch spotted a withered hand protruding from under the refuse. It belonged to a female costermonger from whom Christopher had often purchased muffins on Cheapside. Authorities traced the murder to a vagabond that loitered about Smithfield.

With a shudder, Christopher started toward Rennerstrete. He passed the grounds of Barts, marveling that the four-hundred-year-old hospital escaped the king's chopping block. Like great felled trees, monasteries and churches around London were ransacked or razed in the dissolution, some lying in ruins and others remodeled into places of residence for London's elite. Perhaps the hospital survived because the king needed somewhere for the infirm, especially since he'd abolished the monasteries that cared for them.

The sound of footsteps running up behind him gave him a start. He pulled his dagger from its sheath and spun around, prepared for the worst. Nicholas emerged from the shadows, gasping for breath.

"By God's wounds! What are you doing here?" His hands shaking, Christopher eased his dagger back into its sheath.

"I went by Nathan's to find you, but he said you hadn't arrived from work. I thought I might find you here."

"It appears you found me." Christopher placed his hands on his hips, still trembling.

"'Tis Anne." Nicholas stopped to catch his breath. "She was supposed to meet me and didn't show. Have you seen her?"

Christopher shook his head. "Where were you supposed to meet her?"

"In front of Saint Paul's. She's never failed to show."

"Perchance she's home with Victoria." Christopher kept an eye on a scruffy young man with greasy, shoulder-length hair emerging from the shadows across the market grounds.

"No, I called there. I inquired anywhere and everywhere I could think of, at all the places she frequents."

"Anne is missing?"

"Yes! 'Tis unlike her to not show. I fear for her welfare." Nicholas paced back and forth, his breathing heavy.

"There must be somewhere you missed. She has to be in the city."

Nicholas stopped to crack his knuckles. "Let's put aside our differences," he pleaded. "Help me look for her."

His eyes narrowing, Christopher protested, "You stole her right under my nose! Why should I help you find her—so you can torture me? So I can watch you marry the maiden I love?"

Wringing his hands, Nicholas pleaded, "For her, Christopher. Do it for her. I pray you. She could be in danger."

Christopher flashed a wicked grin. "Very well. But you must grant me one request."

"We have no time to lose. What is it?"

"Delay your marriage."

"Are you mad? What does our marriage have to do with finding her now?"

"Agree to delay your marriage, or I'll find her without you."

Nicholas lowered his head, raised his bushy eyebrows, and scowled. "You want a chance with her. That's it, isn't it?"

"She should marry the man who best suits her. If she chooses you, then I'll leave you well enough alone. But I've barely spoken with her since we came to London. Agree to delay the marriage a month. One month is all I ask."

"Very well. You don't have a chance with her. She hates you after the way you behaved."

Planting his feet and resting his hands on his hips, Christopher demanded, "Swear to me you'll keep your word."

"Very well. You have my word."

Christopher thrust his right hand forward. Nicholas offered a limp handshake. The deal was done.

Bordeaux

Charlotte tucked Gabrielle and Anatole into bed. Exhausted from a day's play at the Garonne River, they fell asleep immediately. With Thomas away to

271

promote his carvings in the Dordogne Valley, she looked forward to a quiet evening to herself—a rare treat.

Settling into her favorite chair to mend the hem on Gabrielle's play dress, she pondered the topic discussed with the last reading group: King Francis' Edict of Fontainebleau. The decree labeled those who studied the new religion as dissidents, guilty of high treason against God and humanity. Conviction led to loss of property, torture, public humiliation and execution.

Charlotte could understand the king's outrage on discovering a placard on the door of his Amboise bedchamber five years earlier, but she thought the resulting edict an overly harsh retribution. One only need consider the recent pillage and slaughter of an entire village of Bible-believing Waldensians in the southeastern part of the kingdom, at Mérindol, to confirm that the king took his edict seriously. She shuddered.

If only Thomas would open his eyes—but he would never stray from the Mother Church, and she knew it. She berated herself for slipping up earlier and mentioning that she met with others to study the Bible. The darkness in his eyes still haunted her.

She tacked the hem of Gabrielle's dress in place with a running stitch, dreaming of a day when she could teach her children the new religion. Alas, doing so would raise Thomas' ire. At least she could teach them stories from the Bible—true stories, not the ones embellished with fables featured on some of the stained glass windows. Thomas wouldn't know the difference. He had no interest in reading the Holy Bible for himself.

A forceful knock at the door jarred her from her musings. After weaving the needle into the fabric, she set the dress on the arm of her chair and hurried across the room. Glancing out the window on her way to the door, she realized the sun had set. Another knock came—*rap-rap-rap*—insistent and frantic.

"Charlotte!" The voice belonged to a female. "Charlotte! Open!"

Charlotte fumbled to lift the latch, and peeked out.

"I must speak with you, quickly!" A gangly woman with dark circles under her eyes pushed her way into the cottage, carrying with her a palpable cloud of tension and fear. Rain water dripped from her mud-splattered cloak onto the oak floor. "Close the door," she gasped. "They might be following me." Charlotte eased the door closed, careful to not wake the children.

"Nicole, you're soaked. Let me get a towel."

"There is no time for that. Quick! You must listen." Fear saturated Nicole's dark brown eyes.

272

Anatole whimpered. Charlotte held her breath, willing him not to wake. The babe stirred and settled back to sleep. "The authorities—they're hunting for those who attend the reading group."

Charlotte's heart sank. "How do they know?"

"Someone informed. They must have informed Father Berger. You must take your children and flee."

Charlotte protested, "Where will I go? Thomas is away. I can't carry the children alone. Where are the authorities now?"

"They're making their rounds, visiting our cottages. They know who we are. You must hurry. Go to your parents. The priest there, Father Maubert, is sympathetic. He'll shelter you."

"But night is falling. I can't travel alone in the dark with the children. It isn't safe."

"It's more perilous to stay here, where they will find you. I'll pray for your safety. Get the children and go, Charlotte. We're all in grave danger. They'll press us to betray one another. I must hurry and warn the others." The two friends embraced. Nicole slipped out the front door, into the cold rain.

Charlotte stood stiff, incredulous. Who had she harmed? Who wished her ill? She could think of no enemies. She came from a respected family. A distant shout propelled her to the children's bedside. She shook them awake, forcing herself to be calm.

"Gabrielle! Anatole! Listen to Maman. Get up and put your shoes on. You must be quiet. Do it for Maman."

Gabrielle's eyes blinked open as she sat up. Anatole lay limp. Charlotte scooped him in her arms and heard screaming, this time closer. Fear sucked the oxygen from her lungs. She fumbled about, looking for Anatole's shoes.

"Gabrielle, put on your shoes. We must hurry to Papi's house." Gabrielle stood stiff, her bottom lip protruding, tears forming in her eyes.

"Maman," she whimpered, "I'm afraid."

"Yes, you are afraid, but you mustn't question. You must get your shoes this minute. Go." Gabrielle ran and returned with her shoes, while Charlotte tucked a shawl around Anatole. Gabrielle whimpered. Kneeling in front of her daughter to slip on the shoes, Charlotte coaxed, "You mustn't cry. Be good and Papi will have a sweet for you." The child's face brightened.

"Sweet?" Anatole yawned. Charlotte put her finger across his lips. "Chut. Yes, you will both have a sweet. Now, let's play a game to see how quiet we can be. It will be like hide and seek. We are the hiders." Gabrielle nodded, biting her lip.

Touching her finger to her lips one more time, Charlotte slipped out to make her way to her parents' estate in the dark.

Dartford

A knock on the door roused Elizabeth from her weary stupor. She folded the wet rag with which she was dabbing William's perspiration-soaked face, and carefully laid it across his forehead.

"I'll be right back," she said, standing up straight. "Someone is rappin' at the door." William managed a weak nod.

Elizabeth dried her hands on her apron and crossed the room, her breathing shallow. She inched the door open and peeked out.

"Master Tisdale!" Her heart skipped a beat.

"Good day." The justice of the peace tipped his hat and crinkled his nose as the pungent aroma of vinegar wafted past. "Amy told me William isn't well. I wished to offer my help." He wedged his boot between the door and doorframe and pushed his way inside, uninvited. "My wife sent this along." With both hands, he extended a warm loaf of rye bread.

"Why, thank you," she lied, hoping he couldn't detect the tension in her voice. "It wasn't necessary." Making a point to leave the door ajar, she turned her back to push the loaf in her bread box. Luke Tisdale's eyes darted about the room, noting its arrangement—the table and stools, the loom, William's tools, a twig broom, a barrel.

"He's been bedridden since yesterday morn." Elizabeth turned back to face her visitor. "He hasn't responded to the licorice and comfrey tincture Molly gave me. Barely says a thing, and managed to eat only a spoonful or two of Amy's pottage."

"Have you tried leeches?"

"No, money is scarce, so I haven't called on the apothecary yet. But I invoked Saint Genevieve to heal him."

Tisdale removed his cap and clutched it over his abdomen with both hands. "It appears you've done all you can, save calling on the doctor. 'Twould please me to watch with him while you fetch Doctor Hubbard. I've heard the new doctor has a fine healing touch. He learned his trade in London. Amy and I discussed it and, knowing of your situation, we want to pitch in to help you pay."

274

Elizabeth's eyes narrowed. She longed to reprimand him, to tell him she knew about his scheme, but summoned her restraint. "'Tis kind of you and Amy, but I don't think we'll be needin' the doctor's help at this time. I'll give the tincture some time to work and call on him later, if it looks to be needful."

Luke crossed the room to William's bedside. Placing the back of his hand on William's cheek, he frowned. "I don't wish to alarm you, but he looks nigh to death. I take no joy in saying it, Goodwife, but you'll be attending his funeral if you don't get the apothecary here in haste. Mind you, I don't mean to upset you. 'Tis Christian concern that brought me here. You've already lost a son; you can ill afford to lose your husband. It would indeed be a pity if William's death were laid on your conscience." Luke's implication that she might be responsible, if William were to die, turned her cheeks crimson.

William wheezed, his body doubling up with each cough. Elizabeth lifted the rag from his forehead, scurried to a basin of vinegar to dip it and wring it out, and hurried back to dab his face.

"I've some honey there." She pointed with her nose toward the mantle. "If it please you, a spoonful might ease his cough."

Luke crossed the room to retrieve the honey, studying the barrel near the fireplace. Taking long strides to the bedside, he handed the honey crock and a spoon to Elizabeth. She waited for a break in William's cough, then gently pried his lips open to coax the sweet nectar into his mouth. William clamped his lips around the spoon and gazed up at her with swollen, sticky eyes, his face pale and clammy.

"Do fetch the apothecary," he pleaded, swallowing the honey with great effort. "I feel wretched."

"There you have it." Luke hopped to her side. "Don't trouble yourself for a moment; I'll take great care with him." He stretched his hand toward the rag. "Go on, I'll take your place."

Elizabeth pulled her hand away and took a step back. William writhed under another coughing fit. Perspiration trickled from his temples, while his body shivered under his damp nightshirt. He wheezed out the words, "Fetch the doctor."

Reaching toward the rag, Elizabeth insisted, "'Luke, 'twould be most helpful if you could fetch Doctor Hubbard while I stay with William. I know what he needs."

The justice of the peace dabbed William's cheeks. "I can't describe William's symptoms as you can," he insisted. "The doctor will need to know precisely what remedies to bring with him. You're better equipped than I to inform him."

"Go, Lizzie." William rolled onto his side with a moan. He closed his eyes and breathed heavily, his chest rattling. Within seconds, the sound of his snoring resonated within the cottage.

Her heart sinking, Elizabeth finally relented. "Very well. I shall be gone only a few minutes." She tugged her cloak from the hook next to the door and swung it around her shoulders. With a last desperate look at William, she uttered a silent prayer and slipped out, stopping at the blackthorn hedge between her cottage and the neighboring one to contemplate a course of action. After a few moments' reflection, she tiptoed to the window on the side of her cottage and, ever so slowly, raised up to peek in.

As expected, Luke was not at William's bedside; rather, he had his arms plunged elbow-deep in the barley barrel. Indignant, she watched him burrow for several seconds before he turned to look elsewhere. His eyes moved past the window. She ducked. A minute or so passed. Her thoughts bounced back and forth between confronting him and holding back. Finally, deciding she had no choice, she took a deep breath, stormed to the front of the cottage and flung the door open.

Luke sat on the stool, holding the rag against William's forehead.

"I...I forgot something," she stammered. Had her eyes played tricks on her? No, as sure as the sun rose that morning, she'd witnessed Luke rummaging through the barley barrel just a minute earlier. A sideways glance confirmed the lid sitting askew. She crossed the room to fetch a small crock, watching Luke fidget when she straightened the barrel lid. After retrieving the crock she explained, "I meant to get a refill of salve while I'm out." Luke dabbed William's face while she approached and laid the back of her hand against her husband's forehead. "He's ablaze, he is," she lamented.

Luke shifted his position on the stool. She eyed the corner of a book protruding from under his buttocks. He wiggled and shifted his weight to the other side.

With eyes slanted, she growled, "I know what you're doin', and I'll not have it."

"What do you mean?" he said blankly.

She rolled her eyes. "How dare you play the fool with me, Luke Tisdale. The book. The Bible. You're after it. Your arse is on it this very minute. 'Twas not in the barrel. How did you find it?"

Luke took his hand off the rag and pulled the book out from under him. He jumped up, lifted it high in his right hand, and declared, "This book is banned. Your husband is defying the injunctions, defying his monarch. This book must burn."

"I've told him he must be rid of it, and he won't hear of it."

"William is a rebel to his king. He must be dealt with accordingly."

"Give me the book, and I'll dispose of it. Then leave us in peace. No more spyin', no more harassin'. The matter will be done with. Give it to me." She stretched her arm forward. Luke stretched his arm high above her head. "Give me the book," she demanded, jumping up to swipe at it.

"Shall I allow lawlessness to reign in this parish?" Clutching the Bible to his chest, Tisdale hurried toward the door. Elizabeth lunged in front of him and clawed at the book. He butted her with his right shoulder and stood stiff, daring her to come at him again. After regaining her balance she rushed at him, boiling with adrenaline. Using her fingernails as weapons, she dug into his arms and pulled with all her might. His grip loosened. She stomped on his foot. Recoiling, he dropped the Bible. She scooped it up, darted to the fireplace and tossed the book in the flames.

"There." She turned and glared at Luke, her chest rising and falling rapidly. Folding her arms and thrusting her chin in the air she proclaimed, "Now, perhaps, we shall have some peace."

Luke smoothed his disheveled jerkin and cloak. Shaking his finger he scolded, "Woman, you're mad. I've a mind to send you to the whipping post."

"If you try to harm me, I shall accuse you of assault."

"Who will believe you? You, wife to a Lollard and mother to a prodigal? Will they take your word over mine?" He turned to leave. Intent on getting in the last word, he looked over his shoulder and taunted, "I suppose explaining to your husband what happened to his Bible shall be punishment enough."

She locked the door and crossed the room to the hearth, her body shivering like a wet dog. After checking to see that William was still asleep, she pulled a handful of twigs from the kindling pile and placed them atop the book, as if she were laying flowers atop a casket. Once they caught, she added some sticks and two small logs. As soon as the logs exploded into flames, she poked the remains of the book into the hungry fire and watched it burn until all traces were gone.

Curate Reede descended the gallery stairs in All Hallow's church, startled to discover Anne Cooper slumped forward on a pew, resting her head in her hands. When he reached the bottom of the stairs, he set his lantern on a table and approached her.

"I thought myself alone in the building," Reede remarked. "May I help you?"

Anne straightened and looked up into the kindly man's face, her eyes swollen and red. She dabbed at her eyes with a handkerchief. "I don't know that anyone can help me," she sniffled. "I need answers, and I don't know where to find them."

The curate chuckled inside. She'd managed to express the common lot of humanity in eleven simple words. He eased himself onto the bench next to her and caressed the newly upholstered pew. "Do you like the green saye? Came from the south of England." He cleared his throat and probed, "What seems to be the trouble?"

"'Tis lovely," she stammered, a bit flummoxed that he chose to speak of fabric in her time of distress. Could she trust him? Would he understand? Fearing her trouble might sound silly, she deliberated on whether to open her heart. However, the desire for advice overcame her reticence. Through her sniffles, she asked, "You've gotten to know Nicholas Hall. What do you think of him?" Dabbing at her nose with the damp handkerchief she leaned forward, anxious for his response.

"Nicholas Hall? He's a good man. Hard-working, honest, a man of genuine faith. He's always willing to help in any way necessary. Would you agree?" The curate sat back. He'd learned most folks would arrive at their own answers if they could confide in someone with a good listening ear. She nodded. Reede leaned forward and continued, "I've watched him at the meetings. He's an earnest student of the new learning, it appears?"

"Yes, he's all of the things you said. We're to be married in a fortnight. But when you read the banns last week, I felt as if perhaps it was I who should express a reason we should not be married." She closed her eyes and choked, "Shouldn't I be happy?"

The curate swallowed. "Having never been in your situation, I don't know that I'm the best to offer advice on the topic. But I've observed that folks behave in many different ways when it comes to getting married. How are your wedding plans coming?"

Anne bit down on her quivering bottom lip. "I fear making a mistake."

"What is there to fear in giving your hand to a good man like Nicholas? Is there some sort of shadow in his character known only to you?"

"No, 'tis nothing of the sort. He's a good man. I can think of no better."

"Now you have me confused. You have doubts about giving your hand to a man about whom you can say there is no better?"

Anne snickered through her tears. "I knew I would sound mad." A loud sigh escaped her lips. "There's another. His name is Christopher. He came to London with Nicholas. The two are friends from childhood. Christopher and I took a fancy to one another when we lived in Dartford, and my father sent me here, to London, to separate us. Christopher's father has Lollard sympathies, and my father couldn't tolerate my taking to a Lollard's son."

"The picture is becoming clearer." Reede leaned back against the pew. "Do you still have an interest in this lad, Christopher?"

"I don't know. When the two arrived in London, Nicholas began attending meetings and embraced the new learning. Christopher did just the opposite. According to Nicholas, he began to frequent taverns, and became ever more bitter and angry. He secured a job on a Dutch vessel traveling from London to Bordeaux, and spent several weeks away. During that time Nicholas courted me. We've gotten on well, as you can see. But Christopher lately returned to London. He claims to have changed. Now I find myself utterly torn. I haven't been able to find out what happened with Christopher, because I'm obliged to spend my time with Nicholas."

"Many a maiden would love to have your problem." Reede leaned forward and scratched his chin. "Some who come to me can't lure a lad's attention to save their life. Yet, here I sit with a maiden who can't choose between two."

Anne smiled through her tears. "'Tis silly, isn't it?" They sat in silence for several seconds before she spoke. "Have you any advice?"

Of all the duties involved in the care of souls, playing matchmaker was one Reede refused to take upon himself. He searched the forlorn maiden's eyes and asked, "What does your heart tell you?"

She thought for a few moments. "It tells me I must go forward as if…"

The church door handle rattled. When the door flew open, Anne's jaw dropped.

Feeling painfully self-conscious, Thomas knelt next to the grille in the confessional booth, made the sign of the cross, and spoke just above a whisper.

"Bless me, Father, for I have sinned." He paused to muster the courage to continue. "It has been six years since my last confession."

At the sound of Thomas Nix's voice, Father Berger sat up straight. Having long puzzled over what brought the impressive young man to France, he hoped to unravel the mystery through the confessional.

"You haven't participated in the yearly Easter confession, as required." The priest's rebuke was pointed, but kind.

"No. In that I have grievously sinned."

"Yes, but let us put that aside for the moment. I commend you for your courage in coming to the sacrament of penance after this long absence. May your soul find peace. Please, continue."

"I accuse myself of the following sins." Thomas again fell silent.

"You're struggling, my son?"

"Yes, Father. I don't know where to begin. My sins are many, but not deliberate. I was only defending the church the night I confronted a commissioner in the tavern, and I fled because I feared for my safety. They looted Canterbury Cathedral! Do I not have a duty to speak up? And I never planned on stabbing a man in Maidstone. The two imposters were highwaymen who would have killed me."

The priest swallowed.

"On several occasions, I didn't tell the truth about who I was when I arrived in this kingdom—but I feared for my life." Thomas paused, searching for words to exorcise the demons that had tormented his conscience the past six years.

Father Berger seized the silence. "You've spoken of acting out of fear. Do you believe fear justifies sin?"

"Well, no. But it didn't seem to me that, in my homeland, I should be persecuted for my allegiance to the Mother Church after Englishmen safely held those same beliefs for centuries. When the king broke with Rome, all of a sudden even the best in the land—including His Majesty's closest friends—were suspect."

"The English king's impetuosity put his subjects in a difficult position, to be sure. He has allowed heresy to run rampant, and placed himself above the Holy Father. You faced a contradiction of your allegiance—to God, or to your king."

"Some say kings are placed over us by God, but I question such in light of King Henry's actions. I believe a man's first allegiance must be to God, but the entire world has been set ablaze by folks of different persuasions professing allegiance to Him. My allegiance to the Holy Mother Church led me here. Whether I'm in the wrong or the right, I'm not certain. What is truth, Father?"

Taking a deep breath, the priest replied, "That to which one pays allegiance is life's central question, something for which we must each account to God. I can't give you an answer; I can only admonish you to seek heaven's guidance and choose carefully."

Thomas came hoping to find answers. Father Berger's vague reply left him frustrated.

"Let us continue with your confession. Can you recite the tenth commandment?" Growing stiff in the confession booth, the priest rolled his neck and wiggled his toes.

"Yes. Thou shalt not kill."

"You confessed that you stabbed a man. Did you kill him?"

"I don't know. I fled before I could learn what happened to him, but my conscience won't let me alone."

"You committed this act in a moment of passion?"

"Yes, they pretended to be a constable and justice of the peace. They tried to steal my begging license."

"*Your* begging license?"

"Well, no, 'twas not mine. I stole it from a beggar named Harry."

"Did you steal this license out of fear as well?"

"I thought it would help me survive, to secure food while I was traveling."

"Did you harm the man from whom you took this license?"

"Yes, I hit Harry in the head with a rock. But I left some coins to recompense him for the trouble. I took his cloak as well. But it was tattered and torn, and I left him mine, which was quite handsome."

The priest sighed within himself. Theft, false witness, potential murder— God himself would have trouble sorting out this long list of misdeeds.

"Have you continued to bear false witness?"

"No, I haven't done so since I revealed my true identity to the family of my wife many years ago."

"Have you harmed anyone since these incidents you have confessed?"

"No. I strive earnestly to do good and not ill to my neighbors, wherever I may be."

"Have you been guilty of theft?"

"No."

"Very well. Anything else?" Father Berger heard Thomas' knees pop as the Englishman shifted his position on the other side of the screen. Several seconds passed. "Is anything else troubling you?" the priest probed.

Exhaling slowly, Thomas replied, "Yes. Something else has been troubling my conscience, something of an entirely different nature. I discovered my wife was meeting with a group to secretly study heretical writings. She didn't obey me when I told her to stop, and found it necessary to go into hiding when someone within the group informed authorities. I know where she is and haven't insisted that she return home. Am I guilty of harboring a heretic?"

A wicked smile crossed the priest's face. He responded, "What does your conscience tell you?"

"I suppose if I didn't feel guilty, I wouldn't be speaking to you about it."

"Let me pose a question. What will happen to the church if heresy is allowed to spread, unchecked? Think of your mother country."

Thomas' heart sank. He realized, too late, he had unwittingly opened a Pandora's Box.

Father Berger continued, "The church fathers have clearly spoken on this issue. Heretics must be cleansed from the body of Christ. Saint Paul wrote, 'If thy right hand offend thee, cut it off.' Do you know where she is?" The priest sensed Thomas' reticence to continue. "You understand," he coaxed, "I can't betray the confidences you share with me. To do so would bring upon me powerful censure. I would be stripped of my benefice, and sent to a monastery to live out the remainder of my days."

"Yes."

"Do you know where she is hiding?"

"Yes." Thomas gulped.

"You'll receive a plenary indulgence for your assistance in rooting out heresy—in other words, you will receive full and unconditional pardon for all of the sins which you have confessed here."

"Yes." Thomas swallowed his anxiety. "I know what that means."

"It appears you again face a question of your allegiance."

Thomas massaged a pinch in his stomach.

Curate Reede and Anne looked at one another, then at Christopher. Christopher looked at Anne, then at the curate, with equal surprise.

"What are you doing here?" Anne blurted, staring at large gashes in Christopher's tunic and stockings.

Panting, Christopher replied, "Looking for you." He peeked his head out the door, glanced up and down the street, then closed the door and approached his startled audience. "I waited for you at the gate until eight o'clock, sick with worry. London after dark is not exactly a safe place for a beautiful maiden like you."

She looked at the floor and smiled.

"London isn't especially safe for anyone at this hour," the curate interjected. The passing torch of a night watchman outside a window caught his eye. "Might I accompany the two of you someplace convenient?"

"The watchman is out? Marry! I lost track of time," Anne lamented. "Victoria will be worried about me."

Christopher offered his elbow. "Milady, I know someone who would be happy to walk you home."

"Grand idea," the curate proclaimed, sensing the answer to Anne's problem had entered the building. As Reede crossed the room to retrieve his lantern, he remarked, "'Tis not prudent to be out without a light; let me accompany you."

Christopher raised a hand to stop him. "McMillan's gate is but a stone's throw away. Could you, perchance, wait here on the step and hold up the lantern until we arrive at the porch? I would like to speak with Anne privately."

"Of course. Actually, here." Reede offered the lantern to Christopher. "You may return it to me on the morrow." Christopher accepted the offer with an appreciative nod.

Upon arriving at Anne's doorstep, Christopher extinguished the lantern and set it on the porch, willing his heart to stop its thunderous drumbeat. As Anne reached for the door handle, he leaned in close behind her—so close, she felt the warmth of his chest on her back and his breath on her neck. He placed his hand over hers. Breathless, she turned. As he studied her face in the moonlight, Christopher recalled the first time he saw her at the market in Dartford. He pulled her closer.

"At last," his voice wobbled. He wrapped his arms around her waist, anticipating resistance but finding none. She laid her cheek against his chest, absorbing his warmth and listening to his heart race. When she lifted her eyes to meet his, he leaned down and allowed his lips to tickle and tease their way across her cheek until they met her lips, moist and eager.

After a long kiss, she cradled her head against his shoulder and sighed, "You came for me."

"I would be a fool to lose you," he swooned, holding her tighter. "I've been mad with longing, with fear of one day finding you and learning another had your hand, or of never seeing you again. Nothing could compare to the wretchedness of the eve you told me you were betrothed to Nicholas. After the news, I thought I would never be able to face another day of my miserable existence."

"About Nicholas." She pulled back, searching his eyes. "I was to meet him this evening, but I couldn't bring myself to do it. I wanted to speak with you, but I didn't dare lest he find out. So I avoided you both."

The *clip-clop-clip* of footsteps on Honey Lane silenced them. Anne held her breath.

"Could be Nicholas," Christopher whispered. "Follow me." He led her by the hand behind a hawthorn hedge, where they crouched, listening as the footsteps slowed to a walk. A shuffle on the porch was followed by *crash! tink-tink-tink-tink* when the visitor tripped over the lantern and sent it skidding across the cobblestone street. Seconds of tense silence followed a mumbled expletive before the stranger broke into a run. They waited for the sound of footsteps to fade into the distance before they emerged from behind the bush and tiptoed to the porch, hand in hand.

"He's looking for you," Christopher whispered. "He should at least know you're safe, lest he put himself in danger roaming the streets all night."

"There's little we can do now. I'll pay him a visit tomorrow, and let him know I was at the church tonight."

Slipping his arms around her waist, he asked, "Will you let him know about us—about tonight?"

With a groan, she averted her gaze.

Christopher persisted, "Will you let him know tomorrow?"

She took a step backwards and stammered, "Victoria must be sick with worry."

"Hurry back," Christopher teased. "I've waited a long time for this."

To occupy himself while she was inside, Christopher retrieved the lantern and examined it for damage in the moonlight. The candle had dislodged from its holder, but the metal casing appeared unmarred. He secured the candle and suspended the lantern on a scrolled metal porch hook.

Ten minutes passed, then fifteen. A shout and a wail drifted from the direction of Smithfield. A dog barked. Another dog responded to the first, then a third joined in to form a haunting canine chorus. Christopher heard more shouts, but he couldn't make out any words. A terrifying thought occurred to him: what if Nicholas were in trouble?

Anne slipped out, calm and unruffled, cradling something in a towel. Christopher forgot about the commotion in the distance.

"How did she respond?" He was staring at the towel when he asked.

"She was asleep in her chair. I put a blanket over her, and waited several minutes to make sure she was soundly asleep before coming back out. I think we're safe." She motioned for Christopher to sit beside her on the porch step. After setting the bundle on her lap, she unfolded it.

His nose detected the sweet aroma of pastry and lemon. "Taffaty tart?"

A coy smile crossed her lips. She lifted the bundle toward him.

"I haven't had one since I left Dartford," he said, reaching eagerly. "Did you make them?"

"Yes, Victoria taught me how."

His first bite transported him to Dartford, to Market Day, to wheeling a wobbly cart full of linens down East Hill on his way to Abby's pastry stand. "By God's teeth," he swooned, "they're better than Abby's." He pushed a crumb into his mouth and licked his lips.

"Thank you," she beamed. "And now that I've given you a gift, you must return the favor. Please, finish telling me about your sea journey."

After wiping his hands on his tunic to remove the sticky residue, he reached for her hand.

She asked about his torn clothing. With a chuckle, he ran his fingers along the frayed edge of the gash in his tunic and explained, "Earlier, Nicholas and I had a small—disagreement. But we settled fair and square."

"Who won?"

"I'll give you three guesses." She pointed at him with a smile. "Correct," he said. "But I have to keep asking myself, am I dreaming? When tomorrow comes, will you return to Nicholas and pretend tonight didn't happen?"

"I think not." She gave his hand a reassuring squeeze. "But so I can be sure, do, *please*, tell me your story. My patience is wearing thin."

"Where did I leave off?"

"You were on the masthead. Something happened—you heard a voice?"

"Oh, yes. The masthead. 'Twas in the midst of a terrible storm, the ship listing this way and that. At last I determined to let go, come what may. Whether that meant to be washed away at sea, or to break my neck in the fall, I was so miserable I no longer cared. I tried with all my might to open my fingers, but they wouldn't open. Just as I was cursing my fingers for betraying me, a sensation of warmth came over me. A presence enveloped me, and a still voice—a peaceful voice—spoke to my mind and told me to not be afraid, that all would be well.

"I surrendered, and knew nothing more until I woke up in the ship bosun's arms. This mate, Patrick, told me he sensed that I have a work to do. I must tell you, after being cursed as a Lollard's son my entire life, to be told God sees something in me—it awakened my heart. I believe God is aware of me, though I don't, as of yet, know why. But I do wish to chart a better course going forward—to mend my ways."

"Quite remarkable, I'd say." A long pause ensued while Anne retreated into her thoughts. "Then you've had a change of heart since you first came to London? That is to say…"

He interrupted. "My behavior when I first came to London—well, I understand you wanting to avoid me. Yes, I've had a change of heart. I no longer wish to spend my time in taverns, yet I don't know what I'm fit for at the moment. I feel a bit like a sparrow without a nest."

"If God spoke to you, as you say, He will find you a nest."

"You speak of God as if you know him. I can't say the same."

"You may feel that you don't know him, but 'tis my sense that God knows you. It appears he is tapping you on the shoulder, so to speak, trying to get your attention." He took a moment to digest her words, when the door cracked open.

"Anne!" Victoria emerged in her nightshirt and cap, rubbing her eyes. "How long have you been on the porch? And who is this with you?"

"I came inside to let you know I was on the porch, but you were asleep."

"And your visitor? You were to meet Nicholas."

Christopher stood, and with a polite nod introduced himself. Victoria's eyes bulged with alarm.

Anne stood and explained, "Christopher and I are settling some affairs. He was about to be on his way."

"Very well, but come in soon. Vagabonds are about—remember the body at City Ditch." Victoria cast a warning glance at Christopher and retreated inside.

"That went well," he said gloomily.

Anne sighed. "We have much to sort out. The light of a new day will help us see more clearly."

"I hope so." He pulled her close and pressed his lips against hers for a lingering kiss, then pinched himself.

"Why did you do that?" she demanded.

"To make sure I'm not dreaming." With a playful smile, he pinched her waist.

She giggled. "Why did you do that?"

"I want you to know you're not dreaming, either. Promise me when you awake tomorrow, you won't have forgotten this night."

"Not a chance."

"On the morrow, then?"

"On the morrow."

He turned to leave, then stopped. "I almost forgot. Close your eyes and open your hands." Fishing through his purse with a wide grin, he extracted something and extended it to her. "Open."

She squealed. Turning the comb back and forth in her hands, she ran her fingertips across its carved hearts. "I love it," she exclaimed, throwing her arms around him. "'Tis absolutely beautiful!"

"I purchased it in the kingdom of France. Lay it next to your bedside. When you awake in the morning, you'll have proof that this night happened."

"Christopher, stop. I will keep it by my bedside," she promised, "but I need no proof."

He leaned down to kiss the tip of her nose, his eyes dancing. "Never forget, Milady, I will always come back for you."

"I trust you will, Milord." She curtsied.

He practically floated to his uncle's cottage, feeling as if his soul had wings.

END OF BOOK ONE

COMING – WINTER 2018
Shining City on a Hill

Book Two
Fanning the Flames

Excerpt

Anne led Christopher by the hand to a bench in the garden. In a low voice, she continued, "All of my life, I've seen myself as a loyal subject of my king, not as a rebel or a traitor. I have no ill designs against King Henry or the realm; on the contrary. And yet, the king's laws have branded me a traitor. The only safety seems to be in stifling one's convictions."

Christopher considered her words. "One would think the growing number of dissenters might soften the hearts of those above us, but His Majesty seems intent on snuffing them out. Many are fleeing to the Continent—to Basel, or Geneva. When a kingdom silences or chases away its most virtuous subjects, what is to become of it?"

She whispered, "The future seems dim; I won't lie. I'm almost afraid to voice the doubts that plague me at times. Sometimes I wonder, where is God? Why doesn't he step in to protect those who stand for his word?"

Christopher studied a bee flitting from rose to rose. "I suppose that question has riddled mankind since Adam and Eve were banished from the garden."

Anne bowed her head. "I don't know if I want to be seen with Lady Askew. I'm ready to retreat from the meetings, to attend mass and hold my peace."

Seconds passed while he waited for her to look up into his eyes. He continued, "But that is their aim. If they succeed in silencing the truth tellers, they will have won."

She shrugged her shoulders. "What does one gain by standing against a monarch? How can one man or one woman overcome the power of a king and his officers? He has an entire navy at his disposal, as well as sheriffs, constables, bishops, and priests, to name but a few. We're but gnats—fragile, powerless gnats."

"I can't believe you're saying this. You're one of the folks who opened my eyes—although I don't know whether to thank you or curse you."

Anne's jaw dropped. "Curse me? How could you say such a thing?"

"Life is so much simpler when one's only intent is to eat, drink and be merry. Belching out vulgar obscenities in a tavern beats watching over your shoulder to see who might be noting every word you say. I've been contemplating the topics we discuss at our meetings, such as whether folks should adhere to injunctions and rituals they don't believe in. The reformers speak with such boldness and conviction, I can't dismiss the things they say. Whether we win or lose is in God's hands, but choosing sides is in our own. Does heaven reward a coward?"

"But 'tis futile to stand against a monarch. He has all power, power over life and death."

"Stop." He grabbed her wrists. "I can't let what you just said go unchallenged. There is but one who has power over life and death—one alone—and 'tis not King Henry."

"You know what I mean," she argued. "The king gives no thought to executing his closest advisors. You and I are but flies to him. If we disobey, he has the power smite us as mere pests that flit about creating trouble."

Victoria peeked her head out the back door, her lips taut. "There's a man at the front door," she said in a low voice. "He's asking for you, Christopher. I don't recognize him."

Christopher's heart skipped a beat. "Do you have a back gate?" he asked, his voice heavy with fear.

℗

For additional historical background on the *Shining City on a Hill* series, visit the author's website at

www.karenedmonds.com

289